Agent of Equilibrium

N.J. Mercer

Clink
Street

London | New York

Published by Clink Street Publishing 2015

ISBN: 978-1-910782-04-0
E-Book: 978-1-910782-05-7

For Rabab

Thanks to my parents

Prologue

Edward watched the desperate, naked figures scramble out of the pit; they were covered in five days' worth of their own and each other's filth. The smell of excrement and stale bodily fluids made him recoil; the old man who stood alongside him smiled wickedly at this. A pair of obese women stepped forward from an assembly of figures clad in black leather smocks who lurked in the shadows and were never far away; they herded the disorientated group down a long, dim corridor to the next chamber. Edward and the old one followed.

"Get back in line!" screeched one of the herders as a confused youth groped his way along the wall he had just walked into. When he was unable to fall in with the rest, a few swift kicks that struck his bare backside with a resonating slap were enough to make him stumble onto the correct route again. One of the bedraggled members of the group rocked with uncontrolled laughter at this; tears rolled down his cheeks. He too received a few kicks for his troubles, but it didn't make him stop. *Very interesting*, thought Edward. *Now here is a chap with potential.* It was what he was looking for.

The pit, as it was affectionately known, was actually a small stone chamber with barely enough room for the six youths to lie alongside each other. They had been left there for five whole days, mostly in complete darkness. A hatch in the ceiling allowed food and drink to be dropped in occasionally, and it was also opened to provide them with a mere hour of light each day. This was all a part of their test; they had known what to expect and had volunteered willingly. They had suffered numerous trials prior to their days in the pit, but it was widely accepted that it was only after entering the pit that a prospect's worth could be truly ascertained. Edward hadn't finished with them yet.

They followed the wobbling flesh of the lead herder through several narrow stone corridors, her vast thighs brushing against the walls on either side. The disparate group reached an impossibly long staircase that they started to ascend. The climb was exhausting at the best of times; however, weakened as they were from their days in the pit, it was almost intolerable. Several of the youths protested at the severity of their trial, only to have their leather-clad herders laugh at their plight, spit on their bare bodies and shove them along regardless. Naturally, progress was slow.

"Come now! Stop there. Our friends need some help," announced Edward with a single loud clap of the hands to emphasise his point. "Will the Pharmacist please see to them?"

A tall, sinister man stepped forward from the very rear of the trailing entourage, his powerful frame and physical presence matched only by that of Edward himself. He wore a suit and a long rectangle of black leather was tied around the circumference of his head, hanging over his face; cold eyes looked out from two steel-ringed holes that were punched into this mask. He produced a syringe from an old-fashioned medical bag at his side. It was the usual energising mix of synthetic amphetamines; Edward had deemed it appropriate for the Pharmacist to add a hint of mild LSD to the blend on this occasion. He was examining these young men and women, and what most interested him about them was their mind. It was through this current, rather prolonged, process that he might find an initiate amongst these youths. Edward's burly associates grabbed each prospect in turn, and the Pharmacist injected the potent mixture into one of their buttocks. Edward himself watched each subject's reaction with interest. Mostly they protested and questioned the contents of the injection before struggling against the fat women who held them down; this was to be expected, all quite normal, but there were two who particularly drew his attention. A tall, gangly fellow, the one who had been laughing earlier, and another who was apparently in the midst of an emotional breakdown, gibbering uncontrollably, overcome by the horror of his recent trials; he had accepted the injection without resistance, probably unaware of the needle that had just penetrated his skin. Edward had been watching both him and the tall fellow closely as they proceeded with the group. *Yes, these two are showing potential*, he thought.

It wasn't long before the prospects were climbing the staircase quite enthusiastically, their spirits artificially lifted by the drugs in their bloodstream. They clambered upwards, away from the lower levels, away from the inversion tables, away from the chains and grateful to be away from the pit. This ascent was to take them back to the surface. Each prospect had done well to come this far, they had passed the trial and a sense of euphoria was creeping into their mood. Edward noted that the tall fellow's disposition remained unaffected – probably because he had been euphoric to the point of laughter throughout his ordeal regardless of any drug. The persisting darkness of the pit and the many humiliations of the days prior had not affected him, in fact, it seemed he had found it all amusing; *a welcome change to the mundane experiences of daily living, no doubt*, thought Edward. The one who gibbered was also unchanged; he continued to mumble to himself and furtively scan the ground before him as if he were chasing unseen vermin. Edward noted all of this.

Finally, the stairway ended, and the whole group found themselves in an inconspicuous barn. A set of large double doors was opened; the prospects ran outside. Fresh air filled their lungs, so different from the underground stench they had endured for the past week. Its effect was cleansing and refreshing, the stimulant properties of the drugs in their body fortified this feeling and heightened their emotions; they had passed the trial! They ran free into an empty field where the damp grass wiped the filth from their unwashed feet. They drank in the daylight and appreciated more than ever the sun's warmth touching their skin. The gibbering fool was unmoved and merely raised a single eyebrow in acknowledgement of his new situation as he continued to scan the ground, blowing an occasional raspberry, or sobbing briefly. Edward wondered at this individual who had been quite normal before the trials, indistinguishable from the rest; now, he was in a unique place. Just look at him, what was in his mind's eye? He was elsewhere, seeing and perceiving so differently from all those around him. Edward's gaze shifted to the tall chap, the one who had laughed throughout; as his fellow prospects celebrated, he seemed almost disappointed. This was interesting, another unique reaction, so illogical, so unexpected; this was certainly evidence of a chaotic mindset. Edward was pleased; the trial might yield two initiates. This was unusual: to find one would be reason to celebrate, but two! He turned with a grin to the old man who had been beside him for the entire ascent, his associate nodded in response. Edward knew he had been thinking along similar lines; after all, the old man was his lifelong companion, he who would ultimately take any initiates under his own wing.

The celebrating prospects were rounded up by several leather-clad herders. Their faces reflected both the joy of completing this test to which they had proffered themselves and the fact that they were high.

Arranged in a loose congregation, they awaited Edward's address. "You stand here after days of being deprived of your basic human dignities. You have overcome isolation, humiliation and countless other internal battles of the psyche. The sky must seem more beautiful to you than at any other time in your lives, and I swear the air must never have tasted sweeter than it does now."

The gathered nodded fervently, they felt strong, worthy of standing before the great man in front of them. From the corner of his eye, Edward glanced at the pair who had previously captured his attention. The gibbering fool was laid out on the damp grass with arms and legs outstretched, while the tall fellow now seemed positively upset at how things had turned out. These were two very interesting individuals.

"I thank you all for being here today, but we have not finished! For now you must all go back down!" announced Edward. The prospects looked at each other in disbelief, wondering if they had heard correctly. The reopening of the double doors confirmed their worst fear. They wailed in protest and despair. A few tried to run away, only to be caught by the herders (whose size belied their agility) and forced back to the doors. Some were dragged along by their legs, clawing at the ground, screaming for mercy.

"How long, Edward? How long must we endure?" cried

another as he was pulled along the grass, a herder on each arm.

"Oh, I'm not sure at the moment; I think it will be at least a week!" replied Edward. The prospect broke down in tears, his misery compounded by drug induced paranoia. Some lost control of their bodily functions at the horror of being taken back underground. There was a sudden, unexpected whoop of celebration.

"A week?" shouted the tall fellow irreverently. Edward turned to face him.

"Yes, do you have a problem with that?"

"It's far too short!" he replied and burst out laughing at this; Edward joined him, unable to contain his own amusement. The herders didn't have to struggle with this one, he wandered back through the double doors voluntarily, looking happier than at any other point in the ordeal.

Wonderful, thought Edward, *a mind that truly transcends the limitations of this physical world! How marvellous.* He looked at his other favourite, who was gibbering away as he was guided back to the double doors, nodding solemn greetings to unseen others around him, indifferent to his destination. This was what Edward wanted; the other prospects had demonstrated responses that were so very predictable, the joy of release from their trials and the despair of return, feelings heightened by the drugs. What Edward sought was the unpredictable; he had always reached for the unknowable. He worshipped disorder, and sometimes it was so hard to find it. These two would make fine Disciples; the rest would be welcome to stay, but these two would go far – if they could bear having their eyelids stitched shut first.

Chapter 1

Johnny awoke with a grunt from his feverish sleep. Sweat had soaked through his clothing and into the worn leather armchair he was sprawled upon; he rubbed his face before taking a few deep breaths. The green LED display of the digital clock radio on his bedside table across the room read: 17:07. Johnny was concerned, he never fell asleep during the daytime, in fact, getting to sleep at night was usually difficult enough for him. The hot, restless slumber his body had been recently succumbing to was worrying. There had been three episodes this week. He had not been particularly tired prior to this latest one, and he had slept reasonably well the night before, so why then should he be waking up in his armchair? This time it had lasted half an hour; he wondered if he was unwell. *Maybe it was TB? Didn't that give you feverish sleep?* Unsure of the answer, Johnny resolved to see his doctor if it happened again – there was a chance, however, that these episodes, and especially the vivid dreams he was experiencing during them, were not linked to any illness at all. A few minutes later, he sat cross-legged on the floor of his studio apartment wearing only a pair of loose kung fu trousers.

Johnny lived alone in a converted loft in north-west London. His cluttered residence had the appearance of an antique store, the type that gets filled with junk but still contains real treasures that reveal themselves only to those who look carefully. It housed, amongst other things, dozens of old books on rickety shelves, several pot plants on a desk, and a collection of guitars that leant against a large amplifier stack surrounded by vinyl records and CDs, all of which dominated one corner of his abode. A low ceiling sloped down on two sides and in it sat four large skylights which filled the loft with fading autumn daylight. There was a noticeable stillness this evening – the streets lay mostly empty outside and their calm permeated the atmosphere indoors.

It was time to exercise; with legs tightly crossed in the lotus position, Johnny M. closed his eyes. There were several flickering candles about the room, some free-standing, and others atop old wine bottles covered in solidified wax drippings. Johnny had already selected a deep purple coloured candle and fixed it to a tall wrought-iron base with an endlessly twisting design. He had placed it about a foot in front of himself with the unlit wick at the same level as his closed eyes. To any onlooker he would have appeared blissfully calm; this would have been a false impression because he was performing his daily mind exercises, and his will was straining immensely as he dug deep into reserves of psychic energy. Johnny had performed this particular exercise on many occasions and always believed that spending a similar amount of time weight lifting in a gym would have expended less effort. After seven seconds of intense concentration, he opened his eyes to begin witnessing the fruit of his labour. The tip of the candle started to glow, releasing a small whiff of smoke. A further three seconds later, there was a flame; Johnny had managed to light it by only using energy directed through his will.

He found that it was easier to perform psychic exercises at the weekends, when his neighbours who lived in the many apartments nearby were generally feeling less anxious; otherwise, the energy radiating from their collective consciousness (to which he was very sensitive) interrupted his focus. With the candle lit, Johnny let his mind relax once more; it was only for twenty seconds – the exercise was half-complete. He closed his eyes again and focused, this time using his psychic energy to starve the flame of oxygen; a few seconds later it was snuffed out. The tip of the candle, its flame extinguished, smouldered, and smoke drifted across the room.

He continued the exercise until he reached a total of twenty-five repetitions. The last performance was the most difficult due to the fatigue that had set in; Johnny had, nonetheless, achieved something that most (but not all) people would have found impossible. As he watched the smoke from the final extinguished flame, he noticed that it was drifting in a disconcertingly unnatural pattern. The blue-grey mist was no longer in random Brownian motion, it instead seemed to snake its way through the air with purpose. Johnny observed intently with one of his dark eyebrows raised. He was unhappy at the invasion of his privacy; somebody was evidently using psychokinetic energy on the candle smoke and had the audacity to be doing it within his own home during the intimate moments of psychic exercise. In response to this potential threat, he used his willpower to surround himself with a psychic shield. The simple manipulation of smoke he was now witnessing could easily become a full-blown assault on his very person. After all, in his line of work he had enemies; many who were as gifted as he was.

Johnny watched the smoke carefully. Its long, convoluted route was taking the form of letters, like stunt planes leaving a trail; someone was writing a message. By the time he had projected a full-strength shield the smoky text was complete and hung suspended in the air.

"What's with the candle? Did I miss someone's birthday?" asked the impertinent message, disturbing the sombre ambience of meditation. Somebody was messing around and Johnny knew exactly who it was. He broke up the smoke with a lazy wave of his hand; preparing for psychic combat had expended unnecessary energy when there was no threat present. Uncrossing his legs, he got up, slipped off the loose trousers he wore, and made his way to the small, damp bathroom. The moment he entered, he felt a static electrical charge in the air, and the skin all over his body started to tingle with a gradually increasing intensity. He had experienced this sensation many times before: it was the precursor to a psychic event and brought on by the presence of subatomic particles known as Presarium, the spirit-substance that lay within all matter. Of the life-forms that dwelled upon this dimensional plane, there were only a few individuals (a mere drop in the ocean of existence) who were receptive to Presarium. With time and sufficient training, they could develop their sensitivity to the point where they were able to recognise the multifarious patterns in which Presarium presented itself; this was the gift of psychic perception. Through further rigorous training they could eventually go on to manipulate Presarium particles with their will and thereby control matter itself; this was the cornerstone of psycho-kinetic ability. Johnny was one of the few people on Earth who could do both.

The tingling sensation in his skin intensified further along with the airborne static electrical charge. Johnny was sufficiently versed in matters psychic to recognise that the changes he perceived corresponded to the opening of an inter-dimensional gateway, albeit a very small one, and at any moment now he expected a visitor to come through it, no doubt the perpetrator of the mischief with the candle smoke. Not being one to waste any time, he decided to continue with his ablutions rather than stand on ceremony for this guest who had probably travelled light years to reach him; he smeared his face with foam and started to shave. After the first few strokes of his razor, a disembodied chorus of a voice echoed through the air; it was faint and seemed to be projected from a great distance.

"I'm on my way, Johnny baby!" it said from no particular direction or visible source, eerily filling the small bathroom.

"Baccharus! Long time no see!" Johnny replied to the familiar voice. As he stood rinsing his razor before the bathroom mirror, he saw in its reflection a small blurred shape slowly materialising in the air over his right shoulder. The tingling sensation and the atmospheric charge reached a crescendo, and Johnny felt as if he was submerged in an electrified pool of water. Not for the first time he wondered what it must feel like to be 'normal', non-psychic, and oblivious to such a great disturbance in the environment as this. Suddenly it all stopped. The air around Johnny was still once again and his skin tingled no more. The gate had closed and there was another presence in the bathroom, the vague blur over his right shoulder had completely materialised into a living entity. Where there had previously been nothing was now the oddest of creatures, the hovering form of a twelve-month infant with coffee coloured skin, black hair (in short bouncy curls) and brilliant white angel wings. The wings were small, far too small for flight, and yet they flapped slowly upwards and downwards, and the little being managed to stay suspended in the air. There was something distinctly male about this cherub, if not in appearance then certainly in manner. He was clothed in nothing more than a voluminous diaper-like loincloth that clung to his body and, like its wearer, also seemed to defy gravity. His face was chubby and the dark eyes mischievous. The strange being at Johnny's side was his familiar, Baccharus, fabricated for him in a distant galaxy, an eternal companion, a link between its keeper and the worlds and dimensions that constituted reality. Baccharus was also gifted with psychic ability, although his was rather more modest when compared with that of Johnny.

"Yo, Johnny! How are you doing, amigo?" Baccharus greeted his keeper enthusiastically, his voice no longer sounding so strange and distant. If his wings did not mark him out as being something other than human, his speech certainly would have; despite his infant larynx, Baccharus was as articulate as any adult.

"Did you miss me?" asked the cherub, his wings continuing to flap lazily.

Johnny paused mid-stroke with the razor held gently against his cheek; he had a quick think, "No, not really. I was quite enjoying the peace and quiet actually." He continued shaving.

"Awww, you're hurting my feelings, Johnny. Well, I would have missed you, if I only had the time – that's what being your personal assistant for eternity is like, I'm afraid, please have some sympathy." Baccharus was grinning cheekily.

Johnny smiled as he washed shaving foam from his face; the water ran off his elbows and soaked the floor. He didn't doubt that his familiar had been busy. Baccharus had been summoned by the Agency two days ago to be briefed on a new assignment; now that he was back, it was time to find out what the plan was. "So what have you got for us?" Johnny asked, prompting Baccharus to disgorge the information he had brought with him.

"There's quite a tricky case to present to you, my friend. We have a lot of work to do. I have been back and forth to the Agency several times now, gathering and receiving information. To be honest, I'm getting quite fed up of inter-dimensional travel; I wish they would open a branch office or something nearer to this galaxy. It's an ego thing you know, setting yourself up at the centre of the universe! Anyway, are you ready for the briefing?"

Johnny did not relish the prospect of a 'tricky case'. "Well … let me have my shower first, then tell me all about it over a cigar and coffee," he suggested.

"Sounds good," replied the cherub, never one to turn down either indulgence.

As he showered, Johnny considered what mission Baccharus might have returned with from the Agency. A possible answer occurred to him, and the more he thought about it the more he anticipated that the days ahead were not going to be restful ones. After towelling himself dry, Johnny paused to look critically at his body in the mirror; he had been trying to pump up and was unhappy at the lack of progress. He made a promise to redouble his efforts as soon as he got the chance. He was twenty-five years old, probably at his physical peak, with a lot still to learn about his psychic ability. Clad in a bathrobe, he made his way to the sitting area of his studio apartment where Baccharus was flicking through endless home shopping channels.

"Smoke?" enquired Johnny, holding out the tin of cigarillos he had just retrieved from a drawer.

"Don't mind if I do," came the reply. Stubby fingers reached out and took one of the miniature cigars. Baccharus placed it between his lips, and a few seconds later it lit spontaneously. He had performed a similar psychic manipulation to the one Johnny had used earlier when lighting the candles, a simple matter of using the will to excite Presarium particles within the substance of the tobacco until it lit. Even though it had been over ten years since Baccharus first appeared on the scene, Johnny still couldn't help watching the small creature with wonder; here was a hovering infant, smoking. It all seemed rather novel even to this day.

"Nice smoke," complimented the cherub, closely scrutinising the cigarillo like a connoisseur.

"What kept you so long, Bach?" asked Johnny, exhaling.

"Bad news chief, bad news," Baccharus replied, looking grave.

Johnny tested his hunch. "It's to do with all that aberrant psychic energy emanating from somewhere up in the north, isn't it? I've been sensing it on and off for a few months now; it has been fluctuating a lot recently. Is that what this is about?"

"You're good, Johnny; very good. I knew that energy disturbance wouldn't pass you by unnoticed," Baccharus said, genuinely impressed. "That's why the Agency has chosen you as its main man in these parts!"

Johnny laughed sardonically. "I'm the main man!? No wonder the planet is always in so much bloody trouble."

"Johnny, I've met other agents, some of them may be older and more experienced, but you, Johnny, you've got potential. The agency has high hopes for you, pal; high hopes, that's what they're always telling me."

As his familiar, Baccharus would never hear Johnny talked down, even by Johnny himself. Such was the nature of the familiar. Baccharus blew three consecutive smoke rings which Johnny dispersed with a jab of psychokinetic energy.

"Well, maybe I should go to the centre of the universe, knock on the door of the Agency and meet the mighty Council of Seven myself some time," Johnny suggested audaciously.

"Oh, they'd love that, Johnny; they really would."

"Well, not just yet. Anyway, what do they want us to do, then?"

Baccharus recounted the information he'd received concerning their next assignment. "I was briefed by a high-ranking familiar directly affiliated to the Council of Seven, which indicates the importance of what I am about to pass on. As you correctly pointed out, Johnny, there is fluctuating, aberrant psychic energy somewhere north of here – lots of it. What we have are powerful Presarium particle waves; their seemingly random nature means that their exact source has been impossible to pinpoint. All we know regarding their origin is that it's somewhere towards the north and not too far from here. If an agent was to head in that direction and investigate further then he might be able to discover where the heck it was all coming from. Oh, and if there is a problem there then he can sort it out too. You, my friend, are the closest agent to the hypothetical source."

Johnny, who was listening carefully, had a question. "I have been sensing this disturbance on and off now for some time, Baccharus. Why has it taken so long for the Agency to assign somebody the task of investigating it?"

"Well, that question also occurred to me so I asked the familiar. It was a miniature unicorn type thing, by the way; very cute. The unicorn explained that there were disturbances like this all the time in the universe. It's the type of thing agents scattered throughout various galaxies have to constantly deal with. It's difficult sometimes to discriminate between freak background psychic activity and genuine matters of concern. Ninety-nine per cent of the time these disturbances amount to nothing."

"So what made the Council of Seven decide this was a 'genuine matter of concern'?" Johnny asked, sensing there was more to come.

"Well, some of the fluctuations from this aberrant psychic energy have had enormous peaks recently, real gazongas, massive spikes lasting for only a few milliseconds; not very long, although long enough for the Council to detect them when everyone else missed them altogether. These are energy fluxes beyond the ability of normal rogue psychics who, as you know, are the main problem agents are called in to deal with. More importantly, the frequency and shape of these waves has the signature of Disorder all over it."

Disorder … the word hung heavily in the room. Johnny looked concerned now. Resisting the Disciples of Disorder was one of the reasons the organisation he worked for existed. As one of its agents, it was his duty to confront any threat from this old enemy.

"So it seems the forces of Disorder are trying to make a breakthrough on Earth again, and it's up to me to find out how? I suppose I have to stop them while I'm at it! Do we have any idea at all as to what they intend doing, Bach?"

"I'm afraid not. There is something obscuring the exact nature of this psychic activity at its very source. There is no clarity in the picture we have so far, the Disciples of Disorder have gone to great lengths to cover their tracks. What we can tell is that the frequency and energy behind the aberrant Presarium waves has not been seen on Earth for many thousands of years, since the times of … ummm, I don't know, say, ancient Egypt … or the Druids … those cats. Basically, a frigging long time ago."

Baccharus was prone to use profanity, he couldn't help it.

Every familiar was unique, designed to fit whatever keeper it was created for, a life-form fabricated by the Council of Seven. The knowledge for creating a familiar was known only to a few advanced alien races. Whatever Baccharus was, from his bizarre appearance to his colourful use of language, it all had a purpose, and that was to be the ideal companion for Johnny; he was crafted to possess the physical form, language and manner to which Johnny would be most receptive, consciously and subconsciously. He was an ideal companion for Johnny by design, engendering healthy levels of trust and mistrust, love and hate, amusement and anger, and myriad more emotional responses, both negative and positive. Observing Baccharus told you more about Johnny than Johnny could tell you about himself. The Council of Seven had even used strands of Johnny's own DNA in the familiar's construction.

Baccharus flicked his cigar butt out of the skylight, which dismayed Johnny; his landlord was always irate about smoking on the premises. Trying to ignore this infraction, he paced up and down the apartment in deep thought, deciding upon a plan of action; Baccharus flew in reverse a few feet ahead of him.

"There must be some more in the way of guidance from the Council," insisted Johnny without a break in his stride.

"I'm afraid not, Johnny. At the moment they don't seem to know a great deal themselves. They just want you to go there, investigate, and then sort this mess out."

Johnny laughed in disbelief. "There is a manipulation of psychic energy so great that it hasn't been experienced on Earth for thousands of years, and they want me to sort it out? I take it they don't plan on sending any help?"

"I'm not finished yet, Johnny. I don't quite know how to tell you this ..." Baccharus paused to draw a deep breath,

"… we have about forty-eight hours before it's too late."

Johnny thought he was hearing incorrectly. "Sorry, Bach, how long have we got?" he asked.

"Forty-eight hours," said Baccharus again, rather sheepishly.

"Why forty-eight hours?" asked Johnny, incredulous.

"Okay, listen carefully, you're going to love this, it's what the unicorn told me. The aberrant Presarium waves converge at a point in time which is forty-eight hours from now, which in turn corresponds to the night when Jupiter, Venus, Mars and Earth are in alignment; which, as you may or may not know, are the four main psychocentric planets of this solar system. The alignment will amplify certain forms of psychic energy; probably something the Disciples of Disorder will try to take advantage of. So the upshot of all this is that we know when we have to sort things out by, and because of the attempts to obscure the signal, nobody seems to know exactly *where* we need to be to do this."

"And if we're late?"

Baccharus shrugged his shoulders. "I don't know; nobody knows exactly. Whenever the Disciples of Disorder make a power move, things get pretty nasty. I know of a planet that was almost destroyed when—"

"Okay, Baccharus, I get the message!" interrupted Johnny. "Enough talk; let's start preparing before it's too late."

The time for action had come; it was what Baccharus lived for. "Yeah! Let's do it!" yelled the floating infant with enthusiasm that was not in any way shared by Johnny. "So where are we going, J-man?"

"Well, let's just head north for now I suppose … I have a strange feeling that it's not only the Council of Seven who wants me out there."

"What do you mean, Johnny?"

"I think there is a voice out there, Bach, calling to me psychically," said Johnny, frowning, recollecting the recent dreams that had been invading his mind.

"What?"

"Don't worry about it, pal. Go and tell Sascha to get ready, I'll pack a few things here. We leave in an hour."

"Okay, Johnny. I do want to know more about that psychic call for help though."

"Yeah, I'll tell you later; just get Sascha ready."

"Right away! Oh! And how about that coffee?"

"No chance! And before you disappear, make sure you tell Sascha everything you told me, he needs to know *all* the details of this assignment."

Nodding in agreement, Baccharus dematerialised from Johnny's apartment. Sascha was Johnny's oldest companion, and the little cherub knew his house very well; such familiarity with a location was essential for cross-dimensional travel. *Sure beats walking there*, thought Baccharus as he faded from view. *Hell! It even beats flying*.

Alone once again, Johnny looked pensively out of the skylight. He had an ominous feeling about this mission; there seemed to be some desperation about it. The Council of Seven were amongst the most powerful psychic entities in the universe, and for them to be forced into such a tight deadline, only forty-eight hours, was a bad sign, very bad indeed.

Johnny swung the skylight open to its widest, and a cool wind blew over him. He took a deep breath; it felt good. The dampness from his shower and the tobacco smoke had made the air indoors stale and heavy. From his vantage point, he closed his eyes and reached out with his mind into the world around him and sensed it in ways few other people could. His consciousness had now stretched beyond the five senses and the three dimensions of space. Now he was aware of the psychic energy innate in all matter, particularly living organisms. Johnny's eyes may have been closed; his perception, however, was wide open. He felt as if he was submerged in a mysterious sensual sea in which he could feel ripples and currents everywhere. Only after careful guidance, experience and supreme concentration could a psychic come to make sense of these strange feelings. He recognised a sensation that streamed over his body, slowly and regularly, as having originated from the garden outside with its assorted plant and insect life. A subtle vibration swept through his face and scalp which corresponded to a flock of pigeons that had landed on the roof. Some of the vibrations surrounding his body varied widely in their frequency and intensity, and Johnny knew they were from the other tenants in the apartments below; with his years of practice Johnny could name the person from whom each vibration originated, how they were feeling, and even a little of what they were thinking. All over his body, there were thousands more of these ripples and oscillations, all occurring at once, each a function of the world around him; he was a radar receiving multiple microscopic signals. Over the past few months there had been a new feeling in the air; it was the result of disordered psychic energy originating from many miles to the north. Even now, Johnny could sense its aberrant vibration: destructive, untamed and quite repulsive. It had been there, in the background, for a few weeks now, stronger at times and weaker at others. He wondered what it was. He had definitely chosen a bad week to try to give up smoking.

Chapter 2

In the Scottish Highlands, almost five hundred miles away from Johnny's apartment in London, Martin Butler stealthily skirted around the outside of a substantial brick perimeter wall. The daunting structure approached ten feet in height and encircled a vast plot of land at the centre of which, hidden from view, stood a magnificent country mansion. It was inside these grounds, beyond this very wall, two months ago, that he had seen the beast walking with the man in the coat. Seeing them that night had set his life on its present, dangerous course.

Martin moved furtively, doing his utmost to remain unseen, concealing himself amongst the surrounding woodland whenever possible; there was purpose etched on his face. It was dusk, the temperature had dropped; he found the cold air bracing. The damp leafy ground felt springy underfoot, and the moisture from it seeped through his black trainers, soaking his feet.

He picked his way quickly through the trees and shrubs, always remaining close to the high brick wall, his shoulder sometimes brushing against its moss and lichen-covered surface. To camouflage himself, he had intentionally chosen dull, earthy colours for the cotton army trousers and tightly zipped sailing jacket that he wore.

Martin was trespassing on land that belonged to an important and influential man, a man with whom he had fallen out of favour, a man who would not hesitate to do everything in his considerable power to eradicate him if he ever discovered that he was so close to his property. Martin did not expose himself to such danger lightly; he had a message to convey, a warning for the girl, Rachel, who lived here in the mansion house. The man whose attention he was trying to avoid was her foster father. In his attempts to reach Rachel alone, he had returned to the property time and time again; finding her had proven more difficult than he had anticipated when first setting out on this most desperate of missions.

Martin was not relying on blind luck to achieve his end; he knew Rachel well and it did not surprise him when he learned that she often wandered alone in the vast grounds of the house, without even her foster sisters for company. He had decided some time ago that keeping a close eye on the gardens would therefore give him his best chance of meeting her. She was someone who enjoyed good company and, despite her youth, also valued moments of solitude; she needed time for quiet reflection – there had been plenty in her life for her to reflect upon.

It was imperative that he find her without her foster parents knowing about it because the warning he carried was about them. Her foster parents, her father in particular, had been responsible for the suffering of too many good people, and soon it would be Rachel's turn, he was sure of it. He knew all this because there was a time, not very long ago, when he himself was closely associated with them. Martin had been a companion of evil and reaped his own selfish benefit in the process. With time though came deeper understanding, and he slowly turned against all the wrong he was witnessing. Had he been too slow in this? He didn't know. He had sat back and done nothing for too long, colluded through his silence. Now he would take action and make amends because with his warning he also brought a plan, a way to save the girl; he just had to make sure she would hear him out. It was going to be difficult. Her foster parents had become increasingly possessive of her, and despite being fifteen years old she was under virtual house arrest without even knowing it.

He continued his progress around the wall, fearful of discovery and determined to complete what he had set out to do. By his reckoning, he had about three nights before the plans involving Rachel and her sisters were executed in this very house. He did not know exactly what was going to happen; he *could* guess that it would be something unpleasant beyond comprehension. *Three nights to save three girls*, he thought to himself, because by saving Rachel he was sure her two foster sisters would also be spared.

Ahead, Martin could see the first of four gates that were housed within the wall at regular intervals; each constructed with thick metal rods and possessing its own complex lock. Many times, in the dead of night, he had tried to coax these gates open; unfortunately, their simple, solid design had proven resistant to any forced entry. They were well maintained and as impenetrable as the wall. On reaching the first gate, he stopped suddenly, convinced that his senses were deceiving him; inside it, only a few feet away, was Rachel, leaning against an aged oak tree. This was the moment he had been waiting for! He guessed it was probably the tenth visit he had made here to look for the girl; however, having lost count some time ago, he could not be sure. It seemed that on this occasion his persistence would pay dividends.

Adrenalin surged through Martin's body; he was like a hunter catching sight of its prey. All the time spent hanging around this damned wall, he thought to himself, all the cold damp days spying on the gardens; finally, here was an opportunity. His heart pounded with anticipation, and his mind became fraught with anxiety at the thought of blowing what could be his only chance of meeting Rachel alone and in the absence of her obsessive foster parents. A chance to pass on his warning before time ran out. For Martin, this was not just an opportunity to help a loved one, it was also an opening to redeem himself.

He thought quickly. Knowing what he had to tell her, he was undecided about the best way to do it. Not being one to work from a script, Martin decided to play everything by ear just as he always did, adapt to the girl's reactions, improvise, this would be his strength … he hoped to God it would not be his downfall.

He took a few seconds to carefully scan the grounds beyond where Rachel stood; when satisfied that there was nobody else around, Martin made his move. Crouching down low to maintain some degree of cover from the surrounding woodland foliage, he edged towards the metal gate, closer to the teenager.

She was turned away from him. He could make out her familiar figure and short dark hair. She was dressed casually in jeans, trainers and a thick hooded top. Her slim frame leaned closely against the broad tree trunk, staring out towards the house as if she was concealing herself from somebody. *Could she have found out already?* Martin asked himself hopefully as he approached her. Now, close enough to make contact, he ducked behind a low branch, ensuring the girl could still see his face from amongst the leaves.

"Rachel," he whispered guardedly; she did not hear him. The fear of giving himself away and losing this opportunity had made him overly cautious so he called out to her again, a little louder, "Rachel!"

The dark-haired girl suddenly spun her head around. Martin saw the startled look on her elfin face, her brown eyes wide with alarm. He smiled nervously, afraid that she might do something to give him away; she looked beautiful he thought, like her mother had. It took Rachel a few moments longer than expected to recognise what should have been a familiar face; Martin reasoned that he was probably one of the last people she had expected to see while strolling alone in the garden. The old oak tree that she was standing beside reminded him of a place from the past where she often stopped to spend a few brooding minutes on her walks.

"Martin?" she whispered, the look on her face quizzical rather than startled.

Martin was pleased that her voice remained so hushed. *Bright girl*, he thought. He had intentionally adopted an approach that demanded secrecy, and she had picked up on this straight away. As she stared at him, Martin spoke. "Rachel, stay behind the tree, don't move … Please … you must keep quiet and listen carefully, there's something very important I have to tell you." He kept his voice low, unable to hide the desperation in it. He watched her intently, unsure how she would react.

Rachel, still looking confused, answered his question with her own, "Why don't you meet me in the house?" As far as she was concerned, he was still welcome in the big old mansion, Martin thought. She did not realise how times and circumstances had changed, that if he entered her home again it would be unlikely that her foster parents would ever allow him to leave. Martin looked into her face, and he could tell they had not managed to turn her against him … yet.

The matter that brought him here was complex and

desperately urgent; he would not be able to explain its every detail during this impromptu meeting. Instead, he would have to depend on the trust that existed between the two of them. "Rachel, when your mother was alive, I loved her more than anything in this world," he said. "Now, as far as I'm concerned, you're the closest person to me … we're like family. I would do anything to make sure you weren't harmed in any way. You know that's true, don't you?" He was edging towards emotional blackmail and didn't like it, but time was scarce.

"Martin, you know you don't have to ask me that," Rachel replied. Before Martin could say another word, Rachel spoke up again, her voice wavering with emotion, "Where have you been, Martin? I was left here alone; seeing you was all I ever looked forward to. I haven't heard a thing from you for so long, no goodbye, no phone call, no explanation. Where were you?"

Martin was taken aback by the mixture of blame and disappointment loaded in the question. The last thing he ever wanted to do was hurt Rachel. "Rachel, I'm sorry. It wasn't my fault. I tried to see you and they stopped me … your foster parents stopped me. That's what all this is about, they started to suspect that I had turned against them and the terrible things they did. That's why I am here now, Rachel."

"What are you saying, Martin? What terrible things?"

Martin could see that hearing him speak in this way was frightening her; he had been the only true father figure in her life, and Rachel trusted whatever he told her. Martin paused, wondering how to word what he was going to say next. There was going to be no easy way to do it. "Rachel, you're in danger in this house, you might have sensed it yourself already, umm … I don't know, maybe you've noticed everyone acting a bit differently recently, a bit strange … something like that?" Martin looked at her; she was still listening so he continued. "Have your foster parents been acting like they're preparing for something, something big that they haven't told you about, you know what I mean? Running around doing things urgently? You might have sensed that they are hiding stuff from you … have you noticed anything like that at all, Rach?"

Rachel nodded quietly; Martin continued, "Have you seen people coming to the house? Strange guests you haven't seen before, coming and going at all hours and no one tells you about them, important-looking people, you might have been introduced to some of them, maybe even recognised them from the newspapers? And the noises, Rach! Have you heard strange sounds in the dead of night? Voices and … and vibrations as if they are coming from deep underground? Have you heard this stuff?" Martin could see that he really had her attention now; she must have been woken up time and time again by the disturbances he described.

"What's going on, Martin?" Rachel asked nervously.

"There's too much bad stuff going on to tell you everything now; just trust me, honey, you've got to get out of here. *All* these things, the noises, the visitors, it's all bad. Tomorrow night I'm going to take you away. I want to sneak you out of your bedroom; it'll be easy, the portico is just under your window. I'll help you from there with a friend who's good at stuff like this. Your foster father is an evil, wicked person, if only you knew half the things he did, Rach. Two thirty a.m. I'll be there on the portico roof to take you away."

"How did you find out about all this?" she asked anxiously.

"I learned about these things because, I am sorry to say, I was once a part of them. I didn't fully understand what they were up to at the time … then I found this and it all became clearer." From the inside of his jacket he took out a battered black diary.

Rachel gasped, "Mum's diary – I thought it had been lost!" Her eyes welled up with tears at the sight of something so intimate from the mother she had loved so dearly; it opened a floodgate of emotion.

"Martin, I'm scared!" she said tearfully. "I've been scared for a long time, and hearing all this has made me *really* scared. Let's go! Please take me with you." It was Rachel's and not Martin's voice that sounded desperate now, she shifted from behind the large oak tree towards him, as if he could open the gate and take her away immediately.

"Don't move, Rach! Stay there, behind the tree!" Martin ordered her almost angrily; he looked around the grounds and towards the house to ensure nobody was there. It was essential they were not spotted. Rachel, taken aback by the commanding tone of Martin's voice, quickly retreated to the tree again.

Seeing her afraid magnified the paternal instincts Martin felt towards the girl, and he spoke reassuringly, "We can't leave now or they will find us both. They have a lot of very scary friends, Rach. You must go back to the house, pretend nothing has happened. I'll come back for you tomorrow night. I'll be outside your window, on top of the portico, at two thirty a.m. with my friend. We'll take you away; I have it planned. Okay? Tomorrow at two thirty a.m. – I already know your foster father will be out then. I'm sure I don't have to say this … nobody must know that I've been here and spoken to you, or they will make sure I never see you again."

Rachel nodded. *She looks so scared, so vulnerable,* thought Martin. He wanted to take some time to comfort her; with the risk of giving themselves away by doing so, it was not a chance worth taking. He gave her a wink and a smile instead, it was the best he could do. A small smile managed to find its way past the frightened look on her face. *She's a plucky girl*, Martin told himself, *she will be fine.*

He suddenly remembered something. "Oh, and before I go, take these," he said reaching into his jacket pocket, "and if you're still unsure about leaving, then read the diary." From his jacket he produced an amulet. It had a long gold chain from which there hung a large amber sphere. Its surface was carved with runic letters, and embedded at its very centre was a small skull, shaped from an unknown black metal. He carefully wrapped it around the old diary and tossed them both through the gates to land at Rachel's feet.

"What's this?" she asked, unravelling the strange item of jewellery.

"It's something my sister gave to me before she … changed. Anyway, keep it with you, and make sure you have it when I come back tomorrow night. It'll keep you safe, don't show anybody. That's it, Rach. I'm going, hon."

Rachel put the two items into the large pocket of her baggy hooded top. Martin smiled at her before drifting back into the woodland from which he had so mysteriously appeared.

"Martin, wait … I …" started Rachel.

Martin turned around. "Rachel, I can't hang about …"

Rachel gave a sad nod.

Martin hesitated for a moment to choose his words carefully. "I *will* come back and get you, Rachel, but if for any reason I don't, then you must get away … you must get away alone." With a final smile he disappeared into the woods. As he made his way through the trees he hoped Rachel would be ready for him. He knew she would trust him, certainly over her foster parents, probably over anybody; if she had any doubts, then he was sure the diary would convince her.

Martin moved quickly, stray branches whipped and clawed at his face; they could not slow him down. Before long, he had cleared the woods and emerged at a narrow winding B-road. He followed the road on foot for about a hundred metres to a discreet passing point where the rental car he had hired under a false name was parked. Looking over each shoulder to reassure himself that he was not being followed, he entered the vehicle. Despite wanting to drive away quickly, he chose to sit quietly for a few moments to calm his agitated mind; there was every chance that he would make a mistake if he did not. He was glad Rachel had the amulet; it was something his sister had given to him when she was still the good, loving person he always tried to remember her as. 'If things change, Martin, this will keep you safe,' she had told him. He did not know where on earth she had got it from; she was right though, things had changed, everything was so much stranger now, and whenever he had the amulet he was safer. It was not just psychological, things actually *were* different. Somehow, he was able to evade the Disciples far more effectively with the amulet.

Meeting Rachel had brought back cherished memories, those of the girl's mother in particular whom he had loved so profoundly; although not formally engaged, they had planned to marry. During the course of that relationship, he had become very close to the young Rachel. If Louise had not died so prematurely, he was convinced they would all be living as a family now. Fate had been cruel and decided otherwise. Without further hesitation, Martin started the car and drove away.

**

He's gone. Rachel was left in the garden feeling very alone. She had felt lonely before, especially since moving in with her foster parents two years ago; never had she felt alone as intensely as she did now. She pressed her body against the large oak tree; it was her only source of comfort.

Martin's uncannily accurate words raced through her mind. There had been a definite sense of something unusual going on in the house recently. She had tried to ignore it. On a few occasions, she had ventured far enough to mention these noises to her foster mother in the hope of finding an explanation; her queries had been brushed aside with an excuse and a smile. The rumbling and vibrations would be blamed on old plumbing in the cellar. The voices and the visitors who came at odd hours also had a convenient explanation; apparently, they were business contacts of her foster father's. They were coming from abroad, she would say, that's why their timings were so unsociable. There was always something unconvincing about these explanations. On one occasion, Rachel heard a group of these men outside her bedroom at four a.m. They seemed to be speaking in perfect Scottish and English accents, discussing something mundane like how wet the weather had been over the past few days, or their gardens; they were certainly not visitors from overseas. The only reason she didn't push the issue any further was because of a realisation she had come to a long time ago; that despite their kindness, her foster parents were both quite eccentric and secretive. If they didn't want you to know, then you wouldn't; it was as simple as that.

She stood alone, wondering exactly what Martin had found out. It had been a few months since they last met.

The familiar brown ruffled hair, narrow sideburns and keen greyish eyes had not changed; but his face, always so youthful and mischievous, now appeared exhausted and harassed. His looks now reflected every one of his forty years and more.

Still unsure about what to make of the strange meeting, she found precious memories of her mother flashing through her mind. Of all the people Rachel had known in her life, her mother had been the best, and after her mother, the person who had done the most for her, far more than her father ever did, was Martin. Following her mother's death, he would meet her at least once every week just to make sure she was all right. It had been months since she last saw him. *So he hadn't been around for a while; that didn't mean he had stopped caring. Maybe there was a reason for his absence ...* Lost in these thoughts, she did not notice her two foster sisters calling to her until they were only a few metres away.

"Rachel! We thought we would find you hiding away somewhere around here!" Meredith called out.

They had known each other for five years, and Meredith was quite aware of the various secluded spots Rachel frequented in the garden. Rachel fumbled with the amulet and the diary in her large pockets, ensuring they were concealed and secure; she smiled at her two approaching sisters as she did so.

"Trying to get away from everyone again?" asked Lisa with a cheeky grin.

Meredith was almost a year older than Rachel. She was a good-natured girl with auburn hair and a bulky frame; she cut a contrasting figure to the slim, dark Rachel. Following her was Lisa, the youngest of the foster sisters. She had green eyes and frizzy light brown hair tied back in a tight ponytail. Of the three girls, Lisa had by far the bubbliest and most temperamental personality, their foster mother referred to her as a livewire and she seemed to revel in this reputation. Like Rachel, they were both dressed casually in jeans and sports tops.

"I just wanted to get out of the house. You know I can't stay indoors as much as you two, it's just so suffocating," Rachel replied quite honestly.

"Yeah, I know what you mean. We just got bored and thought we'd come out to find you," said Lisa.

"So now you've found me, what's the plan?" Rachel asked. Her two sisters looked at each other and shrugged, all three of them laughed. Meredith looked at her watch.

"Shall we go in? There'll be some good stuff on TV now." In agreement, they all walked back to the house.

Meredith had intuitively sensed Rachel's unease and had allowed Lisa to walk on ahead so she could speak to her sister alone. "Are you okay, Rach?" she asked.

On hearing Meredith's concerned voice, Rachel's mind, which was still ruminating over the strange meeting with Martin, snapped back to the present. "I'm fine … just feeling down about living here, in the middle of nowhere, you know?" she replied, not telling any lies and at the same time not revealing what was really on her mind.

Meredith nodded in agreement. "Tell me about it," she said. "Sometimes I wonder why they're so strict about us going out of the house. I mean, I know there was the accident and all, but it seems like there's more to it than that."

At those words, Rachel turned to Meredith suddenly, wondering if her foster sister knew Martin's secret. The expression on Meredith's face was of someone lost in personal reflection, she had made the statement quite innocently.

Chapter 3

It was approaching 10:00 p.m. Martin was almost a hundred miles from the old country house where he had found Rachel earlier in the day. He walked through darkness and drizzle along Billington Road at the very edge of Glasgow's city centre. It was quiet out and he felt uneasy, which, until recently, was unlike him. He comforted himself by imagining cosy scenes behind the drawn curtains of houses that he passed: children tucked into bed, exhausted parents taking a few precious moments to put their feet up, couples, young and old, sitting in armchairs watching TV together, content in each other's company. He envied all these people in their houses. They were leading the life he had desired since childhood but to this day had never known – and still there was no peace for him.

He was anxious about Rachel and knew he would continue to be until she was safe again; it was to this end that he had arranged tonight's meeting. His plan to remove her from under the noses of those ever-watchful foster parents was audacious; she had to be out of that house before it was too late so there was no other choice. Rachel was a smart girl; she might eventually have escaped by herself even without his intervention – he could see that she had already noticed the subtle abnormalities within her foster home. Given time, they might have disturbed her enough to run away; however, he simply couldn't leave such an outcome to chance, there was too much at stake.

Ahead was the Cavendish Arms pub, his rendezvous, nestled on the corner of two small residential streets. He had arrived earlier than planned; that was the way he liked it. *Leaves enough time to settle the nerves,* he thought. The pub was a twenty-five minute walk from his flat. It was not the nearest place to get a drink; the reason he had chosen this particular venue was for its atmosphere, it felt private. The patrons never seemed concerned about other folk who happened to be around, preferring to keep themselves to themselves. It was something he appreciated. In this meeting, privacy was going to be essential, and he no longer felt this could be achieved in his own home, which was probably under surveillance by now.

Martin entered the dimly lit mock-Tudor building and was bathed in the inviting warmth of its interior, a stark contrast to the chill creeping into the wind outside. Ducking under a low wooden beam, he passed a crackling fireplace before approaching the bar. True to form, the stout, grey landlord, who must have seen him a dozen times before, served him politely with merely a nod of acknowledgement and no banter. *That's why I come here, no conversation and no questions.* He selected a wooden table beside a small side window across from the fireplace; it was set slightly apart from the main seating of the pub. Looking around he noted two sets of drinkers: the first made up of four middle-aged men in quiet, intense discussion and the second, a young couple. He glanced at his watch. Peter Pike, his intimidating, unsavoury, loyal friend would be there in about five minutes.

As he waited, he tried to clear his thoughts. Subtly linked events from the distant and more recent past had been weighing heavily on his mind for months, events like Louise's death, his attempts to find Rachel, and the malign intentions of her foster parents. Mentally, it was all taking its toll, and he wanted to forget the whole lot just for a few minutes before his meeting. He rubbed his temples to ease the tension headache that had been occurring far too frequently of late; the massage helped a little. He sipped his beer quickly and tried to think of other things, anything, and his mind gradually drifted back to a time before this mess. He pictured the rare occasions from his childhood home when his mother was well, happy times. A few minutes into these recollections he was interrupted by a familiar voice.

"Marty boy!" it growled. This far north the cockney accent was out of place and absolutely unmistakable. He looked up to see Peter Pike standing over him. He had been so engrossed in his thoughts that he had not noticed the other man enter.

Martin stood up to greet his trusted old acquaintance. "Petey!" was all he said as the two men exchanged solid handshakes and wide grins, old partners back together again. Martin glanced at his watch. *Bang on time*, he thought, *punctual Pete*. "Hey, big fella! Sit! Let me get you a drink," he offered, gesturing to the empty chair opposite him.

"Lovely, cheers."

"What are you having?"

"Kronenbourg."

Martin walked back to the bar while Peter Pike took off his long, dark coat and sat down, taking in his new surroundings as he waited for his drink. On the way back to the table, Martin could not help smiling at how his massive, balding friend dwarfed the chair on which he sat; he placed the fresh drink before Pike and returned to his own seat.

"So how are you doing, mate?" Martin asked, the refined Home Counties accent he had spent so long trying to cultivate slipping in the presence of his old friend, betraying his own poverty-stricken East London roots.

"Good, thanks – you?"

"All right."

Martin sounded guarded and tense. They had spoken to each other briefly prior to this meeting, and he had given Pike an inkling of what troubled him; he had not yet revealed all. "Look, thanks for coming, Pete."

"Hey, no problem, it's been a long time."

"Too right, how long now?"

"God, it must've been about six months."

"Six months? Oh, yeah! That was when we had that storming night in your mate's club; I remember him giving us an open bar! Bloody generous that."

"Yeah, Mike's old place in Farringdon. It was a good one, wasn't it?"

"Yeah …" Martin hesitated before his next question, "You still doing jobs then, Pete? Last time you mentioned you would consider going straight."

"Oh, I'm still doing jobs; still in the game I'm afraid. I think it was just the booze talking that night. I'm doing pretty good too; you've seen my place haven't you? In Finchley?"

"Yeah, nice."

They talked candidly for a while and filled each other in on the six months from when they last met. Martin learned that most of Pike's income these days was legitimate; it came from a jewellery and watch repair store he now owned. It seemed he still occasionally supplemented his income with a break-in or a drug deal, although these transgressions were much less frequent than in the past.

Their glasses were soon empty. Peter Pike went up to the bar for another round. So far, the meeting had been purely about two friends catching up with each other; on Pike's return to the table there was a noticeably sterner expression on the younger man's face and tension in the air, lots of it. Martin thanked Pike for the drink before he spoke.

"Well, Pete, as you know, I've called you here for a reason."

"Indeed," smiled Pike.

"Did you think about it then, the job I need your help on?"

Peter Pike nodded, his face also looking serious now, a change in expression Martin had seen many times before, the transformation from happy-go-lucky cockney to law-less predator.

"I want to help, Marty boy, God knows you've helped me plenty of times before. You never gave me much to go on in those phone calls though. C'mon, mate, you can't hold back on a potential partner, tell me more."

Martin noticed Pike was careful to emphasise the word 'potential'. He nodded and took a deep breath. "Well, I don't know every detail myself, and that's the honest truth. Basically, there are big problems concerning the people Rachel is living with. I found out stuff about them, things they're into. Basically, we need to get her out of the house before she is harmed."

"What are you talking about? Child abuse? Why don't you go to the police? You don't have to be a vigilante in this day and age."

"No, Pete, it could take too long that way. Besides, in this matter, I don't know if I can even trust the police."

"So it is child abuse then ..." Pike stated with a stony face. There was a pause as the two men looked each other in the eye. "Does Rachel know what you have planned yet?" asked the big man.

Martin hesitated, he had not actually said anything about child abuse, it seemed Peter Pike had reached his own conclusion, and it looked like he was ready to help him for that reason. Martin considered setting his friend straight but reasoned that, in a way, he was right so decided not to say anything that might change his mind. "Yeah, she knows the plan. I've spoken to her, earlier today believe it or not. I told her I will be coming so I assume she will be waiting. We go in, get her out just like I explained to you on the phone. You go your own way after that. If anything happens and I get caught with her, then as far as anybody is concerned, it was just me flying solo." Pike listened carefully; he did not answer. "I need *your* help this time, Pete," said Martin, gently reminding his friend of all the times he had been a lookout for him, or a driver, when Pike was breaking into warehouses.

"Look, Martin, I haven't forgotten anything you've done for me. I'm sure you'll agree that I've done shitloads for you myself. I mean, you could have been dead on the street a dozen times if it weren't for me. Look, I'm not asking for anything, it's just what mates do for each other, isn't it?" Martin nodded sheepishly. Pike's features softened as he continued to speak. "There *is* something different about this request of yours, so don't fret. The way I see it, there's more to it than selfish thieving. This is a chance to help somebody, a child, an innocent. I've got no qualms about people being hurt when they have it coming to them, but a kid, no kid deserved to suffer."

Martin smiled. "So you're in?"

"Okay," nodded Pike slowly, "I'm in … for now. Talk to me about the plan first, the logistics of the operation, tell me what we're up against. If I don't like what I hear, then

I'm afraid I'm out again, okay?"

"Okay, no problem."

For the next half an hour, Martin explained his plan while Peter Pike fired questions at him about security, transport, locations, everything. Martin remembered how thorough his friend was in what he did; once a professional thief, always a professional thief. They spoke intensely in hushed voices, pausing only for Martin to fetch more drinks. When both men were eventually satisfied that there was a workable scheme in place, Pike gave Martin the details of his hotel in the West End and left, explaining that he had other jewellery-related business to see to whilst in Glasgow.

Martin remained behind to finish his drink and savour the pub's relaxed atmosphere a little longer – the fire opposite his table was far too inviting to leave so soon, especially as it would be much colder outside by now. He looked around again. From the original group of four middle-aged men only two remained, they both looked tired, and their faces were flushed from the alcohol they had been steadily consuming. The couple from earlier on had left, and in their place were two young men and two women laughing and drinking. Martin watched them discreetly before his mind drifted to the past once more, and his own drink sat on the table, forgotten. He remembered the time when he first met Peter Pike and thought about the circumstances that had led to that chance encounter, a long train of events that revealed much about his early life.

**

Martin was born in East London. His father was a machine worker in a factory with an alcohol problem that was undoubtedly made worse by the fact that his wife, Martin's mother, was mentally ill. She was a loving woman by nature but subject to long spells of crippling depression during which she was a different person; someone who neglected her children and alienated her husband, sometimes for months at a time. Growing up in this situation created havoc in Martin's early years and eventually caused enough emotional turmoil for him to make the decision to leave the family home and live on the streets despite being only sixteen years old – he remained of no fixed abode until the age of twenty-four, eight long and difficult years. It was the streets where he met Peter Pike in a confrontation over discarded food. Supermarkets routinely dumped sealed and perfectly edible produce past its sell-by date in large padlocked bins, plenty of fodder for those in possession of bolt-cutters and hungry enough to use them. Pike, who was also homeless at the time, turned up scavenging at the bins one night a few minutes later than planned, and was galled to find the young stranger taking the bread that he felt was rightly his. He didn't hesitate in making his feelings on the matter quite clear. Refusing to be intimidated by the bigger, tougher man, Martin stubbornly clung to the food and earned Pike's admiration in the process. Martin soon learned that beneath Peter Pike's street-hardened, flawed exterior, there was a good heart and a man willing to take a bold youth under his wing. Pike, who was a few years older than Martin, had plenty of experience living rough and was also a rising talent in the criminal underworld. He looked after Martin, taught him how to survive on the street and even thrive. In return, he had an able accomplice for his illicit endeavours. Their partnership eventually and inevitably led to one place: prison.

It was only because his older sister was able to track him

down that Martin managed to turn his life around. She had escaped the traumas of their childhood home even before he did by way of a desperately impulsive and short-lived marriage. Her divorce turned out to be the stepping-stone she needed to build a successful life with her second husband. With help from her influential spouse, she had been able to move Martin out of London and set him up with a new life in Scotland, near to her. She helped provide him with training for a career in IT that gave him the means to eventually purchase his own flat.

Peter Pike had no such break. Notorious and already well known to the authorities, he received a longer sentence and, unlike Martin, was more than happy to continue his life of crime on release. Despite going their separate ways, Martin had kept in regular contact with Pike. He appreciated the way the older man had mentored and looked after him for so long; he also accepted that he ended up in jail because of him, but what was twelve months in prison compared with the very real possibilities of a violent end on the streets of London – stabbed, shot or overdosed? At least with Pete he had protection and a ready supply of quality drugs. He never had to take chances with shared needles, unknown concentrations of heroin or aggressive dealers; besides all that, he actually enjoyed the old rogue's company.

They remained good friends, spoke to each other over the phone and met up for drinks if either happened to be nearby. Pike would talk openly about burglaries he had undertaken, the stolen goods he handled and other misdemeanours. He quietly hoped Martin would join him again, just like in the old days. Despite this desire, Pike never applied any undue pressure on Martin because he was genuinely happy that his young partner had found a better life for himself. Martin was, in turn, determined to continue forging ahead with his new, law-abiding existence in Scotland. He did not want to let his sister down and so never felt compelled to join Pike again.

**

The landlord calling last orders interrupted Martin's recollections. His thoughts moved from the past back to the present, and the events around the old country house returned to the forefront of his mind. The meeting with his friend had been positive in many ways, and much of his anxiety was replaced by steely determination. Their plan would be executed the following night, just as he had told Rachel. To contact her now would be impossible. He prayed she would be ready for them.

Chapter 4

As Martin concluded his meeting with Peter Pike, elsewhere, Johnny M. completed his preparation for a journey north to investigate the aberrant psychic energy that had been the source of so much recent concern. He was a light traveller and preferred taking only a single piece of luggage filled with essentials. Johnny had packed according to the forty-eight hour deadline knowing the length of these assignments was notoriously unpredictable.

As he zipped a pocket on his small rucksack, the air became charged with psychoelectrical energy, and Baccharus materialised in his apartment for the second time that day. Preoccupied with running through a mental checklist of the items in his bag, Johnny ignored the cherub, who ended up entertaining himself by playing some of the CDs that were lying around. Four tracks of heavy metal later, Johnny's preparations were complete, and he finally acknowledged his familiar. "So, is Sascha ready?" he asked.

"He said he'll be done by the time we get to his place," replied Baccharus.

Johnny nodded with approval. "Good man to be ready at such short notice."

"The best!"

"Did you tell him everything?"

"Of course."

"Let's get out of here!"

The mission was officially under way. Before he closed the front door, Johnny felt the urge to give his home a long, lingering look, as if he were saying goodbye to an old friend … it was not a good sign.

Baccharus flew slowly alongside Johnny as they left the building. He would have caused quite a stir had he been spotted, but it was late and dark, and being psychic meant that both keeper and familiar could sense that there was nobody around to gawp.

The pair stopped at the top of the apartment building's steep driveway where, parked in all its glory, stood the rusting hulk that was Johnny's motorhome, a Ford Transit van that had undergone a bespoke conversion to camping vehicle. Having owned it for many years, Johnny and Baccharus were oblivious to its rather tatty appearance. It may not have been pretty, however, the camper had proved its worth many times over as the main transport for Johnny and the few friends who helped him in his work for the Agency; of this select group, Sascha was the longest-serving and most important member. Johnny and Baccharus both paused to look fondly at the vehicle before they entered it.

"So, when did you start her up last?" asked the familiar.

"Last week, I start her up regularly – every Sunday morning. Didn't get round to it today though, too busy. You've got to keep the engine ticking over, you know. I think the last time I actually drove her anywhere outside of London was the last mission."

Baccharus shuddered as he remembered the case. "The last mission, oh yeah, that must have been four months ago then, the voodoo-witch soul-thief who was collecting spirits for her doll's house, oh yes, twisted, very twisted. I don't think she'll ever recover from the fright you gave her, Johnny."

Johnny had a wicked smile on his face as he recollected the details of that particular assignment. "Let's get moving, Bach."

Keeper and familiar entered the unexpectedly comfortable living space of the motorhome through its side door. A quick inspection of various meters confirmed that the battery was charged and the water supply topped up. Keeping his transport ready to roll had become a routine for Johnny, one that had proved useful many times over. His frequent checks on oil, engine coolant, tyre pressure and a number of other essentials ensured that despite its run-down appearance, the vehicle remained sound. This was about the limit of his mechanical skills.

Johnny belted himself into the broad, generously padded driver's seat while Baccharus sat in the front beside him. The familiar's usual role on these journeys was to deliver snacks and drinks from the kitchen to the driver's cabin and, more importantly, to brew the coffee. If he got bored with his trips to the fridge and cupboards, which he often did, there was a choice of bunks for him to crash out on. With a single turn of the ignition key, the diesel clattered into life, and after an initial belch of black smoke the engine turned over smoothly. They were on their way, and the first stop was Sascha's house; a light rain prompted Johnny to start the squeaky wipers five minutes into the journey.

The motorhome rumbled gently through London's suburbs, passing endless rows of terraced and semi-detached houses. Neon signs from the occasional parade of shops and take-aways reflected multi-coloured light off the damp road. The wet Sunday evening and late hour ensured the streets were quiet, which not only made it easier to drive, it also meant there was less psychic noise. Every person projected a unique aura, their psychic signature – energy to which Johnny was very sensitive. The more people there were around, the greater their psychic presence, and the disturbance this produced in Johnny's mind could become very tiresome; tonight this was not the case.

Johnny drove with his window open a few inches, enjoying the cool, refreshing breeze that came through the gap. It was not long before he was parking on a quiet dead-end street lined with more of the ubiquitous terrace houses. These ones were particularly old and had front doors that opened onto the footpath. The journey had taken about twenty minutes.

"You just wait in here and keep a look-out," he told Baccharus. Even at this early stage of the mission, Johnny wanted to make sure there was a pair of friendly eyes watching the street. Contrary to their mode of transport, it was not a journey of leisure they had set out upon. They were doing the work of the Agency and there would be enemies around, in this case, some of the worst imaginable, the Disciples of Disorder.

Johnny knocked on the door of house number twenty-four, and a tall, lean figure answered. He had high cheekbones, bulbous light blue eyes behind circular glasses and dark brown hair parted approximately down the centre that extended to his neck. Sascha was an old schoolmate from whom there were no secrets, and at present he looked rather flustered.

"Are you ready to head off?" asked Johnny matter-of-factly. Familiarity had long ago negated the need for pleasantries between the two of them.

"Just give me a few more minutes. Come on in and make

yourself a tea or something," Sascha replied hurriedly before rushing back into the house, leaving his friend standing alone on the doorstep. Johnny supposed Sascha was completing last-minute preparations for the journey ahead. Despite the tight schedule he did not hurry him, just in case he forgot one of his electronic gadgets – important devices that had saved their skins on many occasions.

Johnny stepped inside the porch, closed the door and entered the small front room. Even though Sascha was out of sight, Johnny could hear him frantically rummaging at the top of the nearby staircase. The television had been left on, and the weather forecast drew his attention: it warned of sporadic wind and rain across the country over the next few days, and to Johnny's dismay it appeared to be worse in the north.

"Baccharus is in the van, Sasch. You know how quickly he gets bored, he'll start fiddling and probably end up wrecking something," Johnny shouted up the steps.

"Won't be long, Johnny. Have a seat – chill," Sascha hollered back.

Johnny decided to stand, they had a good few hours of driving ahead of them, and this would probably be the only chance he had to straighten out his legs for a while. With hands in his pockets, he sauntered nosily around the small, cosy lounge. He smirked at the outdated soft furnishings the previous owner had left behind; items Sascha could never be bothered to get rid of. An untidy pile of computing magazines and CDs above the fireplace caught his eye, and he picked up a vintage Gunners album, one he had enjoyed listening to many times over. The CD beneath it raised an eyebrow: a Beethoven symphony – Sascha's musical taste had always been eclectic.

"Nobody seems to know exactly what we're heading

into," Johnny shouted back up the stairs. He wanted to gauge how his friend felt about the new assignment.

"Oh, really … should I be worried about that?" came the entirely honest and unconcerned reply.

Johnny smiled at Sascha's instinctively carefree response and continued to pry. Stacks of A4 paper with scrawled writing and technical diagrams were scattered about the place. Textbooks, mainly on electronics and physics, were piled on every shelf and stuffed into various nooks and crannies. A few old mugs and an open packet of biscuits lay on the coffee table amongst these books and papers; Johnny helped himself to a bourbon cream.

**

Sascha worked as an academic in one of London's prestigious universities; his field was electronic engineering. Gradually gaining recognition as a pioneering researcher, his expertise was becoming increasingly sought after by multinational corporations and even the government. Johnny remembered their school days when, as the new boy, he first struck up a tentative friendship with Sascha, his easy-going genius classmate. They were both thirteen years old at the time. Sascha was by far the brightest student in the year, a truly brilliant mind to whom academic insights came effortlessly. The same quirk of fate that had made him such a brilliant student had also given him a quiet and withdrawn personality, particularly around strangers. These character traits combined with his tall frame and disinterest in most transient adolescent concerns made him a target of low-level school bullying. Johnny had never hesitated in intervening whenever his friend was on the receiving end of any harassment from the other boys. Even as a young man, Johnny found any form of victimisation intolerable, and more than once he found himself playing minder to Sascha. Later in life, Johnny realised that it was not some heroic sense of justice that made him like this, but actually, it was because his mainly dormant psychic ability was functional enough for him to experience the negative energy associated with bullying, even at this early age. Ultimately, he *had* to get involved; it was to stop the pain he felt in himself. For this reason, the young Sascha became quite attached to Johnny, who, at first, did not much care for him; eventually, as they matured and got to know each other better, Johnny started to value and respect his friend's intellect and gentle nature. Sascha never veered from the brilliance he demonstrated in school, going on to write scores of scientific papers and achieving the acclaim of his peers. Many of the journals in which his work had been published were sitting right here, somewhere, in his small front room.

**

Footsteps pounded the stairs, Johnny turned around to see Sascha reappear with a large sports bag and two small backpacks.

"One second!" said his friend as he dropped the luggage at the foot of the stairs, only to run back up and return moments later with a camping rucksack.

"Oh good, you've got your rucksack," said Johnny, "for a moment I thought you were going to take all this crap." He pointed to the first set of bags.

Sascha brushed aside one of his long forelocks indignantly. "I *am* taking all that," he replied. "And it's not crap!" he added.

Johnny paused to carefully choose his words. "Look,

Sascha, will you please try to cut down on the bulk? *But if you think we really need all this then I'll try not to complain."* He said this as diplomatically as possible. Johnny did not want the whole operation bogged down with excess luggage; on the other hand, he was also aware that his friend possessed many useful tools. Sascha, acknowledging Johnny's restraint, rummaged through his luggage to find items that might be discarded, and as he did so, Johnny caught a glimpse of some of the contents.

The sports bag was full of clothing and towels, nothing surprising there, while the two small rucksacks were each full of exercise books and files. Johnny recognised these as the notes he and Sascha had collected over the years as they tried to understand the psychic forces that underpinned reality. Contained within them were various elements of their research such as records of psychic events, early work on auras, observations on paranormal phenomena and measurements taken from experiments on telekinesis; it was work that continued to the present day.

**

Johnny was thirteen when he realised something was happening to him. It started off with dreams, vivid dreams in which he was surrounded by seas of ghostly images, strange people in places he had never been to, all set against a fluid, shifting kaleidoscope of colours. Every feature of this bizarre dreamscape triggered emotions and sensations like nothing he had ever known or experienced before, even as he slept. His mind's eye would move untiringly between every detail in the scene until, eventually, the whole bizarre journey would diminish in its sensual intensity and fade into nothingness; he would awaken from these dreams feeling refreshed and invigorated. He tried to talk about the dreams and the way they made him

feel to his family and even some of his friends; it was difficult to find somebody who would listen because there was
never any narrative or dialogue within these dreams. One
person genuinely intrigued by what Johnny was going
through was his new school friend Sascha; the dreams were
a source of intellectual curiosity for him, puzzles waiting
to be solved. Months passed and the dreams became
increasingly vivid, and every night after his eyes closed,
Johnny found himself exploring ever larger and more
complex psychedelic landscapes – whole cities packed
with ghosts. As the dreams intensified in this way, so did
the barrage of emotions and physical sensations that went
with them, to the point that it was being awake that had
become vague and unclear while within the dreams was
where he truly felt alive. None of this was a problem, until
a few months later, when the dreams, much to Johnny's
distress, started to impinge on his waking life. The colours,
ghostly images and strange sensations refused to end with
his sleep, remaining with him as he went about his day – it
scared him. He thought he was losing his mind, only his
friend Sascha was there to reassure him, to talk to him
and unburden the torment of the haunting, ever-present
images.

Every day, Sascha listened to Johnny as he described
his waking dreams. He spoke of strange lights and halos
around people and, most intriguingly, about how everything that he perceived in the world around him stimu-
lated sensory and emotional responses that simply had not
been there before. It was Sascha who first started to see
the patterns in these descriptions, and it prompted him to
postulate quite correctly that Johnny was no longer inter-
acting with the world solely through the five senses: for
him, the realm of the abstract (in which dwelt thought,
emotion and energy) was now a perceptible function of

reality. The friends explored this new, heightened awareness together and started slowly deciphering the torrent of sensory information Johnny was being subjected to. An example of one of their early findings was how colours, auras and vibrations could all be used to discern people's hidden emotions; soon enough, love, hate, truthfulness and deceit were all laid out for Johnny to read after a few moments of disciplined focus. It was during these strange times that the two youths forged a lifelong friendship.

Johnny was not the first to be awakened to the gift; others had developed psychic ability long before him in a process that had been going on since humankind's earliest history. So long as the human race existed, it would continue to give birth to psychics; it was a characteristic introduced into the species' genetic code at the time of its inception. Most psychics never understood their ability and so never embraced it. The gift remained with them only as a curse and an impediment in their lives – many were considered to be suffering from a psychiatric disease. There were two events that set Johnny apart from these unfortunates: one was meeting his friend Sascha, whose companionship and analytical mind guided him through his ordeal, and the second was the arrival of Baccharus.

**

"Well, I suppose it's no catwalk that we're heading to," said Sascha. Johnny watched him discard half the clothes he had packed and all of the towels. From the two smaller bags he brought downstairs, he selected his most relevant notes and shoved them into the now mostly empty clothes bag, dramatically shrinking the amount of baggage he was to take on the trip.

"Okay, that's that," he said triumphantly, and then with great reverence he held up a separate piece of luggage, his large camping rucksack. "From this ... nothing stays behind," he declared. With a smile, he opened the top of the rucksack to show Johnny its contents.

"Now that's more like it!" said Johnny, nodding in approval. Inside was a plethora of electronics; GPS receivers, infra-red thermometer, night vision scopes, EMF detectors, motion detectors and other unrecognisable, phenomenally useful, gadgetry. All these devices were either homemade or modified in some way; nothing was off the shelf. Sascha unzipped another of the rucksack's compartments to reveal a collection of equipment from an army surplus store: dark camouflage clothing, a compass and a miniature tool kit. "Excellent, Sascha, your war-chest is something we definitely need to take with us," said Johnny.

With luggage sorted, the pair prepared to leave the house. Just as he touched the door handle, Johnny stopped and turned around to face his friend and give voice to a thought that had been bothering him for some time. "When I sent Baccharus earlier, I told him to inform you about everything there was to know regarding the mission."

Sascha noticed a touch of remorse in his voice. "Of course you did, pal. I wouldn't expect anything less," he replied.

"Well, as soon as I sent him I regretted it. I was hoping that Baccharus would come back and tell me you weren't able to make it, that you were too busy or something."

"Why is that?" Sascha asked, looking a little hurt and sounding a little confused.

Johnny took a deep breath. "Ever since I started developing psychic ability, you've been there with me, on a journey in which we've both learned many new things. I think you'll agree with me when I say that one of the important lessons has been that the universe is not this massive benign entity full of nothingness that we were always led to believe; it's a place full of life, sentience, energy and, most of all, danger. On every assignment we have carried out for the Agency, there have been hazards – in this particular investigation I sense there is real danger – if I say our lives are at risk, I don't think I'm exaggerating. What I'm trying to say is that you don't have to risk your life, friend. If anything happened to you, I would feel responsible, and I don't think I could handle it."

Sascha looked sombre. "Johnny, I appreciate your concern. Let me say this though: through my association with you I have been awoken to a whole new world. After coming this far, I can't just go back and continue as if it didn't exist. Knowing the truth about the wider universe really puts our daily struggle on Earth into perspective. I hate to say it, but it makes it look pretty insignificant. I can't just go back to living as normal, Johnny … and besides, I don't abandon my friends."

Johnny gave a single nod of acknowledgement. "Well, let's stop talking and get going then!" he said, deciding not to bring the subject up again … not on this assignment anyway. They left the house and Sascha locked up. Johnny couldn't help noticing that his friend had not bothered tidying away the old biscuits and half-full coffee mugs that were lying around; he expected the scientific genius was attempting to grow new strains of mould or fungus for study on his return, or so he hoped.

A little hand waved at the approaching pair from the motorhome's large side window. Johnny opened the squeaky passenger door, and greetings followed as Sascha and Baccharus were reunited. Luggage was loaded quickly on to the vehicle before it became soaked by the persistent rain, and the party set off into the night. Johnny drove,

Sascha sat in the front passenger seat, and Baccharus hovered about the living section of the vehicle, occupying himself by nosily searching through Sascha's rucksack of gadgets, familiarising himself with the items he thought might be useful.

"So, where are we going?" asked Sascha.

"Just north," replied Johnny, "if we get closer to the source of the aberrant energy waves it may be easier to discover their precise location, or at least some clues, besides, I have a feeling that if we don't find whatever we're looking for, it will find us."

Sascha turned in his seat and asked Baccharus to bring his rucksack over. Rummaging through it, he pulled out a small black plastic device that looked like a mobile phone and fixed it to the dashboard.

"What's that?" asked the familiar, eyeing the item suspiciously.

"Something I hope will help us," replied Sascha. "It's a portable version of my Presarium detector; the graphical display will indicate when we are near any significant source of psychic energy, aberrant or otherwise. It may give us a lead regarding where we need to go or warn us if there is trouble brewing – psychic trouble, that is."

Johnny glanced at the device, intrigued. He was aware of Sascha's Presarium detectors although he had never seen one that was so compact. A question sprang to his mind. "The anomalous psychic energy up north has been there for a while, Sascha. The Council of Seven only became concerned enough to send us after they detected powerful, short-lived Presarium bursts from it. I was wondering if your detector picked up any of these?"

Sacha frowned. "I'm sure it must have. If they lasted milliseconds then there's every chance I didn't notice them. Give me a few minutes, I'll scroll through the device's memory to see if it registered anything significant." Sascha picked up the Presarium detector and started fiddling with some buttons. It bleeped and flashed, and the screen flicked through various graphs and charts. "Baccharus, can you get us a few drinks?" he requested while endeavouring to find the energy peaks. The cherub hovered back to the fridge.

While his friends were occupied, Johnny thought about his recent dream; he wondered where the valley was, if it even existed, and who the people in it calling for help were.

"Earth expires, the children broken,
Chaos fires once more awoken,"

They had cried out to him.

"Here you go, Johnny." Baccharus held out an ice-cold bottle of cola for his keeper, another was offered to Sascha, who took it without taking his eyes away from the device.

It was another minute before Sascha announced his findings. "Bingo! I've found about twenty energy surges over the past week. There could have been more, but they are so short-lived I think that even my detector missed them."

"So what do you make of them?" asked Johnny.

Sascha thought for a few moments. "Well, they're bigger than anything I have ever seen, their peaks are well off the scale of my meter. Obviously produced by a powerful source, the nature of which I don't have a clue about … they could even be extraterrestrial."

The friends were all silenced by this suggestion as their imaginations ran wild with possibilities, none of which were particularly appealing, and each chose wisely to keep his ideas to himself.

Johnny accelerated hard as they left the city and hit the motorway. He drove for a further hour before Sascha relieved him of driving duty; it was how they rotated their night journeys: one man drove for an hour, one man rested, and then they changed places.

Chapter 5

Having persuaded Peter Pike to join him, Martin walked back home from the Cavendish Arms. He moved quickly through the cold night to his apartment block. Sodium lighting illuminated the exterior of the modern, angular building; it bathed him and the surrounding car park in an orange glow.

A swipe from his electronic key fob opened the polished steel and glass front door. He only lived on the second floor but decided to take the lift up rather than the stairs. Martin was tired and it wasn't just because of the walk, months of stress and insomnia were taking their toll. As much as he wanted to, he could not retire for the night just yet, he had another meeting. It was with someone whom he had found only after weeks of persistent searching. Martin had realised a long time ago that if he was to confront the evil from the old house, he would need help; somebody other than Peter Pike. Pike was a good man, able enough, but Martin had not revealed everything to him; he could not. His old friend was far too rooted in a conventional view of reality to understand what he was truly up against. Martin needed the aid of one who was experienced in matters of the occult, someone who understood the true nature of the threat before them. When he initially set out to find this help, it had been without any real hope of success. He had scoured websites associated with the mystical and paranormal for days; he had referred to journals on the subject and contacted groups that he never believed actually existed until he found them: organisations like ghost hunting clubs and witch's covens. As he explored this strange new world, it became apparent to him that there were more people involved in it than he could possibly have imagined, and to his surprise there was (mostly) nothing odd about them. They were normal folk, touched at some point in their lives by the mysterious and the unexplainable, and their response was to set out and discover more of what lay beyond their daily experience of life.

As he searched for help, there emerged a name, mentioned by several different sources, somebody with the potential to aid him: Boyd Tennant. Tennant was a psychic investigator, described by those who knew him as thorough, open-minded and successful (Martin wasn't sure exactly how success was measured in this line of work). With a background in security and the military, Tennant could also handle himself, which was going to be important – hostility was likely, and he needed someone who would not shirk from it.

To find Boyd, Martin had befriended a helpful, middle-aged man with a ponytail called Jan from a local paranormal society who turned out to be the nearest thing to a guide for him through this new world he was exploring. Jan was acquainted with Boyd through their mutual interest in investigating the unexplained and agreed to contact him for Martin. Despite this help, Boyd Tennant proved to be rather secretive and difficult to get hold of; he reputedly only spoke to somebody about his work when he was convinced that they were as serious about it as he was. It did not help that his services had no fee, which meant that

Martin was unable to lure him with the prospect of a big payday; it also led him to wonder exactly where this man's income came from. After weeks of frustrating messaging and persuasion, all carried out through Jan, Boyd eventually agreed to accept a phone call directly from Martin, and a fortnight ago they had spoken for the first time. They had made contact on a few more occasions since then, always by telephone. Over the course of their conversations, Martin had explained everything he knew about what went on in the house and his own past involvement with it. In the beginning, he had been a little cagey about revealing the bizarre activities and strange events he had witnessed; gradually, as his confidence in Boyd increased, he went on to explain all he had seen quite openly. To his relief, Boyd did not turn him away as a lunatic, no matter how strange the tale. "Tell me more," the psychic investigator often urged Martin over the course of their conversations, cajoling more details out of him so he could build up an understanding of what was going on in the isolated building.

Martin had been trying for some time to arrange a meeting in person; Boyd was a busy man, or at least gave the impression of being one, add to this Martin's preoccupation with finding Rachel, and the opportunity for a face-to-face encounter had not arisen – until tonight. Having only ever spoken to him on the phone, Martin wondered about the appearance of the other man. Normally, he would not have bothered himself with such irrelevancies; however, the nature of their conversations and the frankly bizarre subject matter often made him consider what type of person was willing to acknowledge the perversities that he described. All he had to go on was the voice, which was gravelly with the hint of an accent, the origins of which he was unsure of, he had never been particularly good at recognising accents, he guessed there was a touch of Scouse or possibly some Irish there. From the throaty voice he imagined an old withered figure, although he knew this could not be true because it was contrary to the exploits he had heard this man to be responsible for. The stories Jan had told him about Boyd could only have involved someone of notable physical vigour.

Martin sat nervously by the phone with an eye on the clock, waiting for the pre-arranged time to call, a quarter past midnight – a late hour to speak. He could not have arranged anything earlier because of his meeting at the pub; besides, he had heard Boyd Tennant didn't sleep very much. Three more minutes to go according to the clock on his wall; he could wait no longer and dialled the number Jan had passed on to him. After two rings, a coarse voice answered:

"Hello."

"Hello?" Martin ventured nervously; he was still unsure about how to interact with this man he had never met.

"Is that Martin?"

"Yes, it's Martin here, Boyd – are you ready to come over then?"

"Ready whenever you are … it's not past your bedtime is it?"

Martin laughed dryly. Was it a serious question or had he just heard a deadpan joke?

"I'll be awake. Flat twenty-four, Halford House, Harper Street, G L four. Is that all right?" he said.

"That's fine; I'll be there in under an hour."

"Great, see you soon then, bye."

"Bye."

Martin hung up and walked to the kitchen to make a coffee before Boyd arrived. He wanted it strong enough to clear the alcohol and tiredness from his head, not so potent that it would keep him awake all night, that wouldn't be necessary – not tonight anyway.

Chapter 6

Boyd lifted the smouldering cigarette from the ashtray by the phone and took a couple of quick drags – finally he would meet Martin. This last contact was by far the briefest in a series of telephone conversations that had been going on for the past two weeks. During the course of these exchanges, he had listened carefully to everything the other man had said and recognised with great concern that unearthly powers were at work in the old mansion house.

Boyd was an acolyte of the Earthly Eye and Servant of the Grimoires, the archaic treatise on which his quasi-religious global organisation 'the Order of the Earthly Eye' was founded; the Grimoires were the source of his knowledge regarding the true nature of reality. It was through training from the Aged Masters (the high priests of his Order) and by knowledge of the holy texts that he could confirm that the vile rites and rituals described by Martin over the telephone were the observances of the Disciples of Disorder. Martin had also been honest enough to tell him that, for a short time, he had been a follower of this most ancient and wicked way and a prospective Disciple. He had described meetings in the basement where powerful beings were worshipped and revered, demonic deities such as Chrobos, Azzubelarian and Orbok. Boyd prided himself on being a tough man, but even he had shuddered at the mention of each damnable appellation. Martin spoke of them so naively that Boyd could only conclude that the Disciples had kept the full truth of these fearful entities from him. *Maybe they had doubted his commitment*, he thought. These were the names of alien beings that had struck fear into the hearts of man's earliest ancestors and were now mostly forgotten. By forgetting these ancient evil life-forms through the course of time, mankind had indeed brought great misfortune upon itself because a millennium was but a blink of an eye to the immortals, and they would never forget their insatiable hunger for worlds. Except for a vigilant few, such as those who followed the Grimoires, mankind had indeed dropped its guard.

It had taken a few conversations before Boyd sensed that Martin trusted him enough to really open up about the events he had witnessed, events that had upset his sensibilities so profoundly. On one occasion, Martin gave an account of underground passages where strange figures lurked in the shadows, where alien smells and sounds offended the nose and ears. He had described all this as if he were speaking of earthly deviations; Boyd knew otherwise, indeed, they were deviations that Martin described – they were *not* of this world though. Boyd's past encounters with Disorder and his familiarity with the ancient texts allowed him to interpret correctly the evil Martin had seen, and it heralded the worst, for it appeared that the enemy had already swollen its human ranks with demons summoned from the worlds where Disorder ruled. It was a bad situation, already there had been deaths – Martin had told him so. He had mentioned someone called Louise as an example, someone whom he cared for. It was the tall man who Martin blamed for the murder; he called him Mr Kreb, the one who walked with the beast at his side. *That's not a man*, thought Boyd Tennant, recognising the so-called Mr Kreb and the beast as summoned entities.

Through Martin's recollections of events in the house, Boyd had also been made aware of a dangerous and more immediate enemy. Chrobos, Azzubelarian and Orbok, awesome in their own right, were not actually present on Earth; there was another – at the very centre of the abominable developments taking place in the old house. "The man at the top of it all," was how Martin had put it to him. "The boss, the man who dragged everyone in like he had a power over them." These were all ways of describing the leader of the Disciples, and Martin, despite turning against the heinous religion, still spoke of the leader with awe. Boyd knew this was not merely a charismatic manipulator of the type so often found at the heart of religious cults, the one who Martin described was the Warlock, and Boyd doubted whether he was even entirely human. There was always a Warlock to rouse the Disciples of Disorder. The Warlock was a being with genuine power – the only power, psychic control over matter. The Warlock could be identified through the account Martin had given of his psychic ability or 'magic' as he had put it. Over time the Warlock changed – the magic never did, it was still exactly as it had been documented in the Grimoires, ages ago.

Boyd had dealt with the Disciples before; this time there was something different about them, they were more focused, more determined, and it made him uncharacteristically apprehensive. He took comfort in his faith by whispering a few memorised lines from the holy chapters of the third Grimoire thus invoking a ward of protection against the machinations of Disorder. Then he muttered a prayer of thanks to the holy books, for without the knowledge contained within them he would be like Martin: able to recognise that evil was truly present … unable to truly know it. The whole affair perturbed him greatly, especially the demons summoned from hellish worlds to aid their fellow Disciples on Earth.

Boyd inhaled again from his cigarette and shook his head in barely subdued frustration because he might have resolved the matter by now. After the first few conversations, he had wanted to make an immediate move to find the old building and eradicate the psychic vermin within it; Martin had not let him. He had stubbornly withheld certain details, refusing to tell him the names of any of the Disciples and the location of their base, only letting slip once that it was somewhere in the Highlands. Martin even knew the human name of the Warlock; he had kept that to himself also. There was a reason for this apparent irrationality; it was to protect the innocent victims wrapped up in this mess, one of whom he personally wanted to remove from the grip of the Disciples. "There's a girl there who needs my help," he had said.

"A girl?" Boyd had asked over the phone.

"A fifteen-year-old, I've known her since she was a kid. The Disciples need her and her sisters for something; I don't know what but I have to get her out of there."

"Don't be a fool! Don't go in there yourself!" Boyd had urged; Martin had refused to listen. He told him that he would never again entrust the girl's well-being to a stranger, and only after he had removed her from danger would he be willing to share information about the location of the cult and the names of its members.

"Let me help you save her," Boyd had pleaded. He wasn't able to persuade the other man to change his mind. Jan must have painted quite a gung ho picture of him; it

seemed that Martin's impression of Boyd was of someone who would go storming in and probably get the
girl hurt in the process – Boyd had to concede that the
'storming in' part wasn't entirely unfair. He had tried to
prise more information from Martin by appealing to his
sense of wider responsibility and explaining the supernatural danger the world was being exposed to, danger
he had witnessed so many times before; the man would
not budge. Unlike Boyd, his first priority was not to stop
the Disciples of Disorder; it was to remove the girl from
danger. Boyd also feared for the girl, she had a central role
in the aims of the cult; like Martin, he did not know what
… he imagined the worst though.

With cigarette in hand, Boyd wandered to the kitchen.
There wasn't enough time to finish the limp corned beef
sandwich on the table so he brewed a quick coffee instead
and continued to ponder the situation as he did so. Time
was short; Martin had told him that events in the house
would be climaxing in three nights. If only they had been
able to meet sooner … Boyd had been preoccupied with
finally apprehending a psychic pervert of modest ability whom he had been trailing for almost a month. The
rogue may have been caught; however, it meant that in
the meantime it had been difficult for Martin to get hold
of him. When Martin was finally able to bring the danger
from the house to his attention, Boyd regretted that he
had been so distracted all this time. Tonight though, it
seemed everything would change. Martin had told him
earlier that he had a plan for the girl and was now ready
for Boyd's full involvement; tonight he would pass on all
the vital information he was withholding, he would tell
him everything. On a more personal level, Boyd looked
forward to meeting Martin, to not be corrupted by the
Disciples of Disorder after the degree of exposure he was

subjected to showed strong moral resolve; he considered the possibility of recruiting him into the Order afterwards.

Boyd checked the time on his clock, it was late. He wasn't much of a sleeper. Boyd had already reported everything to the high priests of his order, and they had given him their blessing to go ahead and eradicate this new threat. *Surely, it was not Martin that found me; it was the Grimoires that had found Martin so that I may make a stand against Disorder.* Putting out his cigarette, Boyd got ready to leave his home and meet the man at the other end of the phone line. He had an overwhelming feeling that in this mission it would be necessary to prepare for every possible eventuality from the moment he stepped out of his home, and so he set about retrieving some of the charms, spells and tools gifted to him by the Aged Masters to aid his work. These holy artefacts were essential to Boyd because he was part of a world normally experienced only by psychics, and he himself was psychically blunt; this was what he had been told by his master. For him, it was something to take pride in. It made him particularly resistant to any psychic trauma that his enemies might try to inflict upon him, and try they had.

Boyd walked from the sparse, functional kitchen of his cottage, across the corridor, to his bedroom; once there, he folded a corner of the large, worn Persian rug to one side and slid away a section of floorboard. He reached into the newly revealed secret compartment, almost up to his shoulder, and from it he pulled out four leather-bound books of various sizes; with his head bowed in reverence, he carefully placed them to one side, keeping the smallest separate.

He retrieved some more items from concealment: three cylindrical scroll cases, each ornately carved from mahogany and inlaid with ivory, a leather pouch filled with a silvery powder, an amber amulet with a long gold chain, and a box. The box was plain and made of a light-coloured wood, he carefully opened it and gazed at the twenty or so smooth polished stones of red granite that were tightly packed inside, each about the size of a large egg and loosely wrapped in a layer of muslin. Even though he wasn't psychic, he could still vaguely sense the energy from these stones, this was about as close as he got to experiencing the presence of Presarium. He lifted one of them and lobbed it gently into the air before catching it again and replacing it in the wooden box. The stones would definitely be coming with him on this journey, along with the small book which contained a collection of choice verses from the first and third Grimoire. Another item he selected from this secret collection was the Qrwshan amulet which he put around his neck – only after dangling it in front of him long enough to catch a glimpse of the black metal skull embedded at its centre. All the remaining artefacts went back under the floorboards, concealed from view until a time when they would be needed once more. His inventory was still incomplete – it was without his favourite tools. Boyd moved an old chair from his desk and placed it beneath a hatch in the ceiling. He stood on it and reached into the attic just far enough to retrieve an old duffel bag from its hiding place; it was a heavy item and he had to strain against its weight.

Sitting down again, he fumbled around inside the bag and drew two black automatic pistols from it, the first, small and easily concealed, the second, larger and with a higher calibre. He looked at the weapons critically before placing the larger of the two back into the bag. A few more seconds of searching produced another pistol, even bigger than the one he had replaced; a revolver. He felt its familiar weight and balance and held it up in front of him as if he were aiming it. Satisfied with his choices, he placed the pair of handguns on the nearby bed and lugged the duffel bag back into its hiding place; it was still very heavy, plenty of weapons remained within it – ready for use another day. From a locked drawer, he matched up bullets with his guns before carefully packing one pistol, ammunition and psychic paraphernalia into a customised, black leather piece of luggage that already contained toiletries and a change of clothes. Everything went in except for the smaller pistol, which he placed in a specially designed holster that held the gun concealed in the small of his back.

As an acolyte of the Order of the Earthly Eye he had, over the course of many years, been called upon to deal with all manner of rogue psychic entities, including poltergeists, demons, jinn and humans. The items he packed reflected his methods of dealing with these threats: the holy artefacts like the stones and the amulet allowed him, a non-psychic, to confront supernatural enemies on their terms, while the pistols meant he could face them on his, with good old-fashioned violence. Now that he had everything he needed, Boyd secured the luggage, threw on his motorcycle leathers, picked up his helmet and exited the small cottage. Outside, the air was calm and there was a lull in the rain. He could still feel the cold of the night through his protective clothing. He produced a remote control from his jacket and punched a few keys, activating a specialised security system. A minute of mechanical clicks and whirrs from the house followed, confirming it was now secured. Internal steel grilles guarded the windows and doors, lights on random timers lit up in different parts of the house, and a secret CCTV network was activated. He walked to his garage, and with the same remote control device he opened its sliding steel shutter door. Inside, neatly arranged along the walls, were workbenches covered in stripped, exposed engines and parts from old motorbikes. In the very centre of the garage was a large BMW touring motorbike coloured silver and black. He mounted his favoured form of transport and started the engine, which thumped into life. With a final jab at his remote control and a twist of the throttle he sped away into the night, ducking beneath the sliding steel shutter doors before they closed off the garage behind him.

Boyd lived in a village outside Edinburgh; the journey to meet Martin in Glasgow would take him forty-five minutes, door-to-door. The late hour meant the roads were relatively empty, and there was nothing to impede his progress. He travelled well above the speed limit, radar detectors and scramblers on his bike ensuring he never got caught. As he rode, Boyd's mind started mulling over the details Martin had shared with him regarding this case; it led him to worry about what effect the Warlock would have on Earth's alignment. Preoccupied with this thought, he soon found himself in Glasgow.

Boyd only knew the main parts of the city well. He had never been to the area where Martin lived, an industrial corner dominated by old, mostly derelict warehouses; the handlebar-mounted satellite navigation system provided the directions. The atmosphere in this part of Glasgow was grim and desolate although not entirely devoid of hope. Amongst the ruins there were pockets of redevelopment taking place, and new modern apartment blocks and housing estates were springing up. Boyd rode past a row of abandoned houses with boarded windows earmarked for demolition. A little further on from these was one of the new estates where Martin's apartment block, Halford House, was located. A van with blacked-out windows speeding in the opposite direction took a bend in the road too quickly and drifted over to his side, causing him to veer sharply to the left; he cursed the moronic driver under his breath.

Boyd rode into the large, well-lit car park in front of the block, it was late. There were still a few lights on inside the building. He noticed the rain clouds had cleared, and the gibbous moon, along with a few of the brighter stars, was visible. He parked his bike, walked over to the front door of the building and buzzed flat twenty-four through the intercom system. There was no response, which was a little worrying. He buzzed again, still nothing. He buzzed flat twenty-six; a few seconds later a sleepy female voice crackled through the intercom. "Yes, who is it?" she asked.

"Hi, it's Martin from flat twenty-four," lied Boyd calmly. "I came to put some rubbish out and left my keys inside, can you let me in?"

"Yeah, sure," she said, seemingly unconcerned. A harsh buzzing sound activated the entry mechanism, and Boyd strode briskly into the block of flats, grateful that it did not have a video-call system.

The nightlights in the corridor were on and revealed the standard magnolia-painted walls and short pile carpet interior of a new-build apartment block. He took the steps two at a time, working his way quickly to Martin's floor. From the end of the corridor, he could see the front door to his apartment was a few inches ajar; the light was on, and there were thin splinters of wood on the carpet outside it, all signs of forced entry.

Boyd's hand instinctively reached under his jacket to the small of his back, and his fingers wrapped around the handle of the automatic pistol; he found its presence ever so comforting. He didn't draw the handgun, just held it where it was; he was in a public place. As he got closer to the door, he raised the visor on his helmet and slowed his pace. His right hand remained on the pistol grip, and he used his left to unbuckle the helmet and lift it up before changing his mind and deciding that if anybody was going to ambush him then he would rather be wearing the extra protection. He stood outside the apartment, concentrating, listening, trying to detect any signs of life beyond the crack in the door, maybe a cough or a moving shadow; there was nothing. In one swift move, Boyd swung his entire body around, kicked the door fully open and rolled into the room, just like he had been taught by old colleagues from the Special Forces. As he tumbled in, he was able to get an eyeful of the interior, and he finished the lightning-fast manoeuvre in a crouched position with his pistol fully drawn and held with both hands in front of him; his eyes scanned every inch of the apartment – there was nobody. He relaxed and looked at the doorframe, a definite forced entry, it had splintered around the still protruding lock mechanism. The interior of the apartment was pristine; he noticed a warm mug of coffee by the phone and an open newspaper, there was even some milk left out on the counter. *Somebody must be here*, he thought. He checked every room; there was definitely nobody around.

Where was Martin? Why had the door been forced? It was a mystery. Boyd's mind raced, he wondered what to do; he certainly wasn't going to walk away. He was an acolyte under the auspices of the Aged Masters, sworn to protect mankind from rogue psychics. The only way to progress now was to either find Martin or hunt for the Disciples of Disorder himself. He remembered the van that had nearly run him over outside; could it have had something to do with all this?

Boyd lowered his gun to start a quick search of the apartment and, he hoped, find clues to Martin's whereabouts. As he walked across the lounge to investigate the crowded bookshelf, he passed a pair of large glass balcony doors that overlooked the rear car park of the apartment building. Some movement outside caught his attention and made him bolt out of the room with pistol in hand – he had seen a tall figure in black flanked by what looked like a large muscular dog. It could only have been the tall man and the beast Martin had told him about – Mr Kreb! Here he was, just outside this building! The pair were getting into a large, black saloon car with tinted windows; there was no sign of Martin with them. Boyd knew that if he lost sight of those two menacing characters, he would be saying goodbye to his only solid lead and the last chance of tackling this case. The decision to follow their black car had only taken him a split second; he ran from the room and descended the stairs three at a time, almost falling over himself in the process. He exited the apartment block from the front to get to his motorbike. It was parked on the opposite side of the building to Mr Kreb. As he mounted his machine, he could hear the black car driving away with its strange occupants; this didn't worry him unduly because it would be another three hundred metres before they reached any junction. So long as he could see which way the car turned, he would be able to catch up with them.

Boyd quickly put the pistol back into the concealed holster, secured his riding gear and started the bike. The black car had set off first; he, however, had the advantage – two wheels. With a roar, he zipped out of the car park and onto the road in time to see the black saloon make a right turn. He caught up easily and followed at a safe distance; the danger now was getting too close and being spotted. Boyd tailed his quarry using well-established surveillance techniques; at times he would let the car drift ahead, almost out of sight, before relying on his superior acceleration and manoeuvrability to catch up again.

Mr Kreb's car wound its way through the city, and it was soon obvious to Boyd that its general direction of travel was south, towards the motorway. As he rode, he stroked the hard sphere of the Qrwshan amulet through his leather jacket, grateful it was there protecting him. The amulet was a blessed artefact; the holy sigils that were carved into its amber surface were imbued with special properties that masked his psychic presence (limited though it was) by hiding his aura. Without it, there was every chance that the undoubtedly psychic Mr Kreb would sense that he was being followed. The danger of being spotted with the naked eye remained. To prevent this, Boyd would sometimes drop behind up to half a mile, only doing so if the road was straight enough to keep the car in view.

They were on the motorway now, southbound. They drove quickly, without a break. It was only after three hours of unwavering progress that Mr Kreb's car started to be driven erratically. When this happened, Boyd realised that it was because they were now following another vehicle ... a battered old motorhome.

Chapter 7

Johnny had acknowledged a long time ago that he was capable of quite extraordinary feats, flying had never been one of them, or so he thought until now. How else could he explain the apparently effortless way in which he soared over the mountains below him, his clothes flapping and snapping against the powerful headwind? He first thought that he might have been falling but noticed movement along the horizontal plane; he was definitely flying, and for the life of him he could not work out how he had become airborne, nor for how long. His best guess put him as having been in this situation for the past half an hour. He had been unsuccessfully trying to control this strange flight for a while; there were moments when he was certain his course had been altered with a jerk of the body in the desired direction. When it did not happen again, despite his best efforts, he could only conclude that it had occurred previously only by chance.

The wind rushed past his outstretched arms and legs. *Strange*, he thought, flying like this didn't seem entirely new to him, there was something familiar about it, just like there was about the view of the rocky mountain valley below. Giving himself up to whatever force was controlling the flight, he concentrated instead on observing the landscape beneath, and it was a strange view. All the miles of mountainous scenery appeared to have been painted over in a drab, unnatural grey except for a long, vividly coloured valley that lay between three prominent, conical mountain peaks; it had a clear lake at its centre of brilliant azure while the woods and grassland that surrounded it were coloured every conceivable shade of green. He also noticed the outline of every natural feature in this valley as being very precise when compared with its grey surroundings, which looked blurred and indistinct by comparison; he was at a loss to explain why the geography below him should have such a contrasting appearance.

His flight started to descend rapidly as he headed towards the valley. From his vantage point in the air, he became aware of a clearing in some of the dense woodland around the lake and remembered where he had seen all this before – it had been in his dreams. So he probably wasn't really flying after all, only dreaming again. It was worrying; the ability to discern between reality and this particular dream was becoming increasingly difficult.

In his previous dream flights, he had never descended low enough to see what he saw now – people in the woodland clearing, tiny specks running about, dancing or possibly playing. He urged the descent to speed up so he could get a clearer view of them; he strained to thrust his body through the air quicker, it didn't work, the flight was still something beyond his control. He descended close enough to hear voices from the tiny specks on the ground, a chorus. There was another, louder voice, whispering and yet somehow audible over both the background chant and the noise of rushing wind.

"Help us, Johnny, help us ..." it said simply. Unsure about what to make of it, Johnny concentrated on the chanting instead.

"Earth expires, the children broken,
Chaos fires once more awoken."

He could have sworn the chant was in children's voices
and was baffled about what it could possibly mean. He
was still descending, getting closer; just when he thought
he was about to catch his first clear sight of the rhyming
valley-dwellers, the images and landscapes around him
faded away gradually into an all-encompassing blackness.
It wasn't long afterwards that he found himself stirring
uneasily.

"About time! I thought you weren't going to wake up at
all, sleeping beauty! It's your turn to take the wheel."

Johnny had to blink several times and rub his eyes to
orientate himself again, and before he could say a word,
Sascha was pulling into a service station. Tired though
he was, Johnny took his turn at the wheel and drove on,
mesmerised by the road ahead. Eventually, he managed
to glance at his friends to see how they were doing; it had
been four hours since they started the journey, and it was
obvious that nobody had the strength left to even attempt
idle conversation. Sascha was trying to get some sleep
while Baccharus had lit another cigarillo. Johnny found the
presence of the rich, sweet smoke in the enclosed space of
the motorhome nauseating. This was a good sign, giving
up smoking might be easier than he had anticipated. The
smell was probably worse for Sascha who was a lifelong
non-smoker. His familiar, on the other hand, appeared
quite relaxed, lying on one of the bunks with a tatty old
paperback he had found on the kitchen shelf, probably
unaware of the offence he was causing. The radio was on;
nobody listened to the power ballads it was belting out.
The so far uneventful journey had taken the companions
up to north-west England.

Johnny was about to suggest that they stop for the night when the monotony of the journey was unexpectedly broken. As they moved along the motorway, Sascha's Presarium detector gave a beep, and the motorhome's big diesel engine started to splutter before cutting out entirely; this was unusual to say the least. Johnny immediately depressed the clutch so the vehicle coasted and turned the key once, then twice, before the engine reluctantly came back to life.

"What the hell happened there?" Sascha asked, fiddling frantically with the Presarium detector on the dashboard.

"I thought you said you kept her well maintained, Johnny!" added Baccharus accusingly.

"I do!" replied Johnny, frowning with concern. "That has never happened before!"

Sascha stared intently at the tiny display screen on his device. "I hate to say this, guys: my meter just detected a peak in local Presarium activity, I'm pretty sure the engine didn't stall by itself ... there's some psychic interference here." He urgently cycled through various screens on his gadget, trying unsuccessfully to find an error in its reading.

"I didn't sense any psychic activity," Baccharus said.

"Me neither," agreed Johnny.

"Well, I'm not surprised that you guys didn't detect anything, it's been a long drive. Johnny, you look pretty damn tired, and as for you, Bach – chilling out back there with that novel – I think you've just switched off entirely ... must be quite an absorbing read."

"Oh, it is!"

"Sweep the area and see what you can find, Bach," Johnny ordered his familiar.

Baccharus closed his eyes in response and concentrated deeply as he tried to detect any psychic presence in their vicinity. "Oh, yeah! There's definitely something nearby...

in a straight line behind us, I think … reach out, Johnny, see if you can feel it too."

Following Baccharus's directions, Johnny also sensed negative energy in the air, cold and full of malevolence – they were being stalked. The attempt to stall their engine and the presence he had just sensed left him feeling far too exposed on the wide open motorway. "I'm coming off at the next exit," he announced. "Let's see who – or what – is following us. Sascha! What have you got?"

By now, Sascha had powered up a whole host of electronic gadgetry in response to this unknown threat; his laptop computer, which was hooked up to the portable Presarium detector, registered another peak of activity. "Get ready, guys, there's some psychic energy heading our way again," he cautioned.

Sure enough, the unknown energy tried to stall them once more; forewarned, Johnny had already started revving the engine hard. The motorhome juddered and its interior vibrated as the engine complained under the strain of the opposing forces. With a great deal of effort, Johnny kept it running, and the psychic attack faded again. The oil temperature gauge was creeping upwards; he knew their vehicle couldn't take more of this abuse. From a road sign, Johnny estimated it would be less than five minutes to the next exit. His two companions frantically searched the wing mirrors to try to spot what was behind them; the overcast night sky and light rain made it difficult to see. Johnny could feel Baccharus using his mind to scan the road; neither he nor his familiar could get a fix on anything. Johnny drove on tensely, wondering when their progress would once again be psychically impeded. Multiple LEDs started flashing on two small, plastic circuit boxes that lay amongst a tangle of wiring arranged on the dashboard; Johnny glanced at Sascha questioningly. His friend was entirely focused on the screen of his computer. "All right, people," he said eventually as he looked up, "the computer indicates a moving source of combined Presarium and electro-magnetic energy about a quarter of a mile behind us. It's definitely a psychic disturbance and is more than likely the source of our current troubles."

Johnny used this information to tune in to the road behind them with his psychic sense; as the driver, it was difficult for him to concentrate fully on this task, and he had to defer it to Baccharus. The motorway straightened out as he drove, and car headlights stretching back for hundreds of metres became clearly visible. It was disconcerting to think that one of those was out to get them; Johnny was grateful that it wasn't far to the exit now.

"I can feel something!" announced the familiar excitedly, and almost immediately they were attacked again by the unseen psychic force. The motorhome slowed down rapidly and then lurched suddenly into the path of a speeding articulated lorry. With its horn blaring, the lorry swerved onto the hard shoulder, just about avoiding a devastating impact. A terrified Johnny wrestled with the steering wheel to regain control of his vehicle and managed to guide it back into the middle lane. The lorry, its horn still sounding, sped off ahead of them, desperate to be as far as possible from the errant motorhome.

"Everybody okay?" asked Johnny, glancing over his shoulder, only to see Baccharus painfully extract himself from a pile of tuna and baked bean cans on the kitchen shelf he had been thrown into by the wild change of direction. Sascha rubbed his head where it had been knocked against the side window and looked ruefully at the electronic devices that were now strewn across the cabin.

"My equipment! What a mess!" he moaned as he

reached down to pick it all up again.

"Forget your equipment, what about our lives!" shouted Baccharus angrily as he pressed his face against the window, trying vainly to catch sight of their psychic aggressor.

"We've got to get off the road, it's getting dangerous out here," said a grim-looking Johnny, and nobody argued; a very real fear had descended upon the party. Trying to stall their engine was bad enough, forcing them into the path of a lorry was something else, and it did not leave any doubt in their mind as to the intentions of whoever was out there.

"You weren't lying, Johnny!" said Sascha.

"What do you mean?" asked Johnny.

"You weren't lying when you said this mission was going to be the riskiest one to date."

"It's risky all right ... happy to stick around?"

"Wouldn't have it any other way."

It wasn't far to the exit slip road now, Johnny could sense a terrible psychic presence nearby – the enemy was close. "Can you feel it, Bach?" he asked, and the familiar nodded slowly.

Sascha had managed to reconnect some of his equipment again and was trying to interpret a complex graph on his laptop display. "Look for a car in the outside lane, about one hundred and fifty metres behind us," he suggested.

Baccharus pressed his face against the side window and was the first to spot the threat they faced. "Oh, yeah! I think I see it! A black saloon," he reported urgently.

"That's the source of the bad vibes all right," confirmed Johnny, his mind completing a quick psychic evaluation of the vehicle. They reached the exit lane, and everyone's attention quickly returned to the road, the tense silence broken only by the ticking of the indicator as Johnny turned off the motorway. Soon it would be time for confrontation. His friends looked subdued and he knew why. The enemy had found them first, and they had not anticipated this.

They drove onto a short stretch of dual carriageway with the black car following. Johnny and his friends cast frequent nervous glances at their mirrors to watch the trailing headlights that blazed so menacingly at them. The motorhome approached green traffic lights; a nearby sign read HARTNALL 12 MILES. A491 BAINBRIDGE. The place names didn't mean anything to Johnny. His keen eyes probed their new location, eager to find anything in their immediate vicinity that could be turned to their advantage like a building or some natural feature; he had no such luck, only rolling fields were present on either side of the road. The lights changed to red, and Johnny cursed under his breath. Cars, observing the traffic signal, obediently stacked up in both lanes ahead of him. He had not wanted to stop or even slow down so soon after coming off the motorway.

"C'mon, lights; go to green," urged Baccharus.

Johnny sensed his familiar trying to alter the lights psychically. "Baccharus, don't!" he forbade. There was fast traffic moving across the junction ahead, changing the lights would have been disastrous. As they slowed down, the ominous black car rolled closer.

"He's getting too near!" Baccharus warned unnecessarily as all eyes were already fixed on the vehicle in the mirrors. Their stalker was no longer a pair of distant headlights but a large chrome grille mounted on a black luxury car. Even though it was directly behind them, it was impossible to see its occupants as the car's windows were tinted and the night was dark. Reluctantly, Johnny took his turn to stop behind traffic, and the black car followed suit. With the enemy so near, Johnny could clearly sense their malign energy, stronger than ever. It triggered a confusing barrage of random perceptions, subjecting mind, body and soul to every conceivable physical and emotional experience both simultaneously and separately: pleasure, pain, despair and so many more feelings all mixed together to produce a single strange sensation so very characteristic of Disorder. Caught in the chaotic energy field, Johnny understood how this heady mixture could be so seductive and why there was no shortage of recruits for the Disciples of Disorder. "Can you feel that, Sascha?" he asked.

"I'm not sure … there is this weird sensation around isn't there?" replied Sascha. Like all living beings, Sascha possessed a trace of inherent psychic ability; it was not enough to be considered a psychic practitioner, he could perceive only a fraction of what Johnny now experienced – this wasn't going to be the case for much longer. Battle was about to commence.

"Let's get ready to face whatever's in that car," said Johnny resolutely. As soon as he spoke there was a build-up of rapidly increasing psychic energy. It caused Sascha's electronic equipment to light up with flashing LEDs and twitter with increasing urgency. The enemy launched its attack of intensified chaotic energy; the effect was both profound and unpleasant.

The temperature inside the motorhome dropped rapidly, and the vehicle started to vibrate and then rock back and forth on its suspension. Magnified psychic energy overwhelmed the three friends, searing nerve endings and flooding their cerebral synapses, exposing them to a bewildering tide of neural activity. Johnny groaned and gripped his head tightly between his hands, trying to squeeze out the unparalleled agony and obscene ecstasy he simultaneously felt from the confused signalling of his brain. His steadily blurring vision could not conceal his friends' ordeals from him. He watched Baccharus, spread-eagled on the floor, shrieking in pain while Sascha's body convulsed and blood streamed from his nose and across his face. Johnny knew the experience was psychologically less intense for Sascha, but on the physical level it was just as unwelcome.

"Do something, guys ..." begged Sascha between his laboured breaths, looking as if he would lose consciousness at any second.

With great effort, Johnny resisted some of the effects of the psychic assault. All he wanted was a few moments of clear thought so that he could think of a way to get them all out of this mess. "Psychic shield ..." he moaned eventually.

"What?" croaked Sascha weakly. Baccharus, who had also heard Johnny, understood. Johnny looked deep into his own psyche, and amongst the storm of unwelcome neural activity there he found a small region of his mind that was unaffected, a place of calm and strength at the very centre of his consciousness. He focused on this tiny island of peace and was thus no longer affected by the madness the enemy had induced. This was not going to be enough. To take things further, Johnny had to dig deeper into his personal reserves of willpower. With intense concentration honed through years of training, he expanded the size of this tiny island of calm so that it grew outwards, and it pushed the disorder of the enemy's psychic energy field away from his own mind. He didn't stop there. He continued to expand the zone of peace outwards beyond the dimensions of his own consciousness and into the material world around him, neutralising the Disciples' frenzied psychic attack in a radius that extended beyond even the motorhome, creating a zone of protection. Within this psychic shield, Sascha and Baccharus found themselves finally free from the effects of the assault. This gave them a chance to recover, and Johnny felt Baccharus use his own psychic ability to reinforce the shield.

For what seemed like hours, but was in reality merely seconds, the struggle between opposing psychic energies continued; the warmth and calm of Johnny's shield versus the confusion and pain of the enemy's assault. The occupants of the cars nearest to them, caught unwittingly at the edges of this psychic battle, had started to feel very unwell. When the lights changed and they moved out of range, they recovered quickly enough to fire a few angry blasts of their horns at the two stationary vehicles.

The Disciples intensified the attack. Johnny could feel what had started off as a deluge of chaotic psychic energy become a full-blown storm.

"Oh no, not again!" he heard Sascha scream as his friend's body was gripped by convulsions once more. He watched him collapse to his knees with eyes squeezed tightly shut, bloody-nosed and moaning. Johnny sensed Baccharus desperately trying to prop up the psychic shield with his own mind. The power his familiar tried to resist was overwhelming, and he too succumbed to neurological overload.

Johnny could only look on as his friends writhed in pain. He took a sharp intake of breath as his psychic shield was finally crushed and chaotic energy now bombarded his senses too. He searched vainly in his mind for the island of calm he had found earlier – it was lost – there was no way to project the shield again, and he feared that they would all shortly perish, leaving behind only the desiccated husks of their corpses. The sight of his friends' suffering, his own helplessness and the physical pain he felt triggered a powerful emotion deep within him – something he couldn't remember ever feeling at this level of intensity before. It was anger, a bitter, terrible anger that exploded at the very core of his being. Johnny cried out in fear at the strange force growing inside him; expanding rapidly and gathering momentum it knew no bounds. This righteous anger, born as it was within the mind of a psychic like Johnny, manifested itself as a wavefront of potent, untamed energy. It escaped from Johnny's mind and expanded rapidly through the air, blowing out a section of the motorhome's fibreglass rear and then continuing its devastating progress until it struck the enemy's car, shattering its windscreen, ripping off its roof and rolling it backwards ten metres. The car's interior was showered with high-velocity shards of glass that peppered its occupants. The destruction was accompanied by the roar of rushing air and twisting metal, and when it all stopped there was silence. What remained was a quiet autumn night in which there stood an isolated motorhome and a car, both appearing to all intents and purposes to have been involved in a collision.

Johnny had never experienced such a force before, and he looked around in bewilderment. His friends appeared dazed but well and, thankfully, no longer subject to psychic trauma from the enemy's chaos energy field, which was no longer detectable. The tinkling sound of broken glass dropping from the shattered windscreen, alongside the creaking of warped metal and fibreglass, was all that could be heard.

"Was that you, Johnny?" Sascha asked, dabbing his nose with a bloodied handkerchief. He spoke gently, as if his friend was a volatile substance that needed to be handled with care.

"I – I think so," Johnny responded, hesitantly. They both

stared at the gaping hole Johnny's blast of psychic energy had ripped out of the rear of the motorhome. Visible through it was the night sky and the enemy's damaged car.

Sascha excitedly grabbed his Presarium meter from the dashboard and tapped a few keys. "Dude, that was off the scale!" he exclaimed. The meter had recorded a wave of energy from Johnny's blast, and it was unable to register its peak.

Baccharus, who was hovering again, waved a clenched fist through the hole at the roofless car. "Don't fuck with Johnny M.," cried his infant voice. He turned to Johnny with a defiant smile on his face. His triumphant tone was short-lived.

There was movement from the black shape slumped over the steering wheel of the damaged car. Johnny watched, transfixed, as the figure in the driver's seat shifted to sit upright again. The face that had until now been obscured by a broad-brimmed hat became slowly visible, and it was hideous. Black, empty eye sockets set in gnarly, grey skin stared back at him and his companions. The whole effect was made even more terrifying by the many tiny glass shards embedded in the being's flesh, and as if this didn't upset the sensibilities enough, there followed a deep, throaty growl and movement from the back seat – Johnny did not intend on waiting around long enough to see what the source of *that* was.

"Let's get the fuck out of here," whispered Sascha. Johnny looked at his friend, his voice had been calm … wide eyes betrayed his terror. He turned back to the grey, withered face behind the steering wheel that stared intently at them all with hollow eye sockets. Suddenly, the lipless gash that was its mouth opened and produced a terrible hissing sound. Without further delay, Johnny leapt into the driver's seat and restarted the motorhome.

"Let me drive, Johnny, we're going to need you ready for psychic intervention, not concentrating on the road," said Sascha. Johnny agreed and they hurriedly swapped positions.

"Drive, Sascha! Get us out of here!" cried Baccharus, unable to take his eyes off the hideous apparition behind them. "There's something moving in the back seat!" he warned as Sascha engaged first gear and pulled away into the night with spinning wheels – quite an achievement in a bulky old vehicle like the motorhome.

Hanging on tight to the vehicle's fixtures, Johnny ventured over to the rear to find out what his familiar, who was still looking through the hole there, had seen. He reached Baccharus just in time for both of them to catch a fleeting glimpse of a snarling canine face with fierce yellow eyes, drooling and gurgling on the back seat behind the driver. Johnny couldn't accept that what he saw was real; a look from Baccharus confirmed the monstrosity was definitely there. They both decided to keep the knowledge of the shocking vision to themselves for fear of panicking Sascha.

Johnny returned to his seat. The lights had changed in their favour, and Sascha weaved deftly through the few cars that were ahead of them before swerving sharply off the roundabout with tyres squealing.

"We're not safe yet!" shouted Baccharus as he stared out from the rear of the motorhome. "I'm pretty sure their engine is still working." He hovered over to join his friends at the front of the vehicle.

Outrunning the powerful black car in the motorhome would be near impossible, thought Johnny as their engine roared and Sascha engaged a higher gear.

"Johnny, that blast of energy was amazing! Why don't you fire another like it at them? Blow them away to kingdom come once and for all. Man! That driver was too ugly to be allowed to live," Baccharus said.

"I would love to, Bach," replied Johnny, "at this moment in time I'm not sure exactly how I did it."

"Baccharus is right, Johnny; that was incredible!" Sascha exclaimed without taking his eyes off the road. "We will have to sit down and analyse what happened; we'll look at the graphs from my meters, assess how you were feeling at that precise point in time, break it all down … just like in the old days. We'll see if we can harness that psychic energy again."

"Sounds like a great idea, Sascha, if we survive that long," was all Johnny could offer in response.

Sascha overtook another car, and there was an audible cry of relief from his two passengers when he narrowly avoided colliding with oncoming traffic in the process. They were on a long, isolated country lane now. Once again, Johnny started sensing the presence of Disorder and suggested Baccharus hover to the rear of the motorhome to have a look through the hole there. In the distance, the familiar could see a pair of headlights belonging to a black car with a damaged roof, the enemy was mobile again, just as Johnny had suspected.

Sascha was driving well beyond the speed limit; the pursuing vehicle was still gaining on them. The friends sat there in silence. A worried looking Baccharus, still acting as lookout, had a question. "So who's following us, Johnny?" he asked hesitantly, the horrifying visage of their pursuer burned into his mind.

Johnny attempted an answer. "A kind of alien. Some Disciples of Disorder are human, many are not. Exactly where the hell *he* came from – I couldn't tell you. Let's figure that one out when we're safe." They drove on.

Sascha braked hard as they approached a T-junction. "Where are we going?" he asked as he looked left and right uncertainly.

"Take any turn, just don't stop. Put as much distance as you can between us and them," Johnny said. Sascha took a left and drove hard through quiet, winding lanes for a few minutes. It wasn't until the road eventually straightened out that Baccharus caught sight of their pursuers again.

"Oh no!" he said.

"What's up?" asked Sascha anxiously.

"They're closing in fast, that's what!" Baccharus shouted back, panic in his voice. Johnny looked into the wing mirror, and there it was, the roofless black saloon, far too close for comfort; he could just about make out the grey of the driver's face. Sascha stomped hard on the accelerator; the motorhome had nothing more to give.

The old motorhome strained and groaned on every manoeuvre, and all the time the faster, nimbler car was closing the gap. The roads were quieter now, and it wasn't long before the Disciples were directly behind them once again; close enough for Johnny to clearly sense their auras.

"Brace yourself, they're going to r—" was all Baccharus, who continued to keep a vigil in the back, managed to say before the black car rammed the rear of the motorhome. Johnny and Sascha's heads whipped backwards suddenly following the impact. The Disciples were trying to force them off the road again.

"They're crazy!" shouted Baccharus.

Two further collisions followed, and Sascha only just managed to keep the bulky vehicle on the road. If they didn't do something soon, thought Johnny, then the motorhome was likely to end up in one of the ditches that ran alongside the twisting country lanes they were racing down. Without warning, the temperature in the motorhome dropped again and it started to vibrate; pieces of fibreglass fell off the damaged rear wing followed by the bumper.

"Here we go again," said Johnny, recognising an imminent psychic assault.

"No way! Not this time!" shouted Baccharus.

Johnny spun around in his seat at this and saw a glowing streak of energised Presarium materialise in the little cherub's right hand. Baccharus hurled it at the enemy like a javelin, he did this twice. The psychic bolts fizzled out before they reached the pursuing car.

"They must be using a psychic shield themselves!" warned Johnny. The Disciples were evidently doing their utmost not to be caught out again.

"I'll have to try something else!" shouted Baccharus. In a change of strategy, the familiar frantically rifled through cupboards and shelves in the kitchen of the motorhome, retrieving tins, bottles and drink cans before returning to the hole in the rear. Using a flying 'run up', he hurled each of the makeshift projectiles at the hideous occupants of the roofless black car. The grey-faced demon driver ducked and weaved to avoid each item, as did the snarling beast in the back seat. Without the roof or windscreen, there was no protection for them, and they had not readied any psychic defence against so primitive an attack. Baccharus made sure that he also hurled some colourful abuse along with each missile. The familiar's efforts weren't in vain, almost immediately the temperature in the motorhome returned to normal and it stopped vibrating as the concentration of the demonic entities in the car was interrupted. A couple of the tins even made contact, first with the dog-like beast which howled and gnashed its teeth in frustration and then with its keeper, stunning him, not causing any serious injury. Baccharus aimed some of the tins at the car itself, successfully knocking off the radiator grille and causing huge dents at various points of impact; this caused some consternation amongst the Disciples, who knew that if their car was damaged any further then the pursuit would be over. His quick thinking forced their pursuers to retreat to a comfortable distance. It did not take long for Baccharus to run out of ammunition.

Sascha turned onto a rutted lane that led to an unrecognisable building in the distance. He and Johnny had concluded that to continue on the main road, outmanoeuvred as they were, was suicidal. They would have to make their stand soon and the building ahead was as good a place as any to do it. The motorhome bounced and rattled along the uneven lane, enduring its continuing punishment admirably. Johnny looked into the mirrors and saw empty road. It wasn't particularly reassuring; he knew it would not be long before the Disciples closed in on them again. On nearing the building it became apparent that it was an old aircraft hangar and visible beyond it was the crumbling runway of a disused airfield. After two hundred metres, the jarring lane they were on joined a stretch of tarmac leading to the hangar. Sascha slammed on the brakes and the motorhome skidded to a halt opposite a set of large double doors. He released the seat belt and was about to exit the vehicle when Johnny gripped his arm tightly and stopped him.

"We need to get inside," Johnny said firmly. The distant sound of a revving engine cut through the night; the demon driver was also approaching the hangar. There was a concerned look on Sascha's face. "Drive through the doors," ordered Johnny.

"Sorry?"

"Drive through the doors," repeated Johnny; there was no time for discussion.

"Go for it, Sascha!" urged Baccharus.

Sascha shrugged, strapped himself back into the driver's seat and accelerated towards the corrugated metal doors, all passengers braced for impact. With a crash, the motorhome forced its way into the hangar, painfully jolting its occupants. The gamble of driving into the heavy doors had paid off. The front half of the camping vehicle sat relatively undamaged inside the hangar, its headlights illuminating the interior. The building was evidently being used as a workshop and storage area for a farm; inside it lay tonnes of hardware and heavy machinery in various states of repair: skeletons of old tractors, stripped Land Rovers, steel pipes and electrical generators were scattered about the interior. Caught in the motorhome's headlights, all this paraphernalia cast bizarre shadows on the corrugated metal walls.

From his lookout post at the rear of the motorhome, Baccharus could see the car racing towards them along the access lane they had just negotiated. It fishtailed along, throwing up clods of mud from its wheels. He let the others know that the Disciples would soon be upon them.

In desperate moments such as this, the friends naturally turned to Johnny for leadership. Occasionally, he managed to rise to the occasion.

"You gonna tell us what to do, Johnny?" asked Baccharus.

"We hide in the hangar!" he replied, and they all stumbled out through the front doors of the motorhome. "Sascha, find anything we can use as a weapon! The more lethal the better," Johnny instructed. With an earnest nod, Sascha jogged over to a workbench full of hand tools he had spotted in a corner and frantically started to rifle through them. "Baccharus, use whatever power you have to project another psychic shield. Do it from a safe place, away from the door we just busted through."

"Right away, Johnny!" said the cherub as he fluttered into the cabin of an old tractor with no wheels, ready to project a shield around himself and his friends. Sascha dashed over with some interesting items.

"What have you got?" asked Johnny. Sascha presented a large chainsaw, Johnny nodded and even managed to grin when Sascha tugged at its starter cord and the petrol engine spluttered into life before he hastily switched it off again. The next makeshift weapon he held aloft was a rather vicious-looking fire axe.

"So which do you fancy?" asked Johnny.

Without hesitation, Sascha lifted the chainsaw. "This," he said with a psychopathic look in his eyes, the influence of watching too many low-budget horror movies.

"Okay, here's what we do," explained Johnny. "We hide amongst the tractors and machinery, and once those bastards come in we keep a close eye on them. I'll use my mind to hide our auras from psychic detection as best as I can while Baccharus resists any psychic attacks. We wait until prune face and his dog come near either of us and then – bang! We let them have it! Ambush!"

It was the best Johnny could come up with given the circumstances. His friends hesitated, expecting further instruction; when none came they accepted Johnny's proposition with as much enthusiasm as they could muster.

"Simplicity! I like it!" Sascha eventually exclaimed.

Outside, the car skidded to a halt and the friends scattered to opposite sides of the hangar to find suitable hiding places. Sascha climbed into the raised shovel of an old JCB digger and lay flat on his back inside it. Johnny ducked behind a massive steel trailer of the type that would have been pulled by a tractor. They heard car doors slamming shut followed by the metallic scraping sound of their demonic pursuers squeezing past the motorhome and through the damaged hangar doors. Once they were inside, Johnny could sense their chaotic energy field again, stinking of corruption; he focused on hiding the aura projected by himself and his friends so they would be concealed effectively. He cast a fleeting look at Baccharus to make sure he was ready; the familiar's infant eyes were closed, and there was a look of serenity on his face as he concentrated on projecting a psychic shield from the tractor cabin. The three friends waited, hardly daring to breathe as slow, heavy footsteps echoed around the hangar. Johnny stretched his neck around the side of the trailer to try to catch sight of their source. His heart skipped a beat when he heard four padded feet in a very different rhythm to the original footsteps, a heavy panting accompanied them and a deep growl caused blood to flow like ice through his veins.

Having only caught fleeting looks at the enemy, Johnny was intent on seeing exactly who, or what, they were up against. He ducked low under the trailer and, from a distance, saw a pair of black boots and narrow trouser legs moving with a long, slow stride. Following behind were four thick and muscular animal limbs that might have belonged to a large dog except that the paws were broad and had retractile claws, making them more akin to those of a big cat; a trail of drooling saliva preceded these animal feet. All of a sudden, a huge black snout dropped to the ground and started to sniff; an alarmed Johnny realised that nothing had been done to hide their scent … they might have lost their initiative here.

The pair disappeared from his line of sight; he had seen enough to tell him that they were heading to the other side of the hangar – to where Sascha was hidden. He stealthily followed the stalkers, ready to intervene on behalf of his friend should it become necessary; he wasn't going to leave

Sascha to tackle two demons alone. The Disciples of Disorder were only a few feet away from the raised shovel of the JCB now; Johnny wondered how long it would be before they guessed Sascha's hiding place. He just hoped his friend had the chainsaw ready. The beast was thrusting its snout from side to side as it followed the scent trail. Tightly gripping the fire axe, Johnny edged as quietly and as carefully as he could closer to the Disciples, stalking the stalkers. He moved from behind the trailer to a tractor and then ducked behind an off-roader, edging forwards until he eventually had a clear view of the figure in black and the creature. This was the closest he had been to either of them, and they looked more terrible than ever. He could clearly see the back of the tall bipedal Disciple with his long black coat and wide-brimmed hat sitting atop a bald, grey-skinned head that was deeply rutted like an oversized walnut; he also noted a strange jerky quality in his movements. His eyes then shifted to the vile, sniffing animal; Johnny stared, horrified at the drooling creature. It was at least the size of a Great Dane, and its stocky build was more like that of a Rottweiler's. The beast's muscular, bulging body was covered in glossy black fur and sharp, elongated canines protruded from an almost feline jaw. Maybe it was because of the distracting appearance of the beast, or maybe his luck had just plain run out, but as Johnny advanced, he kicked an old spanner that had been lying unnoticed on the floor, sending it spinning a few feet ahead of him, clattering away as it did so. In the tense silence of the hangar it was like a siren going off, and the trigger for all hell to break loose.

The tall, black figure spun around sharply towards the noise and faced Johnny; eyes met eye sockets. Johnny gazed in horror at the demon-man's face; deep skin ruts, heavy brow and sunken, black eye pits were emphasised by the motorhome's headlights. The lipless mouth opened and a sharp hissing sound came from it, sending a cold shiver through all that heard it. The four-legged beast at the demon's side bolted towards Johnny, producing a deep, bellowing roar that he could feel resonating through his chest. It was too late to run; he held his fire axe high, ready to bring it down hard as soon as the beast was in range, knowing he would only get one swing. At the sound of the commotion, Sascha broke cover to stand in the digger's raised shovel. He started the chainsaw with a yank of its cord; the tall demon was only a few feet from him. The noise of the buzzing power tool drowned out all other sounds in the hangar and added to the confusion. He leapt from his hiding place with his improvised weapon arcing in a downwards swing aimed at the tall figure in black. It looked like Sascha had the element of surprise on his side and that he would split the Disciple straight down his middle. The timing and range of the attack had been judged as if the target were human, and this turned out to be a mistake. The demon sidestepped, lightning-fast, quicker than any man could possibly have done, and the screaming chainsaw sliced only through air. Not meeting the expected resistance, Sascha toppled forwards, hit his head on the side of a nearby workbench, and crumpled to the floor, unconscious. He narrowly avoided disembowelling himself on the chainsaw, which fell before him.

The beast leapt at Johnny, who had managed to hold his nerve in anticipation of this very moment. Johnny swung the raised axe; it met the creature in mid-air and became embedded in its side. The black furry body, already full of momentum, continued its flight, knocked Johnny over and landed on top of him, drooling foul saliva. It howled as it lay there, Johnny guessed in pain. Teeth gnashed inches from Johnny's face and claws tore at his clothes and torso.

The axe remained in the beast's side, and a phosphores-cent fluid leaked from the wound. The dog-thing was very much alive despite its injury. With a supreme effort, Johnny managed to scramble free from beneath his attacker only to see the beast twist its thick neck to one side, grab the handle of the protruding fire axe between dagger-sharp teeth and, with alarmingly little effort, pull it out from its body. It bit down hard and snapped the axe handle in a shower of splintered wood; it hardly mattered to Johnny because it wasn't this hideous animal that was his main concern any more – its demon keeper had drawn a pistol from his coat and was aiming it at him. Johnny had taken every precaution to protect himself and his friends against a psychic attack; now, it seemed a weapon of the mate-rial world would be responsible for ending his life. Cor-nered by the advancing beast, he could only watch when a screaming, fluttering Baccharus broke from cover in a blur of speed and was all over the gun-toting demon-man. The familiar flapped wildly about his head, using little fingers to tear at the black eye sockets and his wings to slap the face. The demonic figure's arms flailed around as he tried to bat away the frenzied cherub, and with a lucky strike he managed to flick Baccharus to one side. Undeterred, the faithful familiar flew in for another attack; with inhu-manly fast reflexes, the demon swung its pistol around in time to fire, and Baccharus tumbled to the ground.

"Baccharus!" screamed a distraught Johnny. He took a step towards his downed familiar; a lunge from the beast made him back off again. Johnny looked around in frustration for anything that could be used as a weapon, there was nothing. He watched the beast advance slowly, chomping at the air while the pistol that had dispatched his companion was now aimed at him again; a frown was almost visible on the twisted features of the demon-man as he sadistically considered whether to shoot or let his snarling familiar tear Johnny apart.

Johnny dug deep into his mind to create a psychic force of some description. He hoped for a blast of energy like the one he had managed to produce earlier in the motorhome; surely, another like that would save them all. He fought to focus his will, nothing happened. The last time he didn't even have to think about it; on this desperate occasion, the more he concentrated on bringing forth his powers the harder it seemed. It wasn't anger that gripped him now, only despair. He gazed hopelessly at the emotionless eye sockets of the figure in black, then at the gun barrel, and finally the slavering beast.

There was a volley of gunfire, a deafening sequence of small explosions that echoed throughout the entire hangar and made the eardrums ring. The demon in black jerked and twitched as high-velocity rounds hit home, tearing holes into the front of his long coat; he then stumbled backwards and hit the dirt. There was a barely perceptible pause before another volley was unleashed and met its mark again; this time it was the beast's turn to be targeted. Its body, already injured by the axe, was now pierced with bullets. It rolled to one side, howling in agony. Johnny looked at his own torso in disbelief, expecting it to be bloody and perforated; he was fine, only his enemies had been struck in this timely and unexpected intervention.

Standing silhouetted against the headlights of the motorhome was a strangely proportioned figure with an abnormally large head, holding a raised pistol with both hands. Another off-world creature thought Johnny; it didn't concern him unduly, he was just grateful there was somebody with a gun on *his* side. He squinted past the headlights at this being, unable to make out any details beyond the blackness of the silhouette. Johnny realised the figure did not give off any aura, his presence was psychically imperceptible, which was impossible – all living beings had a psychic signature, unless he was masking it somehow.

The two prone bodies of the Disciples twitched and moved and then clambered back onto their feet. They should have died from the gunshots. Johnny noted that there wasn't any blood from the wounds inflicted on these foul beings, just a phosphorescent discharge; they were, he guessed, animated by dark, disordered energy and not normal physical processes. Observing this regrettable resistance to dying, Johnny was grateful that the two Disciples of Disorder had shifted the focus of their attention away from him. Hissing and snarling, they advanced instead towards the figure in the headlights. Johnny took the opportunity to escape from his corner and run to the aid of his two injured friends starting with Baccharus, and all the time he kept a careful eye on the battle.

The staggering demonic Disciple had managed to hold on to his pistol, which he raised to return fire; before he could get in even a single shot, the silhouette had quickly and smoothly changed the ammunition clip in the handle of his own weapon and, unmoved by the apparent invulnerability of his terrifying foes, fired again, unleashing further devastating rounds. Every bullet in the clip was emptied in quick succession and hit home. Johnny didn't know much about guns, but even he could tell that whoever this new guy was, he could shoot. The two Disciples were sent reeling backwards with chunks of disintegrated flesh and clothing flying from them. They were both on the ground once again, their two bodies twitching as they lay there. To Johnny's horror, they started to slowly rise again; mercifully, they did seem weaker than before.

The silhouette had already put his pistol away and was

reaching into what looked like a bag at his feet. He produced a smooth, oval stone from it, a little smaller than a man's fist, and without a moment's hesitation he lobbed it with a gentle underarm movement. The spinning projectile landed on the ground a few feet from the Disciples, who were almost standing again. As soon as the stone touched the ground, it produced an explosive shockwave of psychoelectrical charge that shook the hangar. Johnny felt a rush of Presarium from the stone and the sudden release of power caused him to recoil. The beast and its demonic master, who were both much closer, bore the brunt of the blast and were thrown backwards, sprawling and sliding along the ground. The stone was a psychic weapon and so its effects were most profoundly felt by those with psychic ability. The stranger didn't wait to gloat at the success of his attack; he followed it up instead with more gunfire, inflicting further wounds.

This time Johnny, who had been nursing Baccharus, didn't just stand by and watch. He gently put his injured familiar back on the ground and used the power of his own will to send a beam of psychic energy at the enemy. It was nowhere near as powerful as the subconscious blast he had produced in the motorhome; it was, however, strong enough to keep his resilient foes at bay. Only now, after this sustained assault, did the Disciples opt to retreat. The demon-man raised himself on one elbow and created a flash of blinding energy with a wave of his free arm, dazzling Johnny and his new ally. By the time their eyes recovered, the only sign left of the two Disciples was a hole gouged through the corrugated iron wall on the opposite side of the old aircraft hangar. The silhouette ran across the hangar to the hole, and Johnny shifted his attention to Baccharus again. He felt pangs of sadness as he cleaned the bullet hole in the upper part of the familiar's chest with a handkerchief; Baccharus grunted and groaned. The familiar had been a faithful companion for many years; until now, Johnny hadn't fully realised how attached he had become to the belligerent little fellow. Using his coat as a blanket, he scooped him up.

Johnny turned as he heard booted footsteps approaching him. He could now see that what he had initially thought was another demon was actually a man in a motorcycle helmet – it was quite a relief. The helmet, which had given the impression of a misshapen head, was now held at his side, and a very human face looked on with grave concern.

"Is he alive?" asked the man in a strange, endearing accent, a mixture of Irish with inflections from a dozen different languages that he had been exposed to over time. Johnny nodded. "We've got to get him to a hospital," the man urged.

"That won't be necessary."

"If he's wounded we could—" started the stranger, pausing abruptly when he noticed little cherub wings poking out from the edge of Johnny's blanketing coat twitching ever so slightly. "Oh, I see," nodded the stranger, and there was some relief in his voice when he realised they weren't actually dealing with a human child, "that's a familiar, isn't it?"

Johnny gave a single nod. He wasn't entirely surprised by the man's knowledge of the hidden psychic world; after all, here was someone who had calmly fought off two demons. "Thanks," said Johnny with a smile, "your timing was impeccable."

"Hey, just think of it as your lucky day. The summoned entity was going to blow your head off, wasn't he? I mean, I don't think you had any more tricks left," said the stranger; it was more of a statement than a question.

"Summoned entity?" enquired Johnny.

"Yeah, that's what I call the tall, ugly fellow in black. What do you know him as then? Demon? Bogeyman? In fact, I've been told this one has a name, Mr Kreb apparently. The creature with Mr Kreb is his familiar, it's a Firehound. Either way, they're not from around here, are they? They were brought to Earth from the worlds of Disorder – summoned here. 'Summoned entities', right?"

"Well, I can't argue with that," said Johnny.

"How long do you reckon your familiar will take to recover?"

"About twelve hours," Johnny replied. Like the demons they had just confronted, the cherub did not rely on the normal internal physiology of earthly organisms to exist; it would take more than a gunshot wound through the chest to end Baccharus. Johnny extended his right hand in greeting from beneath his familiar. He was still concerned that he was unable to sense any aura around the other man but that was no reason to be uncivil.

"My name's Johnny ... I believe you and I have a lot of talking to do."

The other man clasped Johnny's hand in a firm, cold grip. "We do indeed," he said. His hard features softened with a smile that lasted less than a second. "My name's Boyd Tennant."

On hearing a loud groan, they both turned suddenly, only to see Sascha rub his injured head and sit up slowly as he regained consciousness.

Chapter 8

Johnny soon established that he and his new acquaintance had a common enemy in the Disciples of Disorder; for now, it was a good enough reason for them to be working together. He was eager to learn how Boyd had come to be involved in this particular case and in the wider esoteric world of psychic phenomena; it was a feeling, he suspected, that was strongly reciprocated. The world was a lonelier place after one had received knowledge of the alien and intangible forces that controlled the universe, after all, who was there to share this newfound cognisance with? Who would understand? To discover somebody with awareness of this secret was a rare and welcome event. As keen as he was to know Boyd's story, they had both agreed that introductions and personal exchanges would take place after moving to a safer location; there was still a vicious and well-informed enemy somewhere out there.

Johnny laid Baccharus on one of the back seats in the motorhome, holding him in place with a belt around the middle. With Boyd, he helped Sascha, who still felt lightheaded, into the front. There were relentless questions from Sascha about events that had taken place while he was unconscious. Johnny did his best to answer them as he took his place in the driver's seat, and the motorhome rumbled into life again. Reversing carefully, he extracted the vehicle from the broken doorway. The engine rattled noisily and steam snaked its way upwards from under the bonnet. Once out of the hangar, Johnny stopped to assess the damage and had some unexpected help. It turned out that Boyd was quite an accomplished mechanic, and he gave the much abused vehicle a quick but thorough once-over. It had sustained some dented front panels which he pulled roughly back into shape before making some gross adjustments to the steering alignment. There also appeared to be a leakage of fluid from the engine which Boyd fixed by swapping one of the hoses with a similar item from a tractor in the hangar; all this took him no more than fifteen minutes.

Johnny reflected on the good fortune that had allowed them to end up in a place with so many tools, not to mention someone who knew how to use them. Boyd had certainly impressed him; he was turning out to be a very helpful person. In the hangar, Johnny found a large aluminium sheet which had been used for repairing some of the farm machinery; it was just what he needed. With Boyd, he wedged the sheet into position so that it covered the hole that had been blasted through the rear of the motorhome.

"How did they do that?" asked Boyd, referring to the hole.

"It wasn't them," replied Johnny.

"Eh?"

"I'll explain afterwards."

Sascha was feeling better, and despite Johnny advising otherwise, he insisted on going back into the hangar. He returned with the chainsaw and a hatchet, reasoning that until they found something better, these basic tools would have to suffice as weapons; he and Johnny didn't carry anything as lethal as Boyd's guns. Technically, this was stealing, and Johnny admonished his friend for it, only to be accused of hypocrisy as he had taken the aluminium sheet and engine components earlier. The pair eventually agreed that the end justified the means and the issue was dropped.

Johnny walked over to Boyd who was conducting a thorough examination of the damaged black car, which turned out to be an S-class Mercedes. He asked him if he had found anything useful; Boyd let him know that there were no clues present regarding the vehicle's ownership, which was a little unnerving because a car that contained no trace of an owner was very rare. Usually there would be music, maybe an item of clothing, or old petrol receipts; here, there was nothing. Even the radio was tuned in to static with no stations in its memory; it suggested that humans were unlikely to have ever used this car. Boyd scribbled down the number plate details on a small pad he kept in the thigh pocket of his motorbike leathers and then opened the bonnet to scribble the chassis number. After seeing him at work, Johnny guessed that Boyd was a detective or a private investigator – as soon as they were out of here he would find out more about him and, hopefully, this case. For now, he stuck to the agreement: they would leave first and talk later. Almost everything was in place for them to move on. It was unlikely that the authorities would be turning up; the gunfire had taken place inside the hangar, which was set apart from the road, which was itself an isolated rural tract; they had, nevertheless, left a mystery and a mess for whoever the hangar belonged to.

"Let's get out of here before any more Disciples of Disorder turn up," urged Johnny, hauling himself into the motorhome; Sascha slid into the passenger seat. Before they all left the scene, there was something Boyd wanted to share with them. He walked over to Johnny's open window.

"We mustn't let Disorder find us again," he said. Johnny agreed wholeheartedly, that much was obvious. Boyd continued, "They have encountered us already and will be familiar with our psychic signatures, which may lead them straight to us again. For me, this is not a big problem, I am psychically quite blunt. I still give off an aura like all living beings but not very much. I am not easily detectable; however, Johnny, you and your familiar and even Sascha may be found like this."

It was a fair point, and Johnny nodded, wondering where all this was leading. "Baccharus or I can obscure all our auras to protect us from recognition – that's what we were doing for a short time in the hangar," Johnny suggested; Boyd was already shaking his head.

"Sitting in concentration to obscure auras all day and night would be far too difficult, especially as there is an easier way."

Johnny was curious. From around his neck, Boyd removed the amber amulet with the black skull embedded in it.

"What is that?" asked Sascha.

"A Qrwshan amulet, it's a holy artefact with special properties. You fellas take it for now. Stay roughly within a fifteen-metre radius of it and it will hide your aura from psychic detection."

Johnny watched the dangling amulet, hypnotised; it seemed to glow. The carved runes on its surface appeared to move and dance as it slowly twirled on its chain.

"It's beautiful," whispered Sascha.

"That's why I can't sense you!" said Johnny, relieved. "You know what? I was getting quite concerned when I couldn't pick up an aura from you; I wondered if you were even truly human. I just hadn't said anything yet."

"It's the amulet that's responsible," said Boyd. "I think you'll find me very human, Johnny. I hope the same applies to you."

"Where did you get it?" asked Sascha, curiously.

"My teachers from the Order of the Earthly Eye gave it to me when I became an acolyte."

The statement was met with baffled looks, "I'll explain later."

"Yes, let's get going; explanations later, just like we agreed," said Johnny, taking the offered amulet from Boyd.

"So where were you heading?" Boyd asked.

"Just north, we're kind of working things out as we go along," Johnny replied, grinning.

Boyd shrugged. "North it is then, back to Scotland where it all started."

"Scotland, is it?" asked Johnny, who had not guessed that their ultimate destination was likely to be so far away.

"If you wish to find the Disciples of Disorder, it will be in the Highlands."

"That's a pretty big area, don't you have any more information?" asked Johnny.

"Afraid not, those two in the hangar were my only solid leads and now they've disappeared." 'The Highlands' was about as specific as Boyd could be regarding the location of the lair of the Disciples.

"Fine, Scotland it is. We'll keep pushing north until we're too tired to go on; when that happens, let's hope we're well away from here. We'll think of a way to narrow the search later."

"Sounds like a plan. As soon as we reach safety, not only should we introduce ourselves properly as agreed, but also take the chance to compare notes regarding this case." said

Boyd.

"Indeed," agreed Johnny. "I suppose you already have a ride then?" he added, gesturing to the sturdy-looking motorbike with the large panniers slung on either side. "If you don't want to freeze your bollocks off then you're welcome to hitch a lift with us instead," he added cheekily.

"Travel in that heap of shit? You must be joking!" responded Boyd; they both laughed. It was decided that Boyd would follow, simply because the motorhome would struggle to keep up with the motorbike.

Johnny and company were on the road again, heading north. This time they were alongside a man with a gun, something they found quite reassuring in many ways and disconcerting in others. The pursuit and resulting confrontation with Mr Kreb had set them back about two hours.

Sascha stared at the reflection of bike and rider following them in the wing mirrors. "We really don't know who he is yet, do we?"

"No," replied Johnny without taking his eyes off the road.

"Do you trust him?"

"Yep."

Whoever Boyd was, Johnny knew they owed him a lot. He was the reason they were still alive. His faith in the new man was enough to put any doubts in Sascha's mind to rest; over the years, Sascha had learned to trust his friend's instincts and judgement. The pair spent the next half an hour speculating on Boyd's identity, suggesting every possibility from a fellow Agent of the Equilibrium all the way through to a demonic entity sent to lure them to some hellish end. Their stream of increasingly improbable ideas was halted by a groan from Baccharus. Sascha unfastened his belt and tended to the sick familiar, dribbling some water into his mouth from a glass. Baccharus was able to swallow and even managed to moan for some more of the fluid; he was recovering well. Sascha returned to his seat and informed Johnny of his familiar's progress, it was welcome news. Johnny understood that Baccharus would return to health quickly and more completely than any earthly life-form, durability was an important element of the familiar fabrication process. With this thought in mind, Johnny drove on, ignoring the tiredness that was setting in.

"You know what's been troubling me all this time?" Sascha asked a few minutes later. "How did they know?"

Johnny had been unsuccessfully trying to work out the answer to this one himself. How could the Disciples of Disorder have even known of their existence, let alone have found them?

"I don't know. I was hoping you might be able to work it out," was all he could offer.

This prompted them both to discuss the matter at length. They couldn't reach a convincing conclusion and their suggestions were progressively making less and less sense.

"You know what? I can't even think straight right now. Just stick some tunes on and we'll find a place to stop soon," said Johnny eventually. They agreed to let the matter lie … for now.

Johnny drove for another half an hour with heavy metal blaring out of the speakers; the energy of the music kept him fired up. It was almost three a.m. The motorway was largely devoid of cars, and the motorhome slipped quickly between the overnight haulage lorries that dominated the tarmac at this hour; it had been a long, taxing day. Johnny remained vigilant at the steering wheel. He frequently looked into the mirrors to check on Boyd before casting his eye cautiously beyond the man on the motorbike to search the road for any hostile vehicles that might be following them, always grateful when none were apparent. Much to Johnny's envy, Sascha had fallen asleep. He wondered how Boyd managed to maintain his concentration as he rode. Here in the motorhome, loud music and having Sascha for company (when he was awake) kept him going – Boyd was riding alone without the benefit of either.

By the time Johnny considered stopping for the night, the group had crossed the border into Scotland and left the motorway. Travel was now along A-roads and dual carriageways. Parking bays and lay-bys mainly used by hauliers lined their route. Johnny started to look for one in which they could camp discreetly for the rest of the night. He used his mobile phone to call Boyd on his earpiece to warn him they would be stopping soon. Eventually, the route ran through a section of heavy woodland, and it was here that Johnny rolled down the window and gestured that he would be turning off the road; they were about thirty miles away from Glasgow. He followed one of the large, blue parking signs to a lay-by, the far end of which was sheltered by overhanging trees that provided cover from prying eyes; Johnny hoped Boyd's amulet would protect them from psychic detection, just as he had assured them it would.

The motorbike had been travelling close to the motorhome throughout the journey and parked beside it. As Boyd stepped off his machine and stretched his legs, Sascha, awake again, opened the side door of the larger vehicle and invited the biker in for the night, apologising for the lack of space. Boyd told him not to worry and explained how his past life had taken him to the extremes of hardship in different war zones; he was used to roughing it, so being offered a bed for the night was actually a welcome luxury. He entered with the luggage from his motorbike and stretched to loosen joints stiffened through hours of riding. Sascha familiarised Boyd with the vehicle's interior while Johnny ensured Baccharus was comfortable. There was an entry and exit wound in the familiar's shoulder, indicating that there was no bullet lodged inside the body; Johnny was grateful as he didn't relish the prospect of digging around for it, especially at this hour. The cherub's accelerated metabolism had already shrunk the wound to less than half its original size. Johnny left the little creature on the seat, wrapped in a blanket, his attention moved back to his two other companions, one old, one new. Boyd had spotted the homemade electronic devices on the dashboard; soon, he and Sascha were chatting animatedly about the function and design of the gadgets, covering esoteric subjects such as Presarium lore and psychokinesis. Johnny noted once again the ease and familiarity with which Boyd was able to talk about matters psychic, matters the average person would have been ignorant of or, at best, sceptical about.

Before retiring, they all sat around the dining table to sip cold drinks; tiredness had given them pale and drawn faces. Johnny knew that it would be impossible for them to rest for the night without knowing something about who the other was and why they were here. An anticipatory silence had fallen around the table. Johnny spoke first.

"Thanks for saving our skins back there, Boyd; we all owe you one. Not many people, in fact absolutely nobody I know, would have been able to deal with those two back there."

"Yeah, what *was* that stone?" Sascha asked, curious as ever, referring to the projectile Boyd had used earlier.

"I have several, they're blessed artefacts, granite sculpted from sacred tools and charged with psychic energy. They're a little like hand grenades; when thrown in the correct manner the energy from them is released explosively at the point of impact. They were gifted to me by—"

"Your teachers from the Order of the Earthly Eye," Johnny completed the sentence.

"Hey! You're already getting to know me," smiled Boyd. "Actually, I have an idea about who you folks might be. I've heard of agents employed by powerful alien races to promote their agenda. I think that's who you are, one of their agents."

Johnny wasn't surprised by the new man's knowledge; in fact, tonight there wasn't much that could surprise him. He did, nevertheless, object to the tone Boyd was taking regarding his activities.

"My friends and I are not promoting a selfish agenda," clarified Johnny. "We help preserve the equilibrium between the stifling rule of Order and the chaos of Disorder. It's partly through our intervention that we on Earth are not dominated by a psychic minority like so many other worlds out there."

"That's what they tell you, right, the Council of Seven and others? Don't get me wrong, I don't dislike them, or you, as their agent. Your goals are actually similar to mine, but the way I see it, here on Earth we have our own way of dealing with these matters. We don't need interference from any alien groups and organisations, no matter how sincere their intentions to do good. We humans can look after ourselves – outside influences will only subjugate our minds in the long run. Relying on non-humans will be to the detriment of our belief in ourselves as a species. We have our own ancient traditions for maintaining the equilibrium and controlling psychic activity."

"Traditions you follow?" asked Sascha.

"Oh, yes."

"What else do you think you know about our agency then?" asked Johnny, genuinely inquisitive.

"Not much, I confess, though there are references to your organisation in the Grimoires. It has been many, many years since I met an actual agent. Maybe spending time with you will dispense with some of my suspicions," Boyd said, maintaining good humour despite the sensitive subject.

"No need to be suspicious, Boyd. There are aliens out there who aren't just about dominating us or any other species. We can all work together, help each other, learn from each other," responded Johnny with some passion. "Look, the way I see it, in groups like the Disciples we have a common enemy so why not join forces?"

"Mind if I smoke?" Boyd asked.

"Go ahead," said Johnny.

A disgruntled Sascha hurriedly opened a small vent window while Johnny took one of the offered cigarettes and lit it over Boyd's steel Zippo. He would try quitting again *after* this smoke.

"How *did* you find yourself working for an alien agency then?" asked Boyd. "I hope you don't mind me prying, I guess it's the obvious question."

"No, it's fine, I'll tell you. It's why we're all still sitting up tonight isn't it? To learn a bit more about each other?"

"I'm all ears."

"Then I'll begin."

Puffing away, Johnny gathered his thoughts for a few moments before starting to speak.

"I started to develop psychic ability as a teenager. The Council of Seven are always screening the universe with their collective minds for potential agents. They are sensitive to the birth of new psychics and this was how they detected me. I must have been about seventeen when they made their first contact. By this time, Sascha and I were well aware of my gift, or curse, whichever way you wish to look at it.

"One night in my family home, my parents and sister were out. I was just taking it easy, watching TV or something like that, when there was a strange tingling atmosphere in the living room, and Baccharus just materialised out of thin air. I was terrified; I tried to get away from him. I started to run, but you can't escape from something that hovers around like Baccharus. He was speaking to me and seemed to know me very well; he knew *everything* about me. You see, that's how familiars are manufactured, to know their keeper intimately, total devotion. The Council must have secretly got hold of a DNA sample from me to construct Baccharus. When I eventually stopped freaking out, Baccharus asked me to invite Sascha over; it was the only way to convince me that I wasn't seeing things. So I called him on my mobile and told him it was an emergency. He came quickly and, as you can guess, he was flabbergasted. When we had convinced ourselves that this hovering cherub in our midst was real, Baccharus introduced himself and explained his extraterrestrial origins. He insisted that he was our friend and that we would be seeing more of him. We all arranged another meeting and he disappeared. I think Baccharus felt it was wise to explain his existence to us gradually.

"The second encounter took place at Sascha's old house. It was a lot quieter there, and his parents never interfered with anything we did so it was a far better place for a discreet meeting. Just as before, Baccharus materialised out of thin air. We were still amazed by his presence, although there wasn't the shock we felt in that first meeting. Sascha even set up cameras to record what he saw as a momentous event: conclusive evidence of extraterrestrial life. Baccharus was having none of it and secretly wiped the recording with his will. It was in this second meeting that he told us everything. He told us about the Council, the Institution for the Maintenance of the Universal Equilibrium, the Trinity and who he was."

Johnny spent the next thirty minutes as if he were giving a lecture, explaining to Boyd all that he had learned about the forces that governed the universe, conclusions he had reached through his association with psychic extraterrestrials and his own personal earthly experiences.

**

To understand why the Institution existed one had to go back in time many millennia to ages pre-dating even the planet Earth, for sentient life existed long before Earth did. The earliest living beings inhabited a distant segment of the universe, far away. One of the simplest concepts they recognised was the duality of existence. For light there was dark, for hot there was cold, for matter there was antimatter, this was the eternal and defining pattern.

At its most basic level, existence could be defined as the battle to maintain the form and organised complexity that was life against the destruction, decay and dispersal of that order as brought about by death; Order versus Disorder.

Some of these early alien life-forms, through observation of the universe and meditation on this duality, concluded that life could not continue to exist in either extreme. With Order, there was no change, no development, none of the random breakthroughs that illuminated the path to progress so existence became stifled until it ceased altogether. The path of Disorder reached the same tragic result through a different route: the chaos and discord it promoted resulted only in a series of random occurrences, a sensational sea of experience, no worthwhile growth; a route that also led to ultimate self-destruction. So they created a third way, one that could see the flaws in each of these alignments. They made it their purpose to maintain the equilibrium between these two extremes so that life could continue to flourish in the universe.

This philosophy was not accepted by all sentient beings. Its conclusions were crystal clear to those that promoted its ideology, and they failed to see why it should be rejected by so many others. They spent much time pondering this until further observation and meditation revealed to them a painful truth: that both Order and Disorder also existed within the 'essence' of all living entities, within their very souls. Some individuals would always have a tendency to Order while others would always be inclined to Disorder; existence in line with these extremes was their natural state. Disorder, Equilibrium and Order were a continuous spectrum, and there would never be any unification of the three conditions of being. Eternal antagonism between the three sides was the condition of reality, and this struggle was what actually *sustained* reality. Within the early universe, the scale of this antagonism often reached the point of all-out conflict. Aeons passed in this battle and the dominance of each of these three parties was in a state of constant flux. This was the war of 'the Trinity', a term that came to describe collectively the three states of existence.

As the universe moved on from its primordial form and life continued its evolution, there came the knowledge of Presarium and the psychic gift. In the great war of the Trinity, it became clear that the preservation of each state of existence was increasingly being championed by a new breed of life-form, the psychic, so much more capable than its fellow non-psychics. Amongst the most potent psychic entities in the universe was an ancient and highly progressed species that had evolved into pure energy. Seven of them took it upon themselves to aid the work of those that fought to maintain the third way, the Equilibrium. They were able to not only manipulate and detect Presarium but also shift their energy state and become one with it. Their essence had been manifested at the very dawning of life in the universe and would last until its end, and they would dedicate their existence to securing the equilibrium between Order and Disorder. The Council of Seven was thus born, endeavouring to maintain the presence of sentient life in the universe. The Council was immediately mistrusted and despised by the forces of both Order and Disorder, who counted entities just as powerful as the Seven amongst their own number. The eternal battle lines were drawn once again, and spheres of influence in the universe fluctuated between the three groups. Whole galaxy clusters shifted from one side to the other and back. In the process, some galactic ecosystems died, some lived, while others were reborn many times over. Earth itself, an infant planet, its native life-forms primitive, was not exempt from this conflict; however, it was never considered worthy of direct intervention. It was only the gradual emergence of psychic-man that drew any attention to Earth from the rest of the universe. Whether this planet and its highest sentient species continued to exist or not was less than a footnote in the struggle of the Trinity – to humankind it was everything. Some of the higher entities, such as the Council of Seven, saw potential in this infant world.

Despite occupying the centre of the universe, the Council had a perceptual world that extended to its very border; they sensed and monitored psychic activity throughout the whole of existence. When Johnny was born, they became aware of a potential new agent and they watched him carefully as he grew older along with a billion other potentials throughout the universe. The gift, even though present from birth, died so easily in the fragile minds of humans. Johnny, however, progressed and grew in strength and the decision to recruit him was made. Baccharus was constructed and dispatched. And so from the age of seventeen, Johnny's psychic development was nurtured and guided by the Council through the familiar. There were others like him, assigned to different geographical locations on the planet; in fact, there were psychics recruited by the Council of Seven on Earth long before Johnny was even born. It was through these loyal agents and their familiars that the difficult, thankless task of maintaining the equilibrium on planet Earth was continued and the human species flourished.

**

Boyd had listened quietly to all of this. "So you became an agent when you were seventeen?"

"Yup."

"Been on many assignments?"

"A few."

"Battled rogue psychics?"

"A few."

"Never been tempted yourself then?"

"To do what?"

"To go rogue, dominate your fellow man with your ability."

"Nope."

"Why not?"

"I don't know, just not my way I guess."

"What do you get out of it? Working for the Council of Seven?"

"They look after my basic needs; I'm clothed, fed."

"How do they do that? They come and dress you?"

"I don't know, it's what they told me. I really don't know how, I think they can manipulate events, it's very indirect. They say they look after me, but that's not why I stick with them."

"Then why?"

"I think Sascha can put it better than I can."

Sascha had also been listening quietly; it was time for him to speak up. "When your eyes have been opened to what is really out there, you can't just turn back. When you have been awakened to the struggle of the Trinity and what is at stake, your life takes on a newer, more complete meaning which you cannot just turn away from," he said.

Boyd nodded sombrely, a frown on his face.

"Why don't the Seven do more for you? Give you powerful alien weapons or something?"

"Their aim is not to dominate. Besides, in the scale of the universe, I'm only one of a countless number of agents. I won't get any special attention. This Trinity conflict is so big that no side would divert resources to somewhere like Earth when its highest life-form, man, has still got so far to evolve. There are many, many planets like ours where the dominant species has not progressed beyond existing only as a single state of matter. If Earth dies then we just join the list of billions of sentient life-forms that never made it beyond the earliest evolutionary steps."

"So you've never met the Council of Seven then?" Boyd asked.

Johnny shook his head.

"I think we can help each other," declared Boyd and extended his hand to be shaken. "I can appreciate where you guys are coming from."

"Now you know a bit about us. *We* still don't know who *you* are. Why don't you tell us your story? I don't want to be reading your mind; I mean, that would just be rude wouldn't it?" said Johnny with a wink.

Boyd took the comment in the correct spirit and laughed it off before he removed his leather jacket to get comfortable. "As it's so late, I'll just tell you how I ended up here for now. The whole life-story thing will have to wait, if it's all the same to you."

There was no objection. Johnny and Sascha listened as Boyd recounted the circumstances by which he came to be involved in this affair. He filled them in on all that Martin had told him, providing them with the inside information he had gathered from the former Disciple. He went on to describe the events leading up to his timely intervention in the aircraft hangar. His audience got the impression that turning up in the nick of time was a habit for Boyd, who just insisted that he was guided by the Grimoires. Boyd went on to emphasise the importance Martin had given to a deadline that was now two nights away, reiterating what the Council of Seven had already stated. To Johnny, this was all highly valuable information, the assignment had taken a leap forwards – it was still looking tricky though. He knew that Boyd wasn't passing on this wealth of information purely out of generosity; Johnny realised that to fulfil his obligations to his Order it would be very useful for Boyd to have a psychic ally, which is what he saw in him. The benefits of this arrangement were mutual. Boyd had already proven his worth in combat, and through his account of the conversations he had with Martin, Johnny now had some idea about what they were to confront: a group of Disciples based in the Scottish Highlands under the leadership of a powerful psychic who was aided by summoned alien entities, one of whom they had met already, the murderous Mr Kreb. Each man now had the measure of the other, and a bond had been formed.

"How did you get involved with this Order of the Earthly Eye then? It doesn't sound like a club that advertises for members," commented Sascha.

"It's a very long story and like I said, it's late; don't you think we should just sleep for now?" Boyd replied.

Johnny looked at the fatigued faces around him and imagined how bad he must have looked himself. It was about four in the morning; rest was what they needed. Boyd's story would have to wait. A mutual decision to retire was made.

"Mind if I have another cigarette?" Boyd asked as he reached for his packet.

"Sorry, Boyd, but yes, I do mind," said Sascha from his bunk. "This place is stinking."

Boyd apologetically stepped outside for his smoke.

"So, in the morning we go up to Scotland?" Sascha asked Johnny, uncertain as to whether a decision had been made in this respect.

Johnny was lying in his own bunk and had been about to drop off to sleep. He could tell that his friend, who had recently woken from a nap, was finding it hard to switch off. "Probably," he replied. "I have a few ideas. One of them is to try and find this Martin bloke – for now we sleep." Baccharus groaned and tried to get up. "Not so fast, pal," said Johnny, reaching over to gently coax his familiar back onto the seat. "You need more rest. If you're up and about now, it will take longer for you to get back to full strength." Baccharus yielded and lay back down again.

Boyd re-entered and retired to another of the bunks, covering himself with a sleeping bag. The only sound outside was the occasional vehicle speeding along the nearby road. Just before he fell asleep, Johnny allowed his mind to drift into the world of psychic perception that lay beyond the five senses. In the distance he heard a voice calling, the one from the dream, but he was sure he was awake. It beckoned him to proceed northwards, to follow it, to help. An image of the valley flashed through his mind. "Find me here ..." the voice whispered in the distance, echoing around the mountains, and there was the faintest suggestion of a chant in the background.

Chapter 9

As Johnny and his friends fell into restful slumber, Rachel awoke for the second time that night from a light and restless sleep. It was the very early hours and outside it was still dark. She lay alone in her room, the strange meeting with Martin very much on her mind. The previous evening, her foster family had noticed her subdued mood and commented on it, enquiring as to whether she was feeling unwell. She told them she was fine, just a little tired. Rachel was quite sure they weren't suspicious of anything going on and had probably put any change in her manner down to the fickle, sensitive nature she was known for, simply Rachel having an off-day. By telling them she was tired she had not lied; Martin's impromptu visit had brought back memories of her mother and reopened old wounds, acting as if nothing had happened for what remained of the day had been exhausting. The voice inside her that she had suppressed all those years ago was screaming out once again, it cried in anguish for her dead mother and for answers about what happened to her.

It was not just memories Martin had brought with him, there was also the old diary, a poignant physical link to the past. Rachel had managed to keep it stuffed inside her loose top until she had the chance to hide it beneath her mattress where it remained concealed from the rest of the household to be read later; alongside it was the strange amulet.

As she lay awake, the rest of her foster family slept; now, at this most unsociable of hours, was an opportunity to read the old journal. There were a few things to do first … while it was still safe. She got out of bed, turned on the small lamp and crept over to the ornate mahogany wardrobe in the corner of her bedroom. From it she dug out some clothing and a few choice possessions: a framed photograph of her mother, an old paperback and her own scribbled journal. It was depressing to think that in the tiny pile in front of her was all she valued; it had been a difficult life. She removed the amulet Martin had given to her from beneath the mattress. She emptied a little sports bag that she used for PE lessons and placed all the items in it, carefully putting the bag into a corner of the wardrobe then hiding it under a pile of clothes. This was preparation for tomorrow night, the night Martin said he would come and take her.

Rachel tiptoed over to the closed bedroom door, opened it a crack and quietly listened. She could just about hear the slow, steady breathing from her sleeping foster mother in the distance; her foster father was away for the night, as he so often was. There were no other sounds; given time, she was certain that the strange noises and vibrations from beneath the house would start again – plumbing indeed. Satisfied that she was the only person awake, she closed her bedroom door again, reached under the mattress and produced the journal from its hiding place, her heart pounding with anticipation as she did so. She slipped back into bed, holding the old diary close to her. Before she read it, she took the precaution of placing it inside a comic book, thereby concealing it from the view of anyone who might happen to enter her room. Her adrenalin flowed, firstly in response to the ever-present danger of being caught with this book and the questions it would raise, and secondly, from the anticipation of being close to her mother again through her words. Despite the lack of sleep she felt quite awake now.

Before she opened the journal, she noticed that there were pages torn from it and wondered how and when this happened; she would ask Martin the next time she saw him. With a deep breath she let the diary fall open at a random page. The dim light from her bedside lamp illuminated the text. Her first act was to stroke its pages and gently caress the writing with her fingertips; somehow, this brought her closer to the mother whom she had loved so dearly. She looked fondly at the large, curly script, and pangs of sorrow started to fill her. The sense of danger Martin had instilled managed to keep any emotions in check – Rachel remained all too aware that she could also fall victim to whatever it was that had taken her mother away.

She flicked through the diary, just looking at it, occasionally reading a few lines. It brought back distant memories: like the time when she moved to Hilvern village with her mother.

**

When Joseph McFadden passed away, having outlived his own children, he left behind a small bungalow to the only relative with whom he had maintained any contact, his granddaughter Louise Croft.

Recently separated from her negligent husband, it was an unforeseen opportunity for Louise and her young daughter Rachel, aged only seven years old, to move away from the misery of their inner-city Glasgow housing estate and start afresh in the old Highland village of Hilvern. Louise, energetic and hard-working by nature, soon established herself in the community by taking up different jobs in and around the village to make ends meet. She served part-time behind the bar in one of the main village pubs and helped the widow Mrs McGuiness run her farm shop situated a few miles out of town. She also worked as a domestic cleaner, carrying out chores in private households for anybody willing to pay her hourly rate.

The McGuiness store sold all sorts, and to many it was the quickest and easiest source for basic supplies such as groceries, solid fuel or toiletries. To procure more business for her cleaning service, Louise left a card in the store window knowing that the little shop was a hub for the people who lived in the more isolated, and often larger, houses scattered throughout the nearby valleys. If anyone needed help with cleaning, it would be the old couples who lived in them.

Soon enough, the advert was seen by a certain well-to-do lady who was in need of a housekeeper for her rambling country property. Following a few telephone conversations, arrangements were made to start work. For Louise, as a single mother, childcare was the bane of her life, so she was grateful when her new employer didn't object to her bringing Rachel along; in fact, the lady said it would be a good idea as she already had three girls of a similar age.

**

Rachel remembered the day she visited the grand old house during her summer holidays. It was not the first time she had accompanied her mother to work. Doing so was a tedious necessity of her childhood, and she was expecting another boring afternoon of trying to occupy herself as her mother grafted away. To reach the house, they had driven along winding mountain roads and then turned into a long tree-lined lane, uncertain if they had gone the right way until finally their small hatchback car drove onto a magnificent pebbled driveway surrounding an exquisite country mansion house.

Rachel was impressed from the very moment she laid eyes on the vast property with its wild and beautiful gardens. For a girl brought up in a congested city, it really was quite a magical place. They were greeted at the door by an attractive woman who was approaching middle age; she was friendly and welcoming to them both. As Louise got to work, the woman took Rachel upstairs and introduced her to her three daughters. Rachel's age fell somewhere between that of the three girls', who initially struck her as being a little strange, she guessed it was because they lived in such relative isolation in the old house. Like their mother, the three were warm and open, and it wasn't long before they became good friends.

It was funny thought Rachel, not for the first time, as she sat there reading the journal; it was funny how something so simple like the card her mother had left in the window of Mrs McGuiness's shop could end up having such a profound effect on their lives. That card was responsible for her present situation, her new home, her new parents and, if Martin's suspicions were to be believed, her mother's death.

Rachel turned a thick wedge of pages to take the journal forward in time; she scanned the writing on the new page and then turned back a few leaves. She knew exactly what she was looking for. The journal didn't have entries in it for every day, and after turning the pages back and forth a few more times she found what she was after, and it was not far from the section of missing pages. It was the record of an event that was to have far-reaching consequences for Louise, Rachel and the new family they had met. Her mother wrote about it in the following way:

17th March

Terrible day. I was helping Mrs McGuiness when she told me that one of her friends who worked at the hospital had just informed her about a girl who died. It was one of Elizabeth's foster children and it sounded like Chloe. Her husband, whose name I can no longer bring myself to mention, brought her in. It was too late though, and nothing could be done for the child.

I was shocked; despite all that had happened I still cared for Elizabeth and the girls. I dashed over to their house with Rachel. I would have gone with Martin had he been around, but he was on a course in Germany for work.

Rachel was very quiet on the drive there. I had already told her about Chloe before we left; she looked sad and a little lost. I tried to explain that things like this happened sometimes and she quietly nodded, I could see she didn't want to talk about it. I had asked her if she wanted to stay behind, she didn't; actually, she was adamant about seeing the other girls.

During the drive I didn't really think about what had happened with her husband a couple of weeks ago – when I reached the house, the horror of it all came back to me, and I felt sick. I knew he was out on business most days so the odds were he would not be around, there was no guarantee though. Given the circumstances of a death in the family, I think I could face him again, and if I did, I wouldn't want anything to do with him except for saying hello and goodbye. If he was home, I decided I wouldn't stay for very long.

We reached the house; even as I entered the drive I sensed things were different somehow. The place had a gloom hanging over it despite the perfectly sunny and warm day. His car was in the drive, it didn't mean anything because he was often driven around by a chauffeur or a taxi.

I walked with Rachel up to the old building just like I had done so many times before, ignoring the negative vibes. I think Rachel felt them too because she was very quiet. I rung the doorbell, I nearly didn't recognise Elizabeth when she opened the door. She always looked gorgeous, this time her face was pale, her eyes puffy, and her usually immaculate straightened hair was dishevelled. She was surprised to see me. I had already told her that I would no longer be working at the house; I could not bring myself to tell her the reason why, not yet. I don't know if hiding what her husband had done was the best thing to do or confronting her with it. I didn't dwell on the matter though; this visit was solely about consoling a friend.

"Louise, I'm so glad you're here," she said. "Have you heard what happened?" she asked and I nodded, and we hugged each other. She burst into tears; I also had to dry my eyes.

She invited me into the kitchen. Thankfully, there was no sign of her husband. Rachel would usually go up to play with the girls, this time Elizabeth led her into the kitchen with me to hear about the terrible news. She told me how a few days ago Chloe had been playing on her bicycle. Elizabeth was always very strict with the girls, never really allowing them to go beyond the boundaries of the garden. On this occasion, Chloe had managed to take her little bicycle onto the small roads outside without telling anybody. It was about half an hour later before everyone realised that she was missing.

Elizabeth and the girls had searched the massive garden for Chloe. She was nowhere to be seen. Elizabeth called her husband who rushed back home, had a quick look around the grounds, and then went out in his car to try and find her. After an hour of driving he saw her in a roadside ditch lying still and looking pale. He tried to wake her; it was no good. He rushed her to the hospital in his car. He carried her in. All they could do was confirm that she had died, most likely from a head injury. She was found on a route used by tired lorry drivers. The police thought she had been struck by an articulated lorry, probably without the driver even knowing she was there. Elizabeth told me about the difficulty of breaking the news to the rest of the girls and how tough it was for all of them to be dealing with what happened.

We were so upset. Both Rachel and I loved Chloe very much; everybody loved her. She was the youngest of the sisters and I always thought the cutest; she always made everyone laugh with her clowning around. The accident had happened only two days earlier. Since then Elizabeth had been depressed and couldn't bring herself to do anything.

The house was a mess. Even though I didn't work for her any more, I offered to clean up. Elizabeth refused, I insisted; so in the end we did it together. Rachel went upstairs to the other girls; they must have talked amongst themselves about what had happened. I think it must have been good for all of them to talk; kids have their own way of coming to terms with tragedies and often bear up to these things better than us adults.

Before we left, Elizabeth told me that she missed me not coming over every week like I used to and that the girls were missing Rachel. I told her I would always be in touch – what more could I say? I didn't want to let her husband get away with it but, for now, I just didn't know what to do.

On the drive back, Rachel didn't speak. I was worried about her; she vaguely remembered the death of her grandparents and her great-grandfather who gave us the house. I could tell it was difficult for her to understand the death of a friend, another child. I talked to her about it when we got back.

**

Rachel didn't have to read any more of that journal entry; she remembered very well the conversation with her mother that day. She had been confused and could not understand why a child had to suffer something so terrible. Louise had explained the tragedy as best as she could. Rachel had found the talk with her mother reassuring, even though it didn't make things much clearer. Ultimately, it seemed to her that bad stuff happened, and there was no real reason for it. Death, illness and even hopeless people like her father just seemed to happen.

Rachel sat back in her bed and reflected on this rather depressing, disenfranchised view of life she had reached. It was a conclusion confirmed by the premature death of her mother. And try as she might, she couldn't yet bring herself to have a more positive outlook on existence. She wondered what the oblique references to Elizabeth's husband were all about; they were worrying.

Rachel looked at her bedside clock, it was five a.m. The excitement of reading the diary was being gradually replaced by tiredness. She felt awake enough to read on a little longer, to another time that she remembered, a period in her mother's life she needed to know more about

… the days preceding her death.

For a few weeks before she died, Louise had been suffering from a run of bad dreams. Rachel remembered, all those years ago, how she would be woken up by the noise of her mother tossing and turning in her bed. To investigate the disturbance she would walk, frightened, to the doorway of her own bedroom and look into the room across the corridor where the troubled sleeper lay, writhing as if possessed, her appearance feverish with nightclothes soaked in sweat. She would watch for a while, too afraid to awaken her or even enter the room and then go back to her own bed once again, trying to ignore the creaking bed and moans so that she could fall asleep.

It was a strange, worrying time. In the days that led to her death, Louise had seemed distant and anxious. Something had been bothering her, and to this day Rachel was desperate to know what. She grabbed more pages and turned them over. These latter entries made chilling reading.

**

18th November

There's something I haven't mentioned yet that I really feel I should. I have been dreaming about a strange man. When the dreams first started he was barely noticeable, he just used to lurk in the background, and I didn't pay much attention to him. As time went on though, his presence in my dreams became ever more prominent. He doesn't lurk in the distance any more; he is very much in the forefront now. I could be asleep, dreaming normally about pleasant things, like meeting a friend or playing with Rachel; before long, he appears. Last week I dreamed about driving with my mother and Rachel through some crazy city I didn't recognise; it was a pleasant dream that turned into a nightmare. There in the back seat, sitting next to Rachel, visible through the rear-view mirror as I drove, was the man, dressed in black from head to toe. He wore a big hat beneath which I could only see his chin and lips, gnarly and pale they were as if he was sick. I screamed at him. My passengers couldn't see him and thought I had gone mad. I turned around, and sure enough he was still there sitting in the back seat. I screamed at him again. Taking my eyes off the road caused the car to crash, waking me up with a startle. Just like that, he haunts my dreams, turning up when I least expect it. I am filled with dread when he's there.

He has become ever more present in my dreams and I cannot get away from him in them. Last night I woke up in a panic, sweaty and shivering. In that nightmare I was in some sort of bleak desert, alone until he turned up and started to move towards me. He was only walking but his approach was impossibly quick, as if he were running. I started to stumble. He was getting closer, and the closer he got the greater my sense of terror. I couldn't move fast enough to get away. I tripped and fell; he was only a few yards from me. I screamed; the fear became so intense that I awoke. The bed was damp with my sweat. I have never been much of a dreamer and have not experienced nightmares since childhood. I am at a complete loss to explain what is going on. They say the dream reflects the subconscious; in that case, from what deeply rooted fears and anxieties do my nightmares stem? Of course, I will talk about it with Martin. He is no psychologist, but who else is there to discuss this with? Certainly not Rachel, she would be terrified. My nightmares are becoming progressively more intense and awful, I hope they stop soon. I'm getting tired now, sleep is becoming very difficult.

**

Rachel continued to read painfully through further diary entries, and learning the details of her mother's suffering hurt her deeply. The accounts mostly described normal days and nights; however, there was always a sentence or two included somewhere within the text that mentioned the nightmares. Under 23rd November for example, a couple of lines read: 'It happened again. Last night the man in black was there, he was closer and I woke up. It was four a.m. I couldn't get back to sleep.' At the end of another entry, Louise had simply written 'the nightmare was there again, worse than ever'.

It was only in her mother's last diary entry that Rachel read another extended reference to the nightmares.

**

2nd December

I didn't feel well today and it's all because of the night-mares. They have been bad recently. Last night was the worst. I am still shaking as I think about what happened. I was in the desert again; it stretched for miles around me. It was empty, there was nobody around, the skies above were bleak and grey like the sand, and a cold wind chilled me to the bone. In the distance I saw a speck on the horizon, a dark speck. I immediately knew what it was and started to run. Just like before, the more I ran the closer the man in black got to me. He was wearing his hat again and as usual I couldn't see his face, just that terrible mouth. This time he was quicker than ever before. The wind picked up and the clouds zoomed across the grey sky, the cold bitter wind whipped my clothes as I ran and still the man in black got closer. I fell, exhausted, onto the sand and turned to see where he was, only to find him standing over me, the brim of his hat still covering his face. I started crawling backwards away from him. It was useless; he had already caught up with me. For the first time I saw the face of this man that had been haunting my dreams for so long and it was horrible. It was grey and wrinkled with deep sunken sockets; there were no eyes in those sockets, just gaping black cavities. I screamed out as I lay there on the ground, unable to stop myself from staring back at that terrible face. Realising it was a nightmare I tried to wake myself – it didn't work, and I remained asleep. Before my very eyes he changed; his whole body melted into the shape of a fierce black dog, salivating and growling. I crawled backwards to get away from him; it was hopeless, the beast was upon me. The dog started mauling my face until my own blood obscured my vision. I screamed; the pain felt so real. Eventually, mercifully, I awoke. I had obviously been thrashing around as I slept; my sheets and duvet had been thrown off the bed. I cried out as I saw blood stains on the mattress. I ran to the bathroom and in the mirror saw that I had a nosebleed. I tried to turn on the tap, my hands were trembling. I managed to get the cold water running and splashed it over my face. The water was a relief, it calmed me. I went to check on Rachel, praying that she had slept through my ordeal; I would have hated her to see me as I was. She was lying in her bedroom, asleep.

I have spoken to Martin before about the dreams. I spared him all the terrible details. After this last dream I will do as he recommended and speak to my doctor. I must get medical help; I can't go on like this.

**

Rachel finished reading her mother's final and most disturbing journal entry. She sat in her bed, devastated, with tears in her eyes. Reading about the suffering of somebody she loved so much was deeply upsetting. Louise had mentioned her nightmares to Rachel only on a handful of occasions, usually after her daughter had commented on how tired she was looking. She had never divulged the true depth and terror of these experiences to her, not even to Martin. Rachel wished Louise had shared her fear with her when she was alive – maybe she could have helped, she wasn't sure how – she would have done something though. She closed the diary and shuddered. Her mother's final nightmares had been almost prophetic, and the images she described were very close to how she finally met her end. Like Martin had said, something was definitely going on. Louise died on the day following this dream, and after the terrible event, Rachel had undergone seemingly endless counselling. It was only after a year that she was judged by psychologists to be dealing adequately with her loss. An important factor in why she did not fall apart entirely was her new life as a foster child. Being in a house surrounded by people who welcomed her in with open arms and were determined to help her was a huge aid to the recovery process. With their support and professional counselling, the withdrawn, disturbed Rachel had managed to push some of the events of her mother's death deep into the far recesses of her mind – now it was all coming back to haunt her. For the first time in twelve months Rachel allowed herself to recollect the day her mother had died.

**

She was twelve years old and sitting in an English lesson at school. She remembered catching glimpses of strangers through the narrow glass window in the classroom door; they were walking back and forth along the corridor with her headmaster, Mr Abraham. Other children noticed them too; Mr Evans, the teacher taking the class, chided them for becoming distracted so easily.

Usually Rachel would have ignored such a disturbance; although, on this occasion, she was certain that the important-looking adults outside had been watching her. After a while the activity in the corridor died down, and she continued with her English lesson albeit feeling a little uneasy; why should they have been looking at her?

After English was French, the last lesson of the day. As she entered the room with the rest of her class she was sure that her teacher, Mrs Martel, was looking at her a little differently, just holding her gaze ever so slightly longer than normal. It was enough to make her feel uneasy again and wonder what on earth was going on. The lesson ended uneventfully; the class started to file out of the room. Rachel packed her schoolbag and was about to leave with the rest when Mrs Martel asked her to stay behind. A little confused, she waited as the room emptied. She went through the events of the day in her mind wondering what she could possibly have done to warrant this individual attention. She wasn't the type of student who was generally kept behind in class for anything; she never excelled in her work enough to be singled out for special praise and neither did she misbehave or cause trouble. Overall, she was a pretty average, or dare she say it, boring, student. Soon, it was only herself and Mrs Martel left in the room. It felt eerie to her, a classroom so often full of activity now empty of all its students, just her and the teacher alone.

"Don't worry, dear, you haven't done anything wrong. You're not here to be told off," said Mrs Martel, seeing the look on the girl's face. "Mr Abraham wants to see you about something." Rachel noticed a kindness in her voice as she spoke. It wasn't a tone or manner that she used with the rest of the class; she seemed so much nicer this way. "Oh, here he is now; I'll leave you with him."

Mr Abraham, the headmaster, walked into the room. He gave Mrs Martel a nod as she left; there was a lady with him, someone Rachel didn't recognise. Rachel sat quietly, not sure what to make of everything that was going on. Mr Abraham and the new lady sat near to her on the classroom chairs, and Rachel couldn't help thinking that they looked too big for them. The lady sat *very* close.

Rachel looked up at them both, Mr Abraham first with his shock of thinning white hair, his round face and droopy brown eyes, a face that could switch from benign kindness to a mask of rage in a second, a useful trick for disciplining his more wayward pupils. The lady looked like a nice person decided Rachel. She was dressed casually and her dark brown hair was tied up. She wasn't young but dressed like a younger person which suited her. Rachel sat quietly, confused.

"How are you, Rachel?" Mr Abraham asked in a soft voice. Rachel, unsure what to say, just nodded gently. "Good," smiled the headmaster. "You're probably wondering what we all are doing here. This, by the way, is Stephanie, she's a police lady."

"Hello, Rachel," said the child liaison officer.

Again, Rachel just nodded, unsure where all this was going. Mr Abraham's face seemed more serious now. "Rachel," he started, "there has been an accident involving your mother."

Rachel felt a hollowness in her stomach suddenly and

stared back at her headmaster. Mr Abraham had paused to carefully gauge this quiet child's response to the unfortunate news; it was difficult with Rachel to know exactly what she was thinking.

"What happened? Is Mum all right?" she asked finally, her voice quiet and wavering, they were the first words she had spoken in this meeting.

Mr Abraham looked to WPC Stephanie Locke. "Hi, Rachel, before I tell you any more about what happened I just want to wait until your dad gets here," she said.

"My dad?" asked Rachel, perplexed. "I haven't seen him for two years, why is he coming?"

WPC Locke spoke again. "We thought you should have a relative here, Rachel. I know your dad hasn't seen you much. He *did* tell us that he cares for you a lot. Is there anybody else you would like to be here?"

"Just my mum … or Martin," she said.

WPC Locke pursed her lips as she looked at Rachel; her green eyes were wide with genuine concern about the child's well-being. Mr Abraham's gaze lowered slightly.

"Who's Martin?" asked PC Locke.

Rachel briefly described the relationship between Martin and her mother, explaining that he was in Germany, on a business trip. Stephanie Locke carefully noted all these details down. The policewoman promised to speak to him. The shrill ring of her mobile phone made everybody start.

"Hi, there … yeah … okay … we're in the school now … Is he with you then? Okay, fine… yeah, see you in a minute." She hung up. "That was my colleague, PC Andrews, Rachel. He's brought your dad along." Rachel managed a small smile at the news; it did little to mask the anxiety all over her tiny face.

Stephanie Locke turned to Mr Abrahams. "They must

be at the front of the school now," she said to him. He nodded and left the room, giving Rachel a gentle, reassuring squeeze of the shoulder first. Rachel waited for her estranged father with Stephanie Locke, who continued to keep a close eye on her. "How do you get on with your father, Rachel?" she asked. Rachel took a few moments to think about the relationship.

Her mother had probably only ever said two good words about her father; Rachel couldn't recollect them. She had also said uncountable bad words: lazy, clueless and idiot sprang to mind. Even though Rachel hadn't seen her father for two years, he did call her periodically. Her mother had seemed happy for Rachel to keep in touch with him despite her personal feelings about the man. He would ring about once every two weeks and would do most of the talking while Rachel just listened. Conversations often began with his usual greeting: "Hello, how are you doing, babe?" The body of the conversation would be something like: "I've got a new job ..." or, "I saw so and so today," in reference to somebody who was completely unknown to Rachel.

She had lost track of her father's 'jobs'; he seemed incapable of any real stability in his life. The lasting impression in Rachel's mind was of a man who never quite got it right. Despite these shortcomings, she couldn't help feeling a degree of affection for the rambling voice at the end of the phone line and had always wanted to know more about him.

"He's all right," replied Rachel to WPC Locke. "I don't really know him that well any more."

"Is there anybody else, Rachel, relatives or friends who we can get in touch with besides your father and Martin?"

"Meredith and Lisa."

"Who are they?"

"Friends, good friends."

"Are they young girls like you?"

"Yeah."

"I see," said Stephanie Locke, making a record of the names in her notebook.

As she was writing, Rachel spoke again. "Meredith and Lisa they had a sister you know, she was called Chloe; she was my friend – she died."

PC Locke frowned. "How did she die?" she asked. Before Rachel could respond the door to the room opened abruptly.

A tall, thin man with short, dark, almost black hair, very pale skin and a bad complexion resulting from years of drug and alcohol abuse entered behind Mr Abrahams. Even though it had been two years since she had last seen him in person, her father still looked the same. Rachel remembered how hay fever made his eyes red and puffy every summer; he looked just like that now. Since hearing the news about his ex-wife, Steven Croft had been distraught; he felt the loss more for his daughter than himself. Once in the classroom he quickly overtook Mr Abrahams with his long stride and walked over to where Rachel and WPC Locke were sitting; he crouched down opposite to his daughter.

"Rachel, babe," he said before giving her a hug. She hugged him back, tiny against his lanky frame. "Honey, it's so good to see you again," sniffed Steven holding both her hands in his. "Babe, there has been some bad news," he started, he had mentally rehearsed what he was about to say on his journey to the school. Mr Abrahams watched solemnly from the front of the class. WPC Locke sat quietly. "It's about Louise – I mean, Mum ..." he faltered. "There was an accident in the park, babe. Mum died in it."

Rachel sat frozen on the chair opposite her father; he continued to hold her hands. She stared back into his face, the magnitude of what he had said beyond her grasp. Her eyes filled slowly with tears, she continued to stare; the eyes overflowed and the tears gently rolled down her cheeks. Her father pulled her to him and wrapped his arms tightly around her. Her body was limp; she wanted to hug him back, to do something, anything.

"You're coming with me for tonight, honey. Then Stephanie here will look after you, okay?" said Steven. Rachel, still in her father's embrace, nodded.

"I'll take you both back to your father's house for now, Rachel, and be with you again tomorrow morning," said Stephanie Locke as she stood up slowly. She gave Steven a nod, and he also stood up, releasing Rachel from his embrace to hold her by the hand instead. "We'd better go," said WPC Locke. Mr Abrahams looked on sadly.

The little group walked to the front of the building. A uniformed police officer was standing on the drive. Locke went to him. They had a few words and he left in his panda car. She walked back to the great wooden doors of the school's main entrance where Rachel, Steven and Mr Abrahams stood waiting.

"I'll take you both home now," she said. Father and daughter followed her to an unmarked Ford. Just before Rachel got into the vehicle, Stephanie Locke couldn't help giving the girl a hug. "You've been such a brave girl, Rachel; I'll make sure you're going to be okay."

Rachel managed to smile back at her. They drove off down the long slope that led from the school to the road. Rachel saw Mr Abrahams watching their car; he shook his head sadly and made his way to his own car parked nearby.

The mood in the vehicle was sombre and Steven tried to

make small talk with his daughter; after all, this was the most he had seen of her in two years. But the circumstances made it difficult to connect with Rachel who was already looking overwhelmed by events so he gave it a rest. They stopped first at Rachel's home in Hilvern to collect a few personal items. It had always been a lively place; now, the photographs, scattered clothing, and letters were no longer signs of active habitation, they were monuments to someone who was no longer there. Rachel listened to Steven as he started fondly pointing out items from life before the divorce: decorations, cushions, and an old vase. There were also plenty of reminders that Louise had moved on following her divorce; the most potent being a photograph of her with another man.

"Is this Martin?" her father asked her as he looked at the picture of Martin with Louise and Rachel. "Could have been me there," he said poignantly, more to himself.

At this moment in time, WPC Locke, who was trained in counselling and managing bereavement in children, was an essential comfort to Rachel. "Just grab a few important things for now, Rachel love. Take your time deciding what you need," she advised, the kindness in her voice unwavering.

Rachel led the way to her bedroom and the police-woman followed. They sat together on the floor in front of the open wardrobe to sort through clothing and other items Rachel might need. It was still uncertain exactly what would be happening over the next few days.

"Will I have to live with my dad?" Rachel asked WPC Locke while they were in the bedroom.

The police officer had already been briefed about Steven Croft's background. He hadn't a penny to his name and continued to battle with drug and alcohol problems. He was a far from suitable candidate to take on the care of a child; the man could barely take care of himself.

"You stay with your dad for tonight, Rach, I'll see you in the morning. We might let you stay another night depending on how things go, and then we will find someone who can really look after you properly," replied WPC Locke.

Rachel accepted this without any argument. If half the things her mum had told her about Steven were true then she knew she was better off living elsewhere. After packing away her last item, a pair of denim jeans, Rachel asked the question that Stephanie Locke had been preparing for and dreading.

"Stephanie, what happened to my mother?" asked the girl.

**

Rachel quickly closed the diary and the comic book that concealed it. She could hear footsteps and creaking floorboards from the landing moving towards her room. She shoved the books beneath her bed and switched her lamp off before the footsteps got close enough to notice the light spilling out from around her bedroom door. She lay down flat on the bed and pulled the sheets over her body. Someone walked past her room; from the footfall she guessed it was her foster mother. Her ears pricked up at the sound of the bathroom door opening and closing. She continued to listen; the toilet flushed and the footsteps made their way back to one of the rooms across the landing. It was almost morning and she had hardly slept. As she lay in her bed, tiredness finally caught up with her, and she fell into a deep slumber.

Chapter 10

With the motorhome hidden from view in the lay-by and Boyd's amulet concealing them from psychic detection, Johnny and his friends managed to sleep. Having retired late and awoken early it had not been for long enough. They ignored the tiredness, there was too much to do; their deadline was only two nights away and they still had not discussed where they needed to go from here.

From the moment he opened his eyes, Johnny could sense the aberrant psychic energy in the atmosphere; it had become stronger the further north they travelled. The inherently random nature of its waves meant that it remained impossible to pinpoint where it emanated from. He sat up in his bunk and looked around; Boyd was already awake and whispering chapters from a small book while Sascha stirred in his sleeping bag. Johnny carefully watched Boyd; this man's duty was the protection of humanity from rogue psychic activity while his own was the maintenance of the equilibrium between Order and Disorder. For now they were together; he wondered if their interests would ever conflict. What if there was a situation where he himself would be considered by Boyd and his Order as being rogue?

With muttered greetings, Johnny made his way to the

bathroom and splashed cold water onto his face. He thought about the recurrent dream; like the energy disturbance it too was becoming stronger and increasingly vivid the further north he travelled. The call for help came from an old woman and her presence in the dream was more powerful than ever. He was certain that it was a psychic message and not something generated from within his own mind. He had not told anyone about the dream in any detail, mostly because he was not yet sure that he trusted it.

Next, Johnny checked on Baccharus, who remained asleep; his recovery would soon be complete. Johnny knew they would need all the psychic ability they could muster on their side which meant that both he *and* Baccharus had to be on top form.

Once everybody was awake, there was a burst of activity within the enclosed space of the motorhome mostly focused around the bathroom. Soon, they had all gathered around the table for a quick breakfast from the kitchen stores. When the plates and bowls were empty the conversation moved swiftly to the matters at hand and Johnny recapped:

"Both the Council of Seven and Boyd's conversations with Martin tell us that we have until tomorrow evening to find out what the Disciples of Disorders are up to. It seems pretty inevitable that we will also have to do something to stop them. Nobody knows exactly what the consequences of failure will be; needless to say, no good would come of it. If Disorder dominated Order then this world would certainly be a very different place. So on that note, let's decide on our next move."

Lively discussion fuelled by strong coffee followed. The question for now was how to reach the source of the aberrant energy and the Disciples of Disorder; they would worry about what to do once they got there … *if* they got there. Johnny considered their main lead: the energy itself – it had proven to be far too loud and random to take them to a specific source – even Sascha's equipment was unable to pinpoint its origin. Johnny could see that for the mission to progress it was time to follow a more solid, definite direction, not just dreams and psychic energy. Martin, the man who had approached Boyd for help, was their only ally thus far and therefore their best hope for getting deeper into the investigation. Martin had been reluctant to give out many details regarding the Disciples in his early dealings with Boyd; however, judging by their last conversation, he was now prepared to reveal everything. Where was he? Had the Disciples already found him? There was no way of knowing. In fact, he was someone about whom they all knew surprisingly little except for one very important item of information, his address. Johnny proposed a visit to Martin's apartment as their next move.

"I started searching the flat, and it was only a few seconds later that I noticed that bastard Kreb from the balcony window and gave chase, so I never really got to look properly," said Boyd.

"In that case," said Johnny, "I suggest we go back and complete the job. Who knows, we might even find Martin there."

All were in agreement; returning to Martin's apartment for a thorough search could reveal some clues. Johnny's ongoing concern was that the Disciples of Disorder were on to them; they had already sent two of their vicious agents in the form of Mr Kreb and his Firehound to halt their progress. Sascha raised the question once again of how it was that these demons came to know about them; nobody could explain it. There was a sneaking suspicion growing inside Johnny that it might have something to do with his mysterious dreams. He kept this to himself for now; it was only a hunch, and he didn't want to worry the group unduly. Nobody was uncertain about the danger of what they were dealing with here. Only a formidable organisation could have summoned a powerful ally such as Kreb. The Disciples and their leader must have possessed deep knowledge of arcane psychic lore. With these thoughts, the conference reached a natural conclusion; it was time to visit Martin's flat.

The camper rolled onto the road once again. The motorbike, by far the speedier transport, rode on ahead to scout for the main party. Mobile phones were going to be their means of communication. Johnny was grateful that Boyd had left the Qrwshan amulet in the motorhome as he, Sascha and Baccharus were all more likely to be detected psychically than Boyd ever would be.

As Johnny drove, Sascha started some research via the Internet. He looked stubbornly for references to cult and occult activity in Scotland. Judging by the periodic murmurs of satisfaction, Johnny could only assume the search was yielding useful information. Next time he looked over, Sascha was jotting down notes and sketching maps. "I'm charting paranormal activity in different regions of the Scottish Highlands," he explained. "I'm trying to find some clues about where we need to go and maybe establish the source of the aberrant energy and uncover any information as to its origin." Sascha could never be accused of lacking ambition in his endeavours.

The journey was uneventful; Johnny supposed it was because the daytime traffic was enough to conceal their physical presence and also their psychic aura. Even without the amulet it would have been difficult to detect their consciousness amongst that of all the people in the cars that surrounded them; difficult, but not impossible.

**

Boyd reached the apartment twenty minutes before Johnny and the motorhome. He parked a few streets away from the building to remain discreet and then carried out some initial reconnaissance that revealed no cause for concern; nobody suspicious was watching over the building or its surrounding area. With a phone call, he gave his companions trailing behind in the larger vehicle the all clear to approach, and they decided that the best course of action would be for Boyd to go ahead and start searching the apartment whilst waiting for their arrival. Boyd entered the block and made his way to Martin's front door. Once he was there, he noticed that someone had closed it which struck him as being a little strange because he remembered leaving it open. *Could've been anybody,* he thought and tried the door handle, noting the frame was still damaged.

**

The motorhome and its crew arrived on the scene. Johnny and Sascha tentatively made their way to the flat while Baccharus, who was almost back to full strength, remained behind in the vehicle under protest to keep a lookout. When the others entered, Boyd was already standing in the middle of the front room; he held a framed photograph of someone receiving a certificate. The certificate itself was alongside the photo and it bore the name Martin Butler. Boyd had just finished a cursory search of the apartment. The place looked an absolute mess and he reassured his friends that he wasn't responsible.

"Someone beat us here?" asked Johnny.

Boyd nodded. "I've had a look around. Whoever was

here before us didn't leave a stone unturned."

"This place is full of residue," Johnny commented, referring to residual psychic energy in the form of Presarium particles that had been left lingering in the atmosphere. It appeared that the flat had been searched both physically *and* psychically.

"I guess there's no point in us looking through everything again," said Sascha.

"You won't find a thing," Boyd confirmed confidently.

"How about psychically, Johnny? Is there anything useful in the residual energy you're detecting?" added Sascha.

Johnny shook his head slowly as he concentrated. "No … nothing specific so far, just more signs of Disorder," he said, frowning.

The three of them couldn't help feeling dismayed; they had come here to find clues, unfortunately, so had whoever was here before them. Sascha and Boyd turned around with glum faces to leave the room, not knowing what their next move was to be. Johnny, who was about to follow them out, stopped suddenly.

"Don't open the door," he whispered to them.

"What?"

"Pardon?"

"Don't open the door; somebody is watching us."

"Watching us? How?" Sascha asked.

"Shhh…" Johnny replied holding up his hand. "Let me concentrate." Sure enough he could feel somebody watching them, waiting for them to leave.

Boyd listened carefully, trying to detect what Johnny had sensed. He shook his head. "I can't hear anything."

Johnny continued to concentrate and his friends remained silent. In his mind, the physical form of the world fell away, its atoms and molecules vanished and he sensed his surroundings only through Presarium, the ghost particle, present in all matter.

Johnny perceived a flow of particles, and with his mind's eye he traced their source to the opposite flat, across the hall. He interpreted the frequency and amplitude of the waves and concluded there was somebody of insignificant psychic ability trying to spy on them. The aberrant energy in the background masked the picture a little; however, this other individual was so close that Johnny managed to see past it.

"Friend or foe?" asked Boyd.

"Is it the Disciples?" asked Sascha.

"None of them," Johnny replied, "it's somebody who is afraid, very afraid, watching us as prey watches its hunter, and he is concerned for his own safety. He is trying to look at us through the security lens of his front door. I think he's alone in there." The frown of concentration on Johnny's face faded away.

"What do we do?" Sascha asked.

"If he is looking now," said Johnny, "he could have been looking when Martin went missing and when whoever came along to make this mess was here."

"He could have seen what happened!" said Boyd and in his eagerness grabbed the door handle to confront the stranger across the hall.

"Boyd, stop!" Sascha called out. "Johnny said the guy is scared, I say it's probably because he *did* see something. We can't just go charging up to his door, especially not all three of us at once. And with all due respect, Boyd, you're not the most comforting-looking stranger to have knocking at your door."

"Fine, but right now he looks like our only lead," said Boyd, taking his hand away from the door handle.

"Why don't *you* go?" Sascha asked Johnny. "You seem to

have tuned in to how this fellow is feeling, you have the measure of the man."

Johnny nodded. "I'll go then. You guys stay here."

He walked out of Martin's apartment and strolled as casually as possible to the door opposite, aware all the time that he was being observed through the tiny security lens. Johnny mustered a kindly smile and knocked. As expected, he had caught the man behind the door by surprise and sensed his anxiety peak. There was no response to the knock; he was still there though, behind the door, quite afraid and not daring to move just in case he gave himself away by doing so. Johnny projected positive emotional signals to try to create a sense of reassurance. Nothing happened; it was becoming obvious that the man was unwilling to meet any strangers.

"Hi, my name's Johnny. I'm a friend of Martin's," he said aloud in the least threatening way he could manage. "Martin has been missing for a while, I'm just wondering if you saw anything? I'm worried about him. If there is anybody inside, please talk to me." Johnny detected some of the man's fear ebb away; his benign manner seemed to be working, although the man was still far from ready to open the door. *Whatever he had seen must have really put the fear in him.* Johnny stepped away from the door and went back into Martin's flat where Sascha and Boyd awaited him.

"What happened?" asked Boyd as Johnny entered.

"Aren't you going to give him a chance to open the door?" asked Sascha.

"He's not going to open the door," Johnny replied. "Whatever he saw freaked him out too much. It's probably why this place isn't already crawling with police – he's been too afraid to call them."

"Then what do we do now?"

Johnny thought about their options. "At this point, my

friends, time is of the essence, and we still don't have any solid leads." He turned to face Boyd. "I suggest you use your size fourteens and kick down the door so we can all pile in and ask a few questions."

The suggestion was brutal and it surprised his friends; they couldn't think of any alternative so went along with it. Boyd assumed command.

"Okay, let's do this! Johnny, stand behind me; Sascha, in front."

The three of them lined up inside the front door to Martin's flat, ready to charge across the hallway.

"Okay, guys, this is the idea. Sascha, you open the door then me and Johnny run out across the hallway with me in the lead. I kick in the door of the flat opposite and we pile in."

"Can you do it with one kick?" Johnny asked.

"One kick is all it will take," Boyd replied confidently. "Sascha, once we have access follow us in and close the doors to both flats just like nothing happened. Any questions?"

"No."

"No."

"The idea is we *blitz* the place: the whole thing should take a few seconds."

Johnny had little experience in such a direct approach and deferred entirely to his friend's instruction.

"Johnny, use your mind to make sure nobody's coming down the corridor," Boyd said.

Johnny focused his psychic senses to scan the apartment block. There was some activity about two floors up, otherwise, they were clear.

"Go ahead ..." Johnny whispered.

"Stay close!" hissed Boyd as Sascha opened the door and he sped out of the room with Johnny following. Boyd strode across the corridor in only two great steps and in one smooth motion swung his right leg up and kicked outwards in a stamping motion that impacted just below the handle, blasting open the door and ripping off a bit of the frame with a cracking sound. The forced entry was over in the blink of an eye. Seeing Boyd in action left no doubt in Johnny that their new companion had done this before … on more than one occasion.

On the other side of the broken door, a terrified, chubby man ran as fast as his physique would allow him to away from the raiders; in the confined apartment there was no escape. Boyd, charging in, caught sight of him retreating to a far room and gave chase. Johnny followed close behind. Last in was Sascha who, in stark contrast, crept along quietly securing the damaged door behind him as if nothing was going on inside.

Boyd went straight for the kill; he caught up with the other man in the doorway to the sitting room and immediately had him in a headlock which he used to drag his body onto the couch. The poor man was full of fear and he mumbled uncontrollably. He turned his head to look Boyd in the face for the first time.

"Oh, no, it's you!" his faltering voice exclaimed with a strong Glaswegian accent.

Boyd put a finger to his lips and made a 'Ssshhhhhh' sound. The other man opened his mouth to say something; no words came out, just a strange gurgling noise. The terror of the moment prevented him from vocalising correctly. Boyd shook his head at the man and told him to 'sshhhh' again and he slowly fell quiet, just about controlling his shaking body.

"Good boy," said Boyd. "Just keep quiet now."

Sascha remained as guard at the front door while Johnny followed Boyd into the living room. Johnny deplored the violence, and he had to convince himself that the end justified the means. On entering, he saw Boyd with his intimidating six-foot-three frame towering over a terrified man with long, curly brown hair on the couch; a thick-set individual with dark-rimmed glasses. Once Johnny was present, Boyd commenced with a gentle interrogation.

"First of all, let me apologise for the rude interruption. If you had opened the door for my friend here it would have made life a lot easier for us all. Now, my first question is where on earth do you think you have seen me before?"

"You were here last night; I saw you go to Martin's flat," mumbled the man.

"Aahh, a nosy parker," said Boyd, "very good, that's exactly what we need."

"S-s-sorry, it's just that last night freaked me out so much," said the chubby chap in a feeble voice.

"It's okay," said Boyd. "We just have a few questions."

"W-w-who are you?" asked the man.

Boyd looked at Johnny who took this as the cue to take over questioning.

"What's your name?" Johnny asked, ignoring the previous question. The other man hesitated.

"C'mon, son, your name, he's just trying to be friendly," coaxed Boyd with a hint of menace. Johnny could see that he and Boyd were automatically slipping into a 'good cop, bad cop' routine, unintentionally – on his part anyway.

"D-D-Dave," stuttered the unfortunate man.

"Dave. Thank you, that's a good start. I'm not going to tell you *exactly* who we are, Dave; consider us as friends of Martin's," Johnny explained. "Not friends like buddies you have from school or go out drinking with; let's just say we are on his side. He actually came to one of us for help. He was in big trouble, and as far as we can tell the trouble caught up with him. All we want to do is help him out."

Johnny tried to project an aura of warmth and reassurance both psychically and physically as he spoke. He sensed a feeling of relief creep into Dave, even though the overriding emotion was still fear, much of it directed at Boyd unsurprisingly. He continued to speak. "Look, I know you saw what happened, and I know it must have frightened you. We are here to try and sort things out. Martin's a good guy and he needs our help. Will you help us to help him, Dave?"

Johnny could sense that Dave was going to open up to them soon and needed just a little more persuasion. "You saw something but didn't go to the police, Dave," Johnny continued. "I understand you were afraid and have been hiding here; the police might have been able to help. Now we are Martin's only chance. Will you help us, Dave?"

Dave nodded in acquiescence and Johnny sensed all his reservations fall away. The strategy had worked; he would talk to them now.

"Good lad," said Boyd patting Dave on the shoulder just to remind him he was still there.

"What would you like to know?" asked Dave, his voice was calmer.

"Everything," Johnny replied, "from the beginning, how you met Martin, what you know about him, every conversation you had with him and what you saw that scared you so much." Johnny suspected that he already knew the answer to the last question.

"Hey, look, I may not be able to remember everything you need to know," said Dave, worried at the amount of information they were after.

"That's okay," reassured Johnny, "just tell me whatever you can remember. Try your best to recall everything accurately, okay?"

"Yeah, sure," nodded Dave, and he began his story.

Chapter 11

"I've lived in this very flat for five years. When I moved here this place was newly built. Martin came along about twelve months later I reckon," started Dave.

"Do you live here alone?" Boyd cut in abruptly.

A good question, thought Johnny, they didn't want any interruptions.

"Yeah, I live here alone," Dave replied in his broad Glaswegian accent.

"Are you expecting any guests today?" Boyd's tone was brusque.

"No! No, I'm not."

The big man turned to Johnny. "Is he lying?"

Johnny did not sense any deception.

"He's not lying."

"Sascha!" called out Boyd.

"What?" came a distant voice.

"Don't worry about the door for now; come and listen to this."

Sascha, who had been keeping a look out through the security lens, sauntered in.

"Okay, we're all here now; please continue with your story, Dave," said Johnny. Dave took a moment to remember what he had been saying.

"When Martin first moved in he used to be this happy, positive guy; it was only about two months ago that he became – different – like, really … dark."

"Dark how?" Johnny interrupted.

"Just brooding and very antisocial. He used to work for his family or something. For his sister I think, yeah, that's right, his sister and brother-in-law. He used to be really into them."

"Did you know his family personally?" asked Johnny.

"No, not really. He *did* tell me a bit about them. He owed a lot to his sister you see. Martin had a really tough background. As a teenager, he ran away from his home in London and lived rough on the streets before moving in with squatters and getting into crime. He was still a young man when a burglary went wrong and he ended up in jail. It was a really shitty time for him as you can imagine. After a short spell, a couple of years I think, he came back out feeling that he had been screwed by the system and totally convinced he had messed up his future; then his sister found him. She came along and basically saved him from ending up back on the street. She could help him out mainly because of her husband who was some sort of hot-shot businessman.

"They got him back into society, arranged for him to get trained up in IT and found a job he could do in one of his brother-in-law's businesses installing and fixing computer networks. That's another reason why I got to know Martin; I'm into computers too, you see. Martin's a smart guy, I think it was the streets that made him like that you know, razor sharp. He told me that he picked up computer skills really quickly, and eventually he earned enough cash to get the flat opposite mine, his first place.

"Martin was really into those guys, his sister and her husband – he really owed them. He was doing really well, and just when he thought things couldn't get any better, they did! He met Louise."

"Louise?" asked Johnny.

"Yeah, his girlfriend; I think they might have been secretly engaged, just from hints they dropped now and again. She used to work for his sister, nothing major, housekeeping, babysitting, stuff like that, busy girl. I think she also worked behind a bar somewhere. Martin went in for a drink once, not knowing that she would be there, and they got chatting. He did this a few times and then asked her out. That's how they got together."

"Martin told you all this?"

"Yeah, he did, we were all right with each other. He was new to the area and wanted a friend and I was there. We were two guys of similar ages, we both liked a drink, smoking a joint together, going out, things just clicked."

"Where did he live before this flat?"

"As far as I know, he was just moving around for years, renting, working for his sister and brother-in-law and before that it was prison."

"I see," nodded Johnny thoughtfully. "Tell me more about Louise."

"When he started going out with Louise I saw less of him. You know what? That was what I expected; I mean that's what happens to guys when they find a girl, right? They go off the radar for a while. Besides, she was hot!" Dave chortled. "Well, he didn't ditch me entirely, we would still hang out. Eventually I got to know Louise myself, not very well though; like I said, she was a busy lady. Oh, yeah! I just remembered something I should have mentioned earlier; more reasons why she was so busy! She used to work in some general store helping an old lady, *and* she had a kid."

"A kid?"

"Yeah, Martin mentioned the kid a few times. It was a girl from a previous relationship. Let me think now, what was her name, yeah … it was Rachel! He got on with her really well. So for a while it was all cool for him, good job, great relationship, it was cool until about two years ago when the shit hit the fan big time. Martin told me he was going to Germany for training like he did sometimes. He didn't come back for around four weeks; he never went away for that long. I only found out he was back when one night I heard noises in the corridor at about two a.m. I went to investigate and saw Martin stumbling around pissed out of his head, reeking of booze. He couldn't even get his keys into the door. I couldn't leave him there and went over to help; he was muttering and murmuring to himself. 'Hey, let's sort you out,' I said, or something like that and took him into his flat; you know, just helping an old friend. When we got inside I saw his face clearly; he looked wretched, haunted, there were big bags under his eyes, his skin was yellow, he was unshaven; he looked rough. Our conversation went something like this: 'Hey, man, what's going on?' I asked him. 'You all right, bud?' Simple questions you might say, but I wasn't ready for his reaction – he just broke down in tears.

"What is it?" I asked as I sat him down. I just wanted to help him, you know; he looked like he was in some deep shit.

"There's been an accident," he told me between drunken sobs. 'Louise has gone.'

"I thought he was telling me they had broken up. 'What happened?' I asked. He was in such a state that I could hardly make out his words. I kept listening and gathered that Louise had been in an accident in the park – then I knew he wasn't talking about relationship problems.

"Is she all right?" I asked. He shook his head and started

to sob louder. He became withdrawn suddenly and wouldn't even look at me. I thought I had said something wrong. Then he said something like 'Dave, thanks for everything. I need to be alone now.'

"I understood he was upset and left. I couldn't ignore what he had said about Louise being in some sort of accident though. The next morning I went to check on him and he said he was feeling pretty lousy. He remembered that I had helped him get inside the night before. He was really apologetic and I could tell he felt bad that I had seen him like that. I asked him about Louise. I remember that he suddenly found it hard to breathe and said, 'She's dead, Dave.'

"I didn't know what to say; I was shocked. Obviously I had to find out more and asked him what happened. He told me it was all a bit unclear. It appeared that she was attacked by some animal, probably mauled by a dog.

"I couldn't believe what I was hearing. I was shocked, 'Did they catch it?' I vaguely remember asking – it was a useless question; it was all I could think of. He told me something along the lines of: 'The police are dealing with it, don't worry'. He went on to explain that with Louise dead, his sister and brother-in-law were looking after her girl, Rachel.

"I asked him if he was going to be all right, and I don't think he said anything, he might have nodded or something if I remember correctly; either way, I could see he didn't want to talk about it which was cool with me. I think I told him he could call at my place any time and drifted back to my flat again.

"I would still see him after that, we were friends; though not as close as before. Most weekends he went up to his sister's to see Rachel. There was this sadness about him all the time; he must have been depressed."

Johnny sat quietly with his friends in Dave's living room, intrigued by the story. He had heard some of it from Boyd when he was recounting his exchanges with Martin; Dave had filled in many of the details. At the mention of the mauling in the park, thoughts of the Firehound had immediately sprung to mind.

"This girl, Rachel, how old do you reckon she is, Dave?" asked Boyd impatiently. Johnny looked at his friend, he was on to something.

Dave rubbed his chin. "When I first heard about her, when Martin and I were good friends, say four years ago, I'm pretty sure he told me she was ten years old. So now she must be fourteen or fifteen."

Boyd nodded, turned to Johnny and spoke under his breath. "Martin said to me, 'There's a girl who needs help, a fifteen-year-old; I've known her since she was a kid. The Disciples need her and her sisters for something. I don't know what, but I need to get her out of there.'"

Johnny realised that his friend had picked up on what could prove to be a very important piece of information. "Carry on, Dave," he prompted.

Dave continued his story. "Louise died about two years ago. Martin was different after that; like I said, he was probably depressed. Things *really* changed two months ago, when he started to become strange. There was something more to it than just bereavement; he started to look ill again, just like he did when he first told me about Louise. His face was all tired and miserable. He looked really fucked up. I started seeing him even less, not my fault though, I would always try and call, you know, knock on his door, talk to him, try and hang out like we used to; he was rarely up for it. He was polite enough about it and would just make an excuse, be apologetic; from two months ago it was like that *every* time. I got the message and didn't bother calling him much."

"Why did he become like this?" Johnny asked.

"I don't know, he never told me."

"Was there anything else that was unusual after Martin became like this, any new friends? Things he said? Anything you might have picked up on at the time but never thought about?"

Dave sat in recollection for a moment. "There *was* something, you remember when I said how much he was into his sister and brother-in-law, how much they had helped him out? Well, I noticed that when this 'depression' started he never saw them much even though Rachel was living with them. He never even talked about them. It was like these guys who were his saviours never existed. He never told me why; I always thought he must have fallen out with them, maybe that was why he was like that."

Johnny nodded. "Did he ever mention their names to you?"

"Who? His sister's and brother-in-law's?"

"Yes, theirs."

"Yeah, he did, ages ago, don't ask me what they were though; I'm really bad with names."

"Do you know where they live? Where did he go whenever he went to see them?"

Dave shook his head. "I don't know, Martin never told me exactly. It was somewhere really out of the way. I know he used to see them when he went up to stay with Louise. They didn't live far from her; I mean she used to work at their house."

"So where did Louise live then?"

"Hilvern – a wee village in the Highlands."

Sascha, who had been quiet until now, spoke up. "You said Louise was attacked by this dog when she died. Do you have any more details about what happened, descriptions of the animal, anything like that?"

"Not really," Dave shook his head slowly, trying to remember, "except that it happened in the village itself, in a park. I remember Martin mentioned she was in a park in Hilvern when she was attacked."

"Which park?" asked Sascha.

Johnny could almost hear his friend's mind furiously whirring away.

Again, Dave shook his head. "I couldn't tell you, buddy, it's a wonder I have been able to tell you what I have already. I mean, it's a conversation that started two years ago. I only remember what I do because it was so shocking at the time. I'm sorry, I'm a dope-smoker, the old memory ain't what it used to be. It's only a small village; there can't be many parks there."

"So what happened last night? What freaked you out?" Johnny asked Dave, bringing the story forward to more recent events.

A grave look crossed Dave's face, his arms folded and his body language became defensive. He swallowed slowly and almost gagged before he spoke. "I came back home last night at about one in the morning. I had been out at a friend's place playing video games. I had just walked through the main entrance when Martin came down the steps. He had a bag and was running really fast, like he was trying to catch a bus or a train or even trying to get away from something. I was about to say hello. I don't think he noticed me – even though he nearly knocked me over. He wasn't just rushing, he was like properly legging it. I just shook my head and went back up to my room; I had come to expect strange behaviour from Martin by then. I closed and locked the front door to my flat, and as I was taking off my coat and shoes I heard a load of footsteps and a noise from the corridor, a horrible panting sound. It was late, you know? I wondered what on earth was going on so I looked through the lens in my front door. There were these four blokes out there, all big, tough-looking bastards dressed like punk rockers or something: leather chains, studs, the works. I thought there was some sort of eighties theme party somewhere, I'll tell you what though, you wouldn't want to mess with them. I had never seen them before. One of them was taller and looked meaner than the rest. I couldn't see his face clearly because of the big hat he had on. With them was this black dog thing. It was massive I tell you; it wasn't a dog really, more like a massive panther or something. They had stopped right outside my door; I was only feet away from them. I was terrified. I kept watching them and then I realised that they were actually after Martin's flat. I just stared through the lens, I didn't dare to move or even breathe. Like I said, one of the blokes was bigger and just plain uglier than the rest, and to be honest he is the reason why I've been hiding here in the flat, him and that dog-thing. There was something really frightening about them; they filled me with fear – even now I'm still scared. Fuck! I'm sorry, I'm starting to shake."

Dave shuddered at his recollections and sniffed back tears. The poor man had been exposed to demons without knowing it, thought Johnny, recognising the description of Mr Kreb. It was no wonder he was shaking. He gave him a few moments to calm down and then Dave continued his tale.

"Do you remember how I said Martin told me that Louise was attacked in the park by this dog-thing? I don't know if it was a coincidence but there, only feet away from me, was this monster; a fucking black dog-thing." Dave took a few breaths to compose himself. "A couple of the other guys tried to open the door to Martin's flat. It was locked so the big bastard in the hat just grabbed the door handle and pushed it open. There was a crack when the wood or the lock or something broke; he did it so effortlessly, it was unreal. All four blokes and the dog piled in; they weren't there long. Obviously, Martin had left earlier when I had seen him running down the stairs – he must have seen them coming from the back and got out from the front. Anyway, they all left again, three of the blokes minus the scary tall bloke rushed back out of the building. I suppose they were after Martin and realised he had only just got away from them. The tall bloke left separately with the creature, he wasn't rushing. That was when I got a better look at both of them, and I really wish I hadn't. The first thing I noticed was the way that the guy in black and the dog moved; it was weird, unnatural. Suddenly, they stopped in the corridor between Martin's front door and mine, and my heart skipped a few beats. I stood totally still, watching them. He wore this wide hat; beneath it I caught a glimpse of his wrinkled chin and mouth. At that point, most of his face was covered, thank God. Ugly bastard I started to think to myself. Then he slowly raised his head and beneath his hat I saw his face, fully; it was this horrible, grey wrinkled prune, and you know what—"

"He had no eyes, just black sockets," said Sascha.

"Yeah, that's right! Hey, how did you guys know?! No fucking eyes! It was horrible; the scariest thing I have seen! I swear he was looking straight through the security lens at me. I'm not ashamed to say this: I had tears running down my cheeks, and I thought I was going to lose control of my bowels. And then he just walked away again. I don't know if he just stopped to think for a minute or whether he really looked into my room backwards through the security lens, which I know is impossible. I just stood there, too afraid to move. Even after he was gone I stood there staring through the lens; it was like I was keeping a guard over my property. The thought of him being out there and me not knowing it was unbearable. I just stood for a few minutes then suddenly I saw you come: Mr Motorcycle Man here bursting in with a gun then legging it away again."

Dave looked at Boyd accusingly when he said this. "I saw you; you've got a pistol tucked into your trousers or something haven't you? I saw you burst into Martin's flat last night, gun at the ready, and then you ran out again. That was it for me! The last straw! I immediately went back into my bedroom, packed a bag and went away for the rest of that night to my friend's; didn't tell him a thing, just told him I couldn't sleep at my own flat." Dave paused for breath, shaking his head in disbelief as he relived the events.

"I came back this morning, and the door to Martin's flat was shut just like nothing had happened. Someone must have come again during the night and I am sure it wasn't to just shut the door. I was wondering what on earth could happen next, then soon enough you guys turn up, knocking at my door. Are you surprised I didn't open it? The lord Jesus Christ could have been standing there beside Gandhi and I still wouldn't have opened it after last night! What the fuck is going on? If you guys are really here to help Martin then I'm relieved; he looked like he was in big trouble."

"You didn't see anything else? Cars? Number plates? Anything?" asked Boyd.

Dave shook his head. "My window doesn't overlook the car park like Martin's does." They all sat in silence while Johnny and his friends digested the information Dave had given to them.

"Good work, Dave," said Boyd. "If there's no more

questions from my friends I guess we're gonna have to love you and leave you."

"What? Leave me?" said Dave, distraught. "Am I safe here? Hey, I answered your questions now answer mine: what the hell is going on?! Take me with you guys!"

Johnny stared at Dave with some pity; he was involved in something that would take a lifetime to understand and still leave many questions unanswered. "Like you said, Dave, Martin is in trouble. It probably wasn't his fault. He was dragged into the wrong crowd. My advice to you is to call in sick to work tomorrow then go and stay with somebody who lives far from here. Take a holiday for a week. By the time you return it'll be like all this never happened and hopefully Martin will be back too, safe and sound," Johnny said. They got up to leave Dave's apartment.

Boyd pulled out some cash from his wallet. "Sorry about the door," he said simply as he left the money on the coffee table.

"Wait! How did you know I was in the flat? What's going on?!" Dave protested.

They left Dave as rudely as they had found him. All three made their way to the car park and into the motorhome where an excitable Baccharus bombarded them with questions about what had happened; he was almost fully recovered. Sascha took it upon himself to inform the familiar of Dave's story while they drove to a petrol station. Before re-commencing their journey, they gathered around the dining table for another makeshift conference.

"Boyd, you were onto something in there," said Johnny.

"By the sacred Grimoires, I know exactly what we need to do," declared Boyd to his surprised friends.

"What have you got?" asked Sascha.

"Follow what I say carefully – Martin told me the Disciples are based in some big mansion house somewhere, he didn't tell me where it was or who owned it. He was worried about a fifteen-year-old girl who was living in that house whom he felt was in danger."

"Rachel!" said Sascha.

"Exactly!" Boyd responded. "If we find where Rachel lives, we find the mansion house and the Disciples. If you were listening carefully you will already know that Dave told us roughly where!"

Sascha started to think aloud, recalling Dave's words. "After Louise died, her daughter Rachel was adopted by Martin's sister and brother-in-law. They lived near to Louise's village, a place called Hilvern. I think that's what Dave said."

"Precisely," said Boyd.

Johnny put it all together. "Well, that's it then. We go to Hilvern, learn of Rachel's whereabouts and find out who Martin's sister and brother-in-law are. Being a 'hot-shot businessman' I'm guessing he owns a big mansion house near Hilvern. We find this big house, we reach our goal. Just like a treasure hunt!"

"Except that it's the Disciples of Disorder that we find as our reward," added Sascha gloomily.

An Internet search by Sascha produced directions to Hilvern village and confirmed that there was indeed only one small park there, Page's Park. The destination was entered into the navigation systems for both the motorhome and Boyd's motorbike before the group set off.

Dave also packed a bag and left his apartment. He was going to take Johnny's advice and disappear for a week.

Chapter 12

The drive to Hilvern took them through some of the world's most ruggedly beautiful mountain scenery. Johnny had little experience of living outside a town or city, and now that he was exposed to the serenity and drama of the landscape around him he could see why so many people settled down in places like this; it made him reconsider his life in London. The capital was somewhere he had ended up by default rather than desire.

**

His family home had been in the suburbs of one of the commuter towns outside the city limits. He was the youngest of four children with a big age gap between himself and the rest of his siblings, and even though nobody said so, it was generally considered that Johnny's birth had been unplanned – but certainly not unwanted.

He had two older sisters, one was an accountant and the other owned a flower shop. His only brother was a doctor, and they were all doing very well for themselves. Johnny could never envision himself going down similar career paths and was always more focused on the arts, where he demonstrated some degree of talent. Following their retirement, his parents moved to Portugal. Johnny, only seventeen at the time, insisted on staying behind to live with his brother, who worked in a London hospital. He had left formal full-time education to play the guitar and was undergoing advanced tuition in the instrument. He paid for his lessons by taking a part-time job on a supermarket customer services team. He despised the role and only persevered with it for the money. To supplement his income further, he also worked as an assistant in a recording studio where he would occasionally do session guitar work. Eventually, he had saved enough to rent a place of his own. As he matured, his psychic ability also progressed, and the demands of working for the Equilibrium increased; his dreams of guitar excellence were thus forced to take a back seat.

**

There was no hostile contact on the way to Hilvern; it seemed the protective amulet was performing its function admirably. The further they travelled into the Highlands the sparser the traffic became. The danger now was not from psychic detection, it was from being spotted in the conventional sense. On these quiet roads the motorhome, and even Boyd's motorbike, could be easily viewed all the way from nearby vehicles to distant vantage points on the many surrounding mountains. As usual, Johnny and Sascha arranged to split the driving between them. Johnny drove for the first half of the estimated three-hour journey while Sascha used the time to scour the Internet for clues regarding what might lie ahead, announcing any interesting facts to whoever would listen. When it was Sascha's turn to drive, Johnny used the time rather less constructively by trying to sleep in the passenger seat. As

Johnny lay there with his eyes closed, Baccharus, who was no longer showing any signs of his injury, hovered over to take up a position beside Sascha while he drove. Johnny listened in on their conversation as he drifted off.

"I'm glad you're feeling so much stronger now, Bach. We'll need your psychic ability in addition to Johnny's," said Sascha.

"Thanks, Sasch, I'm flattered. You know what though? Johnny can handle this himself if necessary. You haven't seen half of what he can do yet; nobody has, not even him. The Council of Seven know *everything* and I heard how they rated Johnny. They reckon his full potential has yet to be awoken."

With his eyes still closed, Johnny grinned; nobody noticed.

"I hope you're right, pal. It's still good to have you around though, powers or no powers."

"Thanks! And you're all right too."

They laughed together.

"So what do you think of this Martin guy then? Didn't he tell Boyd that he used to be one of the Disciples?" asked Baccharus.

"I think he was being vetted or something, Boyd called him a prospective Disciple," replied Sascha without taking his eyes off the road.

"He *was* closely associated with them; people just don't change their alignment that easily, you know!"

"He probably had second thoughts. These groups like the Disciples of Disorder are most attractive to people when they are vulnerable and lonely, it's when they make perfect targets for recruitment. If Martin had just come out of prison then he would have been easy meat for them."

"Why would he be so lonely? He had his sister and

brother-in-law for support."

"True. It seems, however, that they are both tied up in this mess and not in a good way."

This was the last portion of their exchange to be overheard by Johnny before he fell asleep and dreamed the same dream that had been haunting him for so long. His body was carried effortlessly through the air, above the now-familiar valley between the three peaks. Just as before, his dream flight descended towards the same woodland clearing beside a lake. The valley itself was beautiful and coloured as intensely as ever, visible to him in precise detail while the rest of the landscape that surrounded it remained a sea of ashen grey and black. This time, he noticed with some concern that the grey and black region was not static as he had first thought; it was actually growing and encroaching upon the valley. From his flying vantage point he could see that even the lake was losing the azure around its edges. The three surrounding peaks had already been drained of their natural hue, and closer observation revealed that it was their very vitality that had been lost alongside their colour. The plants and trees that grew on their slopes were withered, while rocks and boulders had crumbled and collapsed. What was actually left behind looked like the ash from a fire. *No*, thought Johnny, *not ash*. This change in appearance was more like fruit left in a bowl to rot. What he saw was decay growing over the land below him. At the very centre of this change lay the woodland clearing, a place of beauty, full of brightly dressed people moving around. How long would they last? As he flew lower, he heard their voices chanting,

"Earth expires, the children broken,
Chaos fires once more awoken."

"Help us, Johnny," came the whisper, just as it always did. Johnny could hear it clearer than ever before. This time he was flying close enough to see the chanters, they were definitely children, all of them running and playing joyfully in the valley. He looked around to find where the whispering call for help was coming from and he saw her. Seated at the very centre of the clearing, surrounded by the moving and playing children, was a huddled figure, an old white-haired gypsy woman, plump and ancient. She was sitting cross-legged on the ground, wrapped in a boldly patterned shawl, and her face was turned down, away from Johnny.

He flew closer and the chanting became louder. He could see that the children all had their eyes closed even as they ran and played, and yet somehow they didn't collide or have any difficulty in locating each other. All of this was going on as the black and grey death, flowing down the sides of the surrounding mountains, slowly swallowed the valley. By now it had claimed the entire lake and wood-land – all that remained was the clearing with its inhabi-tants. Gradually, the decay impinged on this too, edging forwards, threatening to wipe out the colourful little space forever. As it grew, the children, with terrified looks on their faces, stopped playing and huddled together around the old woman, as far as possible from the creeping death. Their chanting had stopped. Johnny was in the air directly above the terrified group, descending towards them rap-idly, almost falling. This was the closest he had ever been to them. He wondered how the dream events would end. Would the old woman and the children be swallowed up by the decay? Would he land right on top of them? Would he too be swallowed by the grey and black? The children bunched up together, their eyes closed tight. Suddenly, unexpectedly, the old woman, who had been facing the ground, threw her head back to stare right at Johnny with milky grey eyes, directly acknowledging his presence for the first time. "Help us, Johnny!" was all she said. The message was simple enough, and her voice, despite being many hundreds of feet below him, sounded as if she had just whispered right into his ear; so loud that Johnny woke from his dream with a start.

"Whoa, Johnny!"

"Hey, Johnny, what's going on?"

Johnny took a sharp intake of breath and twitched convulsively. It took him a few seconds to orientate himself; the dream had been so intense and vivid that he had forgotten his current situation. Sascha flashed him an amused glance as he drove.

"That must have been some dream you were having, or was it a nightmare?!" asked Baccharus, intrigued.

Johnny rubbed his eyes. "A really vivid dream; really weird," he said, stretching.

"You must be tired; don't blame you, I feel exhausted," said Sascha.

Johnny thought about this. "See, that's strange. I'm *tired* − not *exhausted*. Actually, I've been more tired than this many times before … This dream is different; like it's not a dream."

"Is this something to do with what you were telling me in your apartment?" asked Baccharus.

"Yeah, it's like … someone's trying to send a message … a message straight into my mind."

"What message? What did you see?" asked Sascha.

"How far have we got now?"

Sascha glanced at the navigation system. "Nearly there," he replied, "about fifteen minutes to go."

"Okay, not enough time to tell you guys about the dream. I don't want to skim over details; there could be something useful in there. I'll tell you later. Right now, we should be thinking about what we're going to do when we get to Hilvern."

They agreed to discuss dreams later. Sascha had one last question. "You've had the dream before, haven't you, Johnny?"

Johnny nodded slowly. "Yes, but not so intensely."

A sign indicating Hilvern was seven miles away changed the subject of conversation. Johnny made a call to Boyd's earpiece and let him know their location. Boyd had travelled ahead on the nimbler motorbike and was already in Page's Park. He said he would stroll around to get a feel for the village and take the chance to have a few smokes before Sascha turned up.

It wasn't long after the phone call that the motorhome also entered Hilvern. Johnny noticed, with some consternation, that aberrant, psychic energy was particularly prominent in the village. He could feel very little of the natural collective aura from its inhabitants, which was unusual because every place of habitation, from a house to an entire city, possessed this quality in abundance. Johnny thought about what Sascha had discovered regarding Hilvern on the Internet. It had started life as a small market village, a centre of trade for local farm produce and livestock. Even though these activities around which it was built had long ago faded away, the place remained the nearest thing to a commercial hub for the surrounding farms, and a home for many of the people who worked on them.

The satellite navigation system led the motorhome to Page's Park, a grass-covered field bordered by mature trees and paths leading to the surrounding streets. At its centre was a tall lamppost beside a dilapidated bandstand. It was getting dark and the lamp was lit. Sascha drove slowly alongside the green expanse while his friends gazed out of the windows; Boyd waited further ahead. Johnny felt a sense of sadness brought on by knowledge of the events that had taken place here.

"Well this is it, boys, Page's Park," Sascha said. "You guys don't seem too happy," he added after seeing the looks on Baccharus and Johnny's faces. There was something obviously worrying the two psychics.

"There's residual energy all over the park," Baccharus muttered.

Sascha reached over and flicked some switches on the devices he had positioned on the dashboard; a small screen with an oscillating green line that formed a delta wave was activated.

"What do you make of it?" he asked.

"Disorder," Baccharus replied.

"Yeah," agreed Johnny, "there is a layer of chaotic energy clinging to the park along with the psychic signature of a traumatic event."

"Louise?" asked Sascha.

"More than likely," replied Johnny.

"Well at least we know it's the right place then," said Sascha.

Johnny closed his eyes, focused, and tried to form a picture of what happened here. Traces of Mr Kreb's aura and the Firehound drifted into his mind; the time it related to was so long ago that he could not obtain a clear image. The atmosphere inside the motorhome was grave, a direct reflection of the negative energy emanating from Page's Park.

They eventually came to a halt beside Boyd's motorbike. He had dismounted and was standing facing the park with his holy book open in front of him, reciting under his breath.

"What on earth is he doing? This is no time to read," said Baccharus as he watched curiously.

A minute later, Boyd had closed his book, and Johnny could sense the atmosphere about the park become lighter and less oppressive.

"What were you doing there?" asked Baccharus as soon as Boyd stepped through the door of the motorhome.

"Clearing the stench of Disorder," offered Boyd as an explanation. "I am instructed by the high priests to recite this particular verse wherever there has been aberrant psychic activity; it dispels the influence of Disorder when it is recited."

Sascha confirmed that his electronic meters indicated reduced Presarium activity following Boyd's reading. Johnny could see the value of a psychic police force like Boyd's Order; without such collectives the whole world could easily be awash with residual energy and rogue psychic activity.

Being so close to the enemy, Johnny felt an increased sense of unease and he could see that his companions felt the same; there was nothing psychic about it.

"So this is where Louise was attacked," said Baccharus to nobody in particular as he hovered by the window and looked out across Page's Park.

"This is the place," confirmed Sascha, taking up a position beside the familiar.

"So what now?" Baccharus asked aloud.

Johnny glanced at the clock on the dash. It was around nine thirty p.m. and the village was dead; everything was shut and there was nobody about on the streets. This was where they would have to find their next lead. They had slept very little the previous night and it had been a long journey; now was the time to rest. Refreshments were distributed from the stores as options were considered.

"I suggest we move outside Hilvern, find a place to stop and make an early start tomorrow," said Johnny. He did not feel the village was a safe place to call it a night. He sensed they were being watched, maybe by locals, maybe by Disciples; he didn't like it. Each of his companions was visibly relieved at the suggestion; they too felt uncomfortable here and any opportunity to sleep was most welcome. Boyd returned to his motorbike and they all promptly left Hilvern. As they drove, Johnny mentioned how strange it was that there had been neither a moving car nor a person on the village streets even though it was not particularly late. "Maybe there's very little to be awake for," Sascha had suggested. "Or maybe everyone's just too afraid to come out at night," Baccharus had added mischievously.

They drove for about ten miles along the main carriageway; Johnny counted only a single lorry followed by two cars going in the opposite direction on this short journey. Sascha spotted a lay-by which appeared discreet enough for another overnight stay, and they parked up. Boyd entered the larger vehicle to join his companions. With the entire team together, the motorhome became a bustle of activity as an evening meal was prepared. Sascha connected to the Internet once again and scoured it for information on Hilvern Village, its surrounding region, and any significant events. Outside, the night was still. Having left Hilvern, Johnny felt more relaxed; he didn't expect this state of affairs to last for very long.

With the meal over, coffee was served; Boyd and Baccharus lit cigarillos. Despite craving the comfort of his bunk, Johnny instead insisted that Sascha take the opportunity to present his research findings, and the others were soon giving their undivided attention to the fascinating information he had discovered.

**

The Hilvern Valley region of Scotland had been considered since time immemorial to be a centre of witchcraft and arcane lore. At its very heart, both geographically and spiritually, once stood the mysterious Dunain Castle.

Historical archives of the region were littered with strange reports of people with superhuman powers. For example: individuals who were capable of flight, others who could appear in two places at once, or those who dispensed powerful curses that afflicted people, livestock and even crops with disease.

The sparsely populated region always had a steady trickle of people migrating from it who took with them frightening stories that bolstered the valley's reputed association with witchcraft and the paranormal. The witches of Hilvern were said to forge allegiances with demons more ancient than Earth itself: beings who gifted them with favours and control over natural laws, allowing them to perform seemingly miraculous acts.

A popular legend that became ingrained in the folklore of the region was of dark-robed men from Dunain Castle entering poorly secured houses and cottages to remove the inhabitants, especially young children. Strangers who visited Hilvern inevitably felt an atmosphere of unease about the valley, and it was uncertain whether this was due simply to its reputation or a primeval sixth sense warning them of hidden, supernatural danger.

During the years when the Church promoted the persecution of witches, and in the earliest days of the witch-hunt, Hilvern's reputation naturally attracted zealots and opportunists by the legion; it wasn't long before the God-fearing avoided Hilvern altogether. The earliest witch-hunters who had enthusiastically sought to cleanse

Hilvern of its magic were finding themselves afflicted with madness, blindness or worse. These invaders realised that there was every chance they had stumbled upon true witchcraft and demon magic, a power they could not fight, and so were quick to avoid Hilvern, especially Dunain Castle, to whose estate much of the land in the valley belonged. They promptly returned to victimising and exploiting vulnerable peasants again.

It was common knowledge that Dunain Castle had been home to a long line of lords, each as mysterious and elusive as the previous one. Some were recognised as sinister, cruel men while others revelled in reputations as carefree playboys or even learned professors. The lords never took any measures to curb the disreputable activity on their estate, which always prompted speculation that they were themselves somehow associated with the wicked goings on. Over time, the castle fell into ruin and its precise location was forgotten; there was much conjecture suggesting that a grand house had been built on its site by the twelfth lord.

Interest in the region and its notorious reputation had long since diminished. The present lord, by all accounts, had proven to be more secretive than all his predecessors. He continued to maintain close links with those in positions of authority and the establishment. There had generally been very little in the way of dealings with the current lord and the public, except in affairs that directly concerned his land.

**

Why here? Johnny thought to himself. It was as if Disorder had always managed to exert its influence in Hilvern and establish some sort of base in this isolated, rural region.

"I'm not finished yet. Listen to this!" Sascha continued, "It's a report I found in a local newspaper website: the *Hilvern Village Herald.* Let me read it out to you."

"Louise Croft, who had been living in Hilvern for eight years, was tragically killed in Page's Park last Wednesday. She was mauled to death by a large dog of unknown breed. Mr David Matthews, a local resident, confirmed that he witnessed a man dressed in black walking with the animal in the park before the incident. Another witness, who wished to remain anonymous, reported seeing the dog, which was without a lead, dart away from its owner before the attack. The owner, it seemed, did not attempt to restrain the animal. Dog and owner were seen leaving the park by another local resident, Arthur Moore. Mr Moore, who was unaware at the time of what had happened, described a tall and very old man dressed in black walking past him followed a few seconds later by the large dog. He did not have much in the way of a description because the man's face was mostly covered by a wide-brimmed hat.

"Police have been trying to follow up leads on the man and dog but have thus far been unsuccessful. Hilvern is a small village, and it can be said with some certainty that neither the dog nor its keeper match the description of any resident.

"Louise Croft, daughter of the late life-long Hilvern resident Joseph McFadden, was a well-known local character. She was a member of staff at the Stone's Throw Pub and worked with Mrs McGuiness at McGuiness's general store just outside the village. She leaves behind a thirteen-year-old daughter who is being cared for, with a view to adoption, by a family friend. He has asked to remain anonymous to afford the child some privacy through these difficult times. Police have a dedicated phone number for any information regarding this incident."

Sascha looked up from his computer screen. Johnny and the rest of the team quietly absorbed the information from the article.

"So what do you make of it all, Sascha?" prompted Johnny, always interested in his friend's take on any matter.

Sascha was happy to share his thoughts. "Well, it certainly sounds like Mr Kreb and the Firehound killed Louise, which is no revelation, it's what we suspected already. What is important though are the new clues. Do you remember Dave telling us Louise worked in a bar and a general store? Well, we have names now: the Stone's Throw Pub and Mrs McGuiness's general store. We'll go to these places and ask questions to find out where Rachel and the big house she now lives in are. I'm assuming the store will be open before the pub tomorrow morning so I propose we go there as soon as we can. If we don't learn anything useful then we try the pub. The landlord might know a thing or two, and if he can't help, well – then at least we're in the right place for a few drinks."

When Sascha had finished, Johnny looked at the rest of his companions; there was no objection to the plan.

"Sounds good," Boyd said, "I bet the police and social workers have all the information we need on file. You know, stuff like where Rachel went and all that."

"You're right," Sascha replied, "obviously they won't share it with a group of misfits such as ourselves, and I suppose to even have a sniff of those files would mean going through impossible layers of bureaucracy first."

"Grand, well then in that case we stick to finding Mrs McGuiness's store or the pub," said Boyd. "Good work, Sascha."

Everybody cleared up and prepared for sleep; for the psychics there remained an important final act to perform. Johnny and Baccharus exited the motorhome and used the vehicle's integrated ladder to climb onto its broad, rectangular roof, not for the intended purpose of loading luggage; instead, they sat facing each other, cross-legged and with eyes closed, concentrating deeply. Above them was a clear, beautiful night sky, an astronomer's dream.

Johnny had been instructed by the Council of Seven to provide an update at least twenty-four hours before the projected deadline, and now was as good an opportunity as any to transfer this information.

As they sat cross-legged on the roof in meditation, the air around them filled with static that made each hair stand on end; occasionally, a spark of electricity would leapfrog from Johnny to Baccharus. Johnny entered the mind of his familiar with his own and transferred every thought and memory regarding the mission so far to the faithful cherub. He included every one of the dream sequences he had experienced and his reflections on what they could mean. Once the transfer was complete, the static charge disappeared and they opened their eyes simultaneously. Baccharus was instantly knowledgeable about his keeper's thoughts regarding the case, and the biggest revelation to him was the significance Johnny placed on the strange dreams he was having. There was no need to discuss anything further; Baccharus now knew Johnny's mind like his own, and it included the knowledge that Johnny wished to continue keeping the details of the dreams a secret from the rest of his companions.

Even at the speed of light, it would take millions of years for messages sent by conventional physical methods to reach the centre of the universe. For those who understood the structure of reality there was a way around this rather major inconvenience: travel between dimensions. To fulfil his role as a familiar, Baccharus was designed to do this intuitively; it was integral to his purpose as the vector of information between Johnny and the Council. Baccharus had tried to explain this process to Johnny on a number of occasions – it only seemed to confuse his keeper further. As a human, Johnny was not really designed for this form of travel, and in the end they both agreed that the only way of understanding how to do it was if you had actually done it yourself. So until such a day, Johnny accepted that the mysterious process of inter-dimensional travel would remain a mystery.

"Have a good trip, pal! Pass on my love!" said Johnny.

Baccharus, waving goodbye, warped and twisted as if he were a reflection in a hall of mirrors. The air filled with static, Baccharus dematerialised, and blue sparks leapt from where his previously solid form had been to the roof of the motorhome where they travelled in a circuit around the vehicle's exterior and faded away.

The warping familiar disappeared from view entirely in a few seconds leaving Johnny alone on the roof. The solitary man stood up again, stretched and took in a lungful of the clear crisp Highland air. The night was still once more, and the stars were visible despite the light cloud that had started to collect; he wondered at their beauty and meditated on the infinite worlds and possibilities that lay in them. It occurred to him that at that precise moment he could be viewing light from the distant galaxy where the Council of Seven resided – it made him feel connected to a far greater reality than the one he experienced on Earth. Quietly, Johnny re-entered the motorhome; his friends had already retired to various bunks to get some much-needed rest.

Chapter 13

Not far from the motorhome and its slumbering occupants, a rental car hired under a false identity drove through the city. Martin was at the wheel. He was tired and haggard but determined to carry out his plan. It was this resolve that kept his mind focused and alert; tonight he felt prepared to face anything.

Martin knew that he had only narrowly escaped capture, or worse, the previous night; if he had not been waiting in his flat for Boyd at that late hour then he would not have seen the black van and car arriving from his balcony doors – they would have caught him as he lay in bed. He had always known that it was only a matter of time before the Disciples came for him, and when the two vehicles arrived, he had responded instantly by escaping into the heart of the city.

It was not purely good fortune that had allowed him to evade his enemies; he had anticipated a moment such as this and made appropriate arrangements which included a car in a hidden location that would facilitate any flight.

Once in the relative safety of the populous city centre he had found a hotel, and despite the late hour he managed to convince the staff to put him up for the night, playing on their sympathies with a story about having his car stolen.

This had all occurred last night, and the Disciples had not yet caught up with him. This emboldened Martin. He was still free, and that was all that mattered because tonight he would penetrate their lair to find Rachel.

He cruised through the Glasgow streets in his hire car. Above him, the clouds were gathering and gradually obscuring the night sky, hiding the celestial bodies that had previously been so clearly visible. Last night, the streets had been filled with processions of drinkers and revellers; at present, there were only diffuse groups of merry stragglers who wandered on and off the road as they pleased, the weekend was over. Martin hardly noticed them as he drove to the train station. His mind was repeatedly going through the plan, trying to cover all eventualities. He hoped Rachel would be ready; she didn't have to do much, just open the window. *Hell! She doesn't even have to do that, Pete could do it. Just be ready to leave, Rachel,* he thought to himself.

Martin rolled to a halt by the pickup area near a broad figure wearing a long coat who was smoking beside one of the train station exits. On seeing the car, the man put out his cigarette, lifted a bag from the ground and casually walked over. He opened the door and slipped into the passenger seat, placing the bag by his feet. He had been given a description of the vehicle and its number plate earlier in the day.

"All right, sunshine," croaked a deep voice from a smoker's larynx.

Without a word, Martin stuck out his hand for a quick shake before driving off. "How was the journey, Pete?" he eventually asked the burly cockney.

"Shit," was the reply. "I'm getting old; just can't stand crowds any more, bloody train was packed from the start of the journey."

"You took a chance coming by train, Pete. If there was a delay or cancellation or something I would have been fucked."

"You can just as easily have delays and get stuck on the road these days. Anyway, the train is good. I pay for my ticket in cash, and as long as I keep my head down, away from the cameras, it's anonymous; bleeding surveillance everywhere these days. You know they have cameras that can track your number plate now?"

"What's in the bag?"

"Just a few things we might find useful."

"So, you ready for this, Pete?"

"I was born ready, mate," said Peter Pike with a laugh.

Martin remained edgy, tense; Pete, the seasoned campaigner, appeared perfectly relaxed. He was showing no more sign of nerves than if he were going out for a drink or a meal, thought Martin, and he found this comforting. He informed Pike that it would be a fairly long drive from Glasgow to the old house – and Rachel.

Once they were out of the city, Pike started firing questions at Martin. They had been over it all already, but he was a professional and Martin knew details were important to him. He answered all of Pike's queries, telling him the height of the perimeter wall, describing the gates, and he confirmed that there were no dogs or barbed wire; this last piece of information worried Pike.

"Why are you looking so anxious? No fucking dogs or wire – that's good isn't it?" asked Martin.

"It's good," replied Pike, "it just seems so wrong though. A big place like that; I mean what have they got? Cameras? Alarms? Or like most people out in the country – fucking shotguns?"

From the look on Pike's face, Martin could tell that it was

a serious concern. "Pete, there's no cameras, there's no alarms and as far as I know, no shotguns. Look, I won't lie to you; I have been in the house, and I have never seen that stuff. I know the people who live there and they've never mentioned anything about weapons to me. It's a small community out there, nothing happens – they have big houses, some land and not much else. If there's any guns, knives or even police, just get the fuck out of there. I brought you along to help me get in and out, not to get caught or shot. Besides, we won't even be going into the building itself, just up to the window I told you about."

Pike nodded, seeming reassured, and gave his persistent analysis of the details a break. They drove on into the Highlands, eventually leaving the A-roads to follow a route that was mostly made up of twisting, tree-lined mountain passes. Most of the journey was spent chatting and laughing about old times or listening to the radio; they harassed each other about their musical tastes and enthusiastically disagreed about which station to tune in to. Martin welcomed the distraction, although it was only fleeting, and the atmosphere soon changed again.

"We'll be there in about ten minutes, Pete," he announced, and he witnessed all the recent frivolity in Pike's mood evaporate in an instant as his friend mentally prepared for the work ahead.

"Make sure you stop just where you told me you would, all right? I mustn't lose my bearings."

"Sure thing," Martin replied.

There were no more questions; it was time to put the plan into action. The road ahead was lit by their head-lights and whatever pale illumination the almost full moon projected through hazy cloud cover. It was approaching two a.m. Martin couldn't remember the last time they had passed another vehicle. He felt Pike's silence and saw him wistfully observing the bleak beauty of the landscape; driving through it at night felt like a journey into another world. Martin too was silent, not because of the scenery – he was contemplating the task ahead.

Their route became very narrow, trees hung low overhead, and branches scraped the side of their vehicle whenever it veered from the middle of the road. There was not enough room for two cars to pass without one pulling over to the side; at this hour, in this location, it was unlikely that they would encounter any. A few minutes and two left turns later, Martin slowed the car down until it just rolled along at a jogger's pace. He was concentrating on the roadside.

"We here, then?" asked Pike.

"Yeah, just looking for my spot," Martin told him.

Pike took off his seatbelt and stretched. The earlier, relaxed exchanges between the friends were long forgotten. Martin looked at Peter Pike, who appeared deadly serious, face and eyes like a hawk's; he was ready to do what he did best, breaking in.

"Here we go," Martin said. He steered the car onto a patch of flattened grass beside one of the bends in the road, a passing place for vehicles travelling along this narrow course. Martin pointed out how well their car was hidden here amongst the surrounding woodland, invisible until you were about ten feet away. Peter Pike nodded appreciatively.

"Okay, Pete, get your shit together. Beyond these trees is the wall and then beyond that it's the house," said Martin, pointing into the depths of the roadside woods.

Pike looked to where his friend was indicating. "Can't see fuck all yet," he said as they both got out of the car, his eyes unable to penetrate the darkness.

Martin opened the boot; Pike took off his long coat and

placed it inside. He put on a black fleece which he had been carrying in his shoulder bag; it was less cumbersome and more suited to the job at hand. Martin was already dressed in a dark tracksuit.

"Lead the way," said Pike in his conspicuous cockney accent, handing Martin a flashlight from the shoulder bag. With torch in hand, Martin stealthily ducked into the woods and Pike followed. Martin kept looking over his shoulder to make sure his friend was keeping up. Pike did not look as lithe as Martin remembered him, time had taken its toll; however, his movements were as agile as ever, and he followed cat-like through the dark woods without falling behind. After about fifty metres the perimeter wall came into view, and in his eagerness, Martin stumbled over some large roots; Pike caught him, and they moved on without losing any momentum. On reaching the wall they spoke in whispers.

"Right, Pete, here we are, mate. You said you had a few ideas about what we should do now."

Peter Pike nodded thoughtfully; he was carefully observing the wall, measuring it up. "You said there's a gate not far from here?"

"Yeah, that's right."

"Take me to it; I don't like the look of the wall, it's too high. If we need to get out in a hurry we're fucked. I think busting open the gate is the best option."

Martin swiftly led Pike along the perimeter wall until they reached the metal gate. After spending hours staking out this house to try to find Rachel alone, Martin felt as if he knew the wall better than the interior of his own flat.

"Keep the torch low," Pike ordered as he looked through the gate into the garden. Martin did as asked and watched Pike observe the great house.

"You know what, Martin? At first, I didn't believe you

when you said there were no dogs. I thought that out here in the country they all kept them. Since I haven't heard a single bark or growl, I think you might actually be right. They don't even have any modern security features; there's no alarm to this gate, and I can't see any sign of CCTV. It's ridiculous!" Pike reached into his shoulder bag and retrieved what looked like a small, silver Thermos flask from it. "Hold that torch steady now," he told Martin.

Pike unscrewed the lid of the flask and a smoky vapour poured insidiously over its top edges. Martin watched, intrigued, as he lit his friend's work with the torch held low and still as requested. Pike placed the flask on the ground, and from a small plastic case that was also in his bag he produced a long glass pipette. With this device, he drew up some of the flask's smoking content and squirted it into the keyhole of the lock; he aimed the rest at points where the lock sat in the heavy frame of the gate. There was a sizzling sound whenever the liquid from the pipette made contact with metal.

"Acid?" Martin asked.

Pike, engrossed in what he was doing, simply nodded. The metal sizzled and corroded while he carefully packed away pipette and flask, ensuring the latter's lid was screwed on tight. They both stood there watching the lock for about a minute. Martin awaited instructions from his friend.

"Okay, I'll grab the gate here, and you push when I push," Pike said. He was gripping the metal bars around the lock, and together they used their combined body weight to apply steady pressure to the compromised barrier. There was a small amount of resistance that soon gave way with a dull popping sound. They eased the gate open. It squeaked a little so Martin lifted it slightly off its hinges in Pike's direction and it was quiet again.

"Kill the torch," ordered Peter Pike before he took it off his friend and put it into the shoulder bag again. From here on, they relied on Martin's memory and the sporadic moonlight to guide their way towards the house.

Old habits die hard, and Pike's eyes scanned all around for signs of a camera or alarms, anything that might catch them; there was nothing. Together, they closed in on the house steadily.

"Nice garden," commented Pike.

Martin smiled to himself, amused that even in these circumstances Peter Pike found time to appreciate such things. They stopped briefly behind a row of dense bushes, and Martin pointed towards the grand old building at the centre of this large expanse of ground they were in. It was about a hundred metres from them. Peter Pike looked at it solemnly.

**

Its slumber disturbed, the thing beneath the ground stirred. It was the vibration from their movements that had roused it. It was very sensitive to touch. Once they had entered the garden, it could feel their breathing, their hearts beating and even sense the electrical energy of their brainwaves. It could feel all this from its home under the soil by way of its many sensitive, powerful limbs that spread like a network of pipes throughout the whole garden, encircling the house and hidden from view. The Bar-Shiyq recognised one of the intruders; the other was an unknown. Its small brain ticked away. It had been a while since it truly feasted; for too long it had fed merely on creatures of the soil. Occasionally, the master had thrown it a sacrifice; tonight, all that looked like it would change.

**

"The lack of security does worry me; there's not so much as a floodlight here," whispered Pike suspiciously as the pair moved from cover to cover. Martin stopped beside a large privet hedge; they had managed to work their way around the garden to face the front of the house whilst still maintaining a safe distance.

"There!" said Martin. "That's the window."

Pike gazed thoughtfully at the huge building in front of him. Its façade was flat except for the portico that covered the great entrance door and the steps that led up to it. The house possessed three symmetrical rows of large rectangular windows, one for each floor; smaller windows were built into the roof. It was the very middle window above the portico that Martin had indicated.

Peter Pike took it all in for a few moments before speaking. "We can use one of those pillars with the blocks carved into it to get onto that little roof above the front door. The one beside the plant climbing up the wall will be best, once there we get the window open. You said the girl would be waiting?"

"Yeah, that's right," confirmed Martin. "The other bedrooms are at the back of the house so as long as we keep quiet nobody should spot us."

Martin, still looking towards the window, waited for his friend to say something; all he got in response was a stifled grunt. He turned around to see Pike's face looking pale, his eyes wide and filled with sheer panic; he was tugging at his left leg with both arms.

"Pete! What the fuck is going on?!" exclaimed Martin on witnessing his friend's distress. He was barely able to keep his voice down to a whisper.

"I don't know, something's caught my leg. I can't fucking

move," said Pike, straining fiercely. His leg suddenly jerked downwards, pulling his foot into the ground, and he whimpered from the pain. "Fuck me! Fuck me! What's going on?" he begged as he tried to suppress cries of agony.

Confused, Martin weighed up the risk of shining the torchlight to find out exactly what the hell was happening against the possibility of giving themselves away by doing so. Another downwards jerk of Pike's leg and another stifled cry of pain made up his mind. He fumbled through the bag that was still hanging from his friend's shoulder, looking for the torch. Once he had it, he shone it on Pike's leg and took a sharp intake of breath. Martin cringed at what he saw, and now Pike too could see what it was that had him.

"Oh, bloody hell! What the fuck is going on, Martin? Did you know about this?" asked Peter Pike, tears of pain and fear filling his eyes. Martin, terrified and unable to shift his gaze from the horrific sight, shook his head. Pike's left leg was buried underground up to the knee. Wrapped around it, extending all the way up to the middle of his thigh, was a thick tentacle covered in leathery skin. It was about six inches in diameter where it emerged from the soil and tapered to a point at its very end, Martin could not help wondering how much thicker the limb became if one followed it underground to its source – whatever *that* was. The thin pointed tip moved very slowly back and forth. Martin watched helplessly.

"I swear, Pete; I don't know what the fuck that is."

"Well, get it off me! I can't feel my leg any more. There's a knife in the bag."

Martin searched Pike's shoulder bag by torchlight and pulled out a serrated hunting knife. He took it and started to hack at the tentacle, producing only superficial lacerations in the thick, leathery hide. He couldn't get any deeper so he started to stab instead and only achieved a similar result. Changing tack, they tried to peel away the tapering end of the tentacle from the leg together; it shifted slightly then returned to its original position as soon as they became tired and let it go.

"Try the acid," said Pike in an agonised whisper, a look of desperation accompanying the fear already written all over his face. Martin put the knife into his pocket and reached into the bag. As he was about to wrap his fingers around the silver flask, it moved away suddenly, along with the bag and his friend. A downward jerk had pulled Peter Pike's left leg into the ground right up to his buttock; there was a sickening 'thunk' as Pike's hip was dislocated by the impossible splits he was forced into. He screamed in agony, all previous caution and any attempt to remain concealed thrown to the wind in his blind panic. Martin looked around nervously, expecting unwelcome company from the house.

Pike was about to play his last card. Reaching under his black fleece he pulled out an automatic pistol and started to shoot wildly into the ground and at the tentacle; all this achieved was a further series of rhythmical jerks and with each one his body was swallowed, twisting and writhing, deeper into the earth. Each yank was accompanied by the sound of ligaments tearing and joints popping. He was pulled into the soil with his lower limbs twisted at unnatural angles. By the time his upper body came to lie against the ground, he was screaming uncontrollably. More tentacles emerged and wrapped themselves around him; Martin vainly tried to pull Pike away from the monstrous grip and stopped only when he heard the inevitable commotion from the house. A door opened and distant agitated voices became audible alongside his friend's ululations.

He turned to run, hoping that Peter Pike would use the last bullet on himself; he knew the poor man did not stand a chance against whatever evil lurked within the ground. He was already blaming himself for his friend's fate and was far too shaken by what he had seen to attempt any heroics. Fear was his only functioning emotion now and self-preservation his only thought, not for entirely selfish reasons – he had to stay alive to help Rachel.

In sheer panic, Martin ran through the night, heading as quickly as possible back to the gate in the perimeter wall through which he had entered. He tried to duck behind trees and remain under cover as much as possible.

Pike's final scream pierced the air; Martin's ears pricked up and his hair stood on end. Finally, the earth closed over his friend and muffled his cry once and for all. There were only the sounds of shouting and running from the house now, drifting towards the place where Peter Pike had been dragged into the ground.

It was not far to the perimeter wall, if he kept quiet he would make it, and from there it was only a short distance to the car. He could get away and come back for Rachel again with a different plan. He ran quietly through the night, stealthily, fast, putting plenty of metres between himself and the house. *Disciples must be everywhere by now*, he thought. It didn't concern him because even if he was spotted and chased, he would still be able to get to the car before being caught. *I'm on the home straight.*

**

Through the ground, it felt the vibration from Martin's frantic run. It knew Martin; his footfall, his breath and the beat of his heart were all very familiar; it even knew the electrical aura of his body. Its tiny brain started to think:

Why is he running at this time of night? What has happened to him? Why is he causing such a commotion?

The Bar-Shiyq may well have ignored Martin, but the master had sent it a message – no one was to get away. The feast it had already acquired tonight had really whetted its appetite. *Make it one more, it could be years before a chance like this comes along again; treat yourself tonight. Feel him running; feel his heart racing, where does he think he's going? Does he not know that I am everywhere?*

** **

In the darkness, and in his haste, Martin did not notice the line of disrupted soil speeding towards him, heading unavoidably on a trajectory that would intercept his run. He fell and cursed the tree root he believed had tripped him. He got up quickly to continue; his foot would not move. It felt as if it was being squeezed tightly and he thought he must have sprained his ankle – and then there was the sensation of something crawling up his leg.

Still gasping for breath from his run, he strained to pull his leg free, just like Peter Pike had earlier. As he did so, he spotted the long narrow line of upturned soil and lawn which ended at his foot. The leathery tentacle that emerged from it had wrapped itself around his ankle and was now sliding up his leg, slowly, silently all the way to the knee.

Tired and breathless, Martin still found the strength to try to free his trapped limb by desperately twisting and turning his body. As he struggled, he looked over his shoulder for the first time since trying to escape and saw four men in long dark clothing exchanging words over the pile of soil where Peter Pike had been. They seemed unaware of his presence. He still had the hunting knife from Pike's shoulder bag and started slashing at the tentacle – it was all he could do, it hadn't worked before, he didn't expect it to work now. With the circulation strangled, his leg was starting to feel numb – and then the jerks started, just as they had done with Peter Pike. He felt his foot being firmly pulled into the ground and crushed. He stabbed and slashed desperately; the leathery hide of the tentacle remained mostly impenetrable to the knife. The hopelessness of it made his heart sink. He had to do something else; the thing simply was not affected by the knife no matter how he used it. Further, intensely painful jerks pulled his leg underground up to the shin. The portion of his limb beneath the soil felt mangled. There was only one thing he could think of to save himself: he whipped off his leather belt and cut off a small section with the knife to hold between his teeth. The rest of it he strapped tightly around his thigh as a tourniquet.

He brought the knife down steadily, penetrating the tissue of his own leg above the knee, almost biting through the leather between his teeth. The pain was excruciating; his desperation made anything possible. The knife sliced back and forth, and the lower part of his thigh became a bloody mess. More than once he almost passed out. He dreaded the moment when he would reach bone and have to use the hunting knife's serrated edge.

The tentacle tightened and jerked downwards again. He grunted as a new wave of pain shot through him; his leg was now beneath the ground up to his knee.

The sound of laughter interrupted his plight. At first, he thought he was hallucinating; on turning around he saw a familiar figure standing over him – how long this man had been there he did not know.

"Oh, Martin!" said the figure between obscene giggles, gently shaking his head. "Cutting off your own leg –

wonderful, Martin – *a man cutting off his own leg?* Now I *have* seen it all."

"Edward, you fucking bastard," Martin drawled in response to the sadistic figure behind him. He was breathing rapidly, his body suddenly convulsed with pain from the wound in his leg; he let out a scream of frustration and sent the knife spinning through the air towards his tormentor. In a flash, the man in black robes extended his arm and held out the palm of his hand. In defiance of all the laws of physics, the spinning blade rebounded in mid-air as if it were deflected by an invisible wall and completed its flight by landing harmlessly on the grass, not far from its thrower.

"Damn you!" screamed Martin as blood loss from the wound in his leg caused his consciousness to falter. There was another jerk and another agonised scream, and his leg was pulled further into the ground. The dark-caped figure moved closer; Martin was too weak to do anything except lie there and curse repeatedly with fading breaths. The man crouched beside Martin's injured limb and sniggered as he shook his head. He gently stroked the tapering tip of the tentacle as if he were petting a dog or a cat. The ground shook with a distant rumble that emanated from deep within the soil causing Martin to start suddenly.

The tentacle unravelled itself and slid away back into the lawn. The dark figure, still crouching, stared at Martin intently. Martin looked back, panting, no longer having the strength to even swear aloud. Edward reached over and held Martin's head between both his hands and stared deep into his eyes. Martin could feel the man's fingers pressing firmly against his scalp followed by the sensation of ice-cold metal spikes stabbing into his brain. He realised what was happening and allowed himself to pass out, blocking the other man from seeing into his mind.

Edward smiled, kissed Martin's forehead and walked away.

Martin regained consciousness sporadically. He became aware of many hands reaching for him, lifting him off the ground and carrying him away. He tried to thrash around but only had the strength to rock slowly in the grip of his captors, one of whom admonished him gently for his efforts. "Stop moving, it'll do you no good. You'll be dead without medical attention – now that would be a waste, wouldn't it?" There was laughter from the other carriers.

**

Rachel lay in bed. Beneath her nightdress she wore a sports top and tracksuit bottoms. She had not been able to sleep; this was the night Martin told her he would come. She lay in the dark beneath her duvet, earnestly clutching its top edge up against her chin, anxiously waiting for him. *Just be ready*, she remembered him saying; she hoped he would come. She tried to remember what she had packed into her rucksack so that nothing would be forgotten, the little bag sitting in the wardrobe, waiting for her to grab it and run away.

A few moments earlier, she had heard noises outside, loud bangs like firecrackers and even a distant scream, it had frightened her terribly. She was unable to bring herself to the window to see what was going on. *That horrible scream! Who was that?* she had asked herself. *Was it Martin? It didn't sound like him. What were those bangs?*

These questions went through her mind over and over again as she lay there waiting. The clock by the bedside showed 3:13 a.m. *What has happened to Martin? He said he would come.*

She kept her eyes on the timepiece until tearfully she realised nobody would be coming tonight. Finally, tiredness overcame her and she slipped into an uneasy sleep.

Chapter 14

Sleeping amongst his friends in the motorhome, Johnny dreamed. He was descending from the sky towards the old woman in the valley, she looked up at him. Unlike the last time, he did not awaken. Instead, he gazed back into her round, rosy face and milky grey eyes. She spoke to him.

"We only have a day," she said, "a day to maintain Earth's alignment. Hurry, Johnny! Please help."

Johnny woke up suddenly; it was not because of the dream. Somebody was whispering in his ear and a small hand was covering his mouth.

"Hey, Johnny, wake up!" said the voice.

With his tired, puffy eyes he could just about make out a small face in the darkness – it was Baccharus. The familiar had returned from his trip to the Council. Baccharus moved his hand from Johnny's mouth and placed a stubby little finger to his own lips, urging his keeper to remain silent.

"Listen," he whispered, "and keep *very* quiet."

Johnny lay still and listened carefully, just as his familiar had instructed. At first, the only sound he could discern was Boyd snoring away on the lower bunk; then he heard it too. Outside the motorhome there were footsteps scurrying around hurriedly. The steps were too fast and their rhythm too irregular to be human; occasionally, something would gently brush against the outside of the motorhome. He looked towards the window nearest him; the previous cloud cover seemed to have cleared judging by the pale blue moonlight that made the drawn curtains glow, allowing him to see the fleeting silhouettes of nearby figures. He closed his eyes and reached out with his mind to learn who, or what, was out there. The world of the five senses was replaced by abstract imagery and perception. He sensed four living beings around the motorhome; their aura was extraterrestrial and the psychic signature they projected had the distinct flavour of the Disciples of Disorder.

How did they find the motorhome? he asked himself as he lay there, perturbed that their movements had once again been traced. Boyd's amulet would have ensured that they were psychically undetectable; therefore, they must have been seen and followed deduced Johnny. He remembered the feeling of being watched when they stopped at Page's Park earlier; could it be that they had been tailed from there? Whatever the reason, Baccharus had raised the alarm now, so maybe this would be their chance to turn the tables and spring the surprise. Johnny shifted his mind back from psychic to physical perception and opened his eyes again.

"There are four of them and four of us – let's wake everyone up," he whispered to Baccharus.

The pair moved silently and steadily so as not to make a noise or rock the motorhome. Johnny crept over to Boyd who was still snoring and gave the big man a few gentle shakes. Boyd stirred then awoke abruptly, panicking, before settling down quickly on seeing Johnny who gestured for him to remain quiet and get ready. Baccharus had woken Sascha without any drama and both were already preparing for enemy contact. Neither of them moved far from their bunk – to do so might give them away.

Johnny quietly briefed everybody on what he had perceived from his earlier psychic sweep: there were four Disciples of Disorder outside who were unlikely to be human. 'Summoned entity' was the term Boyd had used earlier to describe Mr Kreb, and it could be applied here too, although the aura from this lot outside was nowhere near as potent as that of the demon-man. When Johnny had finished explaining, Sascha quietly retrieved the chainsaw he had found in the airfield hangar. Boyd glanced up at him and quietly commented on how scary the tall, quiet man looked with the power tool, just as Johnny had thought earlier in the hangar. For himself, Boyd took the compact automatic pistol from the special holster and then retrieved the big, high-calibre revolver from his bag. He offered either of his guns to the others; lacking the confidence to use them, they all politely turned him down. With a shrug, he kept a pistol in each hand, loaded and ready. Johnny and Baccharus planned to confront whatever was outside with psychic energy; as a precaution, Johnny also held on to the hatchet Sascha had brought along.

Prepared for combat, the four of them stood quietly and listened while Sascha used a special motion detector of his own design to try to fix a location on the enemy; he stared at the device's miniature radar display and fiddled with one of its dials. There was a mechanical creaking sound from outside followed by a quiet tapping.

"They're fucking with my bike," whispered Boyd angrily, recognising the sounds. Sascha confirmed this with the motion detector. There was a quiet metallic noise from beneath the motorhome and it rocked gently, almost imperceptibly.

"They're messing with our chassis now," said Sascha.

"Let's get the fuck out there before they do some serious sabotage," said Baccharus.

The companions positioned themselves at three different exit points; the motion detector soon indicated that all four Disciples were now in a suitable location for engagement.

"Don't let any of them get away," whispered Baccharus.

Sascha gave a quiet countdown and they attacked. With a blood-curdling battle cry Boyd dived out of the front passenger door, the pistol in each of his hands immediately spitting bullets. On hitting the ground he rolled onto his belly. Much to his personal satisfaction, he was targeting a Demon Disciple while it was in the very act of sabotaging his motorbike, and his aim remained true despite the foul appearance of the creature. The demon was wrapped in a long, black, hooded cloak that barely covered its vile body. It was humanoid in size and shape. Mostly hairless, pale blue skin covered its sinuous build. The face beneath the hood was particularly offensive to behold: the smooth skin was pulled tightly over an elongated, angular skull that housed a wide mouth lined with rows of razor-sharp teeth. Deeply set, beady, yellow eyes looked on hatefully and there was no nose, just the hint of a snout with two cavernous nostrils. Beneath its cloak it was naked, and between its legs there sprouted long, grey pubic hair from amongst which dangled a thick blue member. It moved faster than any human could possibly have done and lashed out with long callused nails that tapered into razor-sharp points on the end of each finger. The demon screamed in anger and pain as Boyd's slugs tore into it; the noise it made was unlike that of any earthly creature, an unnatural combination of cackle and wail, the sound of nature perverted.

Chunks of leathery pale skin flew off its disgusting torso as each bullet hit home. The creature tumbled away from the motorbike, still alive. Boyd reloaded quickly and advanced, his two guns blazing before him. Despite its gunshot wounds, the demon had enough strength left to lunge at its attacker; its movements were inhumanly quick. It flicked out its long arm in an arc that sent one of the pistols spinning out of Boyd's hand while sharp nails removed the very tips of two of his fingers. Ignoring the injury, Boyd continued to shoot with the remaining pistol until it ran out of bullets.

Sascha had exited from the driver's side door to set upon another of the foul beings; it too was wrapped in a black cloak like its brethren. To human eyes they were all identical in appearance, although there were probably ways amongst their own kind for differentiating between themselves. Sascha ran towards his target with chainsaw in hand, and despite desperate yanks at the cord its motor would not start; he changed his strategy and extended one of his lanky legs, catching the pale being squarely in its chest, knocking it backwards to the ground. The creature was stunned by the surprise attack. It tried to scramble up again onto its wiry legs and hideous paddle-like feet; Sascha kept it pinned to the ground with his own foot while frantically pulling the chainsaw cord to deliver the final killing blow. In trying to do this he had lost the initiative. The creature on the ground used its powerful arms and hands to twist Sascha's ankle and simultaneously bring its large foot up to strike his testicles. Sascha recoiled and doubled over from this most painful of attacks, but it also caused him to yank harder on the chainsaw cord for that instant and its motor spluttered into life. He brought the buzzing tool down hard onto the demonic entity that lay beneath him, cutting the muscular torso into two messy halves, flicking vile, malodorous fluid and fleshy chunks into the night air. The Disciple of Disorder writhed in agony as it was sliced; its strange, bald head flicked from side to side, its little yellow eyes rolled, and it too produced the unearthly cackle.

Johnny and Baccharus had exited together from the middle cabin door and were confronted by only one of the demons. They baulked at its twisted face, wild yellow eyes and terrible mouth. Caught by surprise the creature took flight, its powerful limbs pumped away fiercely allowing it to run faster than any man could follow. Baccharus, being capable of actual flight, was most suited to give chase, which he promptly did. Almost immediately, Johnny noticed another Demon Disciple, the one intent on sabotage they had heard beneath the motorhome. It was lying on the ground with its upper body beneath the vehicle, its hairy groin and thin legs exposed. Before this most unfortunate of Disciples could realise that anything was the matter, Johnny had started raining down blows from the hatchet upon the lower half of the trapped demon. He felt the tool penetrate deeply, rupturing internal organs, piercing bowel and shattering bone as it did so. One of his swings almost lopped off the being's mammoth member in its entirety. The demon writhed and kicked from beneath the vehicle; it was a lost struggle, the injuries it had received were mortal. Noxious fumes that stung the eyes poured forth from the pierced creature, a dark red, almost black, tar exuded from its wounds. Johnny could see angular shards of bone breaking through the surface layers of skin from the demon's pulverised legs. He only stopped the onslaught after its agonised screams ebbed away to nothing, thus confirming the life force had left its physical form – he hoped.

The last of the demons, having taken flight into the woods, was now out of sight to all except Baccharus, who remained in close pursuit. The familiar flew fast and low, only a few feet above the ground, dodging in and out of the trees. Ahead of him, the creature grunted and growled as it ran, its powerful legs pounding the ground, driving it on. Baccharus tracked his quarry relentlessly, firing a bolt of psychic energy at it whenever he was presented with a shot. His target managed to deftly dodge some of these projectiles while others struck home, burning skin and muscle, producing great yelps of pain.

Johnny followed the trail of crushed undergrowth and broken branches. He caught the whiff of burning flesh, confirming the hard time Baccharus was giving the demon. As he got closer the smell became stronger, and he could hear sizzling blasts of psychic energy along with cries from the creature at their receiving end. Johnny eventually caught up with his familiar in a small clearing; lying on the ground beneath the hovering cherub was a body engulfed in flames. The demon, barely alive, shrieked and rolled about on the forest floor as it burned. Fighting back the heat from the flames, Johnny approached the Disciple and in an act of mercy, swung the hatchet down with all his might, caving in its skull so that it lay still.

Wearily, familiar and keeper retraced their steps through the woods and returned to their companions. Sascha was dragging the bodies of the other slain demons into a pile while Boyd sat in the open side doorway of the motorhome, he was wrapping a blood-soaked bandage tightly around two fingers. Johnny hoped he was not badly injured; in non-psychic warfare Boyd was their best weapon, the only one with military training and experience in using firearms.

"You all right, tough guy?" he asked as he approached

his friend.

"I'm fine, except my hand really fucking hurts. That blue-skin just wouldn't go down in a hurry. I had to climb on top of it and empty a cartridge point-blank into its ugly face in the end."

"Looks like you got a whipping in the process, and I mean that literally," Johnny said, referring to the slashed clothing and welts on his body and face.

"Yeah, he just wouldn't stop lashing out with those long nails. I lived to tell the tale though, and my trigger finger's working."

By now, Sascha had finished dragging the dead demons into a pile.

"What did you do that for?" asked Johnny.

"Boyd asked me to; apparently these things can be reanimated," Sascha replied.

"Best to burn them with a sacred flame," said Boyd. "If their bodies are recovered, there is a chance they can be brought back to life with the correct alchemy. Where's the one you chased into the woods?" he asked the familiar.

"Oh, he's burning already," said Baccharus.

Johnny noticed that in the pile of bodies one of the chests seemed to be moving up and down slowly as if breathing; it was the demon Sascha had cut in half. He pointed this out to his companions.

"Shit!" said Baccharus. "The sooner we burn these things the better."

With a beam of highly energised Presarium focused by his willpower, Johnny set the pile of bodies ablaze. Boyd read the relevant lines from his abridged holy book causing the flames to turn a purple colour and burn with an increased intensity. The bodies were soon reduced to charred, glowing cinders.

Baccharus noticed that Sascha was still limping. "So do

you think you'll need to be cancelling any future plans for fatherhood?" asked the familiar cheekily.

"Not just yet, Bach. I checked earlier and they're both present, and as soon as I have tested their function I'll let you know," Sascha replied with a broad grin.

Battle-weary, they all entered the motorhome. Boyd and Sascha wondered what good fortune had awoken Johnny; he in turn passed the query over to Baccharus who had raised the alarm. The familiar was only too pleased to explain the circumstances. After delivering Johnny's report to the Council of Seven, Baccharus, on his return to Earth, encountered an unpredictable gravity field from a recent supernova. It had deflected his dimensional entry point, forcing him to correct his course through some improvised calculations, and he materialised a few hundred metres away from the motorhome. Rather miffed with this inconvenience, he made his way through the night, back to the vehicle, and in doing so stumbled upon the demons. Not quite believing what he had discovered, he quietly watched as they went about their mischief before using his will to shake some nearby trees and bushes to distract them. Expending huge amounts of energy, he performed a miniature jump through dimensions back into the motorhome. That was how he woke Johnny up in time. The end of Baccharus's account was met with vocal approval from his companions – much to his pleasure.

Johnny was quiet as Sascha and Boyd considered how it was possible that their party could have been located by the Disciples in the first place, and after some discussion, both settled on the conclusion that they had been followed, most likely from Page's Park. It was a reasonable assumption, thought Johnny, one he had arrived at earlier; there was still the possibility, however, of another reason, and he wasn't yet ready to share it.

Outside, dark had retreated and the early dawn brought with it an increased sense of security – and also one of urgency. Johnny knew that if all the received calculations and guidance were correct then they only had until nightfall to find and confront the Disciples of Disorder.

He stepped out of the motorhome with Boyd and noted how effectively the sacred flame had vaporised the dead demons, leaving behind only a patch of charred ground. Looking up to the sky, he decided that there was just about enough light for them to begin inspecting any sabotage; it was the early start he and his friends had desired – even though it had happened in a somewhat undesirable way. He crouched beside the motorhome with Boyd while Baccharus and Sascha set about collecting the scattered weapons from the recent battle.

"Are you feeling up to this?" asked Johnny, screwdriver in hand, looking at Boyd's bandages.

"It's nothing," insisted Boyd, moving his fingers to demonstrate that he was still able to use them.

The motorhome looked untouched at first glance; underneath it, Johnny found a lump of malleable white material which he pushed and prodded with the screwdriver.

"You don't want to do that," said Boyd sternly, "that's explosive."

Johnny froze and did not even dare to take a breath lest it activate the destructive reaction somehow. Boyd reached over and carefully peeled away the material. "There's not much there," he said, "but they stuck it just beneath the fuel tank – bastards. It doesn't look like they got this thing wired up, usually there's an electronic trigger somewhere."

It was the first time Johnny had been subject to such a calculated attempt on his life. It felt unreal, and he could not believe it was happening to him. Generally, he tried not to annoy people too much. He often wondered at folk who could argue and fight and walk away again without a second thought while he, on the other hand, would seethe over any incident for days. He looked at Boyd, someone whose life had been threatened on many occasions in the past. He seemed unaffected. *That's how I've got to be*, thought Johnny. *Just don't let it get to me.* They both crawled out from under the motorhome. Boyd walked over to inspect his motorbike. Sascha and Baccharus were inside clearing the dishes and bedding in preparation for the next leg of the journey. Johnny went to tell them about the discovery of the explosive material. They had each come of their own free will, fully informed of the risks; he wanted to keep it that way. The explosive was of no great concern to Baccharus. As a familiar, he would follow his keeper to hell and back; for Johnny it was hard not see the cherub as an independent individual. Sascha was also unalarmed. Johnny was often amazed by his friend's disregard for such matters; despite his undeniable intelligence, the important affairs of love, life and death somehow never moved Sascha as much as one would expect.

Boyd, who had managed to dispose of the plastic explosive, entered the motorhome a few minutes later looking upset; he explained that his bike's cables and hoses had been subtly tampered with, making it a death trap for anyone who rode it. To make it safe again would take time. Johnny assumed Boyd would now travel with them in the motorhome; instead, Boyd insisted on staying and fixing his machine first.

"How long will it take?" asked Johnny.

"A couple of hours," Boyd replied. "Look, the mission can't wait. You guys go ahead, follow up the leads, find Mrs McGuiness. If there is a problem, I have my mobile phone. I can catch up with you as soon as I'm finished. We may need the motorbike later so it's important to have it up and running. The more mobility the better, I say."

Although Johnny did not want to leave anybody behind, he saw the logic of Boyd's argument. He knew the man would be very unlikely to continue without his beloved bike, whatever the circumstances.

"Do you think it's safe to be alone out here?" Johnny asked.

"Look, it's daylight now. So far, the Disciples have only attacked us at night. I don't think they will regroup in time after the beating we just gave them; even if they do, I still have my pistols and the book, so don't worry."

Johnny and his friends reluctantly complied with their companion's wishes. Baccharus, who was keen to lend a hand with the repair work, volunteered to stay behind. Boyd took up the offer and Johnny felt far more comfortable with the arrangement. Boyd would not be alone, and should it become necessary, he would now have psychic help with him.

Chapter 15

"Keep the amulet, it's more difficult for me and Bac-charus to be detected than you two," Boyd said as Johnny dangled the sacred artefact from the passenger side window.

With a quick farewell, Johnny was back on the road again alongside Sascha, who was driving. The search for Mrs McGuiness and her general store was on, and they retraced their steps to Hilvern, a distance of about ten miles which did not take long to cover. On entering the village, Johnny could not ignore the same uncomfortable atmosphere he and his friends had all felt the previous night. Even though the morning was bright and the location picturesque, there was a hopelessness about the place and a sense of hidden malice. Buildings, although in good repair, looked empty and unlived in. There were not many people on the streets, and those few who had ventured outdoors seemed inexplicably suspicious. There was a distinct abnormality about Hilvern which Johnny could only put down to its historical exposure to the cha-otic energy of Disorder.

Sascha stopped the motorhome at the first parade of shops they encountered: a launderette, mini-supermarket and shoe shop. All were small privately owned businesses; there were no big chain stores here. It seemed a suitable place for Johnny to start his enquiries. The village was compact and Johnny hoped the Mrs McGuiness store would be easy to locate. Firstly, he entered the mini-super-market, which seemed to be staffed by the village's only teenagers, none of whom were of much help. Next, he entered the shoe shop; behind the till was a frail, elderly man who looked like he had worked in the little shop since time began. He greeted Johnny with a faltering, "Can I help you, sir?" Years of working in a shoe shop meant the old man's gaze had already shifted to Johnny's feet.

"Oh! I can see why you're here," he said with a disap-proving look at Johnny's tattered old canvas trainers.

"I think there's a good few miles left in them yet," Johnny said defensively; the old man looked unconvinced. Before they digressed further from the matter at hand, Johnny asked him about the location of Mrs McGuiness's store.

"Yes, I know where her shop is," he assured him.

Johnny waited as the wrinkled face appeared vacant for a few moments. He could see the old man labori-ously searching ancient memory banks, and then, with a defeated shake of his head, the man turned to the open doorway behind the till.

"Daisy! I say, Daisy, my dear, would you come and help me with this young fellow," he called out in his faltering speech.

"Yes, dear, what size is he?" a croaky old woman's voice answered from deep within the stock room.

"What size are you?" asked the old man to Johnny's dismay.

"No, I'm not after shoes," he reminded him, his patience wearing thin. "I'm after Mrs McGuiness who owns the general store."

"Oh, yes! Of course!"

The old man turned towards the stock room again. "Don't worry about his shoe size, Daisy; just come out here to help will you?"

"Yes, George; there in a sec," Daisy croaked back.

Johnny waited; it certainly took more than a second for Daisy to show herself. After an eternity, a stooped, little old lady shuffled out of the mysterious stock room behind the till; she had fine white hair, pale blue eyes and was wrapped in a floral dress under a baggy yellow cardigan.

"Yes, dear?" she asked her husband behind the till. Daisy had dedicated most of her life to facilitating purchases, and this was obvious in her appearance and manner; her face was fixed in a broad grin that had been perfected over the years to put customers at ease.

"Could you help this young fellow at all, Daisy?"

"Of course," she assured. "What are you after? Formal, evening, or maybe sports shoes? A fashionable young man like you might be interested in…"

They're running on autopilot, thought Johnny before stopping her mid-flow. "Look, Mrs umm – Daisy, I'm looking for a shop, a store owned by someone called Mrs McGuiness."

"Oh, I see! You're not after shoes then?"

"No," Johnny said firmly. "No," he repeated again, slowly, to emphasise the point once and for all. He started again in a gentle voice, "I just need to find Mrs McGuiness. Look, if you don't know her then I'll just leave."

"Hmm, Mrs McGuiness," said the old lady with a frown, "when you leave the shop, turn right, then take the next left, then left again out of Hilvern. Follow the road as it leaves the village for about seven miles then you'll find Mavis McGuiness and her store on the left. It's a farm shop;

the farm itself is called Fasely Farm."

Johnny was stunned that he had actually managed to get a useful answer from the old woman. He repeated the directions back to her.

"Yes, yes, that's right," confirmed Daisy.

"Thank you," said Johnny with relief and gratitude in equal measure.

"Are you sure we can't interest you in another pair of shoes?" asked the old man.

"No, thank you," Johnny told him, "but if I ever need another pair of shoes, *this* is the shop where I will buy them."

The couple smiled appreciatively and he left amongst a chorus of 'thank you's and 'come again soon's.

Johnny plonked himself wearily into the front passenger seat beside Sascha, who had been waiting patiently behind the wheel.

"What the hell kept you?" Sascha asked. "I thought you had been ambushed by demons again."

"No, worse," Johnny muttered in reply.

"You should have traded in those things while you were there; they're a bit past it!" Sascha said, pointing disdainfully at Johnny's trainers.

"Look, there's nothing wrong with my damn shoes, okay!" Johnny retorted sharply, causing Sascha to flinch. "Drive on, partner; right then left, then I'll tell you where from there."

"Okay, let's go!"

The motorhome left Hilvern Village behind. Johnny hoped not to return; it was somewhere his instincts urged him to move on from. The day was bright and windy with gusts strong enough to noticeably rock the motorhome as it sped along the winding road; patchwork fields surrounded the route while mountains were visible in the distance. Daisy's directions, much to Johnny's relief, had been correct. Sascha slowed down to turn through a wooden gate which had a sign to either side of it; one swung from a wooden post and read FASELY FARM. The other was larger and nailed to the fence: FARM SHOP, FRESH EGGS, POTATOES AND OTHER PRODUCE it announced in worn red paint. The motorhome bounced along a rough track that took them to a makeshift car park and a small cluster of farm buildings. They stopped in front of the shop, which was actually an extension of a rustic, whitewashed cottage. It had a wooden entrance door with a large glass window; a simple, neatly painted sign displayed the words 'Farm Shop'. Just as before, Sascha waited inside the motorhome while Johnny went in to investigate. He entered the shop cautiously; opposite the entrance was a counter with a till that nobody was staffing. A woman with dark grey hair in an apron stood at a shelf arranging some vegetables for display; she was facing away from Johnny, he assumed it was Mrs McGuiness.

As she went about her work, Johnny took a moment to get a feel of the little shop. The walls were lined with old-fashioned wooden shelves, a far cry from the steel and plastic fittings found in modern supermarkets. Assorted household goods and fresh food produce were out on display along with outdoor clothing, camping equipment, garden tools and cheap electronics. As a child he had come across places like this on family holidays, nestled along country roads. Mrs McGuiness's shop was not only a convenience store for the rural community, it also served as a meeting point for them. People from the neighbouring farms could bump into each other here, leave messages or even goods to be collected later. Urban dwellers, willing to make the effort, would also visit and pick up fresh locally produced food at the shop; Johnny took a liking to the place. Mrs McGuiness still had not noticed him. According to the news article Sascha had found, she was a close friend of Louise in addition to being her employer; she must therefore have known Rachel personally. The hope was that she would know the identity of the 'family friend' who should, by now, have officially adopted the girl; the very man who was also Martin's brother-in-law and somehow associated with the Disciples. If Mrs McGuiness did indeed know anything, then she would have to be persuaded to share whatever information she possessed.

Johnny was the only person in the shop. He looked over his shoulder, nobody else was approaching; he cleared his throat and the grey head turned slowly.

"Mrs McGuiness?" he ventured.

An old but vigorous face looked back at him and smiled. "Oh, hello, I haven't seen you before. Can I help?" she asked. Mrs McGuiness looked and sounded like somebody who, despite her age, had retained some youthful energy; it might have been her bright eyes that gave this impression. The couple in the shoe shop must have been of a similar age; in contrast to Mrs McGuiness, their faces had been dull and vacant.

"Lovely place you have here," Johnny said as charmingly and conversationally as he could.

"Yes, it's okay," she replied pleasantly.

"I'm not from the country really, been a townie my whole life. I do love it out here, and finding a place like yours, well, it's a real gem."

"Being here almost every day one just doesn't see it in that way. I expect it's nice enough."

Johnny continued to look at her carefully; he could not help feeling that it was him who was being scrutinised.

"So where are you from?" she asked.

"Oh, I'm from London, north-westish. Do you know London at all?"

"I'm afraid not," she replied. "Are you on holiday here?"

"Not really."

There was an awkward silence.

"Mrs McGuiness, I'm here because I am actually looking for somebody."

Mavis McGuiness's face remained impassive and she continued to look him in the eye.

"Who are you looking for?" she asked, as if she knew the answer already.

"I understand Louise Croft was a friend of yours. She had a daughter, Rachel. I'm looking for her, it's important."

At the mention of Louise, Johnny detected an intense sadness in Mrs McGuiness's aura; it would have been impossible to know this without his gift of psychic perception because she did not overtly display any emotion – not even a blink – when he spoke the name. She seemed very defensive.

"Who are you?" she asked, stony-faced.

Johnny had his story prepared. "Do you know Martin?" Johnny asked nervously. His link to Louise and Rachel rested on his connection with Martin; he had no idea what she thought of Martin or if she even knew him. On observation, she appeared unmoved by the mention of this name; psychically, Johnny could sense positive feelings.

"How do you know Martin?" she asked sternly.

"He's a friend," replied Johnny, starting to feel edgy. The initially welcoming atmosphere was becoming distinctly colder.

"Why do you want the girl?" she asked. The tables

had been turned, and it was the old woman who was interrogating the young stranger.

"Martin asked me to find her, to make sure she's all right."

"Why should she not be all right?"

"Martin was concerned about the suitability of her foster parents. He felt Rachel wasn't entirely safe living with his sister and her husband. He disappeared before he could give me any more information. Will you help me find her?" Johnny asked.

"No, I can't help you, goodbye," Mavis McGuiness said curtly, turning around back to her shelves.

Johnny was annoyed; he wanted the information he had come for. There was too much at stake, the Disciples of Disorder had to be prevented from upsetting the equilibrium. There existed a psychic phenomenon called the mind probe in which the psychic practitioner hijacked the brain of the subject and leafed through its memories as if he were reading a book. The problem was that by doing this the subject was often left brain-damaged and suffered symptoms of epilepsy, schizophrenia and a whole host of other neuropsychiatric pathologies for the rest of their life. There were even instances that had resulted in death. Johnny was familiar with the theory and knew how it could be done. He had never attempted one before … Could this be his first time? He promptly admonished himself for even considering inflicting such a cruelty upon the dear old lady, especially as he had not laid all his cards upon the table yet.

"Mrs McGuiness, Martin is a good man, he is concerned about Rachel's well-being and so am I—"

"Where is Martin?" she interrupted.

"I don't know for certain. My friends and I are pretty sure he is in trouble. We have good reason to believe that

Rachel's foster parents are dangerous people, too influential around here for Martin to even go to the police – that's why *I* am helping. I won't let Martin down. There is so much at stake, beyond even Rachel's well-being, so please tell me where I can find her. Believe me, if anyone is going to sort this mess out it's me with my friends." Johnny spoke with a sincerity that was not lost on Mavis McGuiness. He noticed the icy atmosphere thaw and her dour expression soften. The kindly face that had greeted him when he first entered the shop was regarding him once again – it was up to the old lady now.

Mavis McGuiness walked over to the front door of her shop and replaced the 'Open' notice that hung there with one that read: CLOSED, BACK IN 15 MIN. Looking outside she saw the motorhome.

"Is there anybody in there?" she asked.

"Yes, my friend. He's in this with me," Johnny replied, still unsure if he had managed to get through to her.

"Call him in if you like, he may be interested in what I have to tell you," she said, then turned to Johnny. "The last thing I wanted was more disruption in my dear Rachel's life, especially from a stranger, but there's something different about you."

Johnny smiled at her, she smiled back, and he went to fetch Sascha.

Chapter 16

Martin longingly watched the way her fine brown hair caressed her shoulders as she walked through the crowd and drifted further away from him. The subtle smell of her sweet perfume was like a trail that guided him through the throng. He tried to push and jostle his way through the gathered mass of humanity while she, on the other hand, moved through them effortlessly. More than once he thought he had lost her amongst the sea of bobbing heads, only to catch sight of her again and find that she was a little further away. Intent on catching up with the alluring figure, he fought his way through the sea of people; just when he thought he had made some progress he was forced back again by the dense crowd, all of whom seemed oblivious to his struggles no matter how much he tried to shove them out of the way. In frustration, he called out to her and stretched his arm above the multitude so she might see him.

"Louise!" he shouted over the many heads. She turned and fixed him with a look from dark, sensual eyes; he was elated. *She heard me!* he thought. She even smiled and beckoned him to follow before turning around to glide through the crowd.

"Louise!" Martin shouted again; this time, she did not

look back.

Every foot of space in the narrow streets seemed to be full of people and Martin forced his way through them. *Where am I?* he asked himself and took his eyes off Louise to identify the location. It was Hilvern, the village where she lived; he had been here many times before and never seen it so full of people. *Who are they? What are they doing here?* He did not know. He pressed on; she was further away now so he doubled his efforts and pushed frantically through the mob, desperate to reach her. A tall man's bald head obscured his view for an instant and when it moved again, Louise was gone.

He thought he had lost her; just as despair was about to set in he saw her again, standing in the doorway to a small bungalow, her home, away from the wretched crowd. "Louise!" he shouted and waved. She smiled, turned and walked into the building. He struggled all the way to the front door, and just before he went in he stood on its step to see exactly how far the crowd of people extended. It was impossible to say: all around him was the village, and every inch of every street was full of people. Martin shook his head in disbelief at the number of these aimless wanderers. He turned away from them all and entered the empty bungalow; the front door swung gently shut behind him of its own accord.

Inside it was dark and the place was devoid of any furniture or decoration. The walls, ceilings and floorboards of the small entrance hall looked old and musty. The bare interior possessed a distinct absence of colour due to the layers of dust and cobwebs that covered every surface. Outside, it was a bright, beautiful day; indoors, very little illumination seemed able to penetrate the gloom. The light that managed to make its way into the bungalow was made visible by the motes of dust that hung thickly in the air. He had not been here for two years. *Could it have been abandoned all that time?*

There were four doors, only one of them was open, just a crack. He saw a shadow interrupt the light that came from it, and he heard footsteps. The dust and cobwebs on the floor seemed not to have been disturbed by Louise's passage. He pushed open the door and entered slowly. His heart beat quicker, knowing that they would be together again. Light beaming brilliantly through a large window in the far wall dazzled him. Despite the exposed floorboards and plain plastered wall, the intense brightness of this room was in stark contrast to the grey gloom of the rest of the house. There was no dust or grime here. He only noticed this fleetingly because his eyes were fixed on Louise. She was lying stretched out across a four-poster bed that sat in the middle of the room, its fresh silk sheets and lace awning a brilliant white that glowed as it reflected light from the window. He had been in this room many times, it had always been Louise's bedroom; it had never looked like this before. It used to be carpeted and full of furniture, and the bed had been a normal, comfortable double bed, not the exotic four-poster affair before him. She looked more beautiful than ever lying there in her long, silk slip; finally, he had caught up with her.

"Louise…" he whispered. He had missed her so much. She smiled at him, a perfect smile, the skin of her face and arms flawless, her dark eyes as hypnotic as ever. She patted the bed and beckoned Martin to lie with her. Louise was more special to him than all of the women he had ever known and cared for. He felt so different around her, so much better. All this time, he thought she had gone and that he would never again be able to experience that feeling of being whole which he only knew when he was with her.

He sat on the bed, wanting to hold her then and there. He chose to restrain himself, just to savour the moment. He drank in her features then reached out to touch the strands of soft hair that lay on the pillow. He had missed her so much.

"Louise, don't ever go away again. I love you," said Martin, and she moved closer to embrace him. Martin wanted to hold her again more than anything in the world; he leaned over, the subtle rose scent that hung about her engulfed him, and he breathed it in deeply as if he were inhaling a drug. Finally, she was in his arms. "I missed you so much, Louise," he said as he held her. He felt the soft skin of her face against his and closed his eyes to revel in the sense of touch.

Suddenly there was a strange sound, a wet popping that was entirely unexpected. It was followed by confusion; something had happened. He tried to scream at what lay beneath him; no sound came out, the revulsion and horror he felt at that moment was paralysing. Louise's face was turned limply to one side, and her slip was soaked red with blood. Some unknown force had caused her body to implode into a bloody mixture of bones and internal organs. Martin recoiled in terror. His hands, his clothes and the bed were all covered in dark red. His mind and body froze, and he struggled to breathe. His desperate efforts to move away from the remains of his lover caused her head to roll over the side of the bed where it dangled, suspended inches above the floor by a single sinuous strand of tendon from her neck. He lurched backwards and fell. Finally, he managed to scream and did not stop until he awoke from the nightmare.

Martin lay in darkness on the hard floor of his cell, shivering; the air around him felt damp and very still. He had been slipping in and out of consciousness for a while and did not know what time it was or whether it was even day or night. He grimaced as he recollected the strange, disturbing dream. He reached out with one hand to feel his right leg; it remained limp. There was no longer any blood oozing from the self-inflicted wound – someone had seen to his injury and that worried him.

Having been left on his back for some time on the hard floor, numbness had gripped parts of his body. It wasn't all bad news, lying there with the wound closed had given him a chance to rest and he felt fractionally stronger. Martin used his hands to grope around and learn something about his current location. First he felt an uneven cobbled stone surface beneath him; he stretched further, and at the very end of his reach there was a wall which felt smooth and cold. No daylight, a cobbled surface and smooth walls – he had a good idea where he was now – it was not far from where he had been caught. He tried to sit up; the right side of his body, the side with the injured leg, refused to comply with his wishes. He shifted his weight to the left elbow and pushed up from the floor; the effort made him dizzy, his arm gave way and he collapsed. Lying there, he waited to see what would become of him. His destiny was no longer in his hands.

It was after some time that he became aware of a strange pulsing vibration from the floor beneath him and was unsure whether it had been there all along. He concentrated on this strange phenomenon until his bored mind started to wander, and he found himself thinking about the alarming events that had made him a prisoner here. He remembered Peter Pike's screams and the tentacles from beneath the ground. The fear and agony on his friend's face was all too clear in his mind, and he despised himself for dragging someone along to meet such a terrible demise. *What was beneath the ground?* he wondered.

Surely, Edward Devilliers had gone too far now, he was summoning beings that had no place on Earth. To use such beasts as his tools made him a very powerful individual, more powerful than Martin had calculated; he lay there horrified at the thought. Even in this weakened state, disabled and on the brink of death, he tried to think of ways to stop Devilliers. Ideas came aplenty; however, without the physical strength to execute any of them, the helpless reality of his situation was made far too apparent. When despair drifted into his soul, he pushed it away defiantly because there was hope. The man he had spoken to, Boyd Tennant, sounded like he could help; he was still out there. Would he forget about everything and walk away after their failed meeting? *No! No way!* He seemed like an honourable man, he knew what was going on, he would help. Then there was Rachel, she was a plucky girl just like her mother. Surely, when he hadn't turned up she would have taken the initiative to do something herself? Rachel would know what to do. Martin lay there with no real evidence to support these hopes, but hanging on to the idea of Rachel and Boyd somehow defying the Disciples was all he could do.

Chapter 17

Sascha locked the motorhome and followed Johnny to the shop; both were eager to hear what Mrs McGuiness had to say and hoped she could cast some light on whatever they were heading into. Once inside, the old woman secured the front door and ushered the pair behind the till into a storeroom filled with cardboard boxes, food and sacks of farm produce. The three of them walked past these supplies, through an open door in the back and outside again into a small courtyard surrounded by farm buildings. They followed the old lady into a cottage that adjoined the shop and found themselves in a small, rustic kitchen. There was a vase of flowers on the windowsill and along the counters stood jars of tea and coffee, biscuit tins, cakes, a bread-bin and a choice of teapots. An Aga gave off a cosy warmth. It would have been the perfect place to relax over a hot drink and put worries to one side; Johnny, however, remained alert to an ambush from the Disciples, even here.

Mrs McGuiness invited her guests to take a seat at the small, square breakfast table. Johnny couldn't help smiling at the ceramic salt and pepper shakers in the shape of a comical fat farmer and his wife that stood at the centre of the multi-coloured cotton tablecloth, surrounded by doilies.

Mrs McGuiness was already heating up the kettle when she asked them if they would like tea or coffee. Johnny and Sascha both requested tea; it just seemed like the most appropriate choice for this kitchen. As the kettle boiled, she put a plate of biscuits on the table for her guests to enjoy. *A genial host*, thought Johnny, *how old-fashioned*. Mrs McGuiness brought over a tray with a steaming teapot beneath a red tea cosy surrounded by tea-drinking paraphernalia. She took the only remaining seat for herself and asked the pair how they wanted their drinks before pouring from the great pot, smiling as she did so, enjoying the task. When she had finished there was sadness again, and she gazed wistfully down at her own cup before starting to speak.

"I knew that one day somebody would come here asking about Rachel. I always thought it might have been the police or maybe those social services people. Whoever it was, I knew *somebody* would come – and here you are." She looked up from her tea to face Johnny and Sascha. "So you think she's in trouble. I'll tell you where she is. When you find her be gentle with her, she's had a hard life. Do you know much about her?"

"I'm afraid not," Johnny said, pursing his lips and shrugging his shoulders.

"Not really," mumbled Sascha.

"If you want to help then you need to know a little about her background first so please listen to me. I always intended on telling this story to anybody who could really *do* something about it, not like the police and others. I'm getting tired of carrying it everywhere and need to unload some of this burden. There's something about you two I feel I can trust."

Johnny anticipated that he and Sascha were going to obtain some useful information that would add some flesh to the bones of this case. Mavis McGuiness took a few sips of her tea; Johnny sensed a deep melancholy in her as she commenced her tale.

"Louise Croft, Rachel's mother, was from a rural highland family whose past generations had made a living by working the land, rather like my own. As a child, Louise moved with her parents to the city. They were one of the many who broke away from a tradition of country living to relocate. They never really had an alternative; the rural life was getting hard and money was scarce. They moved with young Louise to Glasgow, where they made their home, and it was in the city's factories where they found work. The couple settled in a rough area; it was the best they could do. I don't think Louise ever thought much of her new home in the inner city and grew disillusioned with it quite early on.

"Years later she met her ex-husband, Steven, while they were both still young; he was bad news, a lazy good-for-nothing. They connected somehow, and together they had the rather impetuous idea of starting a family. Rachel was born while they were still unmarried. As you can imagine, it was actually Louise's parents who shouldered much of the responsibility for bringing up the child. Rachel was very fond of her grandparents. Working in the factories and smoking meant they were both in poor health, and when Rachel was only a few years old, her grandfather, Louise's father, died. By that time, Louise's mother had to move to a nursing home. Her grandad's death had a profound impact on young Rachel, she grew up very quickly then, an old head on young shoulders. Louise married Steven soon afterwards, hoping to find some stability in her life after her father passed away; unfortunately, her new husband never had it in his nature to settle down. He got bored easily and spent very little time at home. He had practically abandoned his wife and child; the unhappy couple divorced within a few years.

"Around the time of her separation from Steven, Louise's maternal grandfather, Joseph McFadden, a very old man who had lived here in Hilvern his whole life, passed away, leaving her and Rachel his bungalow. Louise had fond memories of the short time she lived in the country, and even after moving to the city, her parents had made trips back there to meet Joseph. Oh yes! Very fond memories she had of visits to the old bungalow in Hilvern. Given the estrangement from her husband and her dislike of the city, inheriting a little home in the country was a new start for her, one she pursued without any thought of looking back. So she moved to Hilvern with Rachel ... that was about eight years ago.

"Unlike her ex-husband, Louise was a hard worker and set about finding odd jobs in the village to make ends meet. She did all sorts, like working as a barmaid one day or a nanny another. Busy though it was, she actually quite enjoyed her new life and plugged away at it, making a fair few friends in the process, including me. I got to know Louise when she started working for me in the shop. With my arthritis and my granddaughter Serena in full-time education, I needed a hand with cleaning and stocktaking, and Louise was the person I hired. She worked with me for years, I say work, but I was a bad influence on her most of the time, making her just sit and natter over tea and biscuits with me ... you can see I haven't changed." Mrs McGuiness managed a small smile as she said this.

"I helped Louise raise Rachel; I was like another grandmother to the girl. In fact, she even *called* me grandma. Her real grandmother, or 'nana', was stuck in the nursing home with dementia setting in rapidly – poor woman has passed away now. Mother and daughter were both like family to

"After a few dates they got to know, and really like, each other; their tough backgrounds had moulded them into similar characters with lots of common ground. They were a good match. Martin got to know Rachel too and in time loved her as if she was his own daughter, and she loved him back; he was a more than adequate replacement for her estranged father.

"Sometimes, Martin would tell us about Edward Devilliers, the man who was his brother-in-law and also his boss. He had a great deal of respect for him, and whenever he spoke of Edward he did so with a noticeable reverence. There was good reason for this. It was Edward who had arranged for him to work in one of his companies at his wife Elizabeth's request. When Martin spoke of Elizabeth, it was different; you could sense a genuine brotherly affection from him which one suspected did not extend to Edward. Either way, he owed them both a lot and rightfully gave them credit for saving him from the bad life his unfortunate childhood could easily have lead to.

"As somebody who was a relative *and* an employee of the Devilliers, Martin was occasionally invited to their business dinners. He talked very little about these events. Louise would tell me all that went on in them because, as his partner, she would sometimes also be invited. Grand affairs they were, the Devilliers were very well-connected people. Councillors, MPs, police chiefs, they were all there. Our little Louise in the company of the great and the good, we all thought things had surely turned around for her. Rachel too was enjoying her new life away from the city; she had got to know the three Devilliers girls and was having a great time in their company. All four had become great friends. Finally, Louise, Rachel and Martin had some stability and happiness in their lives; they were good times ... then things happened. Sometimes you can't help thinking that happiness is not meant for some people.

"A few years ago, there were two tragic events that closely followed each other. Chloe, the youngest of the Devilliers girls, died in a terrible accident. She was out on her bike and was hit by a lorry. It was a sad time. Rachel took it particularly badly; she was very fond of Chloe. It was a few months after that when Louise died in the park. They said some animal attacked her. I believe it was the devil himself. Witnesses said something about seeing a man in black with the beast; police searched high and low for him and made extensive enquiries – they found nothing.

"Needless to say, Rachel was devastated. Neither Martin nor I could leave her for a second; she was scarred by what happened and really withdrew into herself. Who could blame the poor girl? First her friend died then her mother, all in the space of a few months – she must have been wondering who would be next all that time. Martin and I would spend ages with her, talking to her, keeping her calm, reassuring her that everything would be just fine. It took a year of counselling and support to draw her out of her grief and come to terms with the terrible events. I wouldn't say she got over it because a loss like that is something nobody gets over; you just learn to carry on somehow. She's a tough kid, you know. At her age, I think it would have broken me.

"Following the death of her mother, there was always the question of adoption: who would look after Rachel? Her father, Steven, had all sorts of problems, Martin was a young single man who never had children, and I was a frail widow; it was deemed that none of us was suitable for the responsibility. Social workers were to make the final decision, and after the Devilliers expressed an interest in taking care of Rachel it was a very straightforward one. Here was a family who knew Rachel and had adopted before; they had daughters who were her closest friends, a devoted mother and a father who was a respectable businessman and pillar of the community. The Devilliers had mine and Martin's full support, and when it was confirmed that they were to be her fosters, it was a great weight off our minds. Their big house was a little out of the way, not too far though, which meant we could visit Rachel quite readily – it was the perfect solution. Martin continued to keep an eye on Rachel's well-being. In fact, we would sometimes joke that Martin, being Elizabeth's brother, was now Rachel's uncle.

"All of us who knew little Chloe and Louise were never really the same again. The passing of two young people, such a terrible loss, brought home the reality of how fragile life is. We all hurt very deeply. We tried to keep our spirits up by remembering all the good they had brought into our lives; both of them had such bright energetic personalities.

"A few months after the adoption, Martin and I worked with solicitors to take care of Louise's estate. Her bungalow was to be sold and the money put into a trust fund for Rachel. Together, we sorted through Louise's personal belongings. We had asked Rachel if she wanted to be there; she told us she couldn't face it. Her therapist had actually recommended that we shouldn't expose her so soon to such intimate reminders of her mother; we thought it was only right to ask her first.

"Owning the farm meant I had ample storage space so we left all of Louise's stuff locked in wardrobes in one of the spare rooms of the cottage until such a time as Rachel was ready to receive them. We gave away a few things to charity and anything personal or of value we put in safekeeping.

"One of the items we packed away was a box with a collection of diaries in it. We all knew that Louise kept personal journals. I had never seen them until that time; of course, we didn't read any, it just seemed so disrespectful – that decision was for Rachel to make.

"Rachel eventually settled in with the Devilliers. It was difficult at first; in the end, she managed to do it. Emotionally, she was recovering more quickly and completely than any of us had expected – even her therapist was surprised at her progress. She put it down to living within a solid family environment and I agreed; being with the Devilliers and having their support had made a big difference.

"Martin continued to work for Edward while I struggled on with the shop. We were both in regular contact with Rachel. It carried on like this for almost two years until Martin called at my farm one night. He came in looking very agitated; there was thick, dark stubble on his chin and his face looked so pale. I guessed he hadn't slept for a while, the sight of him that night was frightening. Even though it was so late, he asked for the key to the wardrobe where we stored Louise's old belongings. I hadn't thought about all that stuff for ages and asked him if everything was okay, and when he gave me his reply I couldn't believe what I was hearing. He told me he had some suspicions about Louise's death and that Rachel might be in danger. He told me he needed to see Louise's diaries. I knew Martin, and I knew how much he cared for Rachel and Louise so I didn't hesitate to fetch the key for him. I was so worried about my poor Rachel that I was almost at the point of tears and dithering. I asked if there was anything I could do to help and he simply requested that I bring him a strong coffee; the poor man looked exhausted so I didn't waste any time in making him the drink.

"When I got back up from the kitchen, I saw him from

the corridor, sitting in the spare room, one of the diaries open in his hands. I don't think he heard me returning. I caught a glimpse of him tearing some pages out of the journal before I entered with his coffee. He turned around quickly and snapped the diary shut. His eyes were red and there was the hint of tears; he put on a smile as I entered, I gave him the coffee and sat next to him. We had this tense exchange, it went something like this: 'Martin, what's wrong?' I asked. He told me not to worry and that every-thing will be fine. He would sort things out. There was obviously a problem, he was being quite elusive. 'What is it, Martin?' I asked again, and I also asked him what was in the diary. He had gulped down half his coffee already.

"'Something that confirms Rachel is in trouble. I will sort it out though,' I think he said.

"It wasn't what I wanted to hear, and I could barely keep myself from sounding hysterical. 'What trouble, Martin? What's going on?' I insisted. He stood up to leave the room. 'Rachel will be fine, Mrs McGuiness,' he said, the tears in his eyes had dried up, although they still looked so red and sad. With that, he walked out of the room with the diary, leaving his coffee behind. He looked so tired; I tried to get him to stay. He had this ... this determined look on his face.

"'Don't worry about me and don't worry about Rachel,' he told me. He was at the front door by then.

"'Martin, wait,' I said, and he turned around. I was so worried and I had so many questions that I was dithering and stuttering, it's what happens when an old woman like me gets upset, you know. 'What's in the diary?' I asked again. 'When are you coming back?' He just leaned over, kissed my hair and then gave me a hug.

"'I'll be back soon,' he said and left the cottage, taking the diary with him. I followed. He was moving quickly and was already in the car by the time I got to the door. I watched him drive away. It was the last I saw of him and that was over a month ago.

"I have been worrying ever since about Martin and Rachel and what was in the diary. When you turned up saying you were friends of Martin's I must admit it was a relief. I thought it might be a chance to find out what was going on; I was also suspicious of you because of what Martin had said about Rachel being in trouble – it was the reason why I was so uncooperative at first.

"Louise and Rachel came into my life about five years ago. My husband died a long time before that, and my sons and daughters had moved away while he was still alive leaving only my granddaughter Serena to live with me. Louise, Rachel, Serena and I were each other's family. Martin came along a couple of years later. I loved having him here. He was always keen to lend a hand with anything; I had forgotten how useful it was to have a man around! My arthritis always made work difficult. With Louise and Martin I could keep the shop running no problem; it was a bigger, busier place back then. I'm alone again now, except for when it's the university holidays and Serena visits."

Mrs McGuiness paused and sniffed before drying her tears delicately with the corner of a folded handkerchief. "Please tell me Martin and Rachel are okay, they're like my family," she said. "They *are* my family."

Johnny saw Sascha looking at him uncomfortably and knew what his friend was thinking. He was torn between reassuring the old lady and telling the truth, just like he was.

"I'm not going to lie to you, Mrs McGuiness. We don't know whether Martin is okay or not, that's partly why we are here," said Johnny.

Despite fearing the worst, Mrs McGuiness nodded appreciatively at his honesty.

Johnny needed an update on Rachel's current circumstances; it occurred to him that Mrs McGuiness should still be in contact with her. "I'm guessing it hasn't been long since you last spoke to Rachel?" he ventured.

"Oh, yes," replied the old woman. "I spoke to her a few days ago, she seemed fine to me. I speak to Rachel every week, and I also see her from time to time. She seems happy enough. Although she complains about her foster parents being 'weird', she does get on with them, and her stepsisters are all still her best friends. It appears to me that she is leading a reasonable life. That doesn't change the facts. There was something going on that was worrying Martin. He is a sensible man, and whatever concerns he had – I believe he thought they were quite genuine. I didn't mention anything to Rachel; I didn't want to alarm her. I kept asking her if she was all right, looking for any hint of distress in her answers; there was none. I can only assume that she has been doing fine."

There were no more tears from Mrs McGuiness; she and her guests sat there sipping tea quietly. "I have nothing more to tell you; I'm an old woman, confused about everything that's been happening. I still don't really know who you both are. I hope you can help."

Before they left, Sascha retrieved a map from the motorhome and spread it out over the little kitchen table so Mrs McGuiness could show him and Johnny the location of the big old house where Rachel had been living for the past two years. It was the same place they suspected was the lair of the Disciples and the source of the anomalous psychic energy. It was in a valley about twenty miles from the farm shop.

Johnny thanked Mrs McGuiness for her help and the tea.

As he walked out of the shop, he promised her he would come back with Rachel and Martin or, at the very least, some news about them.

Chapter 18

The ratcheting of a lock woke Martin with a start. With a sharp intake of breath he regained consciousness, just as his cell door was opened. He expected light would flood into his room and replace the absolute darkness he had been lying in for the past few hours; all he got was the dull, flickering glow from a distant fire somewhere in the gloomy corridor beyond. He was unsure how long he had been incarcerated, and he had lost count of the number of times that he had slipped into unconscious sleep; on this last occasion, he did not feel that he had been out for very long. He felt stronger than before; not strong enough, however, to tackle the three sinuous naked men who entered his prison cell. Martin observed the figures through heavy-lidded, half-closed eyes; they moved slowly, warily towards him and only the pad of their footfall on the stone floor was audible. He tilted his head upwards slightly and could see that each wore nothing except for a tightly-fitting, black, leather mask. One of them, taller than the rest, closed the cell door and opened a slat that was housed within it so that the little room continued to receive some of the faint orange firelight. The tall one remained standing while the other two knelt over him. One of the figures used a thumb to lift each of Martin's eyelids in turn, looking at him carefully all the time, as a doctor might examine a patient; this gave Martin the chance to see who was present more clearly. The dim light of the cell, to which he had become accustomed, could not hide the pale blue skin of the pair now crouched beside him, and the leather masks could conceal neither their misshapen heads nor their beady yellow eyes. Their abnormal appearance was complemented by the foetid odour that hung around their bodies. It was only the figure by the door that actually looked human. The masked beings prodded and poked Martin, and after a final look at the wound on his leg they dragged him across the floor and placed him sitting upright against the cold, stone wall of the cell. In this new position, he was afforded the best view yet of his prison; he could see that it was very similar to what he had envisaged whilst lying alone in the darkness, using his hands to feel his surroundings. The floor was uneven and cobbled; the walls were of smooth stone and windowless. The entire chamber appeared as if it had been carved into a single rock edifice. The only place he could liken it to was a medieval dungeon; he was closer to the truth than he could have imagined.

Their inspection completed, the two non-humans left the cell, closing the heavy timber door behind them. The open slat continued to allow in the mere suggestion of light from the corridor beyond, just enough to see the single figure that had remained behind; more importantly, it was enough light for that figure to observe Martin.

"Who are you? What do you want?" challenged Martin.

"Defiant to the last," a voice he knew only too well replied. The man slowly peeled off the tight leather mask and Martin could just about make out his high cheekbones, aquiline nose and strong angular jaw. These distinct features were emphasised further by the dim, uneven

248

lighting in the cell; it made the eyes and cheeks appear like hollow sunken pits. Martin looked into the face of Edward Devilliers. Even though it appeared more terrifying than ever here in the basement, he was past the point of experiencing fear, so resigned to his fate was he.

"What are you doing here, Martin?" enquired Devilliers calmly.

"Where's Peter?" demanded Martin, ignoring the question. Just as Edward Devilliers had mentioned, he was feeling defiant.

"Who?"

"Peter! That thing had his leg. How is he?" Martin suspected he knew the answer already.

There was gentle laughter. "Peter's dead, Martin. Tonight, the Bar-Shiyq has feasted."

"The Barsheek? Is that what you call it?"

"It is its name; it has been here for a long time, Martin, long before you and me. I believe one of my predecessors put it here. It knows who is welcome and who is not; it is all the security I need."

"So what are you going to do with me then, you bastard?"

"How rude, Martin. I mean, we are family after all." He said this with a broad grin. Edward Devilliers was considered by the few who knew him personally to be eccentric in his manner, Martin, on the other hand, always sensed a hint of aberration in the way his brother-in-law spoke and conducted himself; it was apparent now more than ever.

"I know what you've been up to behind my sister's back, you sick fuck!" Martin said.

"Sick fuck?" Edward quietly repeated to himself. "Sick fuck? I always wondered how you found out, Martin. I always thought Louise had told you before she died. I imagined her coming to you crying when she should have been flattered by the attention wasted on her."

"Louise never went crying to anybody, Edward; she was made of sterner stuff than that."

"Well, it doesn't matter now really, does it? My Disciples searched your apartment and found these."

Edward held out his hand. Clutched within it were scraps of paper, barely visible in the poor light of the cell. Martin knew exactly what they were.

"Where's the rest of it, Martin? Were there any more juicy details in there? Is that why you tore these pages out? Did they excite you? Maybe you are a true Disciple of Disorder after all."

"You sick bastard," groaned Martin as a spasm of pain shot up his leg. "If you're going to kill me, I want you to bring Elizabeth here first. I think it's time she learned exactly what you're all about, Edward. Bring her to me if you've got the balls or just sneak around like the coward that you are."

Edward Devilliers laughed arrogantly. "Martin, you don't understand a thing, do you? I love Elizabeth, and I do not sneak around. I had high hopes for you – such a fine young man. Your mind is just incapable of grasping the beauty of what I bring to Earth; not like Elizabeth who understands fully. If you wish to see her you may – only at a time of my choosing. Tell her anything you like; she has become a very worthy Disciple, Martin. Outwardly she looks like her old self, but if you were to scratch the surface you would hardly recognise what was inside her now."

"Bullshit, Edward! Just bring her to me – if you dare. The things I could tell her about you ... I should have told Elizabeth before; she would have walked away a long time ago. You're no good for anybody."

"Don't bore me, Martin, I already said I will bring her.

You tell *me* something. Why are you here? I feel that you wish to hinder my work in some way."

"You're fucked up – you sick bastard."

"Don't ignore the question, Martin. Why are you here?" Edward asked again, raising his previously calm voice. It was his turn to be angry. He loomed over Martin, and when no answer was forthcoming he kicked the large, stitched gash on his injured leg. Martin was in agony. The wound slowly started to ooze blood through its stitches, and he screamed until, strangely, his scream turned into a laugh. Edward, furious, kicked again. There was more pain. Martin's laugh turned to a scream once more, and he collapsed from his sitting position onto the stone floor.

"Why are you here? Do you want to take Rachel away from me?" snarled Edward Devilliers angrily, only to be confronted with more laughter from Martin. This time Devilliers too laughed until tears streamed from the corners of his eyes. The impromptu laughter faded until silence gradually dominated the cell; the mania that had gripped its occupants had passed.

"Is that why you are here, Martin? To take Rachel away from me?" Edward asked; his voice was sad. Martin panted, his body felt weak and limp although his mind was strangely exhilarated by the torture.

"What do you want with Rachel?" Martin managed to ask through struggling breaths.

"I think you might know," was the reply, the voice calculating. "That is why you're here, is it not? You must be aware that we have the ceremony tonight; after all, I nearly made you one of the brothers didn't I? I think that despite our secrecy you might have found out something about Rachel's part in all of this. Tell me, Martin, is that why you're here, to take Rachel away?"

Martin lay on the floor of the cell with his eyes closed.

Edward was half-right, he thought, he was here for Rachel; despite his efforts he still did not know what her role in the ceremony was to be. The Disciples had kept it a well-guarded secret. *Let him speculate. Him not knowing for certain why I am here might give Rachel and Boyd the edge they need.*

"Edward ..." Martin said.

"Yes?" asked Devilliers earnestly.

"Put some fucking clothes on, will you."

There was a silent pause; rage filled Edward Devilliers' face and disappeared as abruptly as it had arrived.

"No thanks, I'm comfortable as I am."

Then it happened for the second time. It was what Martin had been expecting; the only surprise he felt was that it had taken so long. Edward Devilliers' fingers wrapped around his head; they squeezed and stabbed and an icy coldness gripped his brain. Pressure steadily increased in his temples; it was as if his skull was being pressed in a vice. He gritted his teeth and moaned at the pain he felt, pain that far exceeded the agony of his injured leg. The source of Martin's distress was the mind probe Edward Devilliers was subjecting him to. Martin felt information slipping from his mind, images from the past, memories he did not know he possessed; Devilliers was shuffling through them all as if he was looking through a giant filing cabinet. Martin's moans turned into a scream, he started to bleed from his nose and ears, and he could taste the metallic blood in his mouth. The searching became more intense, he saw his life flashing before his eyes and was not sure if it was because he was going to die or whether this was the effect of the probe. Mercifully, his consciousness and vision faded until all he could perceive was the sound of his own breathing filling his ears, and vaguely, in the background, there was the voice of Edward Devilliers questioning him maniacally as his probe failed.

"Why are you here, Martin, you bastard? What do you know? Did you come for Rachel? Is anyone else coming? Did you only bring one moron along to help you? Who else knows?"

Under normal circumstances, Martin's mind would have caved in under Devilliers' persistent mental assault and conceded all its secrets to this master of the psychic way; now, his weakness had become his strength – just as it had done in earlier attempts at probing him. The blood loss from the leg and his injuries meant that the pressure of the psychic probe only caused him to lose consciousness and thereby retain his secrets. As he blacked out, Martin managed a feeble smile at his minor victory. He had realised some time ago why the Disciples had gone to the trouble of patching his leg up, it was to prevent what was happening now. With his mockery and his laughter he had enraged Devilliers enough to re-open his wound and weaken him again. Before everything went black, he could just about perceive his brother-in-law screaming and slapping his face, trying to keep him awake.

**

With a scratch of his bare buttocks, Edward Devilliers turned around to leave the cell while Martin lay limp on the floor. Other nude, masked figures that had been waiting outside opened the door for their leader who walked out silently, pondering his captive's fate. After he had left, they shut the door of the small room once again. For a few moments, dim light from the opening high up in the door fell on Martin's unconscious face, and then its wooden slat was closed with a slide and a click, engulfing the prisoner in darkness.

Chapter 19

"We have an address; what we don't have very much of is time," Sascha said to Johnny as he drove to the rendezvous they had arranged earlier with Boyd and Baccharus.

"Yeah, I know what you mean," Johnny replied. "A few days observing the house would be really useful, just to see who's coming and going. I mean, there could be anything in there, like a whole pack of those Firehounds."

"Considering that all our information points to the shit hitting the fan *tonight*, a few days is a luxury we don't have," Sascha concluded. The elation they had felt on obtaining the location of the Disciples' lair was tarnished by the reality of the situation; they still did not know what they would face once they got there – if they even got that far. "Why don't you try and psychically look inside the house?" Sascha suggested as an alternative.

Johnny nodded. "I could give it a go. We've got to get a lot closer first; with all this aberrant, chaotic energy about it will be difficult. I reckon the Disciples chose this location as their base precisely because it seems to disturb Presarium waves."

"Are you saying that the Disciples aren't the source of the disturbance and this location is?"

"I don't know. The disrupting energy is so strong that I

can't believe it could be generated by *any* psychic, human or not. There's something else out there."

"Well, if we don't know what's lying in store for us then I suggest we send in Boyd with guns blazing; shoot first and ask questions later. I'm sure it would make his day," Sascha said, laughing.

"Yeah! Can't argue with a bullet!" chortled Johnny, reaching for his mobile phone.

"I'd better check on his progress."

Boyd and Baccharus were already at the rendezvous, a car park beside a nature trail popular with tourists. Sascha had found it earlier on an Internet map and chosen it in the belief that a leisure vehicle such as the motorhome would fit in discreetly there.

On the phone, Johnny asked Boyd if the familiar had been behaving himself, and it seemed that they were getting on famously. The motorhome was still a short drive away, and Boyd cheekily suggested that Johnny and Sascha take their time so he could enjoy a few more smokes with Baccharus.

While Sascha drove, Johnny took the opportunity to look around and enjoy the breath-taking mountain scenery. For an uncanny second he thought he recognised the view, when an intense pain suddenly struck at the very centre of his forehead, making him feel ill. It didn't take Sascha long to notice his friend squinting and massaging his head with his fingertips.

"Johnny, are you okay?" he enquired with a concerned look. Johnny nodded and tried to make light of the way he felt; eventually, he could no longer suppress his discomfort. With an apology, he moved from the front of the motorhome to lie on the cushioned bench seat beside the dining table in the rear. His friend's attention kept shifting from the road and back to him. On a couple of occasions,

Sascha asked if he ought to stop; Johnny told him to continue.

Johnny had suffered hangovers and migraines in the past; never had they been as intense as this. He attempted to rationalise why he should feel this way. *Could it be stress? Or lack of sleep?* he asked himself.

As he lay there, with his head resting on the seat, something strange happened. Every time he blinked he glimpsed an image, and so to allow this image to remain in his point of view he closed his eyes altogether. Once again he was confronted by the three prominent sugar loaf-shaped mountains from his dreams and yet he was not asleep. He knew this because he was able to open his eyes and find himself in the motorhome again, lying beside the dining table with Sascha in the background, still asking him if he was okay. Johnny reassured his friend that he felt better now and closed his eyes to let the images play themselves out.

"Earth expires, the children broken,
Chaos fires once more awoken."

He flew above the mountains with the same chant echoing through the air around him. The now familiar words were louder than before and even drowned out the usually dominant noise of the wind. Nestled in the valley was the camp of the old woman with milky grey eyes. She sat cross-legged in the woodland clearing while the children in their bright clothing huddled tightly around her. Johnny was watching the ever-present decay closing in on the small party when he heard another unexpected voice over the existing sounds of the dreamscape.

"Johnny, can you hear me?" it asked, and he recognised it instantly.

"Yeah, I hear you, Sascha," replied Johnny, his eyes remained closed.

"Just making sure you're still with us," said Sascha as he drove, satisfied that his friend was still conscious and responsive.

Johnny's attention returned to the dream. He could not understand how it was able to force itself into his waking consciousness.

"What do you mean?" he found himself whispering to it.

"Sorry, Johnny?" asked Sascha. This time, Johnny ignored his friend; his concentration was solely on his own internal world where, behind closed eyes, in the realms of mental imagery, he could see the tiny woodland clearing again from his vantage point high up in the air.

He descended towards it in a slow spiral, the children's voices chanting without a break. The old woman was looking high up into the sky, her neck arching backwards, and Johnny could see that she was staring right at him. "Find us here …" she called to him over the chant. "Find us here …" she kept repeating.

As he spiralled closer to the ground, he could see that the grey tide of decay had crossed the woodland, draining it too of life and colour. It now surrounded the group in a shrinking circle, threatening to swallow the tiny island of brightly coloured people and intensely green grass forever. Johnny descended quicker, he didn't spiral any more, he dropped from the sky like a stone, accelerating ever faster while the old woman and the children huddled together to escape the decay closing in around them. He was going too fast. Surely, the impact with the little group as he fell from the sky would kill them all, he thought. The wind rushed passed him, the group squeezed together tighter, the children chanted desperately, Johnny plummeted. He could clearly see the face of every child now, full of fear, staring out towards the creeping decay. The old woman alone looked up at him, silent. Just as he was about to land right on top of them, he thrust his arms out in an attempt to protect himself. At the point of impact his eyes opened, and he awoke with a start.

Looking down at him were the three faces of his companions. He blinked a few times to see if the dream was still there and saw nothing. The images had gone and so had the headache along with them; in fact, he felt quite refreshed. He sat up within the familiar confines of the motorhome while his friends watched on with concern. *I must have fallen asleep before we reached the rendezvous*, he thought.

"Are you okay?" asked Baccharus.

"Yeah, I'm fine," said Johnny, still surprised at how well he felt; there wasn't even a trace of the headache. He couldn't work out why they were all staring at him.

"What's wrong?" he asked his familiar.

"You were lying there mumbling away with your face all twisted up, dude. And then your whole head was jerking from side to side, and your body was writhing around. We tried to wake you gently and you just brushed us off. At one point, we even thought you were having a fit. Boyd was just about to call an ambulance – you woke up before he dialled out," Baccharus explained.

Johnny saw the mobile phone ready in Boyd's hand. "Hey, don't worry, I feel absolutely fine."

"You *did* have us all worried. What happened, Johnny?" asked Sascha.

"I don't know, all this aberrant psychic energy must be messing with my head." Johnny was not yet ready to divulge the details of his dream; he knew it would not be long before he had to. Baccharus was the only one who was aware of it – and even he could not guess that it was the source of his keeper's distress. The friends continued to stand anxiously around Johnny, unconvinced by his reassurances that all was well.

"Don't worry about me, I feel just fine," Johnny repeated as he got up. At the same time he was struck by a very important realisation. "We've got to move out of here, straight away! I will explain later."

"What? Now?" asked Boyd, confused.

"Where to?" enquired Sascha.

"We go now! Sascha, drive to the abandoned petrol station we saw on the drive to Mrs McGuiness's, make it fast. Boyd, follow on your bike. Like I said, explanations later; trust me."

Without hesitation, the friends quickly moved away from the nature trail car park just as Johnny had ordered. Motorhome, with motorcycle following close behind, raced all the way to the petrol station which lay isolated on a stretch of quiet road surrounded by fields and mountains. It was only a short journey. Sascha turned into the empty concrete forecourt where the pumps had been removed a long time ago. He passed the boarded-up kiosk building and parked beside the disused carwash to the rear, out of sight of the road. Boyd joined the rest of them as they quickly took up positions around the dining table, their unofficial mobile boardroom. When they sat together like this each team member felt strong and morale lifted (especially with the steaming hot coffee Baccharus had prepared). Johnny knew they would have to separate again sooner than he or any of the others would have wanted.

Johnny listened as Boyd started the proceedings by briefly explaining how he and Baccharus had successfully made the motorbike roadworthy again. With what Johnny suspected was considerable self-restraint, Boyd managed to spare everyone the technical details. Baccharus, who could never miss an opportunity to boost his approval ratings, was quick to point out the depth of his involvement in the job.

Johnny went on to give an account of the meeting with Mrs McGuiness; his familiar listened to him enthusiastically while Boyd sat there nodding and raising his eyebrows at interesting junctures in the story. When Johnny had finished, both were quick to congratulate him and Sascha on discovering the name of Edward Devilliers and the location of his house which was, in all probability, their ultimate destination.

A few minutes of chat and speculation followed as each finished his drink, and Boyd offered his evaluation of the situation. "The way I see it, we have the initiative here; we are the attackers, the raiders. The Disciples of Disorder might know we are coming ... what they don't know is when or how hard. I spent years as a merc and worked with all sorts of personnel. Most of my brethren were ex-Special Forces; they came from all over the world, and the one thing they all agreed upon was that the most valuable commodity, more important than all the guns and ammo put together, was intelligence..." He paused to make sure his three companions were listening, which they were, diligently. "We need to know more; I say we go and stake out this house, see who comes and goes while there is still light, and then, under cover of night – we strike!"

Johnny watched his friends nod and murmur in agreement. They had been thinking along similar lines; Boyd, with his combat background, had articulated the idea admirably. Johnny remained relatively quiet, and he could see that his friends had noticed; the last thing he wanted to do was make them feel uneasy.

"I expect the exact nature of our attack will be decided according to what we learn then?" Sascha added.

"That's right; there's no point fixing a plan here and now without gathering some information first, we know so little at present," Boyd said to more nods of agreement. The group started to chatter about preparations for an assault, discussing the weapons available to them and deciding which of Sascha's electronic devices would be most useful in taking on the enemy. As they spoke, Sascha downloaded maps from the Internet which displayed details of the area around the address Mrs McGuiness had given to them. The discussion swiftly moved on to psychic ability and how it would be implemented in any attack, which inevitably led to Johnny, who remained uncharacteristically quiet at this critical stage of the mission where he would usually be playing an active, vociferous role. His friends noticed his lack of participation and put it down to the strange sleep and headaches he had been suffering from earlier. Johnny sensed discomfort from his companions directed towards him, they needed his full involvement now more than ever – it was time to tell them about the dreams and why he would have to leave them. His cue came when Boyd asked him directly what he thought of the plan, Johnny felt that Boyd suspected he would disapprove. The rest of the group waited in silence for Johnny's answer.

"It's a good plan," started Johnny, "there is something on my mind though." His friends, who had already guessed as much, listened patiently. "I have been having a recurring dream from even before this assignment started, and it has been bothering me. It's a weird dream, very vivid, so real that I wake up wondering if it is a dream at all."

Johnny went on to describe how he flew through the valley, over the three sugar loaf-shaped mountains. He told them about the old woman in her field and the way the children played around her, chanting their strange rhyme. Sascha, Boyd and Baccharus sat there looking quietly intrigued.

"In the beginning I ignored it," continued Johnny, "but when Baccharus came to me with this assignment the other day, I had a hunch that it was linked to the dream. As we progressed further north with the mission and nearer to the disturbance, the dream became more vivid and intense. I started seeing the old woman and the children around her more clearly, and she started to speak to me. 'Help us, Johnny,' she would say. 'Find me here,' she told me once, stretching out her arm and gesturing to the mountains around her. When the dream occurs, I can't begin to tell you how real it is. When I wake up from it, I'm disorientated for a while and left wondering where I am."

Johnny paused again to gauge his friend's reactions. They were looking back at him, frowning, waiting for him to continue. He went on to describe the darkness and decay closing in around the old woman and the children.

Sascha had a question. "Is that what happened just now? When we found you thrashing around in your sleep? Were you dreaming *that* dream?"

"Yes," said Johnny. "I was sitting there wide awake in the passenger seat and then it was as if the dream attacked me. It forced itself into my mind and gave me this intense headache right here." Johnny pointed to the centre of his forehead. "I had no choice besides putting my head down and closing my eyes, and when I did that, all I could see was the dream. Just when I thought it couldn't get any more intense, it starts invading my waking life!"

"I'm sure I speak for everyone when I say this: what the heck does it mean?" Baccharus asked quite reasonably.

"Yeah, is there a message in it?" added Boyd.

"I know there is *something* behind the images, I'm not sure what it is. Here's another thing; I have noticed that every time I dream, it's soon afterwards that we are attacked by the Disciples of Disorder. It happened when that tall bastard Mr Kreb got us; it happened again when those blue-skinned demons tried to creep up on us."

"So that's why you got us to move so quickly to this old petrol station!" Sascha said, realising the reason for their speedy change of location.

"Yes, I thought it was best to move away from the place where I had just experienced the dream again, ASAP!"

Boyd was quick to offer his interpretation of events. "It's a trap, Johnny, ignore the damn dream. And whenever it happens we should move before those Disciples can get us, like we just did! It's your psychic ability, you see; it's not all good. There are pros and cons to it just like everything else in the world. I reckon our enemy is tapping into your mind to trace us."

Sascha had a less cynical take on the matter. "It could be a legitimate call for help; we can't just ignore it," he said.

Boyd wouldn't be dissuaded from his view. "It's a trap by the Disciples, a distraction before they attack; it's bollocks, man. We have a mission, we have an objective, we mustn't be stopped or distracted now." Boyd was jabbing his finger on the table to emphasise the point.

"Well, Johnny, why don't you tell us what you think?" Baccharus asked, and everybody fell silent.

"I reckon someone out there has a message they are desperate to get through to me, and they have been trying to do it for a while. I don't know who or what they are. I don't think they have anything to do with the Disciples of Disorder."

"If it's not the Disciples then how do you explain the dreams occurring before an attack?" Boyd asked.

"I think the Disciples just *follow* the dream message. They tune into it psychically somehow, and that's how they have been onto us from day one. They follow the message all the way from sender to receiver; they haven't stopped it because it's been leading them to us every time."

"So what are you gonna to do about it?" Baccharus asked.

"I'm sorry, guys; you're not going to like this. I'm going to find the source of this dream before doing anything else. It's just a feeling, but I think I'm supposed to find out exactly what this message is all about before moving on to the lair of the Disciples. Time is really tight so I will go by myself. If I don't make it back, you guys move on the old house without me."

Both Sascha and Boyd looked devastated and neither could hide how they felt. "Look at the time, Johnny, it's already seven p.m. It will be dark soon. You yourself said that we had to act tonight. There's at least one kid's life at stake here and God knows what else. You can't be doing this; I propose we move tonight – together." Boyd was almost pleading.

"I'm sorry, Boyd. I have thought it through already. Believe me, it's not been an easy choice. You have got to trust me. Sourcing this message and finding out what it's about is as important a part of this mission as anything else." He turned to Sascha. "Tell me, Sascha, how many times have we relied on my gut instinct? How many times has it pulled us through?"

Boyd looked at Sascha who nodded and said quietly, "I know you, Johnny, and if you think there is a sincere call for help out there, you're not going to ignore it."

Boyd turned to Baccharus for support. As a familiar, Baccharus had unshakeable faith in any decision made by his keeper; he trusted Johnny would always do the right thing. Boyd could see there was no way of getting them to change Johnny's mind so he gave it one last attempt himself. "We'll come with you then. We stick together," he proposed.

Johnny shook his head. "Look, there are two reasons why I go alone. Number one: I am endangering the mission. If these dreams come again, I'm guessing another attack would soon follow. It's better that I am away from you guys, we may not be so lucky next time. Number two: like you said earlier, Boyd, it could all be a trap, and if by finding the dream source I walk into it, the rest of you can finish the mission without me. If we are *all* ambushed then not only do we get screwed, in all likelihood, so does the rest of the world."

"How will we know if you're okay?" Boyd asked, slowly accepting the inevitable.

"Baccharus will come with me. If there's any sign of trouble then he can return to the motorhome and tell you guys what happened so you all can complete the mission. You should know that I aim to be back by midnight."

Sascha and Boyd both sat there with long, sullen faces. Johnny did not have to be psychic to know what they were thinking. After coming this far together, they felt abandoned; the group was broken up again and vulnerable. Together, they believed they had a good chance against the Disciples of Disorder; apart, they were weaker. He knew both his companions felt like this because he felt exactly the same. He had thought it all through though, and he had realised that he must go alone.

Sascha had one last question. "How do you know where

to go to find the dream source?"

Johnny stood up, opened the cabin door and walked out of the motorhome. Sascha and Boyd watched him, puzzled.

"Come here," Johnny shouted from outside. They walked over to join him with Baccharus hovering close behind. All three of them stopped beside Johnny.

"Look," said Johnny, pointing up into the evening dusk. They followed his finger and saw three sugar loaf-shaped mountains towering over them.

Chapter 20

Edward Devilliers sat alone in his ornate oak study amongst antique furnishings, dwarfed by shelving that covered two walls from floor to ceiling. He was staring out of the large bay window at nothing in particular. In the background was the sound of the girls at play, they were in a distant room further along the extravagantly spacious corridor of his house. The three teenagers chattered away excitedly over electronic bleeps and music from a video games console that had been the focus of their attention for the past few hours. He leaned back on his large, reclining leather chair, and it creaked satisfyingly beneath him. He thought about his only son, the next lord, so far away. *What type of world would he inherit?* Edward Devilliers pondered. His thoughts moved to the three girls again; to find them had not been difficult. Adoption for someone in his position of influence was an easy process. Bringing them up had been hard work, a task which he had mostly left to his wife, Elizabeth. It was so difficult in this day and age to ensure a girl remained pure. The only way was to keep a close eye on her from as early on in life as possible, and of course, to keep her disciplined. That was the beauty of Disorder; under its umbrella there was room for everything, discipline included paradoxically enough. In many ways Disorder was so close to the Equilibrium; both encompassed multiple facets of the living experience. One vital difference was that Disorder knew no bounds. There was no code of conduct; any extreme event or act was as acceptable as a moderate one. The Equilibrium stifled this journey to the ends of the spectrum while Disorder positively encouraged it. Order, on the other hand, was all about denial, something he found entirely unacceptable.

A ripple of laughter from the girls carried down the corridor, and Edward's musings shifted to the death of Chloe all those years ago. He cursed whoever had run her over to eternal strife; it had been a blow. He did have Rachel though. *She would do*, he thought. Elizabeth had known her for long enough and he had carried out the necessary checks – she was a perfect replacement. After tonight, there would be no need to constantly check on the girls; doing so had become such a burden over the years. *Soon their purpose will be fulfilled.* Three virgins of an age old enough to conceive was what he needed, and it was what he now had. Three vessels untainted by any man to bear the children of Lord Orbok and usher in a new alignment for planet Earth. Tonight, finally, the time was upon them all to reap the rewards of his efforts and further the domain of Disorder. He had taught Elizabeth many years ago the importance of what they were to do tonight, and he had introduced her to the secret his family had guarded for so many generations.

There was a burst of laughter from along the corridor and he smiled. Over the years he had become fond of the girls; however, simple human failings such as affection would not stand in the way of greater things – he was, after all, the High Lord of Disorder and not entirely human. Edward got up from the leather chair. It was seven p.m. and it was becoming dark outside. He wandered over to the window and looked out into the evening sky; a prominent gibbous moon was becoming progressively visible as the sun set. *Just as it had been calculated all those centuries ago*, he thought. *They knew exactly what this night would be like.*

It was time to start the evening's proceedings; he would have to check up on a few thorns in his side first. He took a silver bowl from one of the higher shelves. It was filled with an inch of water, and its inner surface was carved with many small runes. He gazed at it and directed some of his prodigious psychic energy into the water. The runes lit up with an immaterial, pale amber glow, and a three-dimensional image formed slowly, just beneath the clear liquid surface. He could see five figures before him, each wore long leather robes; four of them had voluminous cowls that hid their faces. The fifth man, with his head uncovered, was seated at the very centre of this sinister collective on a heavy wooden chair. He was aged and possessed an elegant, almost feline, face covered in light wrinkles with the hint of a tan. His long, fine, slightly thinning white hair was brushed back and hung over his shoulders. When he became aware of Edward Devilliers watching him, he opened his piercing blue eyes which had been shut for some time in deep concentration.

"Yes, Edward?" asked the old man; the four around him remained still.

"What news do you have of this Agent of the Equilibrium? Has he been stopped? Have we shut down this call for help that has been directed at him yet?"

"No on all counts, I'm afraid."

"Well, aren't you leaving it all a bit late? I'm going to be heading down in a minute to start the proceedings; I will be very busy, Arkkun, so sort it out!"

"Yes, Edward, soon; we are monitoring the signals very closely."

The four hooded men around Lord Arkkun were some of his initiates: young, inexperienced, but full of potential. At present, he was using their combined focus as an antenna to track psychic activity over an exponentially vaster area than any individual mind could achieve. It was how he had followed the dream signals to Johnny.

Unhappy about the lack of progress, Edward Devilliers broke off his gaze from the bowl; the image of Lord Arkkun and the initiates faded. "What the fuck is taking them so long?" he muttered to himself.

It was time to get going. He looked through the study window again to observe a nearby field. He noted the many cars that had parked in it already, hidden from the road. All sorts of vehicle were present, from affordable compact cars to high-end prestige models. The gathering had commenced.

He pulled out four large books from the corner of an enormous oak shelving unit that dominated an entire wall of his study. Hidden behind them was a safe. He keyed in a code to electronically open its door and reached inside, past a few antiques, to remove a large and ancient leather tome. As the book emerged from its storage place the air in the study seemed to come alive. An electrical charge became palpable in the atmosphere, and the hairs on Edward's head and body stood on end; he could feel the vibration of energy in his fingers where they touched the cover. He closed the safe and walked through his house with the book. He passed the girls' bedroom and had a quick glance through the partially open door to reassure himself that they were all still there: *one, two, three*, he counted and was unable to resist a smile of self-satisfaction.

Edward walked down the broad, opulent stone staircase of the old building, through the magnificent entrance hallway with its chandeliers and marble tiled floor, into a long, narrow, wood-panelled corridor. Some way along this corridor he stopped before a door, one amongst a row of identical wooden doors. He walked through it into a small, untidy utility room, it seemed an unusual place for the master of the house to have entered; Edward knew exactly where he was going. He walked past the old washing machines, mops and domestic paraphernalia that cluttered the poorly lit L-shaped room before proceeding around a corner into the shadows. Here, there was a wooden cupboard built into the far wall. He opened it; there was nothing inside. With a projected thought, he slid the false back of the cupboard sideways, revealing a heavy metal door that would have looked more at home on a bank vault. Edward whispered some secret words, and in response, three clicks sounded from the locking mechanism of the door, which swung open. He walked through, and it slammed shut again, leaving him engulfed in absolute darkness for an instant. With another thought he lit a row of large flame torches that were mounted in the wall adjacent to his entry point.

The illumination revealed a fantastic rectangular stone chamber that plummeted for several storeys beneath him, a vast space that had been cut into underground rock over a thousand years ago. He had entered through a doorway that was positioned high up in the corner of the chamber at a point where his head almost touched the ceiling. An open stone staircase descended from where he now stood. It ran along the wall to his left and led all the way down to the great slabs that made up the floor. Positioned around the centre of this cavernous hall were two massive pillars that stood about fifteen feet apart and supported the ceiling. The stone surfaces of both the pillars and the walls were covered with carved images; not an inch was spared.

Strange beasts, humanoids, men and women were depicted in every conceivable act. Edward walked past a section of wall where they were fighting, eating, sleeping and loving. The carvings came alive in the flickering torchlight here, and a draught whistled eerily through multiple small vents hidden amongst the stone images.

Edward Devilliers walked over to the opposite corner of the chamber. More steps plunged deep into the ground, creating a tunnelled passage broad enough for four men to stand abreast. Any person taller than Edward Devilliers, who was of a considerable height, would have struggled to stand erect in the passage, and it was so long that where it eventually ended was a distant, invisible point. He descended for what seemed like an age. All the way he used his will to light a sequence of small torches set in niches within the passage walls on either side of him – the resulting flickering, orange glow was the only illumination here. Each of the niches was vented, and lengthy hidden channels carried the air that fed the flames and kept the passage oxygenated. On his journey down, he passed two landings from which there extended more corridors to either side of him. Ignoring these, he continued to the last of the stone steps, which terminated under a small archway. He walked through the arch and into a plain rectangular stone room the size of a small church hall; this marked the end of his descent. His new location was rather an anti-climax when one considered the grand carved space from which he had made his way. A blazing fire basket provided some heat and lit up the chamber. It revealed a few arches in the wall to his right similar to the one by which he had just entered; beyond each of these, there were more stone stairs ascending into darkness. It was the wall opposite to him that housed the dominant feature of this otherwise plain room: an ornate Gothic arch covered with carvings depicting more of the strange figures that had adorned the great upstairs hall. Edward Devilliers walked through it and into a place that was far more impressive and unexpected than any he had entered so far.

What he now stood in was a gargantuan subterranean cathedral; its interior was bathed in a mysterious pale purple glow while its walls and even the very air inside it resonated to a gentle throbbing vibration. He loved this place passionately, and his eyes darted around it as if he were seeing it for the first time. The vaulted ceiling above was at least six storeys high, and beneath his feet the floor was made of ancient, uneven granite slabs, worn smooth through centuries of use. Those with an eye for detail would have noticed that there were no building blocks visible in the walls, which had been carved into underground rock. Tall, pointed, Gothic arches lined the perimeter of this enormous rectangular space. Numerous pillars supported an ornate balcony that extended all the way around the mid-level forming a viewing gallery which eventually joined a large mezzanine that defined the far end of the cathedral. Many more, smaller archways opened onto all of the higher levels. Stone friezes were carved into the walls at various heights with scenes similar to those from the first chamber except for the recurring illustration of a particularly fierce humanoid entity. At the centre of this vast, ornate cathedral space was a waist-high circular wall about twenty metres in diameter, crafted of finely cut stone blocks. On first inspection it appeared to form the sides of a large indoor pool; however, it was not water that it contained but a crystal clear purple matter with a flawless glassy surface that produced the purple glow of the cathedral interior. It was the portal, and it was from here that the omnipresent, gentle, ebbing vibration emanated.

Edward Devilliers walked over to this mysterious circular region and extended his arm to hover above it. He did not have to utilise any muscles to hold his limb suspended there: the waves of energy emanating from the purple matter were able to do this for him, like a magnet that repelled its opposite pole. *Tonight, I will make good use of the portal*, thought Edward Devilliers. He withdrew his arm, and his face became lined with deep concentration. As he exerted his will, rows of torches fixed at many points all over the walls of the cathedral spontaneously flamed into life along with several fire baskets scattered throughout this sacred location. Their collective light added to that from the purple matter and made clearly visible another tall pointed arch. It was ten feet across at its base, and its border was decorated with ancient carvings and runes, strange symbols unrecognisable to the uninitiated. Also revealed was a large lectern positioned between this arch and the portal; like everything else in the cathedral, it was a stone piece and decorated with hideous gargoyles that appeared to climb all the way up its stand. Edward stepped up to the lectern. He placed onto it the ancient book he had carried all the way from the safe in his study. Leaving this precious item, he entered one of the nearby arched doorways to emerge a few moments later wearing a leather one-piece suit and a cape of black material with a hood that hid his face. He returned to the lectern and stood before his book. He was facing the portal and its purple glow cast an eerie light over his person. Holding his arms aloft he called out loud; it was not in any recognisable earthly language that he spoke. Only the death priests of ancient Egypt and the initiated could have understood the foul and ancient tongue he used; its words sounded cruel and terrible. A chanting echoed around the apparently empty cathedral in response to him: a low-pitched murmur, repetitive and terrifying, with a beat that was in time to the ebbing vibration from the portal.

Edward Devilliers raised his voice above the ancient chant to cry out once again in the same twisted language. He barked hideous words, and from each of the many archways on both the ground level and in the balcony there filed out a continuous flow of individuals, naked except for leather masks that were stretched tightly over their heads and perforated with small eyeholes and occasionally a slit for the mouth. Most were clearly human, men and women, many were not. More of the foul blue-skinned demons that had attacked Johnny could be identified amongst their number along with numerous other strange beings; like a humanoid covered in wrinkly elephant hide, rigid in its movements, and a squat scaled being that twitched furtively. The humans were more numerous by far. To the uninitiated, there was something offensive about witnessing these faceless naked people interspersed with malformed alien beings. Concealed in a secret room beyond the grand archway behind Edward Devilliers stood a figure who would have been instantly recognisable to Johnny and his friends – a tall man in a black hat with a large, muscular beast by his side. All of these Disciples had gathered in the underground cathedral complex earlier that evening to wait patiently for their leader, and now, at his beckoning, they had each taken a position around the periphery of the great cathedral hall.

About a hundred and fifty Disciples had gathered on the ground level and another hundred and fifty higher up in the viewing gallery and the mezzanine. They all looked upon Edward Devilliers at his lectern and the portal. When his people had settled, Edward Devilliers, who stood nearest to the portal, drew back his hood. His handsome face glowed with reflected purple. He looked around at each gathered figure and smiled affectionately. His was an egalitarian organisation. Before him stood Disciples, poor and destitute, beside men and women of authority and power, all stripped naked, all faceless. Amongst the gathered could be counted a mayor, Members of Parliament, company directors, convicted criminals, the homeless and the infirm. Every stratum of society was covered. What made one rise above the other in the eyes of Edward Devilliers was not wealth or standing (useful though they were to exploit) it was devotion to Disorder. Those with a love for the principles of Disorder were indifferent to material gain and cared little for how they were perceived by those around them; only from increasing disorder did they gain any satisfaction. The demons amongst them were born in worlds of Disorder; they were here as examples and as help. It was good for his human Disciples to know that there were whole segments of the universe inhabited by life dedicated to the principles of Disorder, and the 'way of Disorder' was a gift he wished to bring to Earth.

Chapter 21

Johnny loathed leaving his friends behind; they had followed him this far and found themselves operating well beyond their comfort zones, and now he was abandoning them. He, nonetheless, convinced himself that it was for a good reason. To expose them to the potential danger that lay in the valley of the three mountains was inexcusable. There was still the possibility that the dream signals were from a malevolent source. Even if they were not, it was very likely that if they could be traced by the Disciples to him as the receiver, then they could also be followed all the way back to the sender; the enemy might therefore be lying in wait. If he ended up compromised, the mission itself had to continue unimpeded; it was far too important. Despite these reservations, Johnny decided that he would need to take Baccharus along to convey any messages or items back to the rest.

Johnny tried to return the Qrwshan amulet to Boyd again before he left; the big man insisted that he hang on to it and thereby continue to shield his prominent psychic signature from detection. Johnny exchanged a few encouraging words with his friends, who wished him well; he could see that it was difficult for them to let him go.

"Take care, Johnny," said Sascha, surprising his friend

with an embrace and doing likewise to the familiar. Boyd squeezed both their hands in a crushing shake. Johnny left the motorhome with Baccharus hovering over his right shoulder. Sascha and Boyd looked on like forlorn lovers from the doorway.

The first stage in the trek to the dream valley involved crossing the muddy field behind the old petrol station; it was gloomy and night was closing in. Johnny made his way briskly; it would be dark by the time he reached his destination so he carried a torch to light the way back in his long coat. Baccharus diligently hovered a few feet behind his keeper. Johnny, whose mood was pensive, considered what lay ahead of them.

The pair made good progress across the gradually ascending slope of the muddy field; Johnny calculated that it would be another hour of walking before they had a reasonable view into the valley. He did not bring any maps with him, there was no need, the vivid dreams had firmly imprinted an image of the region in his mind. He felt as if he knew the position of every rock and boulder here. His main concern was that out in the open he was an easy target, and if he were to receive another dream message then it could well give him away entirely. As a precaution, he kept a wide-ranging field of psychic perception about him for security.

"How are you doing, Bach?" Johnny enquired after forty-five minutes of walking in silence.

"I thought you'd never ask!" replied the familiar. "If you must know, I'm worried about those two back in the motorhome. I hope they just hang in there and don't do anything crazy."

"Boyd, not do anything crazy!? He'll do something crazy all right. Providing he doesn't endanger the mission or get himself and Sascha hurt in the process that's fine!"

said Johnny.

There was not much more to say. The setting sun meant that shadows from the mountains engulfed the landscape, and despite this poor light their progress had been good. They were now on a gradual ascent through the foothills of the nearest peak; just before Johnny reached their apex he sent Baccharus ahead to sweep the rocky region with a field of psychic energy to see if he could find any sign of danger. The familiar returned to report that there was none, and so without any concern about being seen, Johnny stepped onto a high ridge of craggy rock. It allowed him to view the entire valley basin. On either side and far ahead, he could see the sugar loaf mountains reaching up to the sky, and directly in front of him, the ridge gradually descended into the valley below. Rocks, boulders and scrubby vegetation marked his trail from here onwards. In the fading light he watched the long, narrow loch, surrounded by woodland; it was where the clearing and the old woman from his dream were supposed to be located. He looked behind him; the motorhome was visible only as a speck sitting in the old petrol station far away. Johnny took a swig of water from his bottle. Baccharus asked him where they were heading; he pointed into the distance, roughly towards the loch, took some more water and replaced the bottle in his long coat before proceeding along the rapidly descending route.

It was tough going; the ground was uneven and his balance was constantly shifting to maintain his footing. Baccharus suggested using the torch to light the way ahead or even implementing psychic energy to do the same; Johnny thought it prudent not to. For the whole duration of the walk, not once did the dreams attempt to invade his mind; it was as if they knew he was nearby, and there was no need for them to summon him any longer. After a further ankle-breaking hour of picking his way through the valley, Johnny reached the edge of the woods; over here, he paused, realising that this could be the most hazardous portion of the trek.

"I vote we go in," he said to his familiar eventually and entered the trees. After getting this far there was no option but to proceed.

There was no sun now. Johnny's eyes had adapted well to the darkness; however, progress was difficult. Silvery moonlight that managed to find its way through the branches guided him. More than once he was tempted to light the torch; fear of discovery prevented him from doing so. He carefully picked a route through the woods, sustaining scratches to his face and the back of his hands which were already raw with the cold and damp of the night. It was a good few minutes before he was able to see the traces of a fire between the trees ahead of him; its location was approximately where the clearing from the dream was supposed to be.

"We go towards the light," Johnny said to Baccharus, who was eyeing the beacon suspiciously.

They walked on, drawn to the fire like moths; its dancing flames becoming increasingly visible the closer they got to the clearing. Johnny carefully concealed himself against a broad trunk to observe the open ground before him; Baccharus did likewise. There was an earthy, sandalwood smell from the fire that hung in the air, and its tallest flames leapt almost to the height of a man. Even in the darkness, Johnny could see that this was the clearing from his dream. Subconsciously, his mind recognised the dimensions and shape of the land; it was only then that he noticed a huddled silhouette sitting beside the fire, facing away from him. He could not make out any of this individual's physical detail because of a thick blanket that was pulled over the head and wrapped around the body, but he had a good idea who it was sitting there. Quietly, he took a single step from behind his tree and into the clearing to present himself to the huddled stranger; Baccharus grabbed his shoulder with a little hand, and he turned to his companion.

"Johnny, are you sure about this?" whispered the hovering cherub, still suspicious of a trap.

Johnny nodded, and without a word he walked towards the blanketed figure; Baccharus followed. Johnny felt the heat of the flames against his face, and warmth enveloped his entire body. He found himself questioning whether it was the fire alone that produced this feeling or if it was the soothing aura projected by the stranger who sat beside it.

Despite Johnny and his familiar's close proximity, the wrapped figure continued to sit, facing the fire, with her head lowered towards the ground, apparently oblivious to their presence. The pair circled; their eyes fixed on the still shape, and it was only when they walked between the bowed head and the fire that the stranger looked up suddenly, as if awakening. Johnny stood there, face to face with the unmistakable rosy cheeks and milky eyes of the old woman from his dreams – just as he had expected. She gestured for Johnny to sit beside her and he did so, cross-legged, to her right, facing the flames. He caught a glimpse of the loose, colourful clothing she wore beneath the blanket as he settled down. Baccharus flitted anxiously from one shoulder to the other behind him, ready to react to any aggressive move.

"Thank you for coming," said the old woman in a rich, melodious voice that defied her age. "Both of you," she added, looking at Baccharus.

Johnny gave her a slow nod of the head before speaking. "I could hardly have ignored your beckoning."

"I had to make sure you would come," she replied. "If you had not … well, that doesn't bear thinking. We have waited a long time for you. I did what I was told. If I did what I was instructed then you would come; this message was passed down the line for a thousand years."

"Why am I here?" Johnny asked.

"You are here to prepare, Johnny M., for what lies ahead. To receive knowledge and to grow. Even amongst psychics, you are gifted. You have hardly realised a fraction of your ability. The potential I see in you I have never seen in anybody else, not even Edward Devilliers."

Johnny was confused. "Who are you? What are you talking about?" he asked, trying to keep his composure in the face of these riddles.

"To know the answers to the very questions you have just asked is the reason that you are here. That was why I sent you the dreams, projecting them from my own mind and the minds of my children."

"Every time I had one of your dreams the Disciples attacked me and my friends."

"They followed the dream message to you; I thought they might do that. I had to take the chance, Johnny. If you didn't come here first then there was no point in going on to the house and facing Edward Devilliers. You *had* to come; it was fated centuries ago to be like that. Don't worry about them finding this place; when I projected the last dream to you it was from somewhere else far away. They may be able to *follow* the dream; they certainly can't read it. Now listen carefully to me; I will explain why you are here."

"Please do!" invited Johnny.

"Yeah! And don't forget to tell us who the heck you are!" Baccharus added.

"I'm Theodora," smiled the old woman.

Johnny adjusted his crossed legs to make himself more comfortable; he anticipated the old lady would have plenty to tell them. The crackling fire continued to bathe him in its heat, and for the first time since leaving his flat, he felt quite calm. Baccharus was hovering diligently beside him when Theodora started to speak.

"This valley we are in, it's beautiful, isn't it? It is a place that has been associated with magic and witchcraft for as long as magic and witchcraft have existed on Earth and, believe me, that is a very long time. Not far from here is another, similar place, a neighbouring valley, and that is where you must go with your friends. It is where you will find Edward Devilliers' residence, your final destination.

"Why here? you may ask. Why is this region associated with magic and matters psychic? There is a good reason for that, it is because the environment here is so rich in Presarium, and believe it or not, there are actually a few more places like it in the world. The next question you may ask: why is there so much Presarium here? Well, there is a reason for this also. Please continue to listen carefully.

"Firstly, you must understand that all life and all substance in the universe is sustained by Presarium – the source of psychic energy. It is like a ghost that dwells both within and apart from every particle of matter. Without it nothing could exist: its presence is one of the properties of this universe.

"Next, I want you to understand this: that there are massive inter-dimensional tunnels linking together distant sections of the universe. Their purpose is to carefully balance the distribution of psychic energy, and they do this by allowing Presarium to flow back and forth through them like a tide. The importance of this function cannot be underestimated! If psychic energy is diminished in any section of the universe then eventually matter in that region would come apart and fade to nothing. It works the other way too. If there is an excess of psychic energy then the result is instability – psychic storms will occur, deforming matter and causing unexplainable phenomena. The inter-dimensional channels prevent either of these potentially catastrophic situations from occurring in any given portion of the universe, and the opening of these channels is called a portal. You can find portals anywhere; on planets, inside stars, or just floating about in space. Mystics and psychics have been flocking to this region throughout history because there is a portal here, in the very same valley where you will find Edward Devilliers. When there is a tide of Presarium flowing through it, whether it be 'into' or 'out of' planet Earth, it greatly increases psychic ability and imparts a sense of wellbeing. A psychic is able to feed off the energy that passes through the portal. That's why the valleys here have always been associated with magical occurrences and mystical experiences. There are three such portals around Earth in concealed locations. There was a time when all three of these earthly portals were controlled by the Disciples of Disorder. The Disciples had placed three kings in three corners of the globe to rule each portal. The portals were supposed to be benign channels for the passage of psychic energy; the Disciples of Disorder, through their warped sciences, hid wormholes connected to their own worlds into these dimensional corridors. It allowed them to easily traverse vast tracts of space, to influence and occupy worlds that they previously had no access to and thereby spread their vile religion.

"When the three kings of Disorder ruled Earth all those millennia ago, the portals and their illicit wormholes were used to summon dark energy and all manner of beast from other worlds to this planet. This age is vaguely remembered through stories handed down by generations of man – tales of strange creatures, witchcraft and wizardry; stories of heroes and their brave deeds. The dragons and demons of legend are thought to have been living beings; entities brought through the wormholes from other planets aligned to Disorder to aid the Disciples here on Earth ... to bolster their rule by enslaving the native life-forms of this planet."

The old woman paused and swallowed. Johnny considered her words. He thought about the demons he had seen over the years, and he felt he could better understand what they were now. The old woman continued.

"As you know, there are three alignments in the universe, three camps: those allied to the preservation of strict Order above all else, those allied to the ways of Disorder, and then there are those who adhere to the ways of the Equilibrium ... some of whom are guided by the Council of Seven ... those like you, Johnny. These three different alignments are known as the Trinity.

"On witnessing Disorder progressively taking control of the universe through their wormholes, the forces of Order and the Equilibrium, usually bitter enemies, made an unlikely alliance to combat the increasingly powerful Disciples of Disorder. Earth was one of their battlegrounds; a minor, almost insignificant battleground in a war that raged throughout the universe, but a battleground nonetheless. The wizards and witches of legend were the psychics of their time, and each gravitated towards an alignment. Some say we have a choice in who we join; others say we are born that way.

"So together, Order and the Equilibrium fought the Disciples of Disorder. After millennia of conflict, Disorder was defeated, and on seeing an opportunity to take control of large portions of the universe, Order turned on its ally. The Equilibrium fought back with its own sorcerers, demons and hosts of unknowable entities, some of whom were under the eternal command of the Council of Seven. In many of these conflicts, Order was victorious. The Equilibrium also had its share of success. On Earth, it just so happened that it was Equilibrium that became the dominant force and the result was that Order and Disorder could co-exist and flourish here without their extremes. I hope you can now see how Earth's alignment shifted from being a planet under Disorder's sphere of influence to one under the influence of the Equilibrium and the Council of Seven. It was this change in alignment that allowed the planet to progress through its many ages to what we see around us. Being a planet of the Equilibrium allowed it to prosper. Had Disorder, or even Order, controlled this world then it would be a very different place. Earth is now part of the Equilibrium, along with many other segments of the universe.

"I want to bring you back to the present again, Johnny; once more, the Disciples of Disorder are restless, and they have secretly gathered in strength. Even as we speak, they vie to control all the earthly portals."

Johnny had been listening carefully and many things were starting to fall into place. Baccharus hovered nearby; wide-eyed and excited by the old woman's words.

"So who *is* Edward Devilliers?" asked the familiar.

"For the past one and a half thousand years, this region of Scotland that houses the portal has been controlled by a long line of aristocrats faithful to Disorder known as the lords of Hilvern. The first lord of Hilvern was a vicious warlord of the Dark Ages who hailed from the north of England. He was guided by an ancient wizard, a wretched, twisted being who had been his companion from childhood – a single look from that wizard was said to fill a person with irrational fear. He would walk with his eyes turned down towards the ground, and when he was displeased with anybody, he would fix them with his terrible stare until they grovelled, whimpering before him, their darkest, subconscious fears realised inside their mind. This wizard was reputed to be over three thousand years old, and in his distant youth he had been a sorcerer, a priest in the temples of Egypt when it was the greatest civilisation on Earth, a disciple of Anubis. He had searched high and low all over the world for the one who would be worthy enough to complete his work, and to this end he found the first lord of Hilvern while he was still an infant, with neither title nor social standing. What the infant lord did possess was incomparable psychic ability, and the wizard surrounded his childhood development with the dark energy of Disorder, corrupting his life essence and moulding it until he became the very personification of Disorder even before reaching adolescence. When the boy reached his depraved manhood, he gathered around him, under direction from the wizard, an army of bandits. They set about looting and terrorising the north, conquering its lands. This band of miscreants grew and gradually they worked their way up to Scotland to take control of the Hilvern Valley; for this was the place where the wizard aimed to enact the final part of his wicked plan. Through his knowledge of Disorder on Earth, the wizard was aware of where the portal was approximately located; and on his private wanderings, which could take weeks at a time, he eventually discovered it for himself. He summoned from it a demoness, daughter of the deity Orbok, and once on Earth she took the form of a beautiful, sultry maiden; skin as white as ivory and hair blacker than the moonless night on which she arrived on this world. Physically, her appeal was irresistible; psychically, she was a potent being and radiated copious energy, a natural magnet for all living things, no matter how dormant their psychic ability.

"The wizard presented her to the one he had nurtured from infancy, and many nights were spent in passion between the demoness in human form and the warlord. She soon disappeared, probably to return through the wormhole to the place from where she came, although it was not before she delivered the fruit of her wicked union, a son, the second lord of Hilvern, half-man, half-demon – born with chaos in his very veins, the stock from which future lords of Hilvern would arise. The wizard's work was nearly done; the warlord died of old age, leaving behind his halfling son as the next lord of Hilvern, the new champion of Disorder on Earth. Like the first lord, he remained under the guidance of the wizard, who was now ready to reveal exactly why he had guided his father's empire north into the Scottish Highlands.

"One day, he took the half-demon with him through the conquered lands to the midst of a valley lined by craggy highland peaks. The valley was full of tall evergreen trees in an unnaturally dense forest. They worked their way to the very centre of this thick wood and the entrance to an underground cave network hidden beneath a boulder. He led the halfling ever deeper underground for hours, using flame and psychic energy to light the way to the final chamber, an enormous subterranean cavern filled with stalactites and stalagmites at the centre of which was a perfectly circular shimmering pool. The young second lord of Hilvern inspected it closely and saw that it did not contain water as he had first thought; contained within was a purple, glowing ether, flat and still without a single ripple upon its mirror-like surface. He wondered at the way it sparkled as if it were filled with diamonds. And when he tried to see how deep it was, he realised that it had no bottom. It seemed instead to plunge into the centre of the planet and then to the infinite unknown beyond. Standing there, he could feel the air, charged and alive, causing every atom within his body to pulse with energy.

"By bringing him here, the wizard had divulged the final secret to his half-man, half-demon creation – the portal. The wizard explained to his awestruck companion what the portal was and described in great detail how it was corrupted by the dormant wormhole hidden within it, placed there by Disorder aeons ago. He taught him how the wormhole linked Earth to the worlds of Disorder, and the way it could be made active again so that he could turn it on or off at will. The portal and its energy tides were to be the source of all strength for the new Disciples of Disorder, and the wormhole within it was to be their connection to the greater realm of Disorder. The introduction to this region of power was the wizard's final gift. After guiding father and son throughout their wicked lives, it was time for him to move on.

"The purpose of the lords from thence forth was to continue the lineage that would guard this portal, and when the time came, they were to follow the instructions that would birth the three kings. Until that time, they could do with the portal what they pleased. They were free to tap into its unlimited energy flow to grow ever stronger, and even use it to summon help from different worlds for the furtherance of Disorder.

"There is no definitive record of what happened to the wizard after these events; the commonly held belief is that he returned via the wormhole to the realm from where he had first come to Earth over three thousand years ago.

"Control over the portal, its wormhole and the Hilvern region was left in the hands of the half-demon son, who, through an iron rule, consolidated his warlike father's land-conquests. He maintained the grip of Disorder over the portal so that when the time came it could be used to place the three kings upon their thrones to control Earth.

"The second Lord Hilvern was already acknowledged locally as landlord through fear, intimidation and the elimination of any rivals. He was also shrewd and took as a bride one of the daughters of the clan to whom his lands had originally belonged, and he killed the rest of them until they stopped laying claim to the valley altogether.

"The second lord was never idle. At great expense he cleared the evergreen forest and built a castle on it, a rugged fortress, definitely not a place of beauty. Its dungeons and foundations were intimately connected to the underground cave network that contained the portal. This was how he intended to guard the wormhole and keep it forever under the control of his wicked family. Successive lords expanded further underground. Potholes and caves were dug out until they became corridors and rooms. Eventually, there came into existence a complex and ornate subterranean dungeon network littered with shrines to the demon gods of Disorder. The largest of the caves, the one that housed the portal, was shaped into a massive underground cathedral, hidden from the view of all except the initiated.

"By offering their particularly vicious and cruel personal militias to aid various kings through the ages, the lords of Hilvern always managed to hold on to power in the valley, which has essentially been under their control ever since; an unbroken blood line – the spawn of the demoness – heirs to Orbok ... Chaos personified."

Theodora fell silent briefly and stared into the flames; the fire's crackling and burning was the only sound now. Johnny did likewise while Baccharus watched the old woman, unsure if she had finished. Johnny was enthralled and a little daunted by what he had heard. It might have been an unbelievable story; however, since he had discovered Baccharus and his own psychic powers, anything seemed possible. The first time Johnny's perception of the world had altered was when he discovered his abilities; the second time was when his familiar materialised in his bedroom and introduced him to the Council of Seven and the Equilibrium. What he had just heard from Theodora felt like a third awakening, a third altering of his view of the universe, this account of portals and dimensional channels, the interlinking of psychic energy throughout the universe, and the battle of the Trinity on Earth. It was another piece of a complex jigsaw puzzle, a puzzle for which he did not yet have the complete picture.

"Why did the Council of Seven never tell me all this themselves?" Johnny asked his little familiar.

"I don't know; this is all news to me!" exclaimed the cherub.

Theodora interceded, "All is revealed, Johnny, when the time is right; nature has its way, the universe has its way, and now you know. A student does not ask the teacher, 'Why did you not teach me this before?' but maintains the faith that all is divulged when it is appropriate. The universe is your teacher, Johnny; the Council of Seven is merely a conduit for its message."

Johnny thought about the statement; he accepted it for now although he couldn't bring himself to agree with it.

"It just makes me wonder what else there is to learn out there, it's just so amazing. So who are you then? Are you also an Agent of the Equilibrium?" he asked the old woman.

"I'm no agent," the old woman replied. "You can consider my companions and I as friends of the Equilibrium."

Johnny and Baccharus looked on, waiting for her to

expand on this.

"Earth is alive. It is filled with psychic energy and has its own aura; just like any person. From the very beginning, there have been people born with a particular sensitivity to the living Earth and the ability to tune in to it. Only those who, like Earth, are aligned to neither Order nor Disorder may connect with its energy. The planet is able to speak to certain women and men. By receiving wisdom from my predecessors, and tuning in to planet Earth, is how I can tell you all that I have. The technique for making this connection to Earth has been passed down and perfected over millennia. I am a witch, an Earth witch or Earth priestess, call it what you may; American Indians call my kind *shaman*, some African tribes might refer to me as *Sangoma*. People like me who talk to the Earth are many and are present in all cultures.

"The Lords of Disorder have controlled and corrupted the portal for many generations while we, the Earth witches, have been keeping a vigil over it, handing down this sacred duty to our successors over the years. The portal is a part of the planet, so we who speak to Earth are well suited to watch over it; it is the planet's link to the greater universe. The portal is not for the Disciples of Disorder, or for Order, or the Equilibrium; it is for Earth only. We will always continue to watch over all the portals.

"Tuning in to Earth and communicating with it over time has made us aware of exactly what has been occurring around this particular portal. We, the priestesses, have for generations been secret witnesses to the evil of the lords. Earth has told us how its portal and its lands have been corrupted; it has told us of the evil beings already summoned through it. By controlling the portal, the forces of Disorder desire once again to place three kings on Earth to rule in their name, and they do this with the aid of demons.

"We priestesses are not witnesses without a reason; we are not here to stand by and merely watch. We may be too weak to directly challenge the Disciples of Disorder, however, our observations and our knowledge need to be passed on to one who would confront them, a son of Earth. We have observed the Disciples for generations only to aid him who would fight them, to call him to us, to show him the evil of Disorder, to guide him and teach him our way so that with our knowledge he may go forth to do battle and end the perverse ambitions of the Disciples of Disorder on this planet. We called to you, sent you the messages in the dream, and just like it was foretold, you came. Now you are here, Johnny, listen to these words: there is a strength that lies in planet Earth, it is a living entity. When the time comes, harness it."

The old woman stopped speaking and turned to Johnny and Baccharus with a broad smile. Johnny looked back, the fire crackled away. It was impossible for the enormity of what Theodora had said to sink in.

"Johnny! Wow! You're gonna fix everything!" said Baccharus, and what disturbed Johnny most was that it was a statement and not a question. He felt afraid; it seemed unfair. He had never asked for any responsibility, especially anything like the one that was being placed on his shoulders now.

"Look, I respect what you have done, and I intend to help you all I can. There's just one thing … I don't think the person you're talking about, the one you have been waiting for all this time … is me," said Johnny, conscious of upsetting or even offending the old woman; Theodora seemed unperturbed by his reaction and possibly even a little amused.

"I always harboured some doubts about whether you

would come," she replied. "Some might even have questioned my faith in the prophecy, but here you are. I can feel your strangely unique aura as we speak, and I have sensed how Earth responds to you, Johnny. Never have I felt the planet's energy drawn into a single person as strongly as it is in you. You are the son who we have been waiting for, Johnny – of this I am certain."

Johnny laughed nervously, still unconvinced, although unwilling to argue the point which was, he decided, academic. He was here for a purpose, and time was short.

"You said something about giving me some help – well, believe me, I need it! Especially now that I know I'm up against the offspring of demons and psychic warlords with summoned alien entities to aid him."

"Fear not, Johnny, I will help you better understand this gift you possess and show you how to draw upon deep strength from within yourself *and* from without also."

With a chuckle, the old woman eased herself onto her feet for the first time. Johnny noted her squat, powerful gait and the way she was swathed in voluminous, colourful, woollen garments. Leaving him sitting where he was, she walked over to one side of the fire and pulled out from its edge a small, metal saucepan which Johnny had not previously noticed. She held the hot handle with a thick sleeve and returned with it to sit back down again; this time it was opposite her new acquaintances.

Johnny and Baccharus looked suspiciously at the contents of the little pan. Inside it were the charred, desiccated remains of seeds, nuts and leaves. It was the source of the sandalwood fragrance in the air so noticeable on first entering the clearing. From a satchel that she wore beneath her blanket wrapping, Theodora produced a clay handle-less mug and a small water bottle from which she emptied a red liquid into the pan. She swished the contents about together before pouring the lot into the little mug and offering the mixture to Johnny.

"What's this?" asked Johnny, looking at the contents of the mug uncertainly.

"You asked for help, Johnny, here it is – drink it." She gestured for Johnny to take some of the mixture.

Doubtfully, he brought the clay vessel to his lips. Baccharus hovered up to grab the mug suddenly.

"Wait, amigo, are you sure about this?" asked the familiar.

Johnny shrugged and sipped the contents; it had an ashen taste with a fruity hint.

"Why did you do that?!" demanded a distraught Baccharus.

"Take more!" urged the old woman, and Johnny gulped a large mouthful.

Chapter 22

Sascha and Boyd studied the maps together; they wanted to use the time spent waiting for Johnny as constructively as possible.

"You're pretty good at this orienteering stuff," Sascha commented as Boyd hurriedly scribbled hazards and possible routes to the Devilliers' house on a scrap of paper.

"Reading maps, assessing terrain, all this stuff was an important part of my old job."

"Oh yeah, your old job; what was that again? You were a soldier, weren't you?"

"No, not exactly."

"You never did get round to telling us about your background."

Boyd continued to examine the map before him intently; he jotted down some more figures, and with a final flourish he put his pencil down. "Sorry, Sascha, you were saying?"

"I have been wondering where you're from. And exactly what the hell is the Order of the Earthly Eye?"

"Where I'm from is a very long story, and 'Boyd', even though it's the name I am known by, is not the name I was born with."

There was a prolonged silence.

Boyd reached for his inside pocket. "Do you mind?" he asked as he flipped open his cigarette packet.

"Oh, just go ahead if you have to. So … are you going to build on what you've just told me?"

"What?"

"The long story! Your real name! It just sounded as if you had more to say!"

"Oh, no! I'm not going into all that."

"Well what about the Order then? The Earthly Eye?"

Boyd took a few puffs and frowned. The cigarette smoke and lack of answers were testing Sascha's patience until, finally, Boyd spoke.

"Let me tell you why the Order of the Earthly Eye exists. There are beings, both human and non-human, born with psychic power, power that should by all rights be earned through discipline and study. For them, it's just there. Take Johnny, for example; if the Equilibrium had not found and recruited him, I dare say he too might have become a Disciple of Disorder or something similar. The Grimoires state that the unchecked power of the psychic is the biggest threat to humanity … according to the Aged Masters."

"So you're anti-psychic then?"

"Not anti-psychic, just very wary of them. I suppose you can say that we in the Order have taken it upon ourselves to police psychic activity on Earth."

"What gives you the right to do that?" Sascha asked reasonably.

"Nothing," replied Boyd, "but someone's got to do it. I mean, didn't you see those two Disciples of Disorder who attacked you earlier in the hangar? Someone has to keep an eye on these beings or they will bring calamity to us mere mortals here on Earth."

"Isn't that what the Equilibrium, the Agency Johnny

works for, does?'"

"To a certain degree, yes," nodded Boyd. "There *are* several important differences though, one of which is that the Equilibrium is alien, and we are human. The Equilibrium will always have the interest of the universe at heart; we, the Order of the Earthly Eye, have the interests of earthly life as our priority above all else. The Grimoires we follow were produced by man's earliest ancestors through ancient, mostly forgotten, knowledge; and most importantly, they are an *earthly* power."

"Well I guess for now it means you and Johnny are both on the same side."

"Oh, yes."

"So who are the Aged Masters?"

"Priests of man's first religion; servants of the Grimoires."

"Oh, yeah, the Grimoires, you mentioned those a few times now. What's all that about?"

"The Grimoires are the only written record of man's first religion. They are an epic story, full of guidance, wisdom and prophecy. They aren't there simply to be read. They differ from other books in that the text transcribed within them is a conduit to the power source that is the essence of the universe. Each letter has been penned and imbibed with energy in such a way that it has become like a switch to control elements of our reality; you can turn the switches on and off by reading, copying, or chanting the writing contained within a Grimoire, and by doing this you can alter the physical world. To those who know, there are many ways of activating the text. If you can use the Grimoires correctly, it is like being born with psychic ability. Only the Aged Masters have studied for long enough to utilise the text to its highest level."

"Is that what you carry with you then, a Grimoire?"

"No, the Grimoires are carefully guarded by high priests in five secret locations around the world. What I have is a selection of choice verses from the original Grimoires prepared in the way of the ancients, a concise, powerful treatise. It is a mere shadow of the great books, and even then, I am hardly able to use it."

"So you follow this religion of the Grimoires as an acolyte then?"

"Whole-heartedly."

Boyd sat patiently and smoked, waiting for his next question; Sascha didn't disappoint.

"Where are you actually from? How did you get into all this?"

Boyd eyed Sascha carefully, internally debating how much to reveal. "Okay then, I will explain a *little* about my past to you. It goes against my principles and it *will* be only a little – believe me, it's more than what most people get!

"As a young man, I got into a lot of trouble in Ireland fighting the Occupation. I was a Republican, and the authorities were on to me. I had contacts; they arranged for me to go abroad and start a new life. I worked with other lads in overseas security firms; basically, we were mercenaries. This was all before I had any knowledge of the Order and all the psychic bullshit that occupies my whole existence now. I met an Aged Master in a posting in Afghanistan, saved his life; three of his men died that day and he would have been next. They had been killed by a summoned entity, some ugly lizard-looking bastard. I blew the thing's brains out. After seeing that lizard man, I had to know more; so the Master took me under his wing. I stayed with the Master for many years and learned; he asked me to join the Order, so I did. Members of the Order are assigned to different parts of the world, and I had to choose a location for myself. There was an opening in Scotland so I took it; it was near to Ireland and my childhood roots. Occasionally, I would secretly visit my family in Ireland. I had very powerful enemies who were still after me. I called myself 'Boyd' and set up as a paranormal investigator – believe me, that job description is the best way to be alerted to any rogue psychic activity … along with a whole heap of other bullshit nonsense, mind you! So here I am, in my parish, here in sweet home Caledonia."

Chapter 23

The chanting stopped, and all eyes fixed on the shimmering purple of the portal. They watched this throbbing heart of the entire underground complex in wonder. They were gathered here for a ceremony, an event each had spent years preparing for as individuals, and as a collective, as the Disciples of Disorder, over a millennium.

Despite the vastness of the cathedral, the presence of so many unclothed bodies had actually raised the temperature within it a few degrees making it uncomfortably warm. A static electrical charge in the air indicated collecting psychic energy, and it certainly wasn't helping matters.

Edward Devilliers opened the dark proceedings according to ancient Disciple protocol; he greeted his loyal associates in the tongue of Disorder, the same harsh language he had spoken earlier when inviting them to gather around the portal. It was a language not of Earth, its words and intonations possessed specialised properties that transcended all verbal and linguistic barriers. It was not only heard by the ears, it was also perceived from within the mind so that the speaker's intentions could be understood by any living entity, even one that did not possess the ability to hear sound. It was a bastardised version of the original tongue; progenitor of all language and communication.

The Disciples replied to Edward Devilliers' greeting in one united voice, a ritual response that palpably shook the walls of the underground chamber. Like their leader, they too spoke in the same ancient, damned tongue – a set response formulated aeons ago for this very ceremony. The tone and frequency of each syllable uttered in the chorus had been calculated to propel psychic energy through the purple of the portal and activate the cancerous wormhole within it, creating a route to the worlds of Disorder beyond.

Before he recited from the leather-bound tome on the lectern before him, Edward Devilliers prepared all those gathered for what was to happen here, he spoke in the earthly tongue so they would know that he was addressing them outside of ceremony protocol.

"My loyal friends, to be present here at this time is indeed an honour for each and every one of us. You will all be remembered in ages to come as those who were with me, who aided me in bringing forth the new reign of Disorder on Earth. Your presence here at the birth of the new age will raise your status to that of the aristocracy of the legions of Disorder on Earth, and your lineage from this point on will be both blessed and worshipped.

"To begin this next stage in Earth's evolution, we summon tonight the Demon King Orbok himself; he who sits amongst the highest monarchs of Disorder. A demon with rank lofty enough to seed the three kings who will rule Earth. We are unworthy of his presence. To aid our cause, he has been charitable enough to enter this minor peripheral galaxy, and indeed, walk upon this inconsequential planetoid that is Earth. He does this only because his blood runs in my veins. The essence of King Orbok himself has been passed down to me from his daughter, the demoness, through my ancestors. If requested in the correct manner through this ceremony, he will come to aid his faltering offspring, so that we may establish our rule in what to him is a mere children's playground. Blessed indeed is the father; kind is he to his misguided children.

"Tonight we offer to him the three virgins. Three who will bear his seed and produce half-human, half-demon princes that will be kings here on Earth. It is only after this happens that Disorder may dominate the planet and make it a force to be reckoned with in the universal struggle of the Trinity.

"What we have before us is the portal through which the psychic energies travel. It is through knowledge liberated by our religion of Disorder that the wormhole within the portal was created, a route to the worlds where Disorder and its Demon Kings rule supreme; it is the same route by which Orbok will arrive in our world.

"I warn you now – when we open the corridor to the worlds of Disorder, beware! Experience has shown us that as we wait for Orbok, all manner of chaos beings from his world will slip through into ours. In King Orbok's realm they are vermin, the equivalent of our mice and cockroaches; in our world they manifest themselves as wild demons and spirits, and some may even be described as powerful. Fear not! Because as their essence enters our planetary sphere, I have arranged for it to be drawn away psychically and stored in a specially prepared and sanctified section of the building above us to be dealt with later.

"I tell you this now because if, by chance, we fail to trap one of these entities as it arrives then it may materialise anywhere, even here in the cathedral. If this happens your focus must not be broken, you must chant with me without wavering, you must repeat the sacred words as I have taught you, even if your fellow Disciple, standing beside you, is mauled alive by an entity so vile it churns your stomach. This is the final trial.

"You each possess a degree of psychic ability; it is present in every being, strong in a few, weak in most. Tonight, we aim to combine and focus this inherent ability so that it may become a more potent force, one that may activate the wormhole and summon Orbok. My superior ability will magnify and direct the efforts of your many wills until the Demon King hears the call, recognises my psychic voice amongst the many, and comes to our aid. Orbok will seed the three kings, and when the three kings are in power, the Disciples of Disorder will walk on Earth freely and openly once more!"

Edward Devilliers finished his address in a wild crescendo that emboldened his Disciples; he then switched to the language of Disorder and burst into recitation from the malign book in front of him. He screamed out sacred words that echoed throughout the chamber, words that were foul and blasphemous to the uninitiated. The gathered Disciples started their own delivery of twisted verse from memory, words of power that had been learned and rehearsed for this very night. They wailed and shouted from behind tight leather masks, producing a cacophony of noise from the galleries above and the ground level. Strange words barely capable of being produced by the human larynx rose up in unison. The noise and the scenes that were playing themselves out would have been enough to drive the uninitiated to insanity. And at their very heart, standing at his lectern, louder than the rest, was Edward Devilliers, waving his arms like a demented conductor before the hellish choir, urging on the chanters.

A frenzied rocking motion gripped sections of the gathered miscreants like an infectious disease passing between them. Naked bodies moved back and forth, some holding their arms aloft in an ecstasy of corruption, some human, others not, an undulating sea of flesh, limbs and hanging organs. With the chants of his followers in full flow, Edward Devilliers became quieter. His eyes closed in concentration, and he started to feed off the psychic energy generated by the many minds around him. With his iron will and superhuman psychic ability he gathered all this new energy, moved it into the purple portal, and enhanced it with the potential of his own mind. The semi-solid purple matter of the portal glowed more strongly, and as the Disciples chanted, it slowly started to rotate until a vortex formed at its centre. Its previously lazy, ebbing vibration increased in both volume and frequency – the activation of the wormhole had begun.

**

While the madness proceeded underground, more sedate preparations were taking place in the house itself.

"Lisa, are you awake? We have someone special coming to visit tonight; your father got you these dresses especially."

"Oh, Mum! It's so late now; can't I just go back to sleep?"

Elizabeth Devilliers stood in her youngest foster child's bedroom. Lisa had been asleep; after spending the day cycling, using the Internet and playing with her sisters, she was very tired. It was the school holidays and up until now the evening had been like any other. She could not remember the last time her mother had intruded so late.

"Please, honey, you'll love the dress, and Dad is relying on us tonight; he wants to introduce his family to his friend. I have a special drink ready too; c'mon, it'll be fun."

"Are Rachel and Meredith getting up too?"

"Well, I've spoken to Meredith and she's up. She said she was too old to go to bed at ten o'clock anyway. I haven't spoken to Rachel yet; I'm sure she'll be awake too. Look! Surprise!"

Elizabeth held out a long dress before her; it was a shapeless lace and silk item.

"What is that!?" asked Lisa grimacing. "Is that, like, old-fashioned or something?"

"It's pretty, you'll look like a little princess in it. Give it a try; there's one for Meredith and Rachel too."

Lisa reluctantly heaved herself out of the bed, walked over to Elizabeth Devilliers and took the dress from her.

"Give it a try, and come down to the kitchen, pet; I'll go and see Rachel."

Rachel was sitting up in her bed, anxious and unable to get to sleep. This was the night Martin had warned her about. The day itself had been quite uneventful, and she had found herself wondering whether Martin had gone mad, but by the evening, just before she went to bed, her suspicions were aroused by what she had seen from the bedroom window. In one of the adjoining fields, not far from the perimeter wall of the house, cars were parking and people were milling around. Now that it was dark, she could no longer see the commotion. Occasionally, a pair of distant headlights crossing the field would become apparent. She knew her foster father was an important man who entertained visitors at all hours; tonight, there seemed to be so much more activity than usual. The field had become a car park, and she did not have a clue why. Rachel checked her bedside clock, it was approaching eleven. She had retired to her bedroom at around 9:45 p.m. It was not particularly late; her foster parents were always strict about bedtimes, and this was earlier than what was expected of her. They were not strict about very much; bedtimes and not wandering out of the grounds were two things they never compromised on.

Rachel was feeling edgy; the strange sounds like fireworks from the previous night, the activity in the field and Martin's warning were all getting to her. She was trying to relax by reading a book when a knock at her bedroom door caused her heart to skip a beat.

"Come in," she invited, hesitantly.

"Hi, love."

"Oh, hi, Mum."

"Rachel, there's someone your dad and I want you to meet tonight; it's a business friend."

Rachel looked confused. Slowly, her worst fears were being confirmed. There was something different about tonight after all.

"It's a bit late isn't it, Mum?" she suggested.

"Well, we weren't entirely expecting him," Elizabeth Devilliers lied, "it's really important to your dad. I'm not too fussed myself, it would mean a lot to him though if you could just come down. This friend is very keen to meet the family."

"Can't I just meet him tomorrow?" Rachel ventured, sensing she was on a losing ticket.

"He's not here tomorrow; c'mon, it won't take long. Your sisters are both getting ready to come down. C'mon, Rach, please."

There was a determination in her foster mother's voice, and at the same time, she was trying to be rational and persuasive. Rachel got the sense that even if Elizabeth had to drag her down tonight, she would be prepared to do so, no matter how uncharacteristic it was of her. To object too strongly now would only raise suspicion.

"Okay," she nodded submissively. It was starting to look

as though Martin had been right; she had really not wanted to believe the things he had told her.

"Here, you're all to wear these dresses before you come down. Look at that, lovely isn't it?" said Elizabeth Devilliers, holding up another one of the silk and lace garments. To Rachel, the dress was hideous. With her heart racing nervously and her hands trembling, she slipped out of bed, walked over to the door and took it from her foster mother. She smiled at Elizabeth as if to let her know everything was fine. Elizabeth smiled back and walked out of the room. Rachel knew she had to do something to get away; first, she would have to pull herself together and start thinking clearly again. *I mustn't let fear get to me.*

**

Elizabeth walked from Rachel's bedroom, down the grand staircase and into the large hallway. From here she proceeded along a wood-panelled corridor into the kitchen. She removed three glasses of pearly white homemade lemonade from the fridge (a recipe she knew the girls loved) and placed the drinks in a line on the heavy pine dining table. From a pocket in her skirt, she produced a tiny crystal bottle decorated with gold filigree; it had a rubber-ended pipette as its lid. She put two drops of clear fluid from the vessel into each glass. The fluid had been prepared with great care by the Pharmacist, a precise mixture designed generations ago specifically for a night such as this. As she stealthily put the bottle back into her skirt, a hand on her shoulder made her start. She spun around to see the tall, dark figure of Edward Devilliers standing beside her, still clad in leather. She smiled with relief at the sight of her husband. "Edward?" she whispered, wondering what he was doing here in the house so soon.

"Elizabeth, my dear, there is someone you must meet before we proceed any further with the evening."

"The girls will be down any minute now."

"Don't worry, I'll send a Disciple up to look after them; you must come to the subterranean levels with me."

"What is it, Edward?" she asked; her husband did not reply and was already making his way to the secret complex that lay beneath the old house. Elizabeth Devilliers put the drinks carefully back into the fridge and followed him to the door in the old utility room.

Chapter 24

Sascha watched Boyd from the corner of his eye as he paced impatiently up and down the motorhome. His new companion had made no secret of the fact that he considered himself to be a man of action, and all this waiting was evidently getting to him. Earlier on they had been studying maps of the region together, and following this, Boyd had given Sascha an impromptu tutorial on the basics of firing handguns. Sascha hadn't asked for the lesson; at the same time, he would never turn down the chance to learn something new. He assumed Boyd had taught him because it was a way of constructively using their time. Boyd was restless; Sascha, on the other hand, was unconcerned about hanging around because it gave him the time to work on his gadgets. He tried to ignore his tense companion and focused instead on the work before him, eager to complete this particular device before they confronted the Disciples. Keeping his head down, he tinkered away on the unproven circuits embedded within a shiny chrome item the size and shape of a large cigar. The purpose of this particular creation was to alter the wavelength of psychic energy and therefore its physical properties. He had wanted to try it out earlier, unfortunately, it was not quite complete, and the opportunity for a convenient trial had not presented itself.

Since the discovery of Johnny's psychic ability, Sascha had made it his goal to reproduce through technology what his friend could do with his mind. Not for an instant did he believe that Johnny's skill, and indeed any psychic capability, was magic; it was his conviction that psychic potential was actually a poorly understood physical property of the universe – one he was gradually figuring out. It was he who first postulated the existence of Presarium, an idea that was confirmed later when they were introduced to Baccharus and the Council of Seven.

"I don't fucking believe it!" said Boyd, half to himself, half to Sascha. "It's almost eleven. Where is he!?"

Sascha had lost count of the number of occasions Boyd had asked that question and now simply refused to respond to it. He had been acquainted with Johnny far longer than the other man and did not doubt that his friend would return at an appropriate time. He concentrated harder on the shiny gadget in front of him, mentally blocking out all complaints as he used the mini screwdriver.

"How long are we supposed to wait?" Boyd ranted on, and then he sat at the dining table opposite to Sascha, who had intentionally not said a word for the past twenty minutes.

"What do you reckon we should do?" Boyd asked directly.

Knowing he could ignore his companion no longer, Sascha took a deep breath, patiently put down his mini-screwdriver, took off his glasses and leaned back in his chair.

"Boyd, I have said this before, and I will say it again: we wait until midnight, just like Johnny asked us to. Personally, I think he will be here before then."

"It's possible that he may not turn up at all, right? He

said so himself, 'If I don't turn up, I will send Baccharus to report back and you're on your own!' That's what he said. Right?"

"Well, yes, in a roundabout way."

"Doesn't it bother you?"

"Yes, it bothers me. Look, it is not yet midnight nor has Baccharus returned to bring us news of any problems. I have decided to use the time to prepare for a possible raid on the house in question because, like Johnny said, it may only be the two of us going in; I suggest you do the same."

"Oh, don't worry about that!" Boyd said. "I'm prepared all right!" He opened the front of his jacket to reveal the larger of his two pistols holstered under an arm.

"You see that, sonny! That's prepared!" While his jacket was open, he fumbled inside for a cigarette packet and lit a Marlboro.

"What's that you got there? Some sort of vibrator?" he asked, looking at the cigar-shaped device and chuckling.

"It creates an electromagnetic signal that disrupts psychic energy by altering its wavelength. You're not psychic, I'm not psychic; if we have to go in without Johnny or Baccharus this may save our arses, so to speak."

"Oh, okay, very good," said Boyd with feigned interest.

Sascha sat still and looked at his agitated companion who inhaled impatiently on the cigarette as his eyes darted around the motorhome. Their team was at half strength; Sascha knew this, and it was worrying for him too. When he was certain there were no more questions he leant forwards, replaced his glasses and set to work on the Disruptor device again.

A few minutes later, Boyd stood up and leaned over to look out of the motorhome's window. Sascha, still sitting, watched him. There was a light drizzle outside; the silvery clouds were not continuous and slivers of moonlight managed to illuminate the rural landscape ever so slightly.

"It's almost a full moon, we'll have to keep our heads low," muttered Boyd before sitting down again to recheck his weapons – something else that was bothering Sascha, he had lost count of the number of times Boyd had done this. Sascha returned to his device. He was about to complete a critical piece of wiring when his friend suddenly got up, and in the process of doing so, jogged the table, interrupting the delicate work. Boyd spoke before Sascha could raise any objection.

"I can't just sit here any more; I'm gonna go and check things out on my motorbike." He took a final drag on his cigarette and threw it out of the narrow gap in the window.

"Are you sure that's a good idea?" Sascha asked with genuine concern in his voice, suddenly distracted from his work by the impulsive suggestion.

"Look, we know there's at least one kid in trouble in that house, probably more. The Disciples have big plans going down tonight, with demons and the like included. I hate to say it, but Johnny *and* Baccharus may be compromised; we can't just sit here fucking around. I'm sorry, mate, I have been in enough combat situations to know that reconnaissance is what it's all about so I'm going to get on my bike and gather some intelligence. We need to get an idea of the terrain, observe any activity in the grounds, check weather conditions, all that kind of thing. As far as anyone's concerned, I'm just a random biker riding by, and before you know it, I'll be back. I'm leaving most of my stuff here. I mustn't carry too much; a gun and my holy book are all I need."

Sascha listened and worried. The potential for blowing their cover was very real; he fully trusted Boyd's abilities, but against a psychic enemy it was only Johnny who could be totally relied upon.

"Just hang on, Boyd; give it another half hour, will you?"

Boyd looked at Sascha; on seeing his concern he agreed to wait. Sascha fiddled distractedly with his device, anxious about what Boyd, who was pacing again like a caged animal, would do. The big man cast fleeting glances at his wristwatch as he smoked yet another cigarette. Every few minutes Sascha would say something like, "Oh, Johnny will be here soon…" to try to keep the other man from going off on his own. It carried on like this for another ten minutes before Boyd decided he could wait no longer.

"Sod this, Sascha, I'm going! I won't be long; thirty minutes max. I will be back with some useful data, you'll see. Here, take this, with one of these at your side you're never alone." He placed his high-calibre revolver hard on the table in front of Sascha, who stood up suddenly and started to stutter; before he could complete his words, Boyd had walked out of the motorhome. Sascha followed as quickly as he could, and by the time he reached the doorway, Boyd was already on his bike with his helmet on.

"Boyd!" called Sascha as the motorbike engine simultaneously fired up, drowning out his cry. He could only watch as his companion rode across the petrol station forecourt, onto the road and then away. Unsure what to do, he cast a few suspicious glances into the night, then went back inside, ensuring the motorhome's door was firmly shut behind him. He returned to his device, worked on it for about five minutes before accepting that he was too concerned about the safety of his friends, and most of all himself, to concentrate on it any more. He felt totally abandoned; as the only one in the motorhome, he suspected that he was also the most exposed target. Determined to wait for Johnny and hoping that Boyd would return sooner rather than later, he made a coffee. The only good news it seemed was that his device was almost complete.

Chapter 25

Johnny gulped the strange brew. Baccharus watched nervously. "Be careful, Johnny," urged the familiar. The taste was not unpleasant decided Johnny; he put the mug down after drinking only a third of the warm liquid. He wasn't particularly thirsty, and much to his relief, the old woman did not insist that he finish the drink. Theodora, who was sitting on the ground in front of him, started to rhythmically tip her head from left to right and chant quietly. He watched her slow movements closely; she seemed oblivious to everything around her.

Johnny waited expectantly for something to happen, and a few minutes later he felt the world around him, as perceived through the five senses, gradually shutting down; it was a most disconcerting experience. His sight slowly faded while sounds became distant and increasingly muffled, he just about managed to hear the old woman say something to him before his ears gave up altogether, it sounded like: "Go to the circle" or possibly, "Go through the circle". All sensation in his body gradually diminished to the point that he was no longer even aware of the ground beneath him. There were positive aspects to this particular sensory deprivation, the ache in his neck that he had felt since their last battle and the general feeling of physical malaise from the exertions of this assignment were no longer present.

When his vision was about to black out entirely, it flickered instead for an instant, like a television tuning in to a weak broadcast signal, and it returned again. He could see that he was still sitting in the woodland clearing, and to his utmost surprise, he was colour-blind. Everything around him was visible only as shades of grey, even the burning camp fire. Fortunately, this lack of colour was compensated for by an increased clarity in the detail of what could be seen. The darkness of the night could hide nothing from Johnny, every feature of the surrounding woodland was there for him to behold.

Baccharus and Theodora had disappeared. He looked around; they were nowhere to be seen. Where the old woman had been sitting facing him, there was instead a strange black circle suspended in the air. He stood up, and as he did so he noted how this simple action felt so different, there was no effort in it, as if the thought alone was enough to make him upright without the message having to pass through its natural route of brain to spinal cord to leg muscle. He felt directly interfaced with the world around him.

It was after standing up like this that Johnny received the shock of his life. He looked down and recoiled as he observed his own physical form sitting dead still on the ground precisely as he had been when drinking the old woman's brew, eyes open and unblinking. He looked closer. There was no doubt in it, here was a flawless replica of himself frozen in time. He reached out to touch it, and his hand passed through the body in such a way that it was impossible to know whether it was he or the replica that was the phantom. Johnny had to grudgingly accept that he was now one of two: a version of him sat cross-legged, still and lifeless on the ground, and the other wandered about in a colourless world in another dimension. This was the only explanation that came even close to explaining the strange state of affairs that confronted him. *Oh well*, thought Johnny, *maybe it was a trap by the Disciples of Disorder after all*. He must have died after being poisoned by the old woman, and now here he was, in spirit form.

His attention focused once again on the circle of perfect blackness which remained suspended before him, about three feet from the ground and three feet across. The only way he could explain it was as a gap in reality, a portion of the picture where the canvas had a hole punched straight through it.

He walked around to investigate this phenomenon. The circle seemed to have only one dimension, there was no side profile to it, and from the rear it was not visible at all. In fact, from behind, one could just walk through the region where it was supposed to be as if it was not present. The circle only existed when it was viewed from the front, where Johnny had first seen it. For a few minutes, Johnny marvelled at this strangest of objects, if indeed it could even be called an object. Then he made the decision to reach out and touch it. As his hand made hesitant contact with the blackness, Johnny became aware of a vibration running through his entire body, a feeling accompanied by the sensation of an electrical charge; it was similar to what he felt in the presence of psychic energy, something with which he was quite familiar. Experimentally, he plunged his hand into the centre of the black circle, and it disappeared up to the wrist, just at the point where he broke through the supposed surface. Promptly, he withdrew his hand and it reappeared again, intact. Johnny tried this a few more times with the same result, his hand disappearing then reappearing, always accompanied by the sensation of static and strange vibrations through his body. He walked a few metres away from the bizarre circle and stood there, looking at it intently, when Theodora's words came to mind. With two determined strides, he threw himself head-first into the blackness, desperately hoping what she had said was go *through* and not *to* the circle. Just like before, he felt the vibration as his body was swallowed by the black surface. He really did not know what to expect as he crossed what he hoped was a gate of sorts.

Having entered the other side, Johnny looked around with expectation and curiosity, and then he panicked – surrounding him was only a void filled with blackness. He turned around sharply to see if there was any sign of an exit. Even if the black circle was still there (which he doubted), it would have been impossible to discern its location within the empty space where he now hung.

He floated in limbo, removed from all that had ever existed. The emptiness was suffocating. With nothing else to focus on, his attention shifted to his own body which he could still see despite there being no illuminating light – which was disconcerting. But he was grateful for this view, just as he was grateful for still being able to move his limbs.

What happened? he asked himself. He must have done something wrong; maybe it was how he entered the black circle, had he taken a wrong turn through the gate and become stuck between dimensions? All these thoughts flew through his mind. He tried to move; there was nothing to move against, nothing to move to. Maybe he *was* moving, without any landmark to judge motion by how would he ever know? Was he falling through infinity? As these questions rapidly entered and left his mind they pushed out the initial blind panic he had felt on entering the void. When his consciousness was too tired to contemplate any more, the fear returned once again. Was this to be his fate, to spend eternity in nothingness? Bleak despair soon replaced the fear.

Except for the view of his body, he existed in complete sensory deprivation. There was nothing to track the passage of time here. Judging by the number of thoughts that had rushed through his mind, and sheer guesswork, he concluded that he must have been in this non-place for a good few hours. He looked around again as he had done on countless previous occasions, and still there was not the hint of anything. He concluded that Boyd *had* been right, that this was all an elaborate trap ... one he had walked right into. He even congratulated the Disciples on the brilliance of how they had got him here, the way they had primed him with the dream, how they had misled him through its images. The old woman, Theodora, was probably a demon in disguise; maybe it was Edward Devilliers himself.

There was only nothingness. Johnny, exhausted by going through the same thoughts over and over again, finally gave himself up to the nothingness; he embraced oblivion. The void that had originally been the source of so much anxiety for him became an increasingly peaceful place. Possessed by a deep melancholy, he closed his eyes, and as he closed his eyes the very form of his body that for so long had been the only thing present in the void faded away from existence altogether. Now it did not matter if Johnny had his eyes open or closed; now he existed only as a thought, his own consciousness, forever contemplating being in the absence of all else. With the passage of time, the thought slowed down. Johnny became a single wave of energy, a consciousness in its simplest form, and he found a strange completeness in this – he knew only peace. He could have remained there, hanging in space, for millennia or just a second. To him it would have been the same.

A voice interrupted this eternal peace, and at first, he paid no heed to it. "Johnny," it whispered repeatedly until it occurred to him that he might have recognised the name.

"Johnny," the voice whispered again. It reminded him of something; something he did not care for, so he returned to peaceful oblivion. "Johnny," the voice whispered back at him. Again, he listened and did not act.

A thousand times came that single whisper, a thousand times he ignored it; a little less on each subsequent occasion. Every time he heard it, it stirred him, ever so slightly, slowly lifting him from his singular state of being.

"Johnny," it whispered again, time and time again.

Following one of these whispers, a mere suggestion of a thought flashed into existence for an instant and died. It continued to do this every time the whisper was repeated until, finally, after countless further repetitions it remained in his mind as a thought fully-formed, a memory returning.

Johnny no longer knew the peace of being a wave of pure energy. A more complex consciousness returned to him. He was able to contemplate again and he remembered a very different existence.

"Johnny," whispered the voice.

Johnny, he thought, *Johnny.*

The whispering voice stopped; a chain reaction had been initiated. The void in which he existed was altered as his consciousness considered once again its previous alternative existence, one filled with the complexities and shortcomings of physical form. There was nothingness no longer. A huge, spinning purple maelstrom of light and gas materialised spontaneously. The void started to strobe violently between the blackness that characterised it and a new, brilliant blinding white. Memory slowly returned to his consciousness, and with it the flashing of the void grew more intense while the spinning purple maelstrom expanded to reach the horizon.

Johnny, repeated his consciousness, its newly born self-awareness overriding the previous singular state of being forever, and the flashing void became multi-co-loured. *Johnny, I am Johnny; I am Johnny.* The purple mael-strom started to coalesce into recognisable shapes.

"I am Johnny," repeated his consciousness. This senti-ment was no longer solely a thought; it now had a voice, a sound. Johnny was substance once again, a solid living mass, a whole body.

"I am Johnny M.!" he cried out aloud into the psyche-delic ether through which he floated.

The vague shapes that were forming around him slowly became recognisable images, misplaced in space and time. Scenes from Johnny's past played themselves out before him as if he were watching a cinema screen that filled his entire visual field. There were giant images of his mother and father, transparent and ghostly, talking to him, bend-ing over him as if he were just an infant. The images faded into mist, and he was left flying through space towards a rapidly spinning planet Earth. He had a perfect view of what he guessed was the solar system; the sun, moon and stars could be seen clearly, and superimposed upon this view of space there flashed countless more ghostly images. They were of all the people he had ever seen or known, acting out unrelated scenes from different points in his life; old girlfriends, school teachers, the man from the corner shop where he bought his comics.

Johnny started to tumble through the ghostly images before him. The spinning Earth which drifted in and out of his point of view as he repeatedly turned head over heels grew ever larger the closer he got. Soon, he was so close that the planet dominated all he could see, and the ghosts from his past stopped. When he finally penetrated the atmosphere, he was no longer tumbling; instead, he plummeted towards the surface, accelerating faster and faster. Now that he was surrounded by air, the sensation of speed was all too apparent. He could feel the wind rushing through his hair and over his body; he felt exhilarated like he had never felt before, even in his dreams. The high velocity of the fall made it almost impossible to breathe so he focused his mind, and through psychic manipulation he deflected the wind, creating a bubble of breathable air around him, mitigating any adverse aerodynamic effects.

It was not long before he was once again close enough to see the three mountains that had haunted his dreams for so long; his descent was taking him to the point where this journey had started, the place where he had sipped the old woman's brew. As the ground approached, the detail of what he could see progressively increased. The trees, the faint point of light that was the fire and, eventually, the figures around it, all became clear. Johnny closed his eyes, controlled his breathing and focused his mind. The muscles clenched in his jaw, and the tendons on his neck sprang up as he concentrated on willing his descent to slow down. Steadily, his free-fall succumbed to his conscious control; this was a level of psychic manipulation he had never before achieved.

Four pairs of eyes watched him as he returned from the sky. Johnny recognised only two of the figures looking up at him as he approached; one was the old woman, who smiled and slowly shook her head from side to side in disbelief, and the other was Baccharus, who appeared to be restrained by two bearded men Johnny had never seen before. He was still quite high up when he heard his familiar yelling at him, "Johnny! Johnny! I don't believe it; you're alive." Finally, slowly, his feet touched down on to Earth once again.

"Johnny, you're alive!" Baccharus shouted again, beside himself with joy, struggling desperately to free his little arms from the two men who held him so tightly.

"Welcome back, Johnny!" Theodora said, and Johnny immediately recognised her voice as the whisper in the void.

"Let him go now," ordered the old woman firmly, and the two bearded men, who looked even younger than Johnny, released Baccharus, who flapped joyously to his keeper.

"What's going on?" asked Johnny; Baccharus was the first to answer.

"I thought you were dead, Johnny! A minute after you took the drink, you just burst into light and flame! I went crazy! I really thought you were dead."

Confused, Johnny looked to where he had been sitting before his journey into the void, only to see charred ground. The scene was entirely consistent with what Baccharus had described and he was glad to have arrived without having to witness his own body alight.

"I'm back; don't worry," Johnny reassured his familiar. Baccharus was intimately linked to Johnny on the psychic plane and did not have to rely solely on the five senses to confirm the presence of his keeper; the psychic beacon projected by the man who had arrived from the sky was undisputedly that of Johnny, and somehow it seemed more potent.

"I saw you glowing and burning right in front of me; I thought you were finished. What happened?" the familiar asked earnestly.

Johnny turned to Theodora. "I might ask you the same

question," he said.

The old woman had not stopped smiling, and there was awe in the way she looked at Johnny. "You have completed a unique personal journey, Johnny, a journey of rebirth, one through which you have entered a higher state of consciousness. You have seen the essence of your being and its link to the universe. Meditate on what happened when you get a chance; for now, utilise all that is new within you. Time is short."

Johnny glanced at his watch. *She's right*, he thought. They did not have long to stop the Disciples. By his own perception he had been away for an age; over here, around the camp fire, very little actual time had passed. It was all very difficult to understand, he would heed the old woman's advice and dwell on what had occurred later.

Theodora turned to the two scruffily dressed young men who had been restraining Baccharus. "Erkan, Ashtiaq, go back and tell the others our work is done. We are leaving."

"Yes, Theodora." They nodded respectfully. With a nervous smile and another nod directed at both Johnny and Baccharus, they ran out of the woods with the old woman's message.

"I owe you an apology, Baccharus, but you had to be restrained," said the old woman before she turned her attention back to Johnny. "When your old form disintegrated, Johnny, your familiar thought we had killed you, and naturally, he went on the warpath."

"I just went crazy. I'm the one who should be apologising," Baccharus said to Theodora. "Firing those bolts and then launching myself at you like that … I am so sorry."

Johnny noticed strands of singed hair sticking out comically from the side of Theodora's head.

"It is what any faithful familiar would have done,"

replied the old woman graciously. Johnny spotted several holes burnt into her blanket wrappings and felt embarrassed.

Baccharus must have caused quite a scene.

"You need to go now, Johnny. You and Baccharus should return to your friends so that you all may confront the lord of Hilvern together."

Johnny nodded, it was time to play out the final scenes of this assignment. *Assignment*, he thought; it no longer seemed a strong enough description for what they were setting out to achieve. What they were on, he decided, was a *mission*.

"I'm sorry, I didn't thank you," he said to the old woman. "Without you calling to me like you did, without your guidance, I would never have been awakened. I would have been lost to the void forever."

"I was serving my purpose, Johnny, I need no thanks. To guide you when you came was the message that was passed down through generations of Earth witches. I'm just honoured that it all happened during my time and that it was I who aided you. I know our efforts have not been in vain because I can sense the changes in you already. In the void, you existed for a while in the form of your most basic life essence: pure consciousness. From this consciousness you became a thought and you knew yourself, and therefore the universe came to be – do not be fooled into believing this process takes place the other way around, that, my young friend, is the oldest trick in the book! It is the will alone that makes us what we are, Johnny. It is what determines where you are, and it is what shapes all around you. Remember this, Johnny, for your will is going to be tested many times."

Johnny tried to absorb every word Theodora spoke. He could see truth in it and desperately wanted to sit down again around the fire to reflect on all she had told him; there simply was not going to be enough time for that. He had to move quickly now and confront Disorder. The old woman walked over to Johnny, took his hand and kissed it. She smiled, and with a wink at Baccharus she turned and walked away. Johnny and his familiar watched her exit the clearing opposite to where they had entered. As she made her way into the surrounding woods, the two young bearded men came back to help. They fussed over her as she walked and she shooed them away, chastising them for their efforts.

"Go to your friends, Johnny!" she called without turning back, before melting into the trees and the darkness with her two companions.

Keeper and familiar stood alone in the clearing. "Shall we head back now?" asked Baccharus.

"Yeah, let's go; it's late."

The pair started to retrace their steps to the motorhome. "What actually happened, Johnny? What was Theodora talking about?" Baccharus asked once they had made their way out of the woods.

"Hmm … I'm still trying to understand it all myself. I'll attempt to explain it to you when this is over; for now, let me just give you a small demonstration."

Johnny stopped walking and concentrated deeply. The world around him slowly warped; it stretched and twisted until it was no longer recognisable. To know his current location in space–time, it was necessary for him to ignore the five senses and perceive his environment only through Presarium. Baccharus watched, mesmerised. From his point of view, it was in fact Johnny that was warping and shape-shifting.

"Whoa!" yelled the familiar, his face a picture of absolute astonishment as his keeper twisted and stretched into a man-shaped blur that rapidly accelerated away. Baccharus tried to follow the blur. He flew quickly; despite his best efforts he could barely keep up. And just when the familiar thought he was going to lose sight of Johnny altogether, he too felt the world suddenly start to twist and blur around him. This was followed by an exhilarating sensation of speed such as he had never felt before. Johnny had evidently decided to give Baccharus a tow.

They were about fifty metres from the motorhome when Johnny slowed down and returned to three-dimensional form with his familiar; the air around both of them remained charged with static.

"Johnny, dude! What the heck was that?" asked Baccharus.

"Like Theodora said, it is the will that determines where we are and whatever is around us. I believe I managed to alter space–time."

"It sure beats walking. Hell! It's even better than flying! Johnny, your psychic ability is awesome! The Council always said they had high hopes for you, and they were totally right! Why don't you take us all the way to the Disciples like that? Give them a surprise attack they will never recover from!"

"There are limitations, unfortunately. You have got to be pretty familiar with your route and your destination to do that trick, and a clear run always helps too. I have a lot to learn still. Let's get back to the boys; they must be missing us."

Johnny walked the rest of the way to the motorhome. The cloud cover that was obscuring the moon cleared just as the wind picked up; for an instant, the man in his flapping long coat and the familiar hovering at his shoulder were silhouetted against a silvery background.

Chapter 26

Boyd roared through the night on his motorbike. He felt bad about leaving Sascha behind. In the short time they had known each other, he had become quite fond of this odd man with whom he shared an interest in mechanics and gadgets. He would have felt worse though if Johnny had not turned up and they had to go in unprepared; to not even attempt some form of reconnaissance was simply not his way of dealing with situations like this. Boyd took some consolation in the fact that he had left his beloved revolver with Sascha and even given him a quick lesson on its use. *True, Sascha had not actually asked for the handgun, but what the hell, it was a pretty generous gesture*, Boyd thought to himself. Johnny, on the other hand, still had his Qrwshan amulet; two of his prized possessions left behind to help his companions. He decided he was not such a bad guy after all.

It was not far from the old petrol station to the residence of Edward Devilliers. Having studied the maps whilst waiting for Johnny meant Boyd had a good idea about how to get there. On a few occasions, he slowed the bike and moved his eyes off the road ahead to look around. With some apprehension, he noted the bright gibbous moon, just as he had earlier from the motorhome's window, it might make it difficult for them to remain concealed outdoors. The fast-moving clouds overhead which sporadically obscured the moonlight could, however, work in their favour.

Despite the dire circumstances, he could still appreciate the scenery on a more aesthetic level, snatching glimpses of beautiful moonlit peaks and valleys that stretched for miles towards the horizon. He regretted not being able to enjoy the ride more; biking was not just a means of transport for him, it was also a source of pleasure. But the evil brewing in this beautiful landscape did not allow any time for such luxury.

He had been riding for about twenty minutes and was up to full speed again. He leaned into a right turn and found himself travelling along country lanes so narrow that no two vehicles larger than a small car would have been able to pass each other along them; he would definitely recommend an alternative route for the motorhome. The ostensibly rash decision he had made earlier to scout ahead was paying off already. The data he had managed to gather on the roads, terrain and weather would make life a little easier for them.

The hedges and fields that had dominated the roadside thus far were now giving way to woodland, and he knew from the maps and Johnny's meeting with Mrs McGuiness that it was not far from here to the rear of Edward Devilliers' house. He was so near to the enemy now that he resorted to taking comfort in the abridged Grimoire tucked into his jacket; he could almost feel the powerful runes on its cover against his skin. Boyd mumbled some of its memorised verses under his breath and kept his keen eyes alert for a suitable place to conceal the motorhome when it was time to raid the house.

Chapter 27

Edward waited for Elizabeth at the foot of the worn stone staircase that led from the humble utility room to the grand, dual-pillared entrance chamber of his hidden underground complex. He was putting his long, black cape on again as his wife caught up with him.

"What is it, Edward?" asked Elizabeth Devilliers, her voice insistent.

There was a cruel smile on her husband's face. "There's someone you need to meet down below. I'm afraid I may choose him to be tonight's offering. I would like to know what you think."

Elizabeth shrugged; she wondered why Edward was so bothered about her thoughts on the sacrifice so late into the proceedings, especially as there were other, more pressing, matters. "What about the girls, Edward? They will be down any time now."

"They can wait, dear. They're not going anywhere. Just hurry along now, would you?"

She briskly followed Edward down the second stone stairway, further underground. As an early initiate into the Disciples, she was familiar with most of the secrets that lay beneath the house and had descended into its labyrinth countless times before. In the beginning, she had found it a dark and frightening place; now, it was akin to sacred ground for her, a place she entered with great reverence. Already, she could feel this night was special; it could be sensed in the atmosphere even by non-psychics. The air was filled with dark energy, and the entire stone complex resonated with the pulse from the portal and the chant of the Disciples; it filled her with excitement. Edward was the master of these unfolding events and so, by association, she too had authority here.

Elizabeth could not fathom why Edward wanted her to see the unfortunate who would be the offering tonight. She followed her husband along a tunnelled corridor that branched off from one of the landings along the stone stairway, far from the underground cathedral. This corridor split and turned a few times before ending in a small stone hall which was lit by a central glowing brazier positioned beneath a vent cut into its low ceiling, yet another part of the ingenious air channel network carved out of the rock beneath the house.

Elizabeth did not know this part of the complex particularly well; she eventually recognised it as the level where the cells were located. It was the place Edward held those who displeased him and those who would be required for ceremonial purposes at some point. Often, Disciples with a masochistic desire for captivity or the need to explore deeper into their own psyche were also found here.

Lurking in the shadows of the hallway were three muscular humanoids, naked and pale-skinned. Standard issue leather masks were stretched over the angular bumps on each one's head, covering their faces. On the arrival of Edward Devilliers and his wife, they unbolted one of the cells. Nobody came out; Elizabeth heard a groan from inside which sounded disconcertingly familiar. Edward turned his head towards her. "Someone has been asking about you," he said in a sinister voice. He gently cupped Elizabeth's face in his massive hands and kissed her lips.

"I know you won't let me down," he whispered before turning and leaving the hall.

Hesitantly, Elizabeth walked past the brazier to the opened door. The three Disciples standing guard parted for her, and she proceeded into the darkness of the cell. Carefully, they closed the door behind her and opened the slat set high within it to allow some of the faint light from the brazier to enter. Even here she could feel the ebb of the portal. Elizabeth saw the vague shape of a person lying prone on the cobbled floor in the shadows; he was beside a small hole that she guessed was used for sluicing excrement from this horrid room. Her eyes darted nervously around the rest of the cell to ensure there was nobody else present, prisoner or otherwise; except for the slumped figure, the place was empty. There was a groan. "Who are you?" she asked firmly.

The captive turned over slowly; her eyes had not fully adapted to the poor light, but she could tell that the man was trying to look at her.

"Who are you?" she asked again, and the figure gasped.

"Elizabeth!" cried Martin in disbelief, his voice weak.

It took a few more seconds for it to dawn on Elizabeth that the broken figure lying on the ground was her younger brother.

"Martin?" She hesitated before going to crouch beside him in the shadows.

"What have we done to you, Martin?" she asked with sisterly concern. She noticed the wound on his leg. "Did the Disciples do this?"

"No," Martin groaned, and with a painful laugh he added, "I did it to myself actually. Something had my leg in the garden."

"Did you stop carrying the amulet I gave you all those years ago? I told you it would keep you safe."

"The amber never really went with any of my outfits."

"Stop joking! What are you doing here?"

"I didn't think he would let me see you."

"Who? Edward? What's going on?"

"Elizabeth, you must stop Edward while there's still a chance. You must end whatever he has planned for tonight; save Rachel and the girls."

To stop the ceremony was unthinkable. Martin's words were akin to blasphemy, and they filled Elizabeth with an anger that started to eclipse the pity she felt for her injured brother. "Nothing can stop what happens tonight; it is the greatest event to occur upon the planet Earth for aeons. What have you done, Martin? You could have been part of it."

"Liz, you sound just like Edward!" gasped Martin between painful breaths.

"What is it, Martin? What made you turn away from the Disciples?"

"I always had my doubts about the road one took as a Disciple. Over time, I got to know what Edward was all about, and I didn't like it. Please, Liz, just get away from him, and take Rachel with you."

"Why?"

Martin fell quiet for a few seconds. "Edward killed Louise," he said finally. He watched closely. Elizabeth showed no reaction and this made Martin hesitate. "Listen to me, Elizabeth, then you will understand what Edward and his filthy friends are all about. My body is hurting everywhere – it's only now that I have the strength to tell you this. Edward can't have corrupted you … you were always such a good person."

Elizabeth did not say a word. Martin opened his mouth

to try to speak; he gasped instead and clutched at his leg. Elizabeth looked at his wound; she had noticed an offensive smell from it as she entered the cell, and she was sure it had become infected. Ignoring his suffering, she waited to hear what he had to say.

"Do you remember when I got out of jail all those years ago, Elizabeth? How you helped me build a new life? I will always be grateful for that. They were good times. I enjoyed belonging, meeting important people and learning the secrets Edward taught us; it was all good. I met Louise a few years after that. Do you remember how I bumped into her for the first time in your house? I saw her again in the village pub, she was behind the bar, and we really hit it off. She was a wonderful girl; the way we connected and the relationship we had was the best feeling I have ever known. I know you liked her too.

"When Chloe died in the accident, Edward began showing an interest in Louise and Rachel. He started to invite Louise to meetings the Disciples were having, and he would ask me to bring her along for his lavish dinners. The poor girl really was blown away by the attention. It was Edward's usual way of luring people in; you know how he is. He introduced her to the Disciples of Disorder like they were harmless work colleagues, and all the time he was slowly brainwashing her, drip-feeding her his philosophy. The more sinister parts, like the ceremonies, always came later, didn't they? It was only afterwards that I realised Edward was after Louise to get Rachel. Even at that time, there were rumours circulating amongst the Disciples that Edward was going to enact one of the cult's most powerful rites, and for this he needed three girls; you must have heard it too. Only now can I see that the rumours were true. When he fostered the girls with you it wasn't through some sense of charity; there was a darker purpose to it, just like in everything else he did. After Chloe died so unexpectedly, Edward needed a quick and suitable replacement for her so that there would be three once again; so he chose Rachel. He tried to influence Louise, hoping she would give Rachel to him willingly; she wouldn't do it though. His solution was simple: he got rid of Louise instead." Martin stopped speaking.

Elizabeth knew he was expecting her to be shocked by these revelations; she was unmoved. She loved her brother dearly; it seemed he did not understand her at all. "Is that it, Martin? Is that all you wanted to tell me? That Edward killed Louise so he could use Rachel for some ceremony?" Elizabeth asked coldly.

Martin looked back at her. His face had lit up on first seeing Elizabeth; now it was distraught.

"Why are you looking at me like that?" he spat. "Are you pitying me? How about Louise ... and Rachel? Don't you care about what happened to them?" He shifted his gaze away from her unblinking eyes. "No," he whispered, "no." And then he turned back to face her. "No, I won't believe it. Edward has not got to you yet; I know he hasn't. I remember how you were always so concerned about the well-being of others. I know there's something still there, some of the big sister I once had. There's more, Liz, please let me finish before you do anything tonight."

Elizabeth said nothing; neither had she stopped listening, so Martin continued. "There were witnesses around when Louise died. They said she had been mauled by a vicious dog belonging to a tall man dressed in black. Well, you know what? The man and the dog were both here, in this house, with Edward. I saw them with my own eyes a couple of months ago. It happened when I was driving back to Glasgow after fixing that computer network in Fort William. It was late; I was a little sleepy and was passing by your house. I thought it would be a good idea to stop for a quick coffee; say hi to you guys and Rachel. Do you remember that night?

"When I got here, I parked on the drive, and before knocking on the door I started to sort through some paperwork in my car. I saw two figures in the distance, walking along the very edge of the garden, talking quietly to each other. One of them I recognised as Edward, the other I had never seen before. He was a tall man in black, and following him was some massive creature, like a dog. Edward walked back into the house while the other man left through a gate in the garden perimeter wall. It was dark, and they never saw my car beside yours. That was the first time I saw Mr Kreb and his pet. There they were, in the garden. I instantly made a link between them and the mysterious attack on Louise, I couldn't be certain though. They looked pretty scary. I remembered that necklace thing you gave me; I took it from the glove compartment and stuffed it into my pocket. I was feeling pretty uneasy; I decided to stick to my plan and call on you all in the house. You opened the door for me, do you remember? Rachel and the girls were already asleep, and the two of us just sat and chatted for a while. Then Edward came in. I didn't say anything to him straight away; when you left to get the coffee, I challenged him about the man in black. He seemed evasive at first; eventually he told me it was the new bloke in charge of security, a Mr Kreb apparently. I asked him up front if there was any chance he could have been the one responsible for Louise's death, just to see his reaction. Edward played everything down; told me I was absurd. He said I was still upset about Louise. There was insincerity in his manner when he stated this … wait, I should rephrase that … let's say there was *more than his usual* insincerity. I wasn't convinced by his reassurances.

He never mentioned Mr Kreb to me again after that night; later on, I asked some of the other Disciples about this new head of security. A few had heard of him, many had not, *nobody* had seen him. I left that night questioning who Mr Kreb was, whether he was the man whose dog had killed Louise, and if so, what did Edward have to do with it. Driving away that night, I remembered Louise's personal journals, the exercise books and diaries Mrs McGuiness and I were keeping for Rachel. There had to be a clue there I thought to myself. And so, despite the late hour, I went to Mrs McGuiness's cottage. I got the poor old woman out of bed and searched through the wardrobe in her spare room until I found what I was looking for. I just sat there and started reading straight away. The things she wrote, they were so strange. She described nightmares, of being haunted by a frightening man in black who turned into a dog and attacked her; I mean, it was like a premonition." Martin fell silent and struggled to sit himself up against the wall of the cell. His breathing was shallow; there was anger in his eyes as he spoke again.

"Have you seen Mr Kreb, this man in black, around here, Elizabeth?"

Elizabeth remained icy. "Edward told me a long time ago about someone new looking after security. I had never seen him or even heard his name – until now."

She glared at Martin and wondered why he was telling her all this. Was he trying to shock her? She walked the path of Disorder, and she accepted the possibility of anything. After all that she had seen in her life, these revelations of Martin's barely registered in her conscience. Her thoughts were interrupted when Martin started to speak.

"There was something else I learned from the journals, not nice at all; however, a lot of things made sense after it. I didn't know how to tell you before, Liz. Something happened in one of Edward's Grand Dinners; the ones in which he invited all those so-called pillars of our society. I realise now that they were all corrupt bastards, really. We were all there at this particular dinner. It went on until quite late, and everyone had been drinking for hours. There was never any shortage of wine at these events, was there? I mean, you should know, you were the hostess. You see, for Louise and me it was an exciting world. Here we were dining with mayors and judges; it was unreal. I mean, where did we come from? Nothing! Anyway, like I said, it was late, and Louise was tired so she went to one of the rooms where it was quieter, away from the noise and chatter in the main dining hall. She was feeling tipsy; she never drank to the point where she lost it, she never had. Edward saw her leave and followed her into the room. She wrote in the journal that he started to speak to her, he told her that with him she was in good hands, and that he would show her great things. He said his aim was to introduce her to the ways of his Disciples, and as he said these things, he kept drawing closer to her. She backed off; he wouldn't stop until he had his hands on her. She struggled as he held her wrists tight, and she started to panic. He just watched and smiled as she tried to pull away. It was like he was playing with her. The next bit is really strange. I know Edward can do some pretty weird things; he has some sort of ability. I don't know what exactly, although it's the only explanation I can think of for what Louise wrote next. She felt a tingling from his hands where he held her wrists, a sensation that quickly spread through her whole body. It was like she was awake without any control over herself, while he could move her like a puppet. Her thoughts were her own though. In that locked room he sought his own sordid pleasure; the rest of us may only have been feet away from the door while it was all going on. She didn't write exactly what happened, although the stuff she hinted at left me with no doubt regarding what he did. After that, he just let her go and returned to the party. She never told me any of this, Elizabeth; I had to read it afterwards … after she died. Following that night, she stopped having anything to do with Edward, the Disciples and even you; it was when she stopped coming here to work. I remember asking her what was going on; she never even hinted at what had happened. She just told me that she wanted a change, to move on and find new challenges in her work. None the wiser, I accepted this; in actual fact, she was protecting me and you, Elizabeth, by not saying anything. I don't know if she thought about going to the police or anything like that, but what can you do if the chief constable is at the dinner parties of the man that assaulted you; it's got to make you think twice, hasn't it?

"It was only after Chloe died that Edward became interested in Louise and started to introduce her to the Disciples. I think that was when he realised he had a perfect replacement for his dead foster daughter in Rachel, another child to serve his sick purposes; however, by assaulting Louise, he had messed up. Her refusal to go back to work at the house and have anything to do with him meant he was about to lose the quick replacement for the girl he had lost already. He also had another problem; if what he did to Louise ever came to light, it would undermine his role as leader of the Disciples. People would know that through his own selfish desires he had jeopardised the goals of the Disciples; by submitting to his lust, he lost the replacement child. The easiest solution for him was clear; get rid of Louise. I have thought about it a lot, and I am sure that's why he had Mr Kreb kill her. It all happened so quickly: Chloe dying, Edward's attempts to lure Louise into the Disciples, the assault, Louise dying, and then Rachel being adopted. It's so clear; can't you see what a sick bastard he is, Liz?" Recounting the tale in his weakened state had exhausted Martin.

Elizabeth could see that it had been harrowing for Martin to recollect what happened to Louise. She could see that he had been trying to protect her all this time from this 'act of betrayal' by her partner. He wanted to convince her that Edward was cruel and dishonest, he even wanted her to stop the ceremony; Martin's motives were brazenly obvious. She watched him looking into her eyes, waiting for her reaction. What did he want now? Tears? Help? He would get neither. It was time to make her position clear.

"You don't see what this is all about, do you, Martin?" she asked coldly.

"W-w-what?" he stuttered.

"In the little time you were with us, as one of the pro-spective Disciples, you didn't learn a thing, did you?"

"Elizabeth, what do you mean?" asked Martin, con-fused.

"You continue to judge; you continue to heed right and wrong. The freedom offered by Disorder is lost on you and those like you, Martin." Elizabeth's lips stretched into a thin smile.

"Elizabeth, what are you saying? What have you become?" Martin whispered incredulously.

"It will not be long before Earth reverts to the true way. Forget about this nonsense you have been telling me, Martin – there are greater things at stake here. I offer you this last chance to join the Disciples. I can speak to Edward, tell him you have had a change of heart, and he will accept you with open arms."

"What are you saying!? Who are you? I'm not join-ing up to anything; just go away … leave me to die."

"I love you, brother, and I wish you too could have been a part of all this." With a shake of her head, Elizabeth left the cell.

"Elizabeth! Come back!" moaned Martin, his voice fading to nothing as guards closed the door to his cell.

"Elizabeth! Come back; I know my sister is still alive!" He directed these words towards the small viewing slat.

Elizabeth made her way back to the house from the secret network of chambers that lay beneath. Martin's foolishness dominated her mind. *Stupid boy,* she thought to herself. He had been brought into the fold, almost become one of them; somewhere along the line, the path of Disorder had become obscured for him. Edward had certainly not helped matters with his indiscretions. Martin might not have been so upset about poor Louise if he had been a full Disciple; to him, Edward's actions were an act of transgression. How faithfully Martin hung on to old, decaying values, she thought; they prevented him from seeing the new world. Now it seemed he would be paying the ultimate price. She could not help feeling a pang of remorse at this; was there something of her old self still alive? *No!* She was a true Disciple; it was good of Edward to let her know what he had planned for Martin. It was time to forget about her brother, there was work to do. She could ignore his words quite easily, although there was something else that bothered her. Martin looked different now, he had aged, as was to be expected, but his eyes were the same as she remembered from their childhood. Elizabeth knew that the connection she felt to him as her kin and the places this could take her might be dangerous.

**

Only now could Martin see why Edward had been so unconcerned about him speaking to his sister; he had corrupted her. Knowing this was just as painful as anything Martin had spoken of so far, knowing this almost broke him. Could he be wrong though? He had seen her flinch as he told the story. Even in that dark cell he noticed a slight pursing of the lips as he spoke of Edward and his lewdness. How could she not care about such a moment as he had described? Maybe there was hope. He did not know what to think any more – so many secrets – the people he thought he knew were like strangers, and his personal judgement suddenly seemed inadequate for navigating this miasma of deceit.

Martin heard footsteps approaching; maybe she had ordered a guard to release him. The footsteps stopped, the door opened again, and an all too familiar shape loomed over him.

"You were listening, weren't you?" moaned Martin bitterly with what little breath he had left.

"I was only next door," replied Edward, gesturing to a neighbouring cell. "Is there anyone else you would like to meet?" he asked gleefully.

"You've brainwashed her, Edward; to the point that she actually believes all your crap. You knew all this before you let her see me."

The gloating smile on Edward Devilliers' face was replaced by a more serious expression. "I didn't know for certain, Martin; I had to make sure that you could not get to her. I needed to know that she was a Disciple of Disorder worthy of her status as my partner. She's beautiful, isn't she? She really does understand what Disorder is all about. Elizabeth is not bound by the foundation-less morals that pathetic creatures like you so revere. I wanted Louise that night; this simple fact does not detract from the love I feel towards my wife. I feel love for all my Disciples. Of course, I don't expect you to appreciate any of this, you … you simpleton. Look at the so-called civilisation around you, see the lives of its people, observe how stifled their souls are, look at them go about their existence with spirits crushed, scared of all that is truly beautiful, scared to indulge their mind, body and soul in sensuality. They have limitless perception that is barely utilised, brains whose higher functions remain unexplored; they live akin to cockroaches … the gift of life wasted. What I bring is an awakening; man will no longer sleepwalk. Be honoured of the role you are to play in this, Martin. Your death, like those of so many others, will not be in vain."

To Martin, the world his brother-in-law proposed was unworkable. He had heard it all before and had stopped listening to the rant near its beginning. There was another question on his mind though. "Tell me something, will you? Why do the Disciples want the three girls?"

Edward raised his eyebrows. "I thought you knew," he said. And with that, he turned around to leave.

"Tell me!" insisted Martin.

"No!" said Edward, sneering at him from the doorway.

"Fuck off, Edward," managed Martin with fading breaths.

"Martin!" exclaimed Edward Devilliers as if disciplining a child. He left the cell, laughing.

The door was slammed shut by guards and the small slat closed. When Edward Devilliers' laughter faded, all Martin could hear was the sound of his own laboured breathing and the ebbing pulse of the portal through the stone floor beneath him.

Chapter 28

Rachel heard a knock and looked up. "Hi, Lisa," she said, fumbling awkwardly with the tie on the back of her dress; her younger foster sister strode over quickly to lend a hand. Both were now wearing the silk and lace garments given to them earlier.

"Oh, my God, Rach," said Lisa, "what on earth are these outfits?" She started to giggle.

Rachel, despite her horror at the situation, also found herself giggling nervously. "It's all very strange, isn't it?" she said.

"I know! Meredith is already downstairs; I wonder who's here to meet us? God! It must be someone from the Victorian age or something!" Lisa giggled again. Rachel did not join her this time; Martin's warning about the night continued to play on her mind, and she was starting to feel quite threatened. If by some miracle she managed to escape from the house tonight, her feelings would be a mixture of elation and guilt; elation at having avoided whatever was planned for her, and guilt for abandoning her sisters to some unknown fate. She wrestled with the question of whether she should involve the others in any plan to run away. The danger was that if such a plan failed, or if it turned out to be unnecessary, then she would be exposing them to the possibility of a severe reprimand. As Rachel grappled with this problem, Lisa playfully pranced about the room in her strange dress.

"Lisa …" started Rachel, slowly.

"I need a wee, Rach," interrupted Lisa with a mischievous grin, and she moved to leave Rachel's bedroom.

"Lisa, wait," Rachel said half-heartedly, still unsure about leaving her sister here.

"Back in a sec, Rach," said Lisa as she left.

Rachel sat on the bed, alone again, contemplating her fears. She started to panic, knowing she would have to act soon if she was going to escape. Memories of her mother flashed through her mind; terrible memories of death, isolation and vicious beasts. Her heart raced quicker as she sat there; Martin's warning rushed through her mind. *I will come and get you, Rachel, but if I don't, you must get away*, he had said. *You must get away. Why had Martin not come back?*

She started to pace up and down the room. She remembered the sounds from the garden, the ones from the night when Martin was supposed to have come for her, she had heard screams and loud bangs. *What had happened to him? Where was he now!?* Her body started to tremble with anxiety. *What had they planned for her tonight? What on earth was going on?* Everything Martin had warned her about was slowly coming true, and it became clear that she could not be here any longer. Before her fear got the better of her, she set herself on a course of action. Rachel moved quickly to shut the bedroom door and then squeezed the doorstop up hard against it. She threw on a light jacket to protect her from the cold, damp night and put on a pair of trainers. She slid open the window to her room and suddenly remembered the amulet Martin said would take care of her. She ran back to the wardrobe and grabbed the piece of strange jewellery, leaving everything else. She returned to the window and climbed out of it onto the portico structure beneath. Once on the small roof, she looked around desperately for ways to reach the ground and noticed a possible route down one of the portico's great supporting pillars. The pillar she chose lay against the wall of the house. It had stone blocks carved into its surface with gaps between them big enough for a fingertip hold that could only really be achieved by a rock climber; as fortune would have it, there was a wooden lattice fixed to the wall alongside it, intertwined with a mature climbing plant. The pillar and the plant, Rachel decided, were the best, if not the only, way down.

She turned and carefully closed the window; it was all she could do to throw anybody off her trail. Never forgetting that time was of the essence and remaining conscious of falling, she slowly lowered herself over the edge. It became painfully apparent that there could not have been more inappropriate clothing for this task than the dress she wore, but what could she do? She had put it on in fear, under pressure from her foster mother, and so desperate was she to get away that there was no time to change. She moved with an agility that would have been impossible for a mature adult to replicate. Scratches to the forearms and face inflicted by the plant stung; she continued the descent, undaunted. With four feet left to go, she lost her grip on some damp lichen and fell backwards onto a flowerbed. Winded by the impact, she paused to catch her breath. The point of no return had passed. Stumbling back onto her feet, she ran silently into the night. Her small frame and light footfall did not make a sound, and with the white dress trailing beneath her jacket she could have been a will-o-the-wisp.

Despite her present circumstances, Rachel felt safe in the garden; she had played hide and seek and many other games with her sisters out here for years. She picked her way past favourite trees and secluded spots, always remaining concealed. Occasionally, an unfamiliar robed figure wandering about the grounds would need to be avoided; this was easy for her, and eventually she reached the perimeter wall.

**

The being underground stirred again from its sleep. Could it be another meal? Its tiny brain considered the pattern of movement and the familiar heartbeat. Not a meal, it was the girl. It knew her well; this was no intruder, only a member of the household. This one was always in the garden. It was an odd hour for her to be playing outside, thought the creature as it drifted back into its slumber.

**

Elizabeth's mind was no longer occupied with thoughts of Martin languishing in his cell. She hastily ascended the stairs and passages that led back to the house and made her way to the kitchen. Meredith was already sitting there waiting, dressed in her ceremonial garb. *Such a good girl*, thought Elizabeth. She smiled at her eldest foster daughter whom she had raised from the age of three years.

"You look great," said Elizabeth as she stood beside the girl.

"Thanks, I don't feel great," said the tired Meredith. Elizabeth ran her fingers through the girl's hair with as much affection as any natural mother.

"I've made you all a drink. Where are your sisters?" Elizabeth asked.

Meredith shrugged. There was the sound of footsteps hurrying down the main staircase, and Lisa entered the kitchen.

"Oh good, you're here. Where's Rach?" asked the foster mother; there was no reply. She noticed disquiet on the girl's face. "Is there a problem, Lisa?" Elizabeth's tone was resolute.

"I can't get into Rachel's room."

"What?"

"I can't get into her room, and when I knocked she didn't say anything either."

Elizabeth dashed out of the kitchen, barely able to keep herself from falling as she ran upstairs. Meredith and Lisa followed, just about managing to keep up. *Rachel!* thought Elizabeth as she pounded up the stairs. *Surely, she wouldn't ruin everything; not tonight! That Rachel!* She was the quietest of the girls and also the most wilful; quietly rebellious – nobody knew what went on in that head of hers. Soon, Elizabeth was at her door.

"Rachel?" she called out aloud. When there was no response, she did not call a second time and turned the door handle instead. The doorstop Rachel had left prevented the door from opening; it took a few moments of pulling and pushing to loosen it enough for Elizabeth to burst into the empty room.

**

Rachel reached the heavy iron gate in the boundary wall of the house. She had intended to try and climb over the metal barrier, and when it opened a little as soon as she put her foot on it, she was pleasantly surprised. Maybe fate was favouring her after all she thought, unaware that it was the gate Martin and Peter Pike had melted open with acid the previous night. She heard a faint scraping sound in the distance, it was unmistakable; back in the house, someone had opened the window to her room. Seconds later, she heard voices and dared to glance over her shoulder to look back at the old building for the first time since making her escape. She saw Elizabeth leaning out of her window, squinting into the dark night; more worryingly, there were three men in black gowns running out of the front door. One of them she recognised as an odd man who visited her foster father from time to time; the other two were a mystery. All three raced into the night, undoubtedly after her. With no time to waste, she slipped out of the grounds, into the woodland around the house. As she ran, she wished she had taken a moment to close the metal gate again behind her. The three pursuing Disciples had separated and were heading towards different gates in the perimeter wall; one of them inevitably made his way towards Rachel's exit point.

She ran panting through the woodland, pleased with herself for having had the presence of mind to put on her trainers before she escaped, the ground here was rough and uneven with dead leaf litter and protruding gnarly roots everywhere. There was shouting in the distance, she could not make out the words; it was closer than she would have liked and it prompted her to run faster. She gasped for more cold air to feed her oxygen-starved blood. One of her pursuers discovered the open gate and was calling to his companions to follow him through it. Rachel pressed on. Soon she would be at the road, and she knew that beyond it there lay a larger, denser body of woodland, one which would provide a better opportunity for concealment. Martin had told her to always keep the amulet nearby; he had insisted and she did not know why. It was a simple instruction, and whatever the reasons behind it were, there was something reassuring about holding on to the strange item.

Chapter 29

Damn, this is narrow! thought Boyd as he rode. Even the widest roads had sections that were only a little broader than a car. Later tonight, when they brought the moto-rhome along, it was vital that there be an absence of oncoming traffic. *Or the final confrontation with the forces of evil would be lost because our camper van couldn't get its fat arse past the traffic.* He chuckled to himself at this. It also occurred to him that the isolation of these routes could work against him and his friends, say, for example, if they required medical attention, or the police, or even just a lift. He dismissed these concerns promptly with an "Aaagh, what the hell!"

Earlier, Boyd had contacted the Order to inform his superiors of the showdown tonight, and he had also put in a request for more manpower. The Aged Masters had sent their response; they had wished him well and told him they would be waiting earnestly for his next report. They had been happy to send the people he needed – unfortunately, there would not be any help arriving in time for tonight. To Boyd, already aware of the scale of Disciple activity, this had been a blow, but one from which he had already recovered.

Boyd's eyes flicked from the road to the digital clock on

his motorbike; midnight was approaching. The boys had not called him, he suspected the mobile phone signal in these parts was pretty poor, no matter; he would soon be turning back. He hoped Johnny would have returned by the time he got to the motorhome.

There was one last thing he wanted to do before retracing his steps and that was to see the house itself; get a first-hand view of the target. *Now that*, thought Boyd, *would be truly valuable*. He calculated that he could look at the building and still return by around Johnny's midnight deadline. The maps in his memory told him there would be a left turn coming up; half a mile along it would be a narrow lane which took him past the front of Edward Devilliers' house. He dabbed the throttle and the bike lurched forward. Boyd leaned into the curves of the road with perfect control; he was a skilful rider with years of experience and was almost touching the tarmac with his knee through the bends. Progress was good.

Suddenly, he was confronted by the unexpected. Out of the bushes ahead of him, right along the bike's trajectory, there emerged a ghost in a white gown. His mind processed the information in a split second; he was about to collide with a small, frail-looking girl. She would not stand a chance of surviving the impending collision, especially out here, miles from any hospital. Instinct took over; he squeezed both his brakes and leaned sharply to the right, overbalancing the bike and making it hit the deck. His motorcycle plunged into a fast slide on its side. He followed a foot behind, his leather trousers and jacket skimming the surface of the road, protecting him across the abrasive tarmac. He hoped the desperate manoeuvre had altered the machine's direction enough to avoid the girl who stood frozen before him, her eyes wide with fear.

Boyd stuck out his arm to grip the road with a gauntleted

hand, trying his best to alter the course of his own slide away from the bike; he preferred ending up in a bush to an impact with almost two hundred and fifty kilograms of metal and toughened plastic. The bike caught in a road-side ditch, it flipped up and bounced off a hedge to end up lying back on the road. Much to Boyd's relief, it had missed the girl entirely. He was soon worrying about himself again as he slid into the same ditch and made heavy contact with the soil embankment on its opposite side; his head absorbed much of the impact – and everything went black.

**

Rachel whimpered when she saw the bike heading towards her. It was travelling too fast to avoid, and her body had reflexively frozen in the middle of the road. She held her arms aloft to brace for impact in a futile, instinctive response that would have been no defence against the speeding mass; if the rider had not acted so quickly, she would not be alive. From her point of view, it was a miracle that the bike had toppled and slid away. She saw the rider land in a ditch; he looked hurt and was not moving. She thought he could be dead and wondered what to do.

Rachel was only metres away from the thick woodland across the road, all she had to do was run into it and hide; she had enough of a head start on her pursuers to do this – *what about the man in the ditch?* Could she just leave him there? The distant sound of snapping branches made up her mind. Leaving the rider, she ran into the trees to look for a place where she could conceal herself and catch her breath. She spotted a crop of wild, mature shrubs and decided they would provide suitable cover. She forced her way into their very centre, sustaining scratches all the way up her arms and legs and another one on the cheek. She crouched in a relatively comfortable spot amongst the lattice of branches; not only was she well hidden, she also had a view of the road where the motorbike and its fallen rider lay.

As Rachel hid, three men in loose gowns burst through the bushes on the opposite side; so afraid was she of making a sound and being seen that she almost stopped breathing. She watched the men look up and down the road as they emerged, and she saw the startled expression on their faces when they noticed the motorbike and the man in leather. They muttered amongst themselves, discussing what to do about the mysterious rider she guessed. Two of the men walked over to the downed rider, the third robed man ran across the road and into the woodland where she now hid, continuing the pursuit. Just as she had hoped, he went looking for her deep in the woods when, in fact, she lay in hiding at their very edge; convinced that he would not be able to find her, she switched her attention back to his two accomplices.

Rachel carefully watched the robed men examine the rider, and when they were sure that he was unconscious they lifted his motorbike; not to stand it up at the side of the road as one would have expected, instead, they pushed and pulled it through the bushes until it was concealed. They returned to the rider, leant over him and examined his face through the open visor; they then lifted him from the ditch and searched his clothing, retrieving a couple of items from his jacket which they closely scrutinised. Rachel strained to see what they had; it looked like a book and, to her surprise, a gun. He had a gun, for heaven's sake! Her heart leapt – could it be Martin? One of the men placed these items in his robe, and they started dragging the biker towards the house with his boot heels scraping along the ground behind them. Just before they were completely out of sight, they called for their companion who emerged from the trees not far from Rachel. He followed them back with a last look over his shoulder; Rachel could have sworn he made eye contact with her, but he walked on. Had they given up on the pursuit? She wasn't surprised, the woodland where she hid was vast; however, she suspected they would soon return with help.

The night was quiet again. Rachel felt terrible; she had already abandoned her foster sisters, and now, because of her, this man who might be Martin was also being dragged off to whatever terrible events were about to take place in the house. Rachel knew she could not leave another person to the mercy of her foster father and decided to help the stranger who had crashed. She slipped out of her hiding place to follow the three men and their captive … even though it meant returning to where she had just escaped from. She did not do this only for the sake of an unconscious motorcyclist, there was also self-preservation in her actions. She realised that the woods would soon be searched thoroughly, probably focusing on the area where the motorbike had crashed – where she had been hiding. It would not be safe outdoors; her foster father had no shortage of people at his disposal. Heading back to the house, paradoxically, could be the safest thing to do.

She crept along, clutching Martin's amulet tightly all the way. She passed the motorbike and felt the warmth radiating from its engine. Who could its rider have been? Was it Martin? A passer-by, maybe? If only they had removed his helmet instead of lifting the visor, then she could have seen his face. She followed them back to the house, always silent, always keeping a safe distance. Her dress was a grubby grey colour now – far more effective as camouflage; she was no longer a stark ghostly figure in the moonlight.

She watched as they dragged the man through the gate in the perimeter wall. She waited, and then, after plucking up all the courage she could muster, she entered the grounds of the fearful house, full of apprehension. She shifted stealthily from tree to tree. On familiar territory again, her confidence increased. She crouched behind a small, ornamental garden wall and observed. The unconscious man was being taken to the great front door of the house, it was open, and waiting inside was her foster mother.

**

Elizabeth Devilliers paced nervously in the entrance hall of her house; she bit one of her carefully manicured nails. *Where are they? All they had to do was catch one teenage girl; surely it couldn't be that difficult for three grown men.* Edward had already started the ceremony, and she shuddered at the thought of disturbing him. It had taken generations of waiting for this night to arrive. He would not be happy; his rage would be monumental. *Where are those three idiots?*

As a precaution, she had already given Meredith and Lisa their lemonade; unlike Rachel, the virgin who had vanished into the night, they would not be going anywhere.

She felt a faint vibration in the floor beneath her and, for the first time, the distant sound of chanting was audible from where she stood, above ground. *They must be coming up to full flow*, she thought. Elizabeth knew that if anybody could find Rachel it would be Edward, who had command over all manner of alien beings; that, however, was not the point. At this stage of the ceremony, he was not to be distracted.

There was a commotion in the garden, Elizabeth walked over to the front door. Her heart raced as she saw the three she had sent out earlier dragging somebody back to the house. *Bloody hell, I hope they haven't hurt her,* she thought. As they got closer, her mood turned sour again because she could see that it was not the girl whom they had; they were returning with a leather-clad man. She waited until they were close enough before letting them know exactly how she felt.

"Who, or what, the fuck is that?" she demanded furiously. "And where is the girl!?"

The three men shifted uneasily and glanced sideways at each other, waiting for the one who would have the courage to tell her they had lost Rachel.

"Well, what's going on? Marshall … you tell me," she said, pointing to the thin man with brown hair Rachel had recognised earlier.

Marshall cleared his throat. "We're going to need help. The girl dived into those woods across the road. We need more men – and dogs – we'd better do this quickly before she gets away for good."

"You fuckwits! So you let her get away then! The whole point of sending you three was to not disturb my husband! When the time comes, you go and tell him what happened," Elizabeth raged. There was more uneasy shifting from the men.

"Do I have to ask you everything?" continued Elizabeth, shaking her head in disbelief. "You haven't told me who this is yet."

Marshall spoke up again. "We found him lying by the road; he's got something to do with what's going on."

"What are you talking about? He just looks like some idiot who crashed to me … this had better be good!"

In response, Marshall handed Boyd's holy book and

small automatic pistol to Elizabeth. She handled the items curiously and scrutinised the strange runes embossed on the leather cover, so similar to the script used in some of Edward's books.

"You may save your skins yet," she said, handing the items back. "Take these to Edward and explain what happened. Bind *him* upstairs first! No doubt, my husband will want to 'mind probe' and I have a feeling he will make it a particularly painful one. Inform the Pharmacist!"

The Disciples dragged Boyd's limp body into the house. Elizabeth stood alone in the front doorway beneath the portico and stared out into the night. "Where are you, Rachel?" she muttered under her breath.

Chapter 30

Hidden in the sprawling garden, Rachel watched the three men take Boyd inside. Elizabeth Devilliers remained in the doorway of her old house, staring out across the lawn – Rachel knew she must have been thinking about her, her wayward foster daughter. After what seemed like an age, Elizabeth turned around, and she also walked back into the house. Not knowing what to do next, Rachel decided to remain where she was, crouching and watching. She felt cold and adjusted her jacket. A part of her wanted to run back into the night, and she questioned how long she would last out there, alone. So instead, Rachel opted to slowly move through the garden, edging ever closer to the house, back to her sisters and the biker. She was about thirty metres from the building when a group of men in black combat fatigues burst out from one of the distant outhouses with dogs that were yelping and straining against their leads. Rachel had to dive behind an old shed to avoid their attention; she was convinced the game was up. How could she possibly hide from these animals? She counted four handlers with a dog each. The men were forcibly dragging their beasts towards the broken gate, fighting and cursing them all the way. Rachel suspected the dogs had picked up her scent within the garden itself while the handlers, who must have been told she had left the grounds, kept coaxing the animals back on to her old trail that exited the premises. The dogs eventually got the message, and the hunting party quickly left the garden; Rachel counted herself very lucky not to have been caught.

When the sound of the yelping dogs faded into the distance, Rachel noticed a light that had not been there before illuminating one of the windows high up in the roof. It was from the big old attic, a large space at the very top of the house, hardly used by anybody except her foster father. *It must be where they have taken the rider,* she thought to herself, and she knew a way up there.

**

He lay on his back, disorientated. He tried to open his eyes; his lids felt heavy and they wouldn't go all the way. He could just about make out the poorly lit room with sloping ceilings he was in; more importantly, he could see the vague outline of two figures nearby. In the background was the sound of water running through pipes and steadily dripping into a tank. *Nice and easy now. Just let yourself recover a bit before trying anything stupid.* Boyd's mind flashed back for a second. *Who was that girl I nearly collided with, and what was she doing out there?* he speculated briefly before his thoughts returned to his current situation.

Slowly, subtly, so as not to draw the attention of the two men, he tried to move. An old fear of his was that one day he would come off his bike and end up paralysed; dying was fine, paralysis, he couldn't bear the thought of. As he lay there, he was convinced that this fear had become reality. It took a little longer before he realised that he had no spinal injury and the reason he could not move was because he was bound. He wondered whether his back was hurting from the accident or from being trussed up on the uncomfortable mattress-less metal bed frame. *Probably both*, he concluded. The backache was part of a bigger picture of pain. His whole body felt sore, every rib hurt and one thigh throbbed; all of this was eclipsed by the terrible burning he felt from the ropes around his hands and ankles.

Slowly, his eyes started to focus again, and he could see the two figures wearing long black gowns far more clearly. They faced away from him and were locked in deep conversation, one which he could not hear the words of.

His limbs felt stiff and were starting to cramp. He tried stretching ever so slightly to encourage the circulation; the bed frame creaked and a head turned around.

"Oh, look, someone's waking up!"

Another head turned, both figures walked to either side of him. The two men were in their late thirties or early forties. The one to his left was tall and well-built with tight curly brown hair; the other, to his right, had a cruel, pointed face with thinning brown hair and a terrible complexion, a face peppered with acne and scars.

Now that they were closer, Boyd could see the long black gown each of them wore was made of soft leather and had an attached hood that hung limply over the back. He caught a glimpse of a suit beneath each of these garments. It concerned Boyd that they were not going to any great lengths to conceal their identity from him; it was a bad sign, they obviously did not reckon he would be sticking around long enough to get them into any trouble. *Oh well, time to say hello*, he thought.

"What's going on? I feel terrible." The words were clear in Boyd's mind, but as he spoke, he became aware of his speech slurring; he needed more time to recover. He strained against his bindings to try to sit up, aching every inch of the way.

"No you don't," said a deep, harsh voice, the accent was thick Glasgow. It was the big man with curly hair; his strong hand pushed Boyd back down.

Boyd looked around to see where they were holding him, it was a large, bare room lit by a single, faint bulb. Sloping ceilings, wooden beams and the noise of a dripping water tank indicated that he was in an attic.

"What's going on, fellas? Why am I tied up?" he managed to croak through his dry mouth. He was going to play the role of a lost biker who accidentally crashed on a tricky stretch of road.

"Why don't *you* tell us that?" replied the smaller, cruel-faced man with a Midlands accent.

"What do you mean? I'm just passing through. What's going on?" Boyd said, trying to sound as sincere as possible.

"Oh, don't worry about him, mate, he's just passing through, completely innocent. Tell you what, why don't we untie him now and let him go on his way, eh?" said the cruel-faced man to his larger companion, his accent soaked in sarcasm. He turned to Boyd. "Shall I untie you now, mate?"

The two captors burst into vicious laughter. Boyd just watched them as he lay there. Their laughter faded slowly. "What are you doing here?" questioned the smaller man.

Boyd kept his nerve. "I don't know who you think I am, but you've got the wrong man; like I said, I'm just passing through. I'm sorry if I've made any mistake."

"Oh, silly us; we've got the wrong person," said the big curly man, wearing the joke thin. He didn't do sarcasm as well as his companion; they each still managed a laugh.

Boyd watched them closely; they were decidedly the two

most wretched and uncharismatic individuals he had met in a very long time. As if he had just read these thoughts, the cruel-faced man leant over Boyd and without warning started to throttle him, sneering as he squeezed his neck. Boyd coughed and spluttered.

"Why are you here, you bastard? Who sent you? We know you know something," demanded the miserable soul as he strangled away, releasing some of the frustration he felt at being part of the trio who had lost Rachel in the woodland earlier. Even if Boyd had wanted to answer he could not have done so, the wiry fingers around his neck and the pressure they exerted made sure of that. He felt his eyeballs bulging … and the man continued to squeeze. Finally, he let go and Boyd found himself gasping for air; both captors towered over him, their faces deadly serious.

The man with bad skin, his chief tormentor, seemed to relish the prospect of inflicting further pain; Boyd sensed the big, curly-haired chap would be more measured in his actions. It could be something to play on – or he would die here.

"By the way, do you always carry a gun and runic text-books with you?" asked thin lips before they curled into a smile at the look on the prisoner's face.

Boyd realised he had been searched already and that his story of being an innocent passer-by was not going to wash.

"Where's the girl?" asked the smaller man sharply, hoping to optimise on the surprise he had sprung.

Boyd just shrugged without saying a word; it was an honest response. With a gentle shake of his head, the man slowly gripped Boyd's neck between his thin fingers before going into a frenzy.

"Who are you?" he repeated as he squeezed.

Boyd felt his eyes bulge, just like they had done before;

this time, his hearing also became muffled as the pressure around his neck cut off oxygen and engorged his veins. The man was strangling harder and longer than on the first occasion and if there was any confirmation required for this fact, the determined look on his cruel face was it. Boyd felt his senses shutting down; the man did not stop. His cackling voice asked the same question over and over. "Who are you?"

Boyd started to go limp, and his eyes rolled upwards so he could not see what was going on. He vaguely heard the other man with curly hair bellowing in his Glaswegian accent, "Stop, you're gonna kill him!" The slackening of the grip around his neck Boyd was hoping for did not occur. There was the sound of a struggle, and his head was tossed from side to side; the grip around his neck remained firm. The big man shouted at his smaller companion again, "The boss wants him alive, for fuck's sake. We didn't find the girl so finding this idiot could save our arses! Don't kill him for fuck's sake or I will knock yo—" Those were the last words Boyd heard before he passed out for the second time following his accident.

**

"Oh, you've done it now! I am going to beat the shit out of you for that," said Curly Hair to his smaller, meaner companion. His face was flushed with anger as he stared at Boyd's limp body.

"Oh calm down, you big girl's blouse! He's alive," said the man with the cruel face, finally releasing his grip and surreptitiously examining Boyd – just in case he *had* gone too far. The curly-haired man leant over their captive and carefully watched his chest; it was slowly moving up and down. He heard the faint sound of breathing and straightened up again, relief apparent all over his face.

"What were you thinking? You could have killed him."

"I just wanted more information. They'll blame us for losing the girl, even though it wasn't our fault she got away in the first place. If we could at least find out who this fucker is or, even better, where the girl is, we could report back with it and that would make us look all right again; don't want to let the team down, you know?"

The curly-haired man shook his head. "You're a fucking psycho. Let's go and inform the Pharmacist, like Mrs Devilliers asked us to."

"What? Leave him here?"

"Well, I think you've made sure he's not going anywhere. Besides, he's still tied up. I'm not facing the Pharmacist by myself; he scares the shit out of me, any other night maybe, but not tonight."

"One of us ought to stay."

"Let me put it this way, either *you* go alone and I stay, or we find the Pharmacist together."

With his pockmarked face screwed into a sneer, the man from the Midlands checked Boyd's wrists and ankle bindings again. "Okay, he's secure; let's go and get the Pharmacist," he said.

They both left the attic by the old creaking staircase.

Chapter 31

Rachel moved from cover to cover, sometimes she hid her waif-like body behind a tree and at others behind a wall. She slipped silently through the night, her feet not making a sound. Gradually, she made her way to the mature Leylandii that grew alongside the south wall of the old house. She knew exactly where she was going; after all, this was her home. Rachel crouched down low to crawl between the hedge and the house until she reached a long-forgotten window, a dirty, narrow pane of glass that sat in a rotting frame a few inches above the ground. Three feet long and less than a foot high, it was too small for an adult to pass through; not for petite Rachel though. She pushed its grubby glass, there was some resistance from the rusted hinges, and her heart leapt when they squeaked gently. The window opened, and she was able to crawl through backward and lower her body into the small, dark coal cellar; a few feet away were the locked wooden doors through which the coal itself would have been deposited. It was a space that had not been used for many years, ever since the house's need for burning coal was superseded by mains electricity and its own diesel generator. At some point there had been an attempt to convert it into a store room of sorts. Rachel had never entered here at night, and it was almost pitch black inside, but even in the daytime, it would have been a dark and dingy place. It was the smallest of three such cellars, and despite the darkness, she felt confident of being able to feel her way along its walls to the old wooden staircase that led back into the house.

As she moved through the dark, she was suddenly gripped by an icy coldness. A sudden short hiss made her turn abruptly; there was nothing to see. She chided herself for being so jumpy, it was a frightening situation. She could not afford to panic – that would lead to mistakes. Once again, there was the faintest suggestion of a hiss. *Get out quick*, she thought, and moved briskly, past some discarded furniture, up the creaking steps to the door at the very top of the cellar where she listened carefully. When she was certain there was nobody beyond it, she tugged hard at the handle; after a few determined jerks, its damp, rotten frame gave way. It opened, just like it had done all those months ago when, together with Lisa, she had first discovered this coal cellar. She proceeded further into the house.

Having cleared the nerve-racking cellar and a small passage, she now stood in a cold corridor, intent on finding the downed biker and any clues to Martin's whereabouts. She hoped desperately that she would not get caught in the process. A damp, musty atmosphere pervaded this part of the vast country mansion. Edward Devilliers had closed the doors on the uninhabited sections of his house many years ago, and this was where Rachel now found herself. For a family of five to be using the whole building was simply impractical, and because Edward had plenty of money, there was no need to open any of the property to paying visitors or the like. Besides, most of his real work took place in the chambers that lay deep beneath the building's foundations.

Rachel felt safer in the emptiness she found in this part of the house and wondered why she had bothered running away from the building at all. The flooring in the corridor where she stood was parquet; layers of dust and mould had long ago dulled the appearance of its once polished surface, and she could smell damp plaster everywhere. From here, Rachel knew a way to the topmost floor and the attic.

Pale moonlight from large windows at the end of the corridor provided the bare minimum of illumination needed to get around, and her progress, although stumbling, was swift. A broad staircase took her up to the first floor. She did not stop here; only a few feet away, there were more stairs that continued on to the second floor where she found herself in yet another wide, long corridor, one she needed to cross. She walked along its musty carpet, nervously eyeing the rows of doors on either side until, finally, she reached the smaller staircase at the other end which took her to the third floor.

This floor was built into attic space, and its appearance was far less distinguished than that of the rest of the house. The sizes of the rooms on this highest of floors were comparable to those in an average urban dwelling. Rachel went straight for the old box room; a square, undecorated space with bare, wooden floorboards and a sloping ceiling. In one of its walls, there was a small hatchway. She crouched before its little door, slid back the bolt and crawled all the way through it into the attic proper.

She could hear him before she could see him, groaning from the opposite end of the huge attic. Using moonlight from the windows to guide her and keeping to the shadows, she followed the sound to its source.

**

Boyd gasped as he felt the sudden cold over his face; it was invigorating. Sharp intakes of breath filled his lungs with air, and he felt life slowly ebb back into him. There was another wave of refreshing coldness, and his level of consciousness increased; he felt as if he was waking from a deep sleep – only to enter a nightmare. Bound, with his body still aching from its recent abuses, he became aware of someone leaning over his prone form, and he braced himself for whatever was to come next; nothing happened. He blinked a few times, and by the light of the bare bulb that lit this part of the attic he could see a slight, dark-haired girl beside his bed, a definite improvement on the two ghastly men who had been here earlier. She had collected water from the nearby tank into an old mug and poured some onto his face.

She stood there, motionless, looking at him with wide eyes. He watched her; strange, he thought, she looked familiar. She put a finger to her lips, the look on her scratched face imploring him to keep quiet. He did not say a word. She wore a loose, sporty jacket over a dirty dress, the fine hair on her head looked dishevelled, and her cheeks were grazed; none of this detracted from her pretty, elfin face.

Good lord! he thought as recognition set in. It was the girl he had nearly run over earlier. How long ago that was, he could not be sure; unconsciousness had altered his sense of time.

"Who are you?" she asked.

"Great! Another interrogation!" Boyd muttered. He took a gamble. "Rachel?" he ventured.

She looked startled. "How do you know me?" she asked innocently.

"I'm a friend of Martin's. What were you doing outside? I could have run you over; in fact, what are you doing here? It's not safe, you know!"

"It's not safe out there either; they're already looking for me. I came back because I thought you needed help and that you might help me. In fact, when I saw them pull a gun out of your jacket I thought you might even be Martin. He said he would do something to get me out … even though he didn't turn up the other night … Is he all right?" She looked at Boyd with pleading eyes.

"I don't know where he is, and I don't know if he is all right," Boyd answered honestly; the sadness in Rachel's face was painful, especially as he knew that the other man was probably not going to be all right.

"See if you can get me out of these ropes, Rachel, then we'll head out of this attic and get you somewhere safe."

She started fumbling at his bindings; despite working furtively, progress was slow. Boyd let out stifled grunts of pain as the rope around his wrist tightened then loosened until it finally became slack, and she moved on to the other side.

"Do you know this house well?" he asked as she tried to free him.

"Uh huh," she responded, without a break in her task.

"Good; I thought as much, sneaking in here like you did. What's going on tonight, Rachel? Why did you try and run away?"

"I don't know what's going on; there have been people coming and going all night. It's something that involves me and my sisters. I know that because Martin told me and because of these strange dresses they gave us to wear."

She had just about managed to loosen the ropes sufficiently for Boyd to yank his hands free from the bed and shake the circulation back into them. Pain signals fired simultaneously from every fingertip; ignoring them, he sat up and got to work frantically on his ankle bindings, not stopping until he pulled his legs out of their tethers with a great heave. He closed his eyes, took a few deep breaths and then stood beside the bed frame, rubbing his stiff neck.

"Martin told me I was in danger; me and my sisters too … I'm scared," said Rachel.

Boyd could see the girl was confused and frightened; she was definitely a brave one. Coming back to this place was probably a bad move for anybody he thought; however, she had done it, and he swore on the Grimoires that he would do whatever he could to get her out again.

"Don't worry, honey, before you know it we'll be leaving," he reassured her; it was the only thing to say. After a few stretches, he limped over to the attic window to see what was going on.

"I'm glad you're here," said Rachel as she watched him. Boyd glanced at her self-consciously, a little uncomfortable about his new responsibility. He managed to flash her a brief smile before looking outside.

"Son of a bitch!" said Boyd as he looked down from the attic window. Rachel walked over to see what it was that had warranted such profanity. Two men in black robes were rolling Boyd's damaged motorbike along the driveway. It seemed that the Disciples were intent on hiding all traces of him being here. He automatically moved a hand to where his pistol was supposed to be holstered; its familiar shape was not there. *That's no surprise*, he thought and turned from the window.

"Okay, Rachel, if we're gonna survive tonight you're going to have to listen to me carefully and be very brave. Okay?"

Rachel nodded meekly.

"There were two men here earlier, nasty pieces of work – we need to get out before they or anybody else gets back."

Almost as soon as he had said this, there was the sound of footsteps from the corridor below. They both turned towards the main staircase that connected the attic to the second floor. Boyd's survival instincts were working overtime.

"Quick, go and stand there." He motioned to a dark corner, and Rachel ran to it. Boyd collected the rope that he had been tied up with. He caught sight of an old, disused water tank lying beside the current one; attached to it was a length of lead pipe. He briskly walked over to it and with a few deft twists, removed the pipe from the tank. The footsteps below were much closer now and definitely heading in their direction. Boyd gave the length of pipe to Rachel as she stood in the shadows. "Use this when you get the chance," he told her.

"When … how?" she asked desperately.

"When you get the chance, you'll know what to do!" he assured her with a wink, and she nodded.

Boyd quickly lay back down on the hard iron bed and arranged the rope around his hands and feet again to give the impression that he was still tied up. A spell of brilliant moonlight spilt in through the windows and added to the illumination from the dim bulb.

There was a click followed by a creak as the door at the foot of the staircase was opened. Heavy footsteps echoed on each wooden step until the ascent was complete, and the Pharmacist was in the attic. He walked towards the bed. Lying on his back, Boyd was unable to see who was coming, so he listened carefully instead to each clunking footfall and the sound of deep, slow breathing that accompanied it. Through partially closed eyes, he could vaguely see Rachel crouched in the corner, clutching the makeshift weapon he had given to her. She looked afraid; he wanted to give her a quick nod, or some other sign for reassurance; he couldn't, the figure that had entered the attic was almost upon him. He lay still; his eyes were slits, just wide enough to see the outline of whoever was approaching without giving the game away. This time *he* would spring the surprise.

Clouds slipped in front of the moon again, and the feeble light bulb barely illuminated the scene. Boyd heard the new arrival come to a halt at the foot of his bed; then he saw him for the first time, a tall man who was unlikely to be either of the two that had been harassing him earlier. This fellow was a little taller than the big, curly-haired Glaswegian, far slimmer, and more athletically built.

Boyd carefully watched the man, intrigued by his strange dress. He was draped from head to toe in long, black robes, heavier than those worn by the two who were here previously. It was the mask that made this Disciple's appearance particularly terrifying; a long piece of rectangular leather hanging in front of the face, tied around the circumference of the head with a strap. Boyd glimpsed grey eyes looking out through two large holes bordered by rings of silver metal. Above this mask, Boyd could see the man's white hair, neatly cut and combed backwards. Confronted by this menacing individual, Boyd had to quell the mild panic that arose within him. *What is going on in this house? Who on earth is under the mask? Will I be able to overcome this mysterious adversary? He looks like a big guy.* He had been in tight situations many times before and knew fear was a healthy response when faced with a threat as blatant as this.

The Pharmacist reached into his robes and produced a black leather case with a zip; it was the size of a large wallet. Boyd diverted his attention for a split second to look at Rachel and make sure she was ready; she remained in the corner, crouching, with both hands tightly clutching the lead pipe. He could also see that she was holding some sort of jewellery, maybe a necklace. *She's got to do it*, he thought; he was relying on her.

The masked Pharmacist unzipped his case and retrieved an item from it that Boyd initially thought was a pen. Closer observation revealed it to be a syringe; a surge of adrenalin accompanied this realisation. Light reflected off the device's glass body and flashed across its long protruding needle. The masked man carefully regarded the tip as he gently squeezed the plunger, releasing a jet of fluid. Boyd considered attacking him now; he was still standing at the foot of the bed, too far away for an effective strike. Boyd decided to wait. Satisfied with his preparation, the Pharmacist walked to Boyd's side and lowered the syringe to his already exposed left forearm; just before the needle touched his skin, Boyd exploded into action. His right arm flicked out of the loose rope and knocked the syringe to the floor; the mask may have covered the face, it could not, however, hide the astonishment in those eyes, something that Boyd savoured. Now he had to press home the advantage. He swung his leg around, aiming it at the robed man's kidneys, making good contact. The kick would have bowled anyone over; the Pharmacist just staggered sideways a few steps. Boyd was dismayed that his adversary had felt so solid against his foot. He got off the bed quickly and stood up, aiming a kidney punch at the same spot; before his fist landed, a hand chopped at the side of his neck, jolting his entire body so that he only hit air. The Pharmacist's strength and speed had caught him off guard. The Disciple grabbed Boyd's shoulders in an attempt to grapple him onto the metal bed frame. Boyd wrestled to release himself from this grip; it was like trying to escape from a vice, and he was slowly pushed backwards. Using his body weight to keep Boyd pinned down, the Pharmacist reached into his robes and pulled out a long dagger. With one arm pressing Boyd against the bed, he stood up straight, ready to plunge the weapon. There was a blur of movement behind the masked man, then a thump. The Pharmacist's head rocked forward violently, the dagger clattered on to the floorboards, and Boyd rolled sideways as his would-be killer fell onto the metal bed. No longer was it a terrifying Disciple of Disorder that was standing before him, only a petite dark-haired girl, panting fiercely, with her lead pipe ready for another strike. Before he could congratulate Rachel on a job well done, Boyd was instead shocked to hear movement and moaning from his downed adversary on the bed beside him; a blow like that should have killed a man, or at least caused unconsciousness. *Tough bastard*, thought Boyd. He turned around in time to see the Pharmacist attempting to get back onto his feet and looped the rope that still hung loosely around his wrists twice around his neck before pulling on the ends, choking him. The Pharmacist grabbed at the rope, attempting to ease it away from his neck; Boyd pulled tighter. The masked man started to slide from the bed and onto the floor; he was making a strange sound and his body rocked up and down. Boyd thought he was witnessing his death throes; he soon realised, to his horror, that it was actually choked laughter. The Pharmacist fell silent suddenly, and then, with a cry, he stood up. Boyd, caught by surprise, was thrown backwards; he managed to keep his grip on the rope. Rachel, still holding the lead pipe, was frozen with fear and unable to get a clean swing as the two combatants were struggling so closely now. The Disciple was tall, well over six feet; Boyd, hanging on to the rope, was lifted off the ground. He was swung to either side and did not dare to let go. Almost a minute later, the Pharmacist, weakened, started to stagger and slowly collapsed to his knees. Boyd gritted his teeth; muscles and veins bulged on either side of his broad neck, and his face took on an inhuman visage as he used whatever strength remained in him to garrotte his opponent. The Pharmacist slumped forwards, his head hit the ground with a crack, he twitched violently for a few seconds and then lay still with Boyd straddling him. The victor cautiously released his grip on the two ends of rope in his hands; the vanquished did not move. Breathing heavily from the exertion of his struggle, Boyd turned to look at Rachel, and she gave him a feeble smile which barely hid her terror.

"Thanks," he said, and Rachel just nodded.

"Are you okay?" he asked, concerned about the effect of the violence she had just witnessed.

"I'm fine," replied Rachel.

"That was one hard bastard; let's see who he was." Boyd rolled the dead body onto its back and pulled the mask off. The face was contorted in its final death throes. Lying in front of him was an older man with rather distinguished features. He had thick, white hair that receded at the temples and remained neatly brushed back over the scalp despite the mêlée. Boyd baulked at the thought of what the outcome would have been had he fought this man in his prime.

Rachel took a few steps towards the body and gasped at the wide open and bloodshot eyes that stared back at her. Boyd sensed it was not purely the shock of seeing the corpse that was responsible for her surprise.

"Have you seen him before?" he asked.

"Yes, he was a friend of my foster father's; some sort of business acquaintance, a very important man if I remember correctly."

"Mr Devilliers has friends in high places," said Boyd.

"Well, I've got a few friends too, and with any luck they're on their way," he added under his breath. He looked from the dead man to Rachel. "What's that in your hand?" he asked, pointing to the amulet dangling between her fingers.

"I don't know; something Martin gave to me."

"Do you mind?"

"No, not at all."

Boyd took the amulet; it was an amber sphere, its surface carved with runes, and a black metal skull was embedded at its very centre.

"By the Grimoires, you have a Qrwshan. We may stand a chance yet! Where did Martin get this from?"

"I don't know."

Boyd returned the amulet to Rachel.

"What shall we do?" she asked.

Her question was met with a frown. Boyd silently considered the situation. There was significant danger in heading outdoors, there would be search parties out looking for Rachel; therefore, it seemed that the safest place to be was somewhere in this house. He decided the best thing to do was to find a place where the girl could hide while he tried his utmost to sabotage the plans Edward Devilliers had made for tonight, and do whatever damage he could until Johnny and company arrived … if they arrived.

He explained his plan to Rachel, only hinting that he had friends on the outside that might be able to help. He did not want the girl to be in a situation where she knew too much information; information which she could potentially be forced to divulge. Rachel was in agreement with what he proposed; having run out of options, she would have agreed with any plan that might give them a chance of surviving this night.

Boyd gestured at the robed figure on the attic floor, "Let's get out of here before this lad's friends turn up." His attention shifted back to Rachel, "Show me a place we can hide you, preferably somewhere you can escape from quickly should the need arise." He gave Rachel some time to think of a suitable place.

"We can go back the way I came in, to the old coal cellar. It's a pretty horrid place. I'm sure nobody will find me inside it. We can pile up some of the junk so I could use it to climb out through the window again if I have to." Rachel suggested.

"Can we get there easily?"

"Yeah – I mean, that's how I got here."

"Sounds good – let's go."

She started to walk.

"Wait! Just a few things to do before we leave our friend," Boyd said, returning to the body of the Pharmacist. He fumbled amongst the dead man's robes and found a bunch of keys in various sizes secreted amongst the folds of voluminous black material. Crouched over the body, he saw the long ceremonial dagger and syringe lying on the floor. The glass of the syringe was broken and its fluid spilled, he ignored it and took the dagger which remained in his hand. The keys went into one of the many zipped pockets of his motorcycle leathers. Boyd noticed that Rachel had left the lead pipe in the corner where she had been hiding; he picked it up and held it out towards her.

"Don't leave this; I thought you were pretty good with it." He offered her back the makeshift weapon.

"Thanks." She took it from him for the second time.

"Have you seen any more masked freaks?" Boyd asked before they left the attic.

"No, I'm quite sure they're around though," Rachel replied. "Judging by the cars I saw in the nearby field, I think there are a lot more."

"Where are they all now?"

"I would say they are wherever the doors lead to."

"What doors?"

"My foster father is a strange man; there are doors throughout this property and its land. There is at least one in this house; there are others in the outbuildings and some in the fields around the house which are more like trapdoors. All of them are locked and kind-of hidden, but not totally, if you know what I mean. I don't think he is really concerned about us knowing about them, we certainly can't go through them. I have seen my foster father use them many times, and other people too. I see strange cars in our driveway and people in the fields at all hours of the night, and yet, the house seems to be empty; it never made any sense."

Boyd thoughtfully scratched the stubble on his chin, "I'm still wondering what all this has got to do with you, Rachel?" he asked.

"I don't know, Martin told me if I stayed then I was in big trouble. My foster mother is part of all this too; she brought me this ridiculous outfit to wear." Her hand swept disdainfully over the front of the dress.

"She's Martin's sister, isn't she? Elizabeth Devilliers."

"Yes."

"As soon as we hide you in the cellar, you must tell me where these secret doors are. I need to find that foster father of yours and his friends. Okay! Let's move! I'll go ahead just in case there's any danger; you follow close behind and tell me where to go."

Under the teenager's instructions, Boyd hastily led the way out of the attic. They moved through the hatch by which the girl had entered earlier and into the box room on the topmost floor. He turned every corner ready to thrust the long knife into any would-be attacker, determined to keep the girl safe. There was still the entire empty wing of the house to negotiate before they reached their objective in the disused coal cellar. They did not know it, but deep underground the summoning of Orbok had begun, and already, unspeakable entities from the realms of Disorder were materialising around them.

Chapter 32

Having successfully warped himself and Baccharus through space–time, Johnny was about to enter the moto-rhome again, eager to be reunited with the friends he had so grudgingly left behind. He gripped the door handle; sensing trouble on the other side, he paused suddenly.

"Baccharus, stay back," he whispered.

"What's going on?" the familiar asked.

"Quiet now! Just stay back."

Baccharus drifted away from the vehicle.

"Sascha! Boyd! It's Johnny and Bach, we're coming in!" Johnny thought it wise to not only project a shield but also announce his arrival before entering; it turned out to be a good move. On hearing the door unlock, he slowly opened it to see his oldest friend clumsily aiming Boyd's heavy revolver straight at him. Johnny had psychically pre-empted danger; he had not, however, expected to see Sascha sitting there, ready to blow the head off whoever walked in. There was a split-second standoff.

"Johnny! Bach! I didn't think you guys were going to make it back! I mean, what the hell kept you?!" exclaimed Sascha in a release of pent-up anxiety. A beaming smile had replaced his frown, and he lunged at his two friends with a welcoming embrace. Sascha explained that his equipment had picked up colossal psychic energy fluctuations, making him nervous enough to pick up the gun. Realising what had happened, Johnny described the space–time warp he had initiated and apologised for not thinking about the alarm its energy field would have caused. There was an excited exchange between the three friends, and Baccharus started to recount the events in the valley for Sascha's benefit.

The crew together again, thought Johnny. "So, where's Boyd?" he asked, interrupting the energetic chatter, half expecting the errant Irishman to appear from the bathroom or the pile of bedding on one of the bunks.

Sascha looked grave and shook his head. "He went off, Johnny. You know Boyd; he was getting edgy and restless. He reckoned he would go and scout around … he's not back yet, and if I told you I wasn't concerned, I would be lying."

"How long has he been gone?" Johnny asked.

"Over an hour … it's too long," was the deflated reply. It was followed by silence.

"Damn! He should have waited!" Baccharus said eventually.

"Boyd can look after himself; I bet he's giving those Disciples hell already!" Johnny said, putting a more positive spin on their friend's absence; it brought a smile to everybody's face. "He'll find a way to catch up. We, on the other hand, have got to get moving," he added, and there was a sense of finality in his words.

"Is it time to confront them?" Sascha asked nervously; Baccharus turned to look at Johnny expectantly. All they got was a nod; it was enough – the order to go over the top.

"I'll fire her up then," said Sascha, taking the driver's seat. Johnny settled into the front passenger seat, and Baccharus perched himself beside his headrest as the diesel rumbled into life for the last time before they faced the Disciples of Disorder. The friends set off.

Johnny listened as Sascha told him about how he and Boyd had been studying maps of the region together; it was reassuring to know that at least one of them had a good working knowledge of the local routes. Sascha went on to explain that after Boyd left, all he could do was work on his Disruptor device to keep himself from worrying excessively.

As his friend talked away, Johnny remained quiet, contemplating the task ahead; this didn't last for long though, because Sascha wanted some answers. "Baccharus told me a little about what happened out there, Johnny," he started, referring to the meeting with Theodora, "he said only you could explain the events."

Johnny considered his response, "It was the next stage, Sascha; the next stage of a journey I originally started with you."

Johnny went on to recount his experiences with the old woman. First, he narrated the story of the Earth witches and the summoning of Orbok, and then he went on to describe his personal journey of psychic realisation. Baccharus was quick to add in odd details that Johnny neglected to mention. Sascha listened in wonder; he did not say a word until Johnny had finished, at which point there was no restraining his enthusiasm.

"So now you can use your will to manipulate matter on a larger scale than ever before, that's great! Propelling yourself within a wave of warped space–time … wow! That's all so amazing! Who knows what else you could be capable of?!"

"You're right, Sascha, I can do more now than ever before, although there is a limit to what can be accomplished. The whole art of psychic manipulation works on the visualisation of what you want to achieve. If you cannot create the task in your own mind with some degree of accuracy, then you cannot perform it. I mean, look at now for example, that's why we're driving. I can't just warp us to somewhere I have never seen, or been, before because I can't visualise the destination. Another problem is that I'm still pretty raw. It takes unwavering concentration to perform complex feats, and that, believe me, is pretty exhausting."

"So from what you're saying, I suppose it will be a few years before you really get to grips with your new skills?"

"It might be more than that; to be honest, I don't know."

"Well, let's hope you've got enough in you to sort out these Disciples before the Demon King himself appears."

"Thanks for the reminder!" said Baccharus.

It was a sobering thought; the possibility of confronting a major demon from the worlds of Disorder. It negated the good news of Johnny's enhanced abilities. As ever, the moment of elation that had dared to present itself was promptly cut short by the reality of their situation. They drove on.

Chapter 33

"Are you sure there's nobody around?" Boyd whispered tensely.

"I was here just before I found you, and it was definitely empty," Rachel replied.

The pair stood in a small corridor, outside the box room, on the very highest floor of Edward Devilliers' house. The absence of any outside windows in the narrow passage meant it was very dark. All things considered, it did feel safer here.

The pervasive silence exaggerated every sound they made as they descended the small staircase to the floor below and yet another corridor. They were in the house proper now, albeit the unlived-in part; the scale of everything here was far grander and its appearance more elegant than anything on the top floor, which lay largely within the loft space.

At the opposite end of this longer corridor was an enormous panelled window through which the moon was visible; its light spilled into the house and lit their way. They hurried to the stately wooden staircase beneath that window and continued their descent to the cellar. As they made their way, Boyd noticed the effects of disrepair on the interior. The walls were a patchwork of mildew and peeling paper that in parts exposed the underlying plaster, and the electric lights that were mounted along either side of them had dusty, cobwebbed silk shades. The floor here was covered with a worn, damp carpet that ran along its entire length and was probably the main source of the musty smell that hung in the air.

They passed eight doors, four in each wall, before reaching the next staircase. Just as they were about to take the steps down to the next level, they froze suddenly. There was what sounded like a voice from behind one of the closed doors they had passed; it was very faint. They listened apprehensively. It took a few more seconds before they could work out what it was repeating. "Boyd!" it called, "Boyd!" There was something unwholesome about the muffled, high-pitched speech.

Rachel looked fearfully at her new companion while he carefully eyed the doors, attempting to locate the strange voice that repeated his name. Eventually, his gaze fixed on the second door in the wall to their left, and he started to move towards it; a small hand grabbed his forearm. He turned around to face Rachel.

"Boyd, don't go there," she implored, almost at the point of tears.

"It might be something important, I have friends who are on their way," he tried to reassure her. "They may be sending me a message; no one else knows my name around here, honey. It's okay, I need to investigate this."

He gently pulled himself away from Rachel's tight grip and walked over to the voice. He stopped outside the door and after making sure the girl was out of harm's way, gripped the round knob and eased it open slowly whilst holding the Pharmacist's long knife in front of him; there was no ambush, only the voice. With the door ajar, its pitch was noticeably higher and it had an odd clicking quality as it eerily, hypnotically repeated his name. Boyd let the door swing fully open, revealing a bedroom that was lit by pale moon glow from a curtain-less bay window in the far wall. Keeping a safe distance, Rachel also looked inside over his broad shoulder. The smell in here was striking: the mustiness that permeated the rest of the house combined with the stink of rotten meat. Ignoring it, Boyd scanned the room. Everything here was covered in a white powdery mess, a result of ceiling plaster which had crumbled in some parts and come away entirely in others. He looked past the antique dresser and cabinet in the corner until his eyes fixed upon the ornate four-poster bed that extended from the far wall to the very centre of this chamber. He was drawn to it, not because of its great size or meticulously carved bedposts, but because of the large moving bulge that lay beneath its covers; the source of the voice.

Boyd edged further into the room; dagger ready, he moved to the bed. The closer he got, the quicker his name was repeated. By the time he was only a few feet away, the voice was manic. He was mesmerised by the odd chant; without his knowledge, Rachel had slipped into the room behind him. "Let's get out of here, Boyd!" she begged, vainly attempting to drag him out by the arm, glancing fearfully at the movement in the bed. Boyd pulled himself away from her without even bothering to look back. There was a hypnotic quality about the chant which seemed to be directed, for whatever sinister purpose, towards him; he could not help being drawn to the strange bulge in the bed. Rachel was pulling at his shirt, tearfully begging him to leave the room. All Boyd could hear was the voice; he was under a spell. When he was close enough, he reached over to draw back the heavy bedding; sensing the worst, Rachel slowly backed away. Boyd had only moved the blankets a few inches before the rest were thrown off and sent hurtling across the room, revealing the hideous living form that lay beneath them. Before he could take any further action, he was grabbed by a grotesque limb, one of many. Rachel screamed; all previous attempts at remaining discreet inside this house were forgotten in the terror of the moment.

Boyd snapped out of his trance, only to realise the full magnitude of the horror that now had him. What lay beneath the sheets was a twisted mockery of the human form. The creature was made up of the bulging central torso of an obese man covered in folds of quivering flesh and hideously misplaced sphincteral orifices spewing mucous and ichor. At the very centre of this foul body, where the umbilicus should have been located, there was instead a large, fleshy-lipped mouth; the origin of the voice that had lured Boyd. The thing had no head, and from around its torso there sprouted six warped limbs; human legs that ended in wiry clutching hands where the feet should have been, and each of these disgusting extremities was speckled with outgrowths of fingers and matted hair.

Boyd, his arms held tightly by long, misshapen fingers, tried to pull himself away from the monstrosity. He jerked his entire body backwards by planting his feet firmly against the edge of the bed; it made no difference. Courageously, Rachel wrapped her arms around his waist and used her slight body to try to tug him away; despite Boyd's straining muscles and Rachel's concerted efforts, they could not loosen the creature's grip, it held on with inhuman strength. What they grappled with was the earthly manifestation of a beast that originated in a world light years from planet Earth. Following its accidental passage through the wormhole, it had hastily altered its chameleon body into a form that might give it a chance of survival in this world; the result was a modified approximation of the human body – the abomination that now lay before them.

More deformed limbs flicked out to grip Boyd with huge fingers, and the orifices continued spouting pungent secretions that scalded the skin on contact. "Get back, Rachel!" Boyd roared as his legs were swept out from beneath him. He now hung upside down with each of his own four limbs under the control of the creature. The dangling man was drawn closer to the torso and the hideously positioned umbilical mouth. Bulbous lips curled back into a snarl, revealing rows of sharp teeth and a large wet tongue that flopped out to one side. The creature no longer repeated Boyd's name; instead, it produced a disturbing gurgle interspersed with high-pitched screams that pained the eardrums.

Desperate to help, Rachel lifted the length of lead piping high and edged forwards, ready to strike the beast. She was almost in range for a swing when Boyd shouted at her to stay away; he had experienced first-hand the brutal strength of this otherworldly creature and did not want Rachel in its grip also. She swung anyway and missed; the remaining limbs that were not holding Boyd grabbed at her, and she just about managed to retreat to a corner of the room out of their range.

"Stay there!" Boyd ordered.

She could only watch as her last hope for surviving this night struggled for his life. The monster continued to coax Boyd towards its terrible mouth, and he resisted with all his might. In his right hand, he still held the long, silver dagger. The creature was either unfamiliar with, or unconcerned about, the danger this weapon posed; it was impossible to say.

As he grappled, Boyd formulated a plan; he eased his

resistance and allowed his body, still held above the bed, to go limp. The creature, sensing its prey was no longer fighting, brought him to its gaping maw with great relish. Boyd was soon close enough to feel the pungent breath of the beast against his cheek and see the pustules around its open mouth. Just when it appeared that he might have a bite taken out of his face, he whipped his right arm free of the beast's grip with a sudden snapping motion, and in that same blur of movement, he brought the knife down hard into the mouth, impaling the creature's flabby tongue against the back of its throat. An unearthly shriek, high-pitched and terrifying, filled the room as a mixture of blood and what looked like pus spurted out from the injury. He felt the grip on his left wrist weaken, and with the same sudden snapping motion, he managed to free it too. With both hands, he withdrew the long ceremonial dagger and brought it down in a series of quick, desperate stabs all over the bloated torso beneath him. He managed to do this three times before the creature, still holding him by the legs, flung him away against one of the walls.

He landed on the floor, winded. The room filled with more blood-curdling wails from the monstrosity. The same thick mixture of bloody pus that had gushed from the mouth wound now oozed from each of the new penetrating injuries he had inflicted. *Surely, the beast must die now,* he hoped. He did not intend on hanging around long enough to find out. Still winded, he picked himself up off the floor and ran for the door. Rachel was standing nearby, open-mouthed and transfixed by the horror of what she had witnessed; he scooped her up by the waist on the way out. Using his free arm, he slammed the door shut behind him. Just before he left the room, and out of the corner of his eye, Boyd managed to see the creature raise itself shakily onto its six deformed limbs.

In the musty corridor, he put Rachel down and dragged her by an arm back towards the staircase; she stumbled and fell but was able to get back onto her feet again without any help. The inhuman shrieks from beyond the door and the thumping of heavy limbs against the floor would let neither Boyd nor Rachel forget the evil of what they had just seen. There was a loud banging, Boyd turned around; the creature was trying to leave the room. Every contact it made with the closed door resulted in an inexplicable blue flash around its edge. Puzzled by this phenomenon and far too afraid to find out what it was, he dashed breathlessly with Rachel to the staircase. Their tribulations, however, had not ended; more voices started to call from behind other closed doors, from this floor and also from the ones below. This time, they beckoned Rachel along with Boyd. Some of these doors even started to demonstrate the strange flash of blue light. Things were looking very bad; Boyd had no doubt that more alien beings dwelled in these other closed rooms, and if *they* did not get them, there was every possibility that the noise would draw the unwanted attention of the house's other equally undesirable inhabitants, the Disciples of Disorder.

Boyd's faith allowed him to keep his wits about him, and he even found a few words of encouragement for the girl as they made their way down the broad, wooden staircase to the next level. Just like the floor above, there were voices from behind the doors; fortunately, on this level there was no need for them to cross the corridor – the next set of stairs lay directly beneath the previous one. They were grateful for this small mercy.

Muttering memorised wards of protection from the First Grimoire, he ushered Rachel down. As they descended, he caught sight of movement at the far end of the corridor; a giant oily shape like a massive slug, bigger than a man, was very slowly edging towards them across the floor, moonlight reflecting off its slick body. He turned to look at Rachel; the girl had not yet seen this new horror so he hastened their descent to the ground floor.

The pair found themselves in another of the house's stately corridors. Wide and high-ceilinged, this one was the longest so far; just like its parallels on the upper floors, there were rows of doors along it on either side; thankfully, there were no voices.

"Which way to the coal cellar, Rachel?" Boyd asked, panting. She pointed to a nearby passage; it lay within the shadows and led off towards the right. They both hurried to it. Boyd was hoping they would find a few moments to regroup and muster their strength once they were in the abandoned cellar. Even though he had never seen it, it had taken on a mythic quality: a haven of safety, deep in enemy territory, a place to reach at all costs, a place of sanity in this madhouse. In truth, it was only an objective, something to focus the efforts of the mind upon. Focus the mind or lose it; that was the stark choice they faced in here.

The malformed creature trapped in the bedroom by Disciple trickery was only one example of the myriad demons that had slipped through the gateway opened by Edward Devilliers' underground ceremony. It was only a matter of luck that Boyd and Rachel had not opened any more doors or encountered more vile beings on their way to the coal cellar – luck that would soon run out.

Chapter 34

Branches from roadside trees thumped against the sides of the speeding motorhome. The vehicle was almost too big for the narrow lanes surrounding the Devilliers' mansion; this did not deter Sascha from driving extremely fast. The engine roared as he shifted up through the gears. The road was still damp from an earlier spell of light rainfall, and on more than one occasion, Johnny's heart leapt as he felt the vehicle slide through another of the tight bends. Even his recently enhanced psychic ability could not predict which way the erratic motorhome would swing next; he did not complain, they were in a hurry, and he had full faith in his friend's road-craft. Baccharus hovered just behind Sascha, one little hand anchoring his floating body to the driver's headrest so that his airborne form would not end up in the rear of the vehicle. The cherub was acting as an extra pair of eyes, desperately calling out instructions which were duly acted upon: "Slow down!" or, "Speed the heck up, man!" or, "Start turning now, for the sake of all that's good!" His direction was interspersed with warnings about oncoming obstacles he was convinced Sascha was about to drive into.

From his passenger seat, it looked like the inside of a rally car to Johnny, driver and co-driver giving it their all to win the race. Sascha followed Baccharus's frantic instructions to the letter, and Johnny could see that this had prevented a collision on more than one occasion. He glanced at the satellite navigation screen; even though Sascha had studied the maps and recognised many of the landmarks en route, there would be no room left for human error tonight.

"We're nearly there," declared Johnny; they were about twenty minutes into the drive.

"Better slow down then, Sasch!" suggested Baccharus, tired of being thrown around the interior of the speeding vehicle. Sascha eased off the accelerator until the motor-home was cruising slowly at the sedate pace for which it was designed.

The route appeared narrower and more twisting now than at any other point in the journey, and except for the occasional, distant mountain peak, Johnny could not see anything beyond the woodland on either side of the road. What he wanted was to have a look, right into the heart of the enemy; so, as Sascha drove, he meditated on Theodora's words, and he reached out further with his mind's eye. His senses were overloaded with the aberrant psychic energy that had drawn them here to the Highlands in the first place; with a supreme effort he saw through this confusion, to the portal and then to the cancerous wormhole within it. There he caught an instantaneous glimpse of the realm to which it was connected, a place of fire and abstract symmetry; one of the chaos worlds of Disorder, the source of all the bad energy presently around them. It was from here that beings like the blue-skins had been brought via the wormhole. It was their passage that had caused the short-lived energy peaks that first drew the attention of the Council; tonight, it was going to be impossible to hide the enormous amount of power being unleashed – the wormhole was fully active and awaiting the passage of Orbok, Demon King.

Johnny altered the focus of his psychic perception to detect the individual auras from dozens of Disciples within the house itself, both human and demon. Their numbers worried him. There were also other disturbing and malevolent presences he could sense from within those damned walls; the picture in his mind was not clear enough to discern their exact nature. Unknowingly, he had detected the vile aliens from the worlds of Disorder that had accidentally passed through the open portal this evening.

Baccharus noticed the concentration on Johnny's face. "What do you sense?" he asked his keeper gently. Unlike Johnny, the familiar was not able to feel any living auras from the house at this range; his psychic capability, effective though it was, could not come close to that of Johnny's and even if it did, it would take something really special to see through the confusing haze of ambient aberrant energy.

Johnny's perception returned abruptly to the world of five senses although he spoke as if his mind was elsewhere, and his eyes looked at nothing in particular. "So many psychic signatures, and all of them followers of Disorder," he said finally, speaking quietly, more to himself than Baccharus; the familiar heard him.

"A lot of them, huh? Well, you know what? When you take all those guys out, it will make our victory taste that much sweeter!" said the cherub nodding away confidently, once again demonstrating a familiar's unshakeable faith in its keeper. Johnny smiled at the display of bravura; it was impossible not to. The motorhome decelerated to a walking pace.

"I think we're as close as we can get to the Devilliers' mansion without giving ourselves away so look for a place to stop," Sascha said. A few minutes of painstakingly gradual progress brought the vehicle to a section of roadside which was devoid of trees and hedges and just about wide enough to drive onto; everyone agreed that it was as good a place as any to stop. Sascha turned off the road to park; the motorhome bounced up and down on its suspension, rocking the friends inside it gently back and forth. There was an instant when the wheels spun freely, churning up the soil, and it looked like they had grounded themselves, until their faithful transport lurched forward and was free once more. It was a good spot; the vehicle appeared to be adequately concealed amongst the surrounding woodland. Baccharus proclaimed it to be a positive sign for what lay ahead. The friends unbuckled themselves from their seats and prepared to enter the enemy stronghold. So near to the Disciples now, Johnny depended more than ever on the Qrwshan amulet Boyd had left for them.

Neither Johnny nor Baccharus had to do much to ready themselves. Johnny considered taking the hatchet and chainsaw they had brought from the hangar, only to decide, several minutes later that he was better off relying solely on his innate, newly improved, psychic ability; anything else would be a distraction – psychic combat was all about concentration. One item he would not be without though was his trench coat: not only did it keep him warm and waterproof, it also provided useful camouflage on nights like this; more than that, it was a charm that had seen him through numerous scrapes and without it he felt naked. He put it on after changing into the dark outdoor clothing he had brought along.

"Your turn!" said Johnny to Sascha, for whom preparation was a more complex affair, mostly because he was not psychic. As Sascha dressed up in his own layers of dark clothing, he gave Johnny careful instructions on selecting gadgets from his rucksack to perform final checks on. For a few moments, the motorhome was alive with flashing LEDs and the noise of twittering electrics. When this job was done, Johnny took a step back; he asked his friend if he was ready, Sascha shook his head, and looking rather reluctant, he commenced a search through Boyd's bag.

"I feel like a trespasser," he said as he did this.

"Do what you have to," Johnny replied.

Sascha seemed to know what he was after; he eventually located some rounds for the revolver and then distributed the ammunition amongst his many pockets. "That crazy bastard must have felt bad about leaving me defenceless. He left his gun and showed me how to use it too; can you believe it!? I didn't even realise he was going to disappear at the time!" Sascha said. He was about to close the bag when a wooden box from within it caught Johnny's eye. He stood up, took it out and opened it. Inside were smooth stones, each one wrapped in muslin.

"Psychic grenades! If I remember correctly – I think that's what Boyd called them," exclaimed Sascha.

Johnny remembered seeing Boyd use these powerful artefacts earlier in the hangar. He passed them over to his companion who carefully placed as many as he could into the deep side pockets of his trousers and jacket.

Finally, hesitantly, Sascha picked up the revolver from the table; he held it away from his body as if it was dirty. Johnny noticed.

"You comfortable with that thing?" he asked.

"No," replied Sascha, fixing the gun with an intense stare.

"Good," replied Johnny. "That's the best way to be with those."

"Well, it's either this or the chainsaw. Do you think I should take it?" Sascha asked without taking his eyes off the weapon.

"Hell, yes!" Johnny replied.

Sascha looked at his friend; there was a wicked smile on Johnny's face, but he meant what he said.

"I guess if there are too many of them then we will need all the help we can get," Sascha said, rationalising the need to take this lethal weapon.

"Baccharus and I have got our psychic powers; you, on the other hand, are going in as a man with only his wits and courage about him. You know I would prefer it if you stayed behind, old friend. I also know that abandoning companions is not in your nature. Keep the gun, and blow the brains out of anything that comes near you in that house."

The decision was made. Sascha slipped the weapon into a large buttoned pocket on the inside of the jacket he wore and finished his preparation by securing any loose zips and catches on his clothing.

They were ready sooner than anticipated.

"A strong coffee before we head off might be helpful …" ventured Sascha.

"Yes, please!" replied Baccharus.

"Hmm, good idea," added Johnny.

Minutes later, it was time to leave the motorhome. The vehicle had been their cocoon. To step out of it was to vacate a place of safety and it wasn't easy. Johnny led the way, Baccharus followed while Sascha, who came last, locked up.

The fresh, crisp night air was filled with the rich aroma of damp bark and leaf litter; it had a reviving effect on Johnny, and any fatigue was soon forgotten as adrenalin-fuelled anticipation took over. He felt a healthy fear, one that sharpened the senses; it was a fear of both the known and unknown.

"I reckon we're about seventy-five metres from the perimeter wall of the house," said Sascha, interrupting Johnny's thoughts.

They stayed close together as they made their way through the woodland. Johnny, who carried the Qrwshan amulet in his long coat, had stressed the importance to each of his companions of staying within a few metres' radius of it. The rain had ceased long ago and patches of silvery cloud cover remained overhead. There were enough evergreens around to ensure that it was dark beneath the canopy despite the shed autumn leaves. The team's progress through this environment was slow and difficult.

On nearing the house, Johnny's mind became clouded by the intense psychic activity from the building; it was the perceptual equivalent of hearing many musical pieces being played together at once. Ignoring the noise, he tried to reach out with his mind to detect Boyd's tune but could not; Boyd always said he was psychically blunt and diffi-cult to detect, so Johnny wasn't overly perturbed by this.

Pressing on through the woodland, the three soon reached the perimeter wall. They stood before the great brick obstacle with no idea about the existence of the iron gates within it. Sascha scratched his head as he considered how they were to cross into the garden; Johnny, not wanting to waste any time, placed his hand on his friend's shoulder. "Brace yourself," he said simply. Sascha gasped as an icy, tingling sensation emanating from Johnny's hand gripped his entire body. Johnny concentrated hard as the world around him fell out of focus. He lifted himself and Sascha off the ground without the aid of any discernible force; his surroundings appeared blurred. He managed to look down and see the top of the wall pass beneath him; it rip-pled as if it were a reflection in a pool of disturbed water.

Steadily, the ground on the other side, which also appeared fluid, came up to meet him, and as soon as it made contact with his feet everything returned to solid normality. Johnny stood there with his hand still on Sascha's shoulder.

It took Sascha a few moments, and a few double-takes, to realise that he had been transported by Johnny, over the wall, on a wave of distorted space–time. Johnny, anticipating that he was about to be barraged with questions, gave Sascha a look that told him now was not the time to ask. "I'll analyse this later," promised Sascha.

To Baccharus, the wall was never an obstacle, and he flew over it to meet his friends on the other side. All three looked warily around the large garden and the grand old country mansion at its centre.

There was one entity that had managed to remain hidden from Johnny's perception, its psychic signature lost amongst the torrent of aberrant energy; even without this cover, it would in all probability have remained undetectable, purely because its aura was so massive and so downright alien.

**

Hello! What is all this, then?

The Bar-Shiyq took less than a second to sense their vital signs. Heart rate, respiratory rate and surface electrical charge gave Johnny and his friends away as intruders.

The master has never invited them before. Hang on; is that a bird with them?

In all its years underground, with its network of hypersensitive limbs that stretched out for many metres through the soil under the garden, the creature known as the Bar-Shiyq had never been surprised; that was until tonight. These three had seemingly materialised out of thin air without so much as a vibration.

Oh well, that makes three unwelcome visitors … a veritable feast.

**

"Sascha, move!" screamed Johnny suddenly, he did not wait for his friend to respond and sent him tumbling sideways with a mighty shove. Sascha, still a little disorientated from the space–time manipulation, was taken aback by the violence; it was nothing compared with the shock he had when a thick, leathery tentacle burst out of the ground where he had just been standing.

"What the heck!" screamed Baccharus, instantly using his will to energise a psychic bolt; he held the glowing linear streak in his left hand like a javelin ready to be hurled.

"Be still!" warned Johnny, and they all froze. The leathery tentacle flicked from left to right, trying to locate its target, which in this case was Sascha. None of them moved. The groping limb closed in on Sascha as he lay on the ground, forcing him to roll away in an evasive manoeuvre which the creature detected and reacted to by suddenly sending three further tentacles bursting out of the ground around the unfortunate man. One wrapped itself around his waist, the other his leg, and the third had his arm. The tentacles immediately tried to yank his body underground; Baccharus had already unleashed his psychic bolt. The energy weapon sizzled through the air towards the tentacle around Sascha's waist, producing the scent of ozone as it homed in on its target. There was not much margin for error. The familiar's aim was true, and the bolt made direct contact with the terrible limb, burning it in a miniature explosion that smelled of charred, rotten flesh. Baccharus had to fire two more bolts in quick succession at the same section of tentacle to bisect it. Sascha continued to writhe and struggle against the remaining alien limbs which increased their pressure on his arm and leg.

Johnny tried desperately to reach his friend; more tentacles appeared in a shower of soil around him. He managed to psychically sense their approach and avoid them; he could see that time was running out for Sascha, who was being pulled into the ground.

"Fire at any new tentacle that emerges, Bach, before it gets anywhere near me!" Johnny cried, and the familiar duly redirected his psychic bolts, allowing Johnny to aid Sascha unimpeded.

Surrounded by giant flailing tentacles and with his familiar's energy bolts exploding around him, Johnny reached Sascha, and in each of his hands he grabbed one of the limbs that had wrapped themselves around his friend's arm and leg.

Maintaining a firm grip on the hideous appendages, he reached deep within his psyche to draw upon his newly awakened powers. In the obscure, dark regions of his sentience, he found concentrated psychic energy which he channelled through his hands, into the substance of the creature beneath the ground. On receiving this surge of energy through its tentacles, the beast felt true pain for the first time in thousands of years and released Sascha, who deftly rolled away, desperate to be beyond the reach of that crushing hold.

Johnny still held on, unleashing megawatts of energy into the creature, electrocuting it with the power output of an urban substation. The Bar-Shiyq tried to withdraw its two limbs that were in contact with the human, it could not; they were paralysed by the current rushing through them. Smoke started to waft from Johnny's hands, and the sickly smell of burning flesh and keratin from the creature gradually filled the air; and still, he would not let go.

More tentacle-limbs burst out from underground and thrashed wildly about Johnny; Baccharus prevented them from causing any real harm by continuing to fire his bolts. The Bar-Shiyq was desperate to attack its tormentors. The surface of the garden, with its lawns, plants and trees, started to undulate rhythmically; the whole landscape moved like a choppy sea of soil and vegetation. Johnny and his friends looked on, wondering how this could possibly be before realising with barely suppressed horror that the tentacles they now battled actually extended underground throughout the whole of this massive garden. What they had seen already was only the tip of the iceberg. Johnny considered whether each tentacle was some sort of living organism in its own right or whether they were all attached to some appalling body. His answer came in the shape of a large mound emerging from the ground about fifty metres away. It grew like a giant molehill before his very eyes, soil rolling off its sides as it steadily increased in size, reaching ten feet in height. His companions watched in terror as a deep growl, which Johnny could feel in his chest, emanated from the great heap. He had been about to release his grip on the tentacles; now, nothing was further from his mind.

Twitching movements from within the mound gradually dislodged more earth, revealing the form that lay beneath; a massive, quivering bell-shaped creature covered in folded, bulging layers of leathery hide. From the flared bottom edge of its bell-body emerged multiple thick tentacles like sinuous roots at the base of a tree; they disappeared into the ground to form the massive maze of subterranean limbs with which the creature detected and attacked its prey.

The surface of this alien organism was featureless except for a large mouth, with teeth like steak knives, positioned half way down one of its sides which it opened so wide it almost unfolded its body. The beast, terrible though it was, seemed to be in trouble; it made rumbling sounds interspersed with an occasional roar while smoke billowed from its body and tentacles.

Despite the urge to run from this awesome sight, Johnny continued instead to hold on. To release his grip on the tentacles now would be suicidal; the semi-paralysing effect of the psychic energy waves he was sending prevented the many lethal limbs from striking the three of them with their full force or even dragging them to that terrible mouth. Sascha helped Baccharus spot stray tentacles that might pose a threat to Johnny, and the familiar duly blasted them away with his bolts. Boyd's revolver was in Sascha's hands, ready to fire into the bell-shaped body should Johnny, who seemed to be just about in control of the situation, give the order; as it turned out, this was not going to be necessary.

"Take it easy, guys," Johnny said finally, when he felt the sustained psychic charge he was delivering overcome the creature. The once rapid motion of the tentacles slowed down into lethargic flops, and increasing amounts of smoke rose from the thing's hide, which had started to burn in some areas and bubble in others. The deep rumbling from the monster ceased, and its body started to quiver more rapidly than before. Johnny hated seeing suffering, even in something as cruel and terrifying as the Bar-Shiyq, so he sent a last, massive surge of power through his hands to devastating effect.

The entire mass of the beast, including its tentacles, began to spasm, uprooting trees and knocking over garden walls. There were small flames around the garden that originated from its burning skin and flesh. The Bar-Shiyq's existence finally ended when its bell-shaped body burst open with a sickening splash, filling the garden with wet chunks of flesh. The writhing tentacles became inanimate, and the whole garden lay still once more; the grounds around the house looked like they had been shelled.

Even a fool could tell that the operation, which had started covertly enough, had now lost any element of surprise. After all, there was little one could do to hide a fight with an extraterrestrial beast that was as large as a building.

Fifteen leather-suited Disciples had gathered at the edge of the garden, near to the house. The cultists had arrived on the scene following the disturbance, and they had wisely decided that crossing the grounds whilst the beast was still alive and churning up the lawn with its tentacles was going to be seriously hazardous. Despite this caution, two of them lay dead, unable to escape the wildly thrashing limbs of the tortured Bar-Shiyq. One of the deceased had a tentacle still wrapped around his body, and the other's neck was twisted at an impossible angle. Now that the creature had expired and the tentacles lay still, there was no need for the rest of the Disciples to hold back. Producing a collective barking sound, they charged at Johnny and his friends, brandishing pistols and knives, not really knowing who or what they were up against, and in their fanaticism, not really caring.

Johnny was wiping pieces of the Bar-Shiyq from his clothes when he heard Sascha's warning. "Get lively, boys! We've got company."

He looked up to see his friend crouching with Boyd's revolver in hand, the enemy was closing in. Sascha fired three shots, each one brought down a charging cultist. Sascha couldn't have missed – there were fifteen fanatics running straight at him; as long as he aimed in their general direction he was bound to hit. Some of the Disciples started shooting back in retaliation, running as they fired; they all missed. Johnny could see that it was not accuracy they hoped to achieve, only to overwhelm the three of them with their greater number.

"Go for it, Bach!" Johnny ordered, refusing to be intimidated, and his familiar was upon them in an instant, blasting away with psychic energy bolts as he flew around like a maddened bumblebee. Between the two of them, Baccharus and Sascha had dispatched half the enemy before they were even within twenty metres. Of the remaining cultists, three had automatic pistols, and they stopped mid-charge to aim them. Johnny saw two of them target Sascha while the third aimed towards the sky to exchange fire with Baccharus. Despite having little opportunity to recover from his recent exertions, Johnny was able to use his will to curve the trajectories of the enemy's bullets away from his companions.

Four of the Disciples did not have guns and continued their rapid advance with long-bladed knives drawn instead. They were getting dangerously close. Sascha was reloading. His unpractised hand fumbled with the bullets, dropping some in the process. The instant he completed the task and snapped shut the drum of the revolver, the first of the knife-wielding lunatics was almost on top of him. Seeing the danger, Johnny launched a tackle at the leather-clad enemy, reaching him before he could bring the knife down. The move sent them both sprawling to the ground, and before either one could get up, Sascha finished the job with two rounds. Johnny looked at his friend gratefully; Sascha appeared disturbed, and he knew why, it was the first time he had killed.

"You had no choice," Johnny said.

As Sascha agonised over his actions, a bullet grazed his arm, and he fell backwards, clutching his wound. The three remaining knifemen were closing in quickly. Johnny could see that he was not going to have enough time to do anything about them. At that moment there was a shower of glowing energy bolts. To aid his keeper, Baccharus had diverted his attack from the gunmen (one of whom he had already taken out with a head shot); in doing so, he had exposed himself to the enemy's fire which came at him thick and fast.

Johnny and his companions were very much on the defensive now and he didn't like it. Baccharus's intervention had bought a little time. *Enough!* he thought and stood up. Using his will, Johnny manipulated psychic energy into a broad wavefront of Presarium, creating a speeding arc of power aimed at his adversaries. The arc pushed a column of rushing air before it. The cultists became unsteady on their feet, and their hooded capes flapped in the psychic wind. A second later, the arc itself made contact. The first of the charging knifemen suddenly found his momentum reversed. No longer was he running towards Johnny and Sascha, he was instead hurled backwards twenty feet through the air. Before he even hit the ground, Johnny's Presarium wave had struck each of his fellow Disciples with the same devastating effect, lifting them up and hurling them away to land painfully on the lawn, winded and incapacitated. With its energy expended, the wavefront of psychic power dispersed. Except for the moans and groans of those who had been on its receiving end, the night was quiet once again.

"Look! They're not all human; some of them are blue-skins!" exclaimed the sharp-eyed Baccharus. Johnny and

Sascha went to investigate and saw that a few of the defeated Disciples were indeed the pale blue demon-men they had encountered in the night attack on the motor-home, helpers summoned by Edward Devilliers from the worlds of Disorder. As the three of them examined their felled opponents, one of the human Disciples, injured but still alive, managed to sneak away unseen back to the house.

"C'mon, guys, let's get going before their friends come along to join the party," Johnny said.

"Where to?" Baccharus asked.

"We go into the house, and then we find a way to go underground," Johnny replied, recalling the old woman Theodora's words about the location of the portal. "Baccharus, you go and keep a look out – silently as possible. Sascha, follow me."

Baccharus flew up high, an eye in the sky to guard against surprise attacks. Johnny and Sascha ran through the devastated garden towards the old mansion.

Chapter 35

Nude bodies writhed and gyrated in the vast under-ground cathedral to Disorder. The dance of the cultists produced the psychic energy required to activate the parasitic wormhole that linked the world of Orbok, Demon King, to Earth.

At the centre of this manic activity stood Edward Dev-illiers, his body steadily rocking back and forth, his eyes closed. His face was contorted and it resembled the hideous gargoyles that adorned the lectern from which he directed the night's proceedings. Beads of sweat dripped from his forehead and off the end of his nose onto the stone floor. His hands moved like a mime artist grappling with a great imaginary weight; doing this helped him manipulate the psychic energy generated by this most ancient of ceremonies. Occasional sparks of electrical charge leapt from his fingertips and were drawn through the air to be swallowed by the glowing purple centre of the portal. There were even a few particularly energetic moments when a continuous bolt of lightning arced from his body along that same route.

As the ceremony progressed, the steady feed of psychic energy generated by the Disciples of Disorder continued to power the hidden wormhole and alter the very character of the portal. Already, its flawless sparkling purple substance had taken on the form of a rotating vortex, one that became increasingly funnelled the quicker it turned; it was as if the purple matter was being shifted by centrifugal force. This was only the beginning of the transformation. The longer the ceremony went on, the faster the vortex rotated, until the funnel at its centre finally widened into a tunnel, the end of which was so far away that it seemed to terminate within the very centre of the planet. In fact, it reached much further than this, into an adjacent dimension. The glowing purple matter was now confined to the walls of this spinning tunnel, and its translucent substance was veined with forked lightning that danced, crackled and leapt across its centre – the portal was now altered completely, and the wormhole was active. Each of its rotations was accompanied by a deep and low-pitched noise, creating a pulse, the vibrations of which coursed through the whole underground cathedral complex.

Occasionally, a golden globe would come bursting through the wormhole, and it would fly through the walls and ceiling of the underground chamber. Each globe represented a living entity from the world of Orbok, the Demon King, unwittingly sucked through the altered portal in the form of pure energy. It travelled across dimensions in this excited state and would become solid living matter once more when it came to rest. The many rooms in the disused wing of the mansion house had been painstakingly prepared as cells to draw in these globes and contain the materialising beasts, while complex incantations guarded the doors. The system was not perfect, and there was every chance that demons would appear in corridors or even the gardens; hopefully, they would be the exceptions. The Disciples planned to round up all of these entities later and either nurture or dispose of them, depending on their usefulness.

Another flash of brilliant forked lightning arced from Edward Devilliers to the wormhole. The whole hall was now synchronised in its swaying and chanting; all present remained focused on the generation of psychic energy.

**

In a separate chamber, accessible via the large and ornate Gothic arch a few metres behind Edward Devilliers, was another group, removed from the events taking place in the main body of the cathedral. While the High Lord was engrossed in conducting the ceremony, the responsibility of directing cult affairs came down to this important gathering of Disciples. Amongst them was an old man with long white hair, swathed in leather ceremonial garments. He was accompanied by four of his initiates; caped youths whose faces were permanently hidden beneath voluminous cowls. Earlier on, they had all been active participants in the ancient rites of the ceremony to summon Orbok; now, they were required to take care of other matters.

Arkkun was an old and much trusted companion of Edward Devilliers, a business partner who had combined much of his financial interests with those of the High Lord's family many years ago. Impossibly old, his psychic ability and the secrets he had divined from the cult of Disorder allowed him to outlive a normal human life span. He was a dedicated servant of Disorder and had been one of the tutors to the child Edward and his father before him.

Not far from Arkkun stood a figure dressed in black; taller, broader and more terrifying than any other Disciple present tonight, possibly with the exception of Edward Devilliers. A fierce-looking beast covered in short, shiny black fur was crouched behind him. Arkkun, sinister and intimidating though he was in his own right, felt much safer giving Mr Kreb and his familiar a wide berth; he could sense that his initiates felt the same way. Like the rest of them, Kreb had been projecting his psychic energy to help power the wormhole, but Arkkun had requested that he accompany him instead to deal with those matters that had started going awry.

Various Disciples entered and left this relatively small chamber through a separate arched doorway from which steps ascended by a convoluted route to the surface; they were runners, and much to Arkkun's dismay, they were bringing bad news. The chanting from the main cathedral hall changed into a new, alien blend of words and sounds. Arkkun recognised it as the next stage of the ceremony; the time to put things right was diminishing rapidly. He had already received reports about the girl, Rachel, disappearing. It appeared that she may have escaped out of her window; nobody knew why, she had no reason to be afraid. After all, everyone had managed to keep the true meaning of tonight from her – hadn't they? To find her again was critical. Without her the ceremony would not be completed. Earlier on he had ensured that men and dogs were out looking for her.

There had been some short-lived good news; the servant of the Grimoires who aided the psychic agent had been captured outside the house. It seemed he had had an accident on the road as he went about his mischief-making and was found by the Disciples. The plan was for the High Lord himself to probe the man's mind, glean his knowledge and, with any luck, zombify him in the process. This, unfortunately, would no longer be happening because the intruder had escaped from under their very noses *and* killed the Pharmacist in the process! The outrage!

Lord Arkkun was displeased; the High Lord would be even more unhappy. No doubt, as second in command, a portion of the blame would lie at his feet. He would therefore find out who was supposed to have been guarding the biker and dispense suitable punishment – he would not shoulder the blame alone.

Chapter 36

They stood before a narrow, innocuous door; its surface was covered with peeling and yellowing white paint. Reaching the entrance to the coal cellar, without being discovered by the Disciples, felt like a small victory to Boyd and Rachel.

Both were shaken by their earlier brush with death at the clutches of the deformed monstrosity. Neither of them knew the origin of that particular horror, nor did they doubt there were more like it within this house. Try as they might, they could not forget what they had seen, and neither could they vanquish from their memory the chorus of inhuman voices that had called to them from behind closed doors upstairs. Despite the assault upon their sensibilities, the pair had managed to make it through the house to stand just outside their goal.

Boyd grasped the dulled brass knob and pulled ajar the cellar door; with Rachel having already forced it open earlier, it provided little resistance. He stood for a moment, looking down onto the rickety wooden staircase that descended towards his right and into darkness; there was not much that could be seen as the cellar space actually started halfway down the steps. The dirty ground-level window through which Rachel had originally entered hardly let in any of the pale and distant moonlight. Boyd wondered how she could possibly have made her way through the cellar and into the house without injuring herself in the darkness, and he commended her efforts; now it was time to retrace her steps.

"Rachel, I'll go in first to check things out. You close the door and wait here at the top step." Rachel hesitantly agreed and moved in behind Boyd. With eyes well adapted to the dim light in the house, Boyd noticed an old worn cord dangling by the door. He pulled on it and a light bulb covered in dust and cobwebs flickered to life at the foot of the stairs; it threw odd shadows and failed to provide adequate illumination to the cellar beyond. He started to walk slowly down.

"Wait," said Rachel urgently after he had only taken two steps. Boyd turned to face her. "When I came through here earlier, something didn't seem right. It felt like there was somebody watching me, and it was so cold; I just wanted to get out of there."

Boyd nodded and looked down the staircase into the darkness again; he could not see anything. He wondered if turning on the electric light had been such a good idea after all; his eyes would have to readjust to darkness again once he entered the cellar proper. There was a fleeting sound like a scrape from the depths of the darkness; it made his heart leap, and it added an ominous quality to what Rachel had just said. It was a sound that might have been ignored under normal circumstances; however, in his state of heightened alertness, it was alarming. Boyd wished he still had the long-bladed dagger; it probably remained where he had left it, embedded in the demon upstairs. He needed a weapon and knew Rachel still had the length of lead pipe. He turned to her and saw she was clutching it along with the amulet. He asked her for the pipe before he went into the cellar and felt terrible about doing it; she seemed only too pleased to give it up.

The sound of his feet and the creak from each step he took on the way down cut through the quietness; he pressed on steadily. The length of lead was raised above his shoulder, ready to swing down hard on anybody or anything that looked hostile; he managed to reach the foot of the stairs without incident. Boyd looked up at Rachel and smiled as if to say "so far, so good". She had been watching him closely as he went down. He was about to enter the zone of darkness beyond the light of the old bulb, and it took only a couple more steps for him to be swallowed by it completely. He knew Rachel wouldn't be able to see him now.

Once he was down there, Boyd found the darkness was not as absolute as it had appeared from the top of the stairs, and he could just about see the walls of the old cellar. It was a small place and contained a few scattered items of junk, mainly old furniture, and there was little room for anybody to hide in it. His initial visual inspection did not reveal anything untoward, then he heard it again, a hissing sound this time; it came from the blackness beneath the staircase.

"Boyd, what was that?" cried Rachel from the top of the stairs.

"Quiet!" Boyd replied curtly, trying to keep his voice down. He was focused entirely on trying to see what was beneath the stairs. He walked slowly and purposefully towards where he guessed the noise had come from, lead pipe ready; his wide-open eyes looked wild and alert. Boyd squinted into the darkness; he noticed a series of pipes running along the wall, and he started to relax. *Old plumbing, so that's what it was*, he thought to himself, and just as soon as he did so, there was a sudden, palpable drop in temperature; not just a draught – it was a real biting cold. A shiver ran down his spine. There was no obvious reason for the uncomfortable chill and he started to back away slowly. As he did so, he became aware of a shallow layer of mist unfurling about his ankles. It appeared from the darkness beneath the staircase, spreading outwards as if it were being blown from a smoke machine; soon it covered the entire floor of the old coal cellar.

Boyd nervously watched this phenomenon while the temperature in the room continued to drop. The chill started to penetrate his flesh and enter his bones; it felt worst around his legs, especially below the knees where the mist touched him. He knew that old buildings could be cold, particularly in their damp cellars – this was something else, totally disproportionate even to the temperature outside. That it was not natural was the only conclusion he could reach as he started to shiver uncontrollably.

"Boyd, what's going on down there? What's that hissing?" called Rachel from the top of the steps once again.

"I don't know. There's something very strange here. I don't think this is as safe a place as we thought."

He took a few hasty steps back to the staircase. As soon as he moved, there was another sudden hiss, the loudest yet. The cloud of mist that had been spreading across the floor burst upwards from the ground in a column that engulfed his entire body, and he was surrounded by freezing vapour; it was as if it had moved of its own accord. Boyd let out a stifled cry as cold, biting frost collected over his clothing and skin. The blood in his veins seemed to freeze, and his muscles stiffened to the point that he was hardly able to move. The nearest experience he could compare to it was falling through a thin layer of frozen ice and into a garden pond as a teenager. The sudden freezing shock that had taken his breath away then was what he experienced now, all over again.

Boyd swung the lead pipe back and forth at the mist, the frigid muscles of his arm made the movement awkward and clumsy. He was not expecting his desperate actions to have much of an effect on the vaporous substance, but it was all he could do.

"Boyd, is everything all right?" called Rachel in a trembling voice.

Boyd couldn't reply. He wanted to call out and tell her it was all fine; knowing full well that it wasn't, he said nothing. He heard her feet echoing and creaking on the bare wooden steps.

"Don't come down, Rachel!" he managed to cry out with great difficulty through chattering teeth. "Stay up there!"

Rachel's response was quick; he heard her take two steps back to the top of the stairs. By now, Boyd was frozen to the spot; the mist danced around his body and wherever it made contact with his skin, he felt the blood drain away. Every breath became an effort as the cold air contracted his airways, at times choking him; all he could do was stiffly thrash his arms and the pipe about in unsuccessful attempts to dissipate the bewildering haze. Intent on leaving the cellar, he managed to stagger forwards a few inches at a time, forcing his cramped leg muscles to respond to his brain. Engulfed by this mist that seemed to have a mind of its own, he did not get very far. It curled and wound its way around him, encircling a leg here or an arm there, essentially disabling the limb. Ice crystals had already formed on his clothes, hair and face; one of his eyes was frozen shut. He fought to keep the remaining eye open, afraid that he would eventually have to blink.

"Boyd! Boyd!" whimpered Rachel. He could just about hear her through painful ears. The exposed areas of his skin turned from pale pink to sickly purple-blue, and maintaining circulation to his tired, frozen limbs was all that mattered now; if he stopped *trying* to move then it would be the end of him.

He stumbled and staggered backwards. His swinging lead pipe succeeded only in parting the hostile mist for a few seconds at a time, and he eventually dropped it with a clang onto the hard floor, his hands having lost the dexterity even to grip this crude weapon. No longer able to stand, he was now on his knees, and still, the mist swirled and danced around him. He thought of the girl; he feared for her in this place of evil.

**

Rachel, in defiance of the previous warning and through concern for her friend, quietly descended into the cellar. She gasped in terror halfway down the stairs. From here she could see Boyd on his knees, shivering helplessly, covered in a layer of glistening frost. He looked back at her with his single open eye and tried to speak; the only sound that came from his frozen mouth and stiff tongue was an unintelligible moan. Rachel wanted to run. Controlling the panic that was building up inside her, she hesitantly edged closer towards him; she could not leave the poor man to his fate. In response to this encroachment, the mist, with a sudden blast, arranged itself into a wall between the girl and Boyd. It swirled and drifted until it took on the form of a dark and menacing face, filled with hatred. Eyes that were black holes stared straight into Rachel's soul, and its gaping mouth produced an angry hiss. It was a face of uncontrolled fury. Rachel stumbled backwards onto the stairs, her eyes fixed on the terrible apparition. She only looked away when she noticed icy mist curling over each step, drifting towards her. The petrified girl screamed and turned to run back up the old staircase. She heard a thump from behind her and glanced over her shoulder to see Boyd toppled over, lying still on the cellar floor. Not knowing whether he was dead or alive, she climbed the steps quickly; the ice mist caught up with her as she neared the cellar exit. Straight away, she could feel its cold fingers grabbing at her ankles and reaching up her legs. She fell just before reaching the top of the stairs, certain she was doomed.

The cellar door, only a few feet away, burst open suddenly. Rachel screamed at the new terror that confronted her: filling the doorway was the silhouette of a huge man dressed in a long black coat and wide-brimmed hat, a sight more frightening and menacing than even the ice mist. Horrified, she noticed an animal of sorts moving frenetically from side to side on all fours behind him; it barked and produced a sound so loud and deep that it sent vibrations through the very staircase on which she lay. From the recent readings of her mother's diary and distant memories of the police investigation, she had a good idea who the pair looming over her were.

The tall figure spoke a single throaty word, "Bikhalas."

Rachel watched as the ice mist receded down the stairs and she instantly felt some warmth return to her body. She gasped as the giant took a single step through the cellar door, swung his mighty arm around, and scooped her off the staircase. It was all too much for Rachel, and she lost consciousness. The last thing she could remember was the smell of decay from the figure as he held on to her body.

**

Mr Kreb prised the Qrwshan amulet from between Rachel's limp fingers. The amulet may have hidden her psychic signature, but Mr Kreb was sensitive to all forms of psychic activity, including that from the demons Boyd and Rachel had disturbed upstairs. The agitation he detected amongst these wild beings had guided him to the abandoned part of the house from where it was easy for his Firehound to pick up the scent.

Chapter 37

Johnny dashed across the ruined garden to the house with Baccharus and Sascha in pursuit. He kept close to the uprooted trees and shrubs for cover while avoiding metres of dead tentacle along the way. He guessed it would not be long before another wave of defenders arrived, and so the sooner they were all out of sight the better. The subterranean creature had been an unexpected obstacle, and it had slowed him and his friends down. The struggle against it had drawn the attention of the cultists; to try to regain the initiative was now paramount. On reaching the house, he crouched beneath one of the windows, his back to the wall.

"Can't you warp us to where we need to be, Johnny?" asked Baccharus impatiently as he joined him.

"I don't know where we need to be! Besides, it's much more difficult negotiating a warp through complex structures like a building!" Johnny replied, equally impatient. "Right now I'm open to suggestions." He was frustrated by the difficulty of trying to sense anything beyond the barrage of psychic energy from the Disciples' ceremony.

Sascha, who was also crouching beside Johnny, frowned. "The old woman said that we needed to be underground, didn't she?" he asked.

"Yes," confirmed Johnny, "the summoning of Orbok will be taking place in a chamber that used to be a cave which contained the original portal." He watched Sascha reach into his rucksack and pull out a weighty electronic device, like many of his designs, its appearance was crude. Johnny knew its beauty would lie in its function.

"What's that?" was the obvious question, and Baccharus was the one to ask it.

"What we have here is a multiple frequency radar and detector. I reckon I can use it to do some geophysics work."

"Do what?"

"Observe."

"Okay, just make it quick! We can't be hanging around here much longer."

Johnny stayed put under the window and let his friend get to work beside him. Sascha powered up the radar device, and holding it just above the ground, he started sweeping it from left to right. Johnny watched the colourful images on Sascha's small LCD screen. To him they looked like random patterns; he could see that it all meant something far more profound to his friend.

"With some luck, this gadget should detect the presence of underground anomalies that might direct us to the lair of the Disciples," declared Sascha. To cover as great an area as possible (whilst continuing to hold the radar inches from the ground) meant walking around doubled over; with Sascha's lanky stature, this was no mean feat. Johnny watched him move both swiftly and awkwardly around the perimeter of the house, oblivious to everything except the graphics on the tiny display in his hand. Baccharus had started hovering high overhead as a lookout for any threats coming their way while Johnny relied on both his eyes and the psychic field he was projecting to do the same, conscious all the time of the difficulty in sensing hostile

Disciples through the plethora of psychic signals surrounding him. His mind remained open to any sign of Boyd's aura or even that of the girl, Rachel; for now, there was none.

Sascha continued to circle the house with his improvised ground radar and when he was about to move out of sight, Johnny followed him. They continued like this for several nerve-racking minutes, trying to find an entry point to the underground chambers. Johnny had often admired Sascha's supreme concentration and did so again on this occasion. His friend, who had been attacked by extraterrestrial beasts and mad cultists, appeared unshaken, completely absorbed by the readings from his device. Finally, Sascha stopped beside a ground-floor window; it had a light on inside. Johnny listened to the results of his survey.

"I have located some underground chambers linked by tunnels. One or two of them look pretty big. They all seem to be leading to somewhere, possibly a larger chamber; it's far too deep for me to tell for certain. If we were to enter the house through this window, we won't be far from the surface entrance to one of the main passages," Sascha said.

Johnny used his mind to detect the presence of any life-forms in their immediate vicinity, especially inside the room beyond the window. This type of close-range psychic perception could still produce an informative picture even with the aberrant background energy. Satisfied that they were alone, he gave the all clear and Baccharus immediately descended to peer directly through the window into a rather spacious and unexpectedly domesticated family kitchen.

"This all looks quite normal. I was, at the very least, expecting an altar with a blood sacrifice at the ready," he said with a hint of disappointment in his voice.

425

"Johnny, why don't you get us inside," suggested Sascha, bracing himself for travel via space–time warp. Johnny nodded, stood with his back against the window and raised an arm. Sascha waited for the hand on his shoulder and closed his eyes, only to open them again suddenly at the sound of shattering glass. He winced as Johnny used his elbow to send the few remaining pieces of the windowpane he had broken flying into the kitchen where they smashed on the floor.

"Okay, let's go in," he said, crawling through the frame.

"That's not quite what I had in mind," mumbled Sascha, following him. He swung his long legs through one at a time and into the kitchen. Baccharus hovered behind both of them, chuckling.

"So, how do we get underground?" asked Johnny as he brushed glistening diamonds of glass from his clothing; there was no response. Sascha was already scanning the floors of the house with his ground radar device, attempting to pick up the readings from the subterranean passage he had detected outside. Johnny watched him intently and continued to project a psychic proximity field. He still carried the Qrwshan, although he suspected that this close to the wormhole all their psychic signatures would be near enough impossible to detect even without it. Sascha, still hunched over his device, drifted out of the kitchen without discussion; Johnny cast Baccharus a worried look, and they both followed.

"Somewhere around here," murmured Sascha to himself thoughtfully, his eyes still locked onto the screen of his device.

"Everything okay, Sasch?" Johnny asked; again, there was no reply. He had seen Sascha like this before, and it was dangerous. He was too distracted by what he was doing to show any concern for being discovered.

They found themselves in a broad, long corridor that led to a distant and impressive-looking hall; above them was a high, rendered ceiling, and on either side there were walls of polished wood panelling lined with doors. It was an old-fashioned interior; its grandeur made an impact not achieved in modern buildings. Johnny could see that all these details were lost on the single-minded Sascha, who was bent double and moving with his device like a bloodhound on a fresh trail. After a few minutes of scanning the corridor floor, the ground radar echo pattern led him to another door, which he pushed open to protests from his friends.

"Wait!"

"Hey, man, don't!" warned Johnny and Baccharus, barely able to contain their alarm.

"What?" asked Sascha, looking slightly annoyed at the interruption.

"Just let us know if you're about to do something or go anywhere, Sasch. I mean, it's great that you're so into this trail, but try and remember that we're amongst the Disciples now; there could be anything waiting for us here … especially behind closed doors," said Johnny.

"I thought you guys would sense it if there was any trouble. That's your department, right? You know what I mean?"

Baccharus intervened. "The whole building is awash with psychic signals; they're bouncing everywhere so it's kind of difficult to detect anything, even where the hell your own friends are, let alone any enemies. Just slow down a bit, amigo, that's all."

"Okay – point taken," Sascha replied.

They all proceeded through the contentious door into a small room filled with old cleaning equipment and washing machines; it was the disused utility room, Edward

Devilliers' favoured entry point into his network of underground chambers. At first inspection, it looked like an insignificant part of the house, just as it was supposed to. Johnny even suspected his friend had taken a wrong turn; however, undaunted, Sascha pressed on past the clutter and around the corner of the L-shaped room where he found, and opened, the storage cupboard. As Johnny and Baccharus watched, he rechecked the display of his ground radar device and then tapped the cupboard's false wooden back, producing a hollow resonant sound.

"It's behind here," he said simply as he tried to push and prise the false back away. With a puzzled look, Johnny helped him, and eventually they were both able to slide the back of the cupboard sideways to reveal the unexpected sight of a massive steel door. A structure like that in a humble utility room was wholly inappropriate, and it confirmed that they had found something important.

"This is it – this is the way down," said Sascha.

Every stage of the journey that brought them closer to the portal had been accompanied by fresh tides of progressively stronger aberrant psychic energy, and the discovery of this door was no different; beyond it, Johnny could sense a vast psychic disturbance – the vibration of Disorder. He focused his mind to see if there were any unwelcome surprises on the other side. It took a few moments to do this; when he was satisfied that the coast beyond was clear, he gripped the massive, cold steel handle and attempted to open it. Sascha, who had already put his radar away, took a step back and drew the revolver. Nothing happened – a couple of quick shoves confirmed that the door was firmly locked. They had not come this far to be thwarted by such means. Johnny focused a tight beam of psychic energy into the door handle and its locking mechanism; both started to give off light whiffs of smoke before glowing red, then pale yellow, and finally turning a bright white, at which point the metal became visibly softer and pliable. He shoved the door once again. The almost liquefied metal of the lock and handle offered no resistance this time, and the mighty steel barrier swung lazily backwards on its hinges. To perform this feat, Johnny had used the same principle that lit the candle in his bedroom magnified many times over, something that could only be achieved following his strange experiences with Theodora.

Johnny and Baccharus almost recoiled at the wave of disordered psychic energy that rushed out of the opened door. It overwhelmed them with a flood of sensations and emotions; the effect was similar to Mr Kreb's earlier psychic assault, although on a lesser scale. With deep concentration, keeper and familiar cleared their minds of the influence of Disorder. Sascha, who was less sensitive in such matters, remained largely unaffected, except for a passing sensation of his skin crawling, particularly over the scalp. There was an electronic bleeping and Sascha reached into his pocket. He took out a small device and observed the miniature screen on its topside before sliding a switch to silence it and putting it away again.

"What was that?" Johnny asked.

"It measures ambient Presarium. The curve was off the scale."

"Damn right it was," said Baccharus.

The opened door gave them all their first exposure to the sounds of the ceremony, a distant murmur that was carried to them through the complex network of underground tunnels. Johnny listened to the illogical melodies and alien phonetics superimposed over the faraway and palpably vibrating pulse of the portal. At times, all he could discern was a cacophony of random screams and shouts, and yet there was no escaping the possibility that under-lying it all was some sort of musical structure. Just when he thought he had recognised the form, it would elusively slip away again. The entire effect was very disorientating; such was the way of Disorder.

"What is that?" asked Baccharus, listening carefully.

"I don't know. It sounds pretty fucking evil to me," was all Johnny could offer. Sascha nodded in agreement. Having come this far, there was no choice except to venture further until they faced whatever lay ahead.

Johnny peered through the doorway and down into a great chamber. The floor of this enormous stone hall was many metres beneath them at the foot of an unenclosed stone stairway hewn masterfully out of solid rock. They were so high up at present that Sascha's head almost touched the ceiling. The old woman, Theodora, had told Johnny that the Devilliers' house was built on the foundations of a medieval castle. Until now, this had not really registered. Standing in the doorway, looking down into the vast stone space lit by the flickering glow of several flaming torches, it felt as if he had taken a step back in time. It was an impressive sight, and the longer he observed the more detail he noticed, and the more impressive it became.

"Well, well … what have we here, then?" said Johnny, placing his foot on the first step, which was worn smooth through centuries of use; the rest followed him as he descended into the strange world beneath the foundations of Edward Devilliers' mansion, the same foundations that once supported the ancient castle of the lords of Hilvern.

Sascha commented on how the many different surfaces here joined seamlessly into each other, and he noted the absence of any building block, leading him to conclude that the whole structure had been carved into bedrock. To Johnny, and indeed any other psychic, the very walls here radiated ancient wickedness.

Two mighty pillars stretched from floor to ceiling at the centre of this immense chamber. Light from flaming torches brought the ornately carved stone gargoyles and friezes that decorated the walls to life. Scenes depicting men and hideous beasts were animated by the dancing flame, and for an instant, the three friends were lost in the hypnotic imagery. All around them, the noise of faraway chanting persisted along with the rhythmical pulse of the wormhole; intimidating though these sights and sounds were, the companions were not discouraged. Awestruck, they continued onwards until they reached the floor of the chamber. They were drawn to the pillars, which, like the walls, were also decorated with carvings; these depicted humans and non-humans worshipping vile alien deities. The unnatural ecstasy of surrendering the soul to Disorder was captured perfectly in their etched features. It was art that intrigued and repelled in equal measure, and had there been any doubts in their minds, it also confirmed that by confronting Disorder they were on their way to doing something right as judged by a more universal standard.

The blazing wall-mounted torches made the great chamber very warm, and it would have been uncomfortable to remain there had it not been for a gentle draught that kept the temperature in this new environment bearable. There was some confusion amongst the friends regarding the source of this underground moving air until closer examination of the walls revealed a series of channels ending in vents incorporated within the stone friezes and carvings. It was through these that the air, alongside the chanting and pulsing that accompanied this new world, travelled.

In a corner of this huge chamber, opposite the stone

stairway by which they had entered, were steps cut into the floor, descending further into the ground; the same ones Edward and Elizabeth Devilliers had been using earlier. Tentatively, Johnny led his companions down them, deeper into the lair of Disorder; it was the only way to go without turning back. Like the entrance chamber, these steps also seemed to have been chiselled painstakingly out of solid rock.

The passage they now proceeded along was a claustrophobic affair. The way was lit by lanterns sitting in functional and undecorated recesses in the walls; looking further ahead, Johnny could see what appeared to be two distant landings with doorways leading off to either side. The inordinately long passage continued way beyond them, and it was not yet possible to see where it ended.

They walked on; all around them the air was becoming increasingly charged with aberrant psychic energy generated from the ceremony deep in the bowels of this complex. Air vents within the lantern recesses carried the hum of the portal and the baleful chanting. Both of these sounds were becoming increasingly audible from the passage itself, a sure indication that they were nearing their source. The persistent, twisted mantras gnawed at the minds of the sane.

"I wish they'd shut up," Baccharus said impatiently, and Johnny felt the same; he was sure Sascha did too.

After a full minute of descent, there was still no end apparent to the subterranean staircase. Eventually, they managed to reach the first of the small landings, and just as they had observed earlier, two side corridors exited from it in opposite directions. After short deliberation, they opted to ignore these passages and continue further down towards the source of the chanting. They had considered separating and exploring individually, in the end they decided against it as all the evidence so far indicated that the enemy preferred to attack in numbers; alone they were likely to be easily picked off.

A few more minutes of progress down the stone stairway allowed Johnny to finally see the vaguest suggestion of where it might terminate. In the distance was what looked like a room; there was still a long way to go to reach it. Much closer was another landing, similar to the one they had passed earlier, complete with another two corridors leading off to either side.

"Hold on!" shouted Johnny at the top of his voice, and before his companions could make a move he was grabbing each of them, Sascha by his shoulder and the floating Baccharus by one of his fat cherub legs. Every nerve ending in the three friends tingled instantaneously as if they had been wired into an electrical current, and their vision suddenly blurred. Even with eyesight distorted, Johnny could still discern a brilliant bright explosion directly ahead of them followed by the appearance of dark menacing shapes. Both Sascha and Baccharus let out a cry that made no sound. Moments later, the blur cleared and their jangled nerves settled. Johnny had warped space–time into a wave that carried him and his friends rapidly back up the stone staircase to a point even before the first landing; somewhere they had been several minutes earlier. There was a very good reason for him to be backtracking like this so suddenly. Pouring out from the side corridors onto each of the two landings ahead were Disciples of Disorder. Some were clad in black leather, some in robes; mostly they were naked. The enemy had been covertly observing their progress and planning an ambush. By attacking simultaneously from front and rear, their aim had been to trap the three intruders between the two landings. It was an offensive led by none other than

Psychic Lord Arkkun himself. He had been shielding the Disciples from detection with his mind. At the last moment he had diverted his mental energy into a huge psychic spear aimed at Johnny and his friends. The resulting shift in Presarium was all the warning Johnny needed to warp him and his company away from danger. Never before had he been able to execute so complex a psychic technique as quickly as he had just managed. The time necessary to focus his mind had been miniscule; a further demonstration of his enhanced ability.

From Johnny's new vantage point, the result of Lord Arkkun's psychic spear was obvious to behold; the steps where he had been standing moments earlier were now scorched and ashen from its impact. Johnny and his friends were safer in their present location, although their exposure to danger was still very apparent. In front of him, upon each landing, now stood two groups of Disciples made up of both men and pale, blue-skinned demons of the same breed that had been encountered several times already. Most were armed with dagger or pistol, a few were empty-handed and Johnny knew they were the ones to look out for as their weapon would be their minds.

Warping away so suddenly had caused confusion amongst friend and foe alike, and when the noise of the psychic spear had gone there was only the persistent sound of disembodied chanting in the air. Johnny prepared to retaliate; his companions had already made their move. The group of Disciples nearest to him was being assailed by energy bolts from Baccharus and bullets from Sascha, who held aloft Boyd's revolver. Almost immediately, the air was filled with the smell of singed flesh.

The Disciples rallied quickly, and a couple of them started firing back with pistols. Their counter-attack was short-lived; two intensely bright flashes of light caused them to stagger about, disorientated and in disarray. Johnny had struck them with an attack of his own unique design; drawing ambient photons into a concentrated mass, he had released the lot in a psychic flare. Most of the Disciples were temporarily blinded, and the unlucky ones were left with permanent retinal scarring.

Sascha started shooting at any cultist who was showing signs of recovering vision; Johnny was impressed with the steady hand demonstrated by his lanky bookworm friend, who was turning out to be quite a sharp-shooter. He could see that Sascha targeted humans and humanoids alike; the desperation of the situation allowed him to strike without the moral consideration that might have crippled his fighting ability. The three friends had quickly killed or incapacitated the Disciples from the first landing; however, there were survivors amongst them who retreated to join their comrades on the landing further down to form a second front that was advancing warily.

Bullets ricocheted off the stone passage around Johnny and his company; they whistled past their ears, forcing them to keep their heads down and back off slowly. As the three of them prepared to launch a counter-strike, they were stopped in their tracks by the prone bodies of Disciples they had already dispatched levitating and hanging limply in the air in such a way that they provided cover to the advancing enemy. It was alarmingly obvious to Johnny that powerful psychic forces aligned to Disorder were now at work against them.

"I can't shoot, Johnny! Those bodies are blocking my view!" Sascha shouted in desperation.

"Yeah, tell me about it!" Baccharus added – the familiar had released a salvo of psychic bolts, only to see them impact ineffectually against the hovering obstacles.

"It's time I gave gravity a hand," Johnny said.

With great effort and supreme concentration, he used his will to try to force the bodies back to the ground, where nature intended them to be, and managed to move them low enough for Sascha and Baccharus to pick off an advancing Disciple each. The hovering bodies descended further still, and Johnny seemed to be winning this battle of wills when his unknown psychic adversary changed tack suddenly. No longer happy to simply levitate the collection of dead and unconscious Disciples, his opponent decided instead to use them as weapons and sent them cartwheeling like rag dolls through the air with incredible velocity. They reached the friends, knocking all three to the ground and then landing on top of them. Even the airborne Baccharus could not avoid the stray leg that struck him squarely on top of his head.

As Johnny lay there, trapped in the tangle of bodies and limbs with his friends, he commended this feat. It would have taken a great effort of will to hurl the limp bodies of so many men and demons at them like that; there was a notable psychic indeed amongst the enemy – he wondered if it was Edward Devilliers himself.

The Disciples were quick to capitalise on their advantage, and the din of their gunfire reverberated through the passage once again; in the enclosed space the noise was deafening. Johnny heard another much closer sound, a dull thumping; it was bullets penetrating the bodies under which they were all buried. Johnny struggled desperately to free himself, knowing that it was only a matter of time before luck ran out and one of them hit home. He produced a psychic field which deflected most of the bullets so that they flew harmlessly around the three of them. Sascha and Baccharus managed to struggle to their feet again under this protection. Johnny got up last, and by the time he was facing the group of nine remaining Disciples,

Sascha was preparing to fire back. Baccharus, quick off the mark as ever, was already sending glowing bolts of fiery psychic energy through the air in his trademark attack. Once Sascha started shooting, they managed to incapacitate, possibly kill (it was impossible to say) three more of the Disciples. Johnny did not attack; instead, he continued to focus on defending against the bullets flying their way. Soon, the friends found their own projectiles being psychically deflected into the stone walls of the passage; neither Sascha nor Baccharus could land a shot on the Disciples – the two sides were in deadlock.

Johnny looked carefully at the cultists. They were a collection of figures, both male and female, half of them naked except for tight leather masks that covered their heads and faces; the other half wore flowing black robes and cowls that hung low over the head. It was amongst this latter group that he believed the hostile psychic was present, and an idea for determining who this individual was occurred to him.

"Sascha, stop firing and chuck one of Boyd's stone things instead. We won't get anywhere unless we strike at the psychics amongst them."

Sascha stopped shooting, and from the knee pocket of his trousers he retrieved one of the smooth stones. Discarding the muslin wrapping, he lobbed it underarm with a spinning rotation, just as Boyd had shown him. The centrifugal force activated the psychokinetic energy stored within the stone as it sailed through the air. The Disciples, unsure about what was heading towards them, watched suspiciously without relenting in their attack. The mystical artefact landed a few feet in front of them; stone met stone with a sharp crack and was followed instantly by a shockwave of psychic power that went off with a flash and the sound of flammable gas being ignited. All of the

Disciples recoiled from the energy that was released; there was one robed figure amongst them who was affected by it far more profoundly than the others were. He was hurled backwards through the air with his arms and legs thrashing around until he landed painfully on the hard steps further down, drawing the attention of all combatants. This exaggerated response to the attack revealed him to be an advanced psychic.

While his fellow Disciples looked on with some distress, he stood up again and drew back the large cowl that hid his face, revealing fierce blue eyes that stared at Johnny through two holes in a tight leather mask. Without wavering, he removed the mask with a deft sweep of the hand.

"If we are to continue battle, then you should know who it is that will defeat you and your pathetic companions!" he announced with a wry smile. Challenging Johnny and his friends was an aged man. He had a narrow-jawed feline face covered in light wrinkles and long, wispy white hair brushed back all the way to his shoulders. His intense eyes never seemed to blink, making his appearance all the more striking.

"So who the fuck are you then?!" retorted Baccharus above the background noise of the chant.

"I am Lord Arkkun, wretch!" shrieked the beloved of Disorder, and with a flick of his hand he fired a beam of highly energised matter at the floating familiar. A glowing line stretched through the air from the white-haired man's palm all the way to Baccharus. The familiar managed to hover nimbly to one side; he was not quick enough to avoid having his head narrowly clipped by the beam, sending him spinning backwards up the stone tunnel. Sascha retaliated by firing two shots from the revolver, Lord Arkkun simply raised his free hand and manipulated the Presarium within the bullets so that they disintegrated in mid-air.

Lord Arkkun was about to throw everything he had at the trespassers and his mind worked furiously to this end. With focused will, he aimed further destructive beams at Johnny and Sascha. Survival relied on Johnny creating a psychic shield to absorb and disperse the concentrated energy directed at them. When his beams did not make any headway, Lord Arkkun again launched the bodies of dead and dying Disciples at the companions, distracting Johnny and thus weakening the shield so he could follow up with further beams which managed to hit home. Johnny's shield ensured that he and Sascha remained alive, but it did not possess sufficient strength to save them from singed clothing and painful minor burns.

The Disciples who had recovered from the concussive effect of the psychic grenade, and were able to fight beside Arkkun, continued their steady ascent along the stone passage; they were closing in on the friends with pistols firing.

This is not looking good, thought Johnny. His psychic stamina was being expended on creating shields and absorbing attacks; he knew they would not defeat Arkkun by relying on defensive measures alone. The Lord of Disorder clearly intended to destroy them before they had a chance to even lay eyes upon Edward Devilliers. Johnny would have to strike back … and soon.

"Both of you, get behind me; I'm dropping the shield!" Johnny shouted to his friends above the sound of gunfire and the electrified crackles of psychic energy.

"What are you going to do?" Sascha asked nervously as Baccharus, who had recovered from his head injury, stopped firing his bolts and hovered to take up position behind his keeper.

"It's time to hit back!" said Johnny as he diverted his psychic energy from projecting the shield into energising an attack. The feeling of frustration at being pushed back, the pain from his burning skin, and the concern for his friends all welled up inside him. In this way, he found the heightened emotional state to give him access to more psychic energy than he had previously thought he could muster. Johnny had hoped to energise a powerful psychic spear to hurl at the enemy; the desperate situation gave him the strength to summon not one but six of these lethal weapons. He diverted the last bit of energy from his shield into the sixth spear, and in his mind all the weapons were fully primed; there was no shield so he did not waste any time. Johnny allowed his thoughts to become substance. Available Presarium contained within his vicinity came together to form the six fiery vessels of energy that he had blueprinted in his consciousness. They seemed to materialise out of thin air before him, and their physical presence was magnificent. Each was longer than a man and glowed with an intensity that pained the eyes. Johnny had arranged them to point at the enemy in a circle of five that reached the very edges of the passage while the sixth hovered in the middle. Almost as soon they appeared, the spears were sent hurtling towards the Disciples with a roar. The followers of Disorder shrieked at the sight, and realising there was no escape from the incoming weapons, they tried fruitlessly to shoot at them instead. The six psychic spears tore through bullets and Disciples alike, setting them alight or vaporising them. Even the bodies of the defeated, lying on the ground, were not spared.

Lord Arkkun, his eyes wide open and staring in terror, reflexively backed away before using his powers to try to quickly warp to another location; despite being a wily old warrior, he was not entirely successful. His dematerialisation shadow made fleeting contact with the high-energy spears resulting in a strange affliction (although one that was not uncommon in psychic battle). From now on, he was to be trapped in the form of a warp phantom; a bizarre existence in which he flickered in and out of reality. Sometimes his body was solid and at others composed only of ether. His physical form moved between these states randomly and beyond conscious control. The three friends watched as Arkkun became transparent for an instant and then disappeared.

The spears had performed their function admirably. Johnny no longer focused his mind on maintaining their form and so their structure dispersed, and they faded out of existence. The noise of combat had peaked with the roar of those spears, the final offensive of the skirmish; now that they were gone, there was only the sound of distant chanting and the ebbing of the portal again. Both were louder than before and their noticeably increased tempo provoked a sense of urgency.

Johnny, Sascha and Baccharus stood, sat and hovered respectively on the stairway, each taking a few precious moments to recover from the battle.

"That chanting, Johnny, how many of them do you think there are? I mean, it's only the three of us," Sascha asked nervously, still shaken from the fight.

"Four," corrected Baccharus. "Boyd is around here somewhere – I know it."

"Still, four against how many? You know what I mean?"

"Doesn't matter! Didn't you see those spears Johnny unleashed? PEEOOWW! Straight through those sons of bitches. There may be a hundred of them, two hundred; Johnny will come up with something."

Sascha could only shake his head at his companion's unfounded enthusiasm. Johnny had also been thinking, and it was along lines similar to Sascha rather than Baccharus. "You're right, Sasch, we can't just go in for a head to head confrontation – they will outnumber us easily. We need to sneak up on them somehow. What we need to know is the layout of this place."

"How the heck are you going to find that out?" Baccharus interjected.

"There is a way," said Johnny simply. His friends watched curiously as he went to examine each of the defeated Disciples, eventually stopping at an injured human who was masked, naked and barely conscious. "What I hope we have in here is a map!" he said tapping the Disciple's head. Johnny pulled off the man's tight leather mask, revealing a middle-aged face with a head of long black hair streaked with white. The Disciple was more conscious than he was letting on, which was going to be important.

"Mind probe?" Sascha asked hesitantly.

Johnny nodded. "I am not a fan of mind probes. I think it's going to be necessary though. We have no time to waste."

On hearing the words 'mind probe' the injured Disciple started moaning and tried to scramble away; unfortunately for him, he was too weak to resist whatever Johnny had planned. Sascha and Baccharus looked on with concern. To be the subject of a probe was usually an unpleasant experience, the Disciple could end up losing his mind; there was also a chance that he would be fine. Nobody would know until the process was complete.

Johnny crouched behind the semi-conscious cultist, placed his outstretched fingers equal distances apart on the man's head, and he closed his eyes. He remembered something and opened his eyes again. "Oh, by the way, Sascha, try and find a robe and mask that fits you, preferably one that isn't too tatty."

"Sure." Sascha wandered off to find a fallen Disciple

whose physique approximated his. Johnny closed his eyes again; he had not yet commenced the mind probe. His subject was already muttering away nervously. Johnny dug his fingers into the man's scalp, firm contact made the process much more effective. As his concentration increased, the Disciple started to struggle.

"Hey! Get off me! What's going on?" mumbled the man in feeble protest; Johnny's focus did not waver despite the objections. It was not long before he had subdued the subject's mind, and the Disciple resisted no more. Johnny poked and prodded the various memory regions of the man's cortex, learning how his wild childhood and tragic personal circumstances had pushed him towards the occult and eventually into Edward Devilliers' hands where he had found liberation through a love of chaos with its forever changing principles and an appreciation of the beauty to be found in anarchy. This was not the information Johnny was after so he searched further through the maze of thoughts and mental images; the longer he searched, the more discomfort the subject experienced. The Disciple started to shake and twitch with steadily increasing ferocity. Sascha, now dressed as one of the robed guards, noticed blood dripping from his nose and urged Johnny to hurry the process; Johnny knew that if the man died it would be a moral disaster, especially if he did not yield any useful secrets. Relevant images finally presented themselves to Johnny; a network of halls, rooms, tunnels and stairways, identical in architecture to their current location. Johnny rapidly flashed the images back and forth in his mind, studying them and noting every detail.

"Come on, man! You've got to stop there; he can't take any more!" Sascha warned.

The nosebleed was gushing now, and the Disciple lay

there with eyes, teeth and fists clenched tightly. Johnny eased his mind away from the subject and decreased the pressure he exerted from his fingertips, finally releasing the man both physically and psychically. The Disciple's body went limp, he was breathing steadily and any signs of distress had passed. He even managed to half-open his eyes; it seemed his brain might have survived intact.

"So did you get anything?" Baccharus asked.

Johnny nodded. "Time I got changed too," he said and started to strip a dead Disciple's leather robes; wrapped up inside was a portly young woman, he had assumed it was a man.

Once in disguise, Johnny briefed his companions on what he had seen. He described the corridors and chambers that lay in this underground complex, and most importantly, he pinpointed the location of the ceremony – the subterranean cathedral where they would have to confront the Disciples. Sascha and Baccharus listened to all of this very carefully, without even speaking a word, and when Johnny went on to describe the plan he had formulated for the final assault they absorbed every detail and nodded along with what he was telling them. Johnny warned them that soon they would truly be entering the heart of this enemy stronghold. The only certainty was that they would be outnumbered … very outnumbered. He also gave them hope; Johnny believed that he had seen memories of Boyd in the mind of the Disciple. Their friend was probably still alive somewhere in this very complex. When he had finished, Johnny gave his companions a few minutes to reflect on everything he had presented to them, and when they voiced no objections he knew it was time to move on.

"Okay, boys, stay close. Bach, you stay low," Johnny ordered.

"Are we going now?" Baccharus asked, his voice sounded uncharacteristically nervous.

"Yup, now that I have accurate knowledge of where we have to go, there is only one worthwhile way of getting there."

"A Warp?" guessed Sascha.

"That's right."

"Let's go and find some Disciples!" declared Baccharus.

Chapter 38

Consciousness returned gradually. Even before he opened his eyes, Boyd could feel that his body was incapacitated. He tried moving an arm and then a leg but found he could do neither. *Fuck's sake, not again* was the first thought to enter his mind.

A strange vibration which he could not explain pulsed through him at regular intervals, and then he noticed the cold; he felt so very cold. His last memory was of the icy mist, how it had engulfed him and sapped him of life and energy. Maybe he was dead now and that was why he could not move his limbs. The weird whispering and moaning mist had killed him with its cold embrace.

What is that noise? Some sort of singing and chanting? Cherubs perhaps, just like Baccharus ... Am I in heaven?

At first, the chanting had seemed distant; as he became increasingly lucid it was clearer and louder ... and the most fearful thing about it was its omnipresence.

There was relief when he felt himself shivering and his chest heaving – both confirmed he was still alive; he *had* survived the mist after all. His moment of relief only lasted for as long as his eyes were shut. On opening them, he thought he was dead once more, and judging by the scene around him, it wasn't heaven where he had ended up … this was definitely hell.

Boyd lay in a wooden ox-cart, wrapped from head to toe in layers of heavy chain that formed a giant metal cocoon around him so tight that he could barely lift a finger. He looked out through the links that covered his face onto a great Gothic hall which was poorly lit by lanterns and flaming torches fixed to its walls. A purple glow tinged the whole scene and indicated an alternative source of light that he could not see; this puzzled him. Even more puzzling were the twisting, gyrating figures that crowded the peripheries of this strange place and the balconies higher up. Despite years of confronting Disorder and witnessing the peculiarities of its followers, he still found himself watching the dancing Disciples with disbelief. Most were naked except for leather masks that tightly gripped their entire heads; others were dressed in black outfits covered by capes, *they* wore leather masks which were a little different. Theirs were plain and long and hung in front of the face so that their wearer looked out onto the world through two large, metal-rimmed eyeholes. It occurred to him that this second lot were dressed like the man with the syringe he had killed earlier. Further examination of the Disciples revealed the anatomy of a few to be non-human; some were like the blue-skins he had encountered earlier with his friends.

Even through his chains, he felt the very hall itself resonating to the Disciples' chant, which he recognised as being recited in the tongue of Disorder (it was like the language of the Grimoires, only twisted). Its vocals ranged from the complex and intricate to the guttural and bestial; somehow, the legions around him remained in chaotic harmony with each other. He had heard this language before, all over the world, and it only confirmed what he knew already: that he was a prisoner of the Disciples once more. Whispering, Boyd recited memorised lines from the Grimoires, a ward of protection. He was interrupted when a nearby moan followed by a nudge startled him – there was somebody else in the ox-cart! His bonds ensured that he could not turn around to see who it was. Was it the girl, Rachel? Surely, they wouldn't treat a child the way they were treating him now. He felt helpless and angry; if anything happened to Rachel, he swore by the Grimoires that even if it was his very last act in this world, some-one would pay. The chanting proceeded unhindered for what seemed like an age to the trussed-up Boyd. Despite the depravity around him, he was grateful for the flam-ing torches and the multitude gyrating reprobates as their combined heat had almost restored his body temperature.

Then the chanting stopped; there was a tense silence, shuffles echoed around the chamber here and there. "Pre-pare the first prisoner," boomed a voice, cold and author-itative; it sent an unexplainable shiver through Boyd, who had never considered himself to be of a nervous disposi-tion. He heard people moving around in response to the disembodied order. Footsteps made their way towards him as he lay helpless. Hands grabbed his chain cocoon and rolled him onto his side, affording him a better view of what was going on through the links around his face. It was not him they had come for; from the corner of his eye, he could see that they were in fact after the figure lying behind him, the one who had been groaning and was also wrapped from head to toe in chain. He watched as four leather-robed Disciples carried this unfortunate away on their shoulders. *Was it Rachel?* he asked himself again. *Can't be – too big.* It looked like another man; it was difficult to tell through the chain. The captive barely moved. Boyd watched carefully to find out who it was bound within those chains; he realised that whatever fate befell his fellow prisoner would probably be what he would have to look forward to for himself.

While the attention of the hall was diverted away from him, he silently struggled against his bonds; twisting and turning, he tried to free himself. His cocoon rocked to either side, and more details of the underground cathedral were revealed, he even saw the wormhole. Flabbergasted, he watched the ethereal spinning tunnel of purple light and gas, and he flinched whenever lightning crackled through its substance. So engrossed was he by this sight that he even forgot his bondage whilst he observed. For what it was worth, he now had an explanation for the purple glow that engulfed the chamber and the deep vibration that pulsed slowly through its walls and floor. Never in all his years of confronting rogue psychic forces had he seen such a bizarre and breathtaking sight as this spinning region of energy – the focus of this grotesque ritual he was caught up in.

The cold voice bellowed more of its chilling orders. "Bring forth the vessels!" it commanded. The strange audience turned to another section of the great hall so Boyd took the chance to further adjust his position. Caterpillar-like, he brought his knees up and then down together until he was able to see the tall, fierce figure that stood at the wickedly carved lectern. He carefully observed the daunting physical presence of the man who was master of this ceremony; he noted his great height, angular nose, square jaw, lean build and thick black hair brushed back over a large forehead. Despite lacking any notable psychic ability, Boyd could sense energy radiating from this distinguished individual like prickly heat on his face, uncomfortable and unpleasant, quite unlike the aura of calm he felt around Johnny – maybe he was not as blunt as he thought. He suddenly felt the urge to turn away; it was beyond his conscious control, as if there was something offensive about observing this chief of the Disciples for too long. He knew it could only be Edward Devilliers standing there – the Warlock.

When a steady drumbeat started to echo around the hall, Boyd's heart leapt. He followed the collective gaze of the gathered Disciples to a wall with three pointed archways and watched as separate processions emerged from each one with great pomp and solemnity. Two giant, muscular Disciples at the centre of each group carried a sedan chair on their shoulders. They were masked and naked like many of their fellows. All the chairs had a passenger who was draped entirely with a large black sheet that reached all the way to the floor, giving the appearance of three great cones making their way towards the wormhole. The processions marched in time to the slow drumbeat, and when each one had entered the cathedral completely, a collective whisper started amongst the Disciples. This new sound, superimposed upon the deep background pulse of the vortex, had an altogether more sinister and unnerving quality than the previous chanting. It was made even more disturbing by the fact that the Disciples all wore masks, which meant there was no evidence of any moving lips amongst them. The whispered mantra adversely affected the minds of sane balanced men, Boyd included, and he wished for them all to stop. Fear and irrational thoughts afflicted him, and he had to fight hard to prevent these primeval instincts from overrunning his consciousness. Such was the effect of hearing one of the spells of Disorder, and to resist it he uttered to himself more of the words he had memorised from the Grimoires, thus fortifying his sanity.

Female Disciples pulled at the corners of each black sheet, revealing the occupants of the sedan chairs; three young girls, all clothed in long dresses of white silk and lace. He felt his stomach clench; just as he had dreaded, one of the girls was Rachel. The three sat there impassively, staring into space without even blinking, oblivious to the madness unfolding around them. Boyd looked at Rachel carefully; her breathing was agonisingly slow. He had no doubt that she and the other girls were in a trance, possibly drug-induced, maybe hypnosis; he had seen both techniques used by rogue psychic elements before. He flexed every muscle in his body against the chain, his efforts now driven by an intense anger; it did not loosen, even a little. He could only continue to watch what was happening from inside his metal cocoon.

The sedan chairs and their processions came to a halt at three points spaced equally apart around the low wall that encircled the wormhole. With nervous glances at the spinning maelstrom beneath them, the muscular Disciples who carried the girls lowered and then fixed the long poles from their chairs to large ornate metal brackets that formed an integral part of the wall structure. They did it in such a way that each chair with its occupant was held suspended over the edge of the rapidly spinning energy tunnel. Throughout this manoeuvring, the girls had remained unresponsive; their eyes blank, their bodies still and upright. They did not even acknowledge the immense electrified purple region that lay beneath them, even though the wind that blew from it ruffled their clothes and hair.

A distant rumble became gradually louder; something massive was approaching from a fourth archway. Boyd watched and shuddered at what came slowly into view. Four burly, topless Disciples with muscular bodies, leather trousers and leather face-masks of the steel eye-ringed type strained to roll in an enormous wooden scaffold on wheels. A long, sturdy cross arm reached out from the device, and from it hung a row of heavy chains with cruel-looking meat hooks dangling at their end.

The crude, medieval appearance of the contraption made it appear more sinister than anything he had seen thus far. It was pushed ominously towards the wormhole; the size of its beams and the rippling muscles of the masked men who moved it so ponderously left no doubt as to its great weight. Even from inside the cart, Boyd could feel the stone floor tremble under the scaffold's bulky metal-rimmed wheels, and as it got closer the clinking of its hanging chains could be heard alongside the rumble of its progress.

He watched with morbid curiosity and the hope of finding a weakness amongst the enemy. What was the meaning of the sedan chairs? What was the strange scaffold and hook device? Like everything else in this hall, their purpose seemed to lie around the wormhole, so central was it to this vast chamber. The baleful wooden frame came to rest at the edge of the spinning dimensional tunnel along with its bearers. Boyd had decided the device resembled a portable gallows. *A rope would be more inviting than those three meat hooks*, he thought to himself.

Now that the structure was closer, he could see that its wooden framework was spattered with dark stains. He had been around long enough to recognise old blood when he saw it, and it took all his inner strength to fight off the panic that threatened to grip his mind as he lay there helpless before those hooks. In this apparently hopeless situation, bound and terribly outnumbered, there were only his friends left to rely on. Knowing that he was in the presence of psychics who could read his mind, he did not dare to dwell on thoughts of his comrades. To give them away now would be to lose everything. What he did not realise though was how close they already were.

One of the four burly Disciples who had rolled in the scaffold swung its cross beam around by tugging on the thick, frayed rope attached to its far end. This brought the hooks to hang over the stone floor of the cathedral where they swayed slowly back and forth. Again, Boyd wondered what twisted purpose these careful preparations were designed to serve. Not being one to lie back and accept his fate, he struggled against his bonds intermittently, just in case, by some fluke, they had slackened; there was no such luck. He would keep trying though because except for watching the ugly scenes before him there was nothing else he could do.

"*Entroth etta faistanor paphomet erra phicaedes* – Orbok! Start the summoning!" shouted Devilliers from the lectern.

The ambient whisper became a full-blown chant again; the Disciples repeating the words of their leader … words from the warped tongue of Disorder. The phrases used in this particular chant were chilling to listen to, particularly as the repetitions steadily increased in volume. Except for the name of Orbok, Boyd could not understand what they were saying. He had dealt with Disciples who worshipped this strange deity before, and lovers of Orbok were notorious for performing secret rites noted for cruelty and depravity that surpassed those practised by Disciples of Disorder affiliated to other deities.

Another command from the lectern echoed around the hall. "Make the offering!" The ones to respond to this order were the robed cultists who were still patiently holding the chained man who had been lying beside Boyd upon their shoulders. They took up the chant, louder than the others, and their deep voices added a new terror to the already chilling chorus. Two of the four muscular scaffold-bearers took the chained man from their robed fellows and carried him back to their device. They held him high and braced themselves as a third scaffold-bearer took firm hold of one of the hanging meat hooks, raised it above his head and swung it towards the prisoner. The force with which he did this was enough to drive the hook between the layers of wrapped chain and into the body beneath which it penetrated just under the ribs. Boyd gasped at the moment of impact, he had expected a scream of agony – there was only the quietest of moans, as if the prisoner was too weak to muster any stronger protest. The scaffold-bearers released their grip. The location of the hook meant the victim's body hung freely, leaning at an angle of almost forty-five degrees. Disgusted by the evil perpetrated before him, Boyd now considered his own fate; there were two more hooks, and there was little doubt left in his mind regarding whom they were intended for.

Two scaffold-bearers started to unravel the chains from around the victim; a steady stream of blood dripped through the links and splashed their bare chests, some of it landed on the stone floor of the chamber and some on the wooden scaffold frame adding to the stains Boyd had noticed there earlier. He watched, horrified. Whom had they sacrificed? The chain was unwound from the head last, and on seeing the face, Boyd filled with impotent rage. It was the face from the photograph in the apartment. Hanging naked from the hook was Martin. Another feeble moan indicated that he was still alive – barely. On his body were other, older injuries, the most noticeable being a deep gash in his thigh. Martin's eyes were closed and his face appeared pale and drawn. He looked as if he had been in bad shape even before this atrocity. Boyd cursed what he thought was the Disciples' incompetence: they had failed to kill him with the hook and now he was suffering. What Boyd did not know was that the Disciples were too skilful in their abhorrent methods to make errors; they needed Martin to live just a little longer.

The scaffold-bearer who held the rope attached to the cross arm pulled it again, swinging the mighty beam so that it now dangled the almost lifeless Martin over the centre of the wormhole. The blood that dripped from his wounds painted an arc that extended across the stone floor and over the low wall, disappearing into the electrified purple ether. What the Disciples needed was a final boost of energy, one that would further accelerate the wormhole and allow it to bring forth the Demon King himself, because until now, it had transported only relatively minor entities from the worlds of Disorder. The perverse sciences practised by the Disciples dictated that the wormhole was to be fed with life force to achieve its highest energy state, and so they had presented it with Martin's as it left his physical body at the point of death. The freshly nourished tunnel glowed more fiercely than ever after swallowing Martin's soul, and it spun even faster. Martin's dead body stretched and warped to impossible proportions until it was finally pulled to an incalculable length all the way from the hooked chain to the dimension that lay at the very end of the wormhole. It became so narrow in this process that it disappeared from view altogether – there would be no afterlife for Martin.

This energising of the wormhole was the signal for chanting to recommence, and it reached new heights of passion and intensity. The cathedral filled with fresh mantras and choruses, their increasing volume matched only by their progressive disorganisation. The whole affair appeared to have descended into a free-for-all as Disciples seemingly shouted whatever came to mind; somehow, the overall effect worked. Each dissonant voice fitted together to produce a depraved melody that defied logic and in doing so remained loyal to the philosophy of Disorder. This madness heightened the psychic energy in the cathedral further; increasingly powerful bolts of forked lightning started to crackle inside the spinning wormhole, leaping from its purple edges to the unknowable depths at its very centre. Some streaks of lightning even crossed the gap from the portal perimeter to strike Edward Devilliers at his lectern; the High Lord rocked his head back in ecstasy at this, and with outstretched arms he thrust his chest forwards to receive more of the stray, invigorating energy. Cultists writhed, gyrated and recited; some shouted, some screamed, some whispered. The electricity crackling through both the vortex and the body of Edward Devilliers became more frequent and powerful; the vibrating pulse of the portal was now a rapid pounding that shook the whole cathedral and coursed through every nerve ending of those present. Each hair on Boyd's head and body seemed to stand on end, and his skin crawled as if infested with mites, a sure sign of high Presarium concentrations in the air. For the first time, he was experiencing what psychics perceived on a daily basis. He had been trying to avoid thinking of his friends all this time, just in case one of the psychic Disciples was to read his mind. But now he had reached the point where he could no longer control his thoughts, and all he wished for was that Johnny would find a way to put an end to the insanity he was witnessing.

**

Alien beasts from the world of Orbok, Demon King, continued to arrive periodically through the wormhole, their essence shaped as glowing clouds of speeding golden matter. Just as the Disciples had planned, they were drawn through the walls of the cathedral to the rooms in the abandoned wing of the house. Meticulous preparation meant that so far none of these creatures had materialised within the hall itself. These were glorious moments for the Disciples, they were moving closer to beholding Orbok, Demon King, and establishing their new age.

There was one of them, however, who was feeling unsettled following the ceremony, and it frustrated her that she felt this way at such an important time; something inside her was obscuring the path, asking questions that should not be asked. She had always considered her faith in Disorder to be rock solid, so why did she feel herself wavering? Surely, this should not be a problem – was it not said that Disorder rejected nothing; therefore, could it not be concluded that even her doubts had validity within the philosophy of Disorder? Her thoughts were going around in circles; she didn't like it, although she knew why this was happening. During the offering, she, like her fellow Disciples, had felt elation at having moved closer to the goals of Disorder. The knowledge of her brother's sacrifice had been acceptable, welcomed even, and then the chains were unwrapped. Something changed deep inside her. The sight of the pierced, broken man had produced a visceral reaction, one that rekindled the dying flame that was her old self, the thoughtful, caring sister with very human traits; and now, after many years, she was seeing the world through those eyes again. Elizabeth Devilliers found that she existed in a strange duality, the love of Disorder instilled in her through years of soul-corrupting exposure was unchanged – alongside this was the renewed presence of an earlier personality, driving her in a different direction.

Chapter 39

Edward Devilliers looked on approvingly from the stone lectern at the forces he had set in motion. As a powerful psychic, he could feel the energy around him far more intensely than anybody else present. To him the air was electric, saturated with Presarium, and his very substance resonated synergistically with each pulse from the portal. Lightning arced back and forth between the vortex and his body, lighting up the underground cathedral with brilliant white flashes that lasted for seconds at a time. Finally, he was satisfied that the wormhole, the corridor between Orbok's world of Disorder and his cathedral, was ready. It had grown in potency ever since the beginning of the ceremony, and now it was strong enough to carry the essence of the living deity that was the Demon King.

Standing at his lectern, Devilliers felt intense sensations such as he had never experienced before; pleasure that no orgasm could match, alertness no stimulant could achieve, pain to which no torture could compare. He was enjoying himself; it was a shame he would have to be leaving all this, even if it was only for a few minutes … Arkkun was requesting an urgent audience. Faithful Arkkun had wisely allowed the ceremony to commence without interruption to a stage where the wormhole did not require the

High Lord's full attention. As he stepped away from the lectern, Edward Devilliers wondered exactly what it was that troubled his chief Disciple. He had already been informed that little Rachel, always unpredictable, had run away at the last minute, only to be found again by Mr Kreb and his hound. *Mr Kreb*, thought Edward Devilliers distractedly as he made his way to Arkkun, *now there's a fine specimen*. His trusted enforcer, Kreb, was summoned several years ago through the wormhole to be his personal aide. Here to struggle with him until the kingdom of Disorder on Earth was established; loyal only to him, Edward Devilliers, in whose veins ran the blood of the demoness, daughter of Orbok, Demon King.

Edward sighed and shook his head as he walked through the large Gothic arch to the smaller administrative corridors at the rear of the cathedral where Arkkun awaited. After being on the lectern for so long it felt nice to stretch the legs; this was the sole reason why the High Lord had not bothered to summon Arkkun to him. *What is the problem now?* he wondered, guessing it had something to do with that persistent Agent of the Equilibrium; it was unfortunate, he thought, that this whole endeavour continued to flirt with failure. He consoled himself with the knowledge that despite all the hiccoughs, the ceremony was still on track; the sacrifice, a human soul, had now been offered. *Martin had made himself useful after all*. Keeping things on track was vital now; it would be generations before the positions of the celestial bodies (both within and outside this solar system) were in an ideal alignment for repeating this ceremony. On this particular night, the tide of Presarium flowing through the portal was just right, exactly as it had been predicted by past lords. If the flow was too weak then there would be no way that Orbok, Demon King, could complete his journey to reach Earth, and if it was too strong then any life force, including one as great as that of Orbok's, would be torn apart by the currents. Indeed, tonight the conditions were ideal for the Demon King to manifest on Earth and touch the womb of each of the three virgins, making them carriers of his seed. A simple touch would be sufficient to implant his life force – *so much more efficient than the human equivalent* – and then the virgins would bear three kings; human–demon hybrids to rule Earth in the name of Disorder once again. Three kings to command each portal, another battle won in the Trinity War – the struggle for the alignment of the universe.

Soon, Orbok will be here in his full majesty to tread upon this world, thought Edward Devilliers joyously. It would be a dangerous time when the deity arrived; direct physical contact would mean instant death to all humans, except for the virgins, who had been chemically treated and blessed, and himself, of course, for he already had the blood of demons within him and was therefore immune to the death touch.

As he walked, Edward Devilliers listened with plea-sure to the now distant, devoted chanting. It was a psy-chically potent piece called *The Diabolicium*, a collection of mantras imploring Orbok, Demon King, to appear. He was in a narrow stone corridor lined with numerous wooden doors, a far cry from the grandeur of the main cathedral hall where the ceremony continued without his presence. The fifth administrative chamber was where Arkkun would be waiting; Edward found the room and entered. He was in a small stone space that, despite its ancient origins, was now furnished and fitted out with the latest modern office furniture and electronics; carefully, he closed the door behind him. Inside the carpeted office waited Arkkun, although not as Edward had ever seen him. Arkkun the warp phantom's physical form flickered in and out of existence. His molecules switched randomly between alternative energy states for a few seconds at a time. For an instant he would appear to be transparent, as if he were a projection of light, only to become solid suddenly or even disappear from view altogether. Edward raised one of his dark eyebrows at his old teacher's predicament; there was going to be some explaining to do.

It took a full fifteen minutes for Arkkun to update Edward on the disruption caused by Johnny and his friends. On completing his account, he stood quietly as the High Lord of Chaos pondered. *There is a powerful enemy in our midst*, thought Edward, *but one who has yet to perform a psychic feat that I myself would not be able to.*

He was irritated at the invasion. He had complete faith in his own abilities on both the psychic and physical planes and so was not overly concerned regarding this matter, just irritated. *Should the time come, I will personally cut down this intruder.*

"How many more guards do we have to spare, Arkkun?" he asked.

"We have fifty remaining, about half of them armed. Five of them are lower grade psychics, four of them are my initiates; I will be happy to remove the stitching from their eyes so they may seek out and destroy the intruders." Arkkun was referring to the practice of stitching shut the eyelids of new psychic initiates to encourage them to rely on inner perception over the five senses; in these dire circumstances, training would have to be suspended.

"Unstitch the initiates. Keep them as part of the ceremony for now; we still need to maintain the wormhole. Send the remaining psychics out with half the guards, Arkkun; the rest are to stay in the cathedral hall. The order is: 'if they cannot stop this agent, then they are to resist him to their last breath'. I'm sure they won't defeat him; hopefully, they can hold him off long enough to complete the ceremony. Only then will I be free to give my full attention to the eradication of this pest. I emphasise that the ceremony must not be disturbed! Orbok, Demon King – must not be disturbed!"

"Shall we send out Mr Kreb? With his beast? Together they would be quite able to track the intruder down. They are exceeded in ability and ferocity only by you, Edward."

Devilliers shook his head. "No, Arkkun, we will not yet play all our cards. Mr Kreb is to remain in and around the cathedral."

"As you wish."

"By the way, how are you? Can you use your psychic ability any more as a warp phantom?"

"I am weakened, lord; my powers have become unpredictable, and they fluctuate as I have never known them to."

Devilliers nodded with a frown, unsure how useful his lieutenant was going to be in any confrontation. "Send out the men," he ordered.

With those words, he left the fifth administrative chamber to rejoin the ceremony. *Poor Arkkun,* thought Edward. Johnny's psychic spear had struck him just as he was about to shift his physical form through space–time, thus inflicting a warp injury. Now Arkkun would spend the rest of his life as a warp phantom, to flutter in and out of existence, to be there but not really be there. That was the lot of a warp phantom. Edward felt sorry for his old teacher, to be suffering such indignities in his latter years was unfitting; he *did* find himself a little amused by the unfortunate flickering individual – undeniably, there was a wicked streak within Edward Devilliers. He returned to his lectern.

The ceremony was already in full flow. The High Lord's presence produced a renewed fervour amongst his followers, who chanted and gyrated their naked bodies harder than ever in the presence of their spiritual leader. Edward was proud of them, his Disciples. He looked expectantly to the centre of the spinning purple portal, waiting for the first signs of the manifestation of Orbok; something would happen soon – he could feel it. As he stared, entranced, into the portal, he thought about Johnny's intrusion. The attack on the cathedral complex had not been altogether unexpected; there was never any doubt that the Equilibrium would send agents to stop him sooner or later. He had gone to great lengths to try to disguise his activities; the location itself and the energy from the portal would have provided adequate cover for a while. To activate the wormhole, the corridor to the worlds of Disorder, meant harnessing huge amounts of psychic power which would have been impossible to hide indefinitely. It was only a matter of time before he was found. In fact, it was not he who had been slack, by leaving it this late to intervene in the ceremony it was *his enemies* who had not been paying sufficient attention.

Who is this agent? he wondered. Usually these matters could be left solely to Arkkun; this time, the old man had come unstuck. He looked up to the high balconies of the cathedral's viewing gallery and mezzanine; he opened his senses. Arkkun was there already, projecting his orders as a psychic message to his initiates who passed it on verbally to the guards, causing as little disruption as possible to the ceremony. The guards and psychics could be differentiated from most Disciples by the simple fact that they were the robed and clothed ones. There were a few others performing specific tasks who also wore some form of dress. The majority of the gathered were required solely to participate in the ceremony and were therefore naked except for the leather masks stretched across their heads. Edward's eye wandered around the hall, and he noticed the proportion of flesh on display become more prevalent as the robed guards were dispatched to start the hunt for any interlopers, leaving the nudes behind.

Standing at his lectern in anticipation of Orbok, Edward Devilliers felt a gentle, subtle psychic disturbance in the atmosphere which quickly disappeared. It did not possess the essence of Disorder and should not have been there. He looked around the cathedral urgently to see what it could possibly have been; he did not see or sense anything unexpected, the ceremony was proceeding as normal. He looked up to a balcony, towards the flickering form of Lord Arkkun, also a potent psychic; his old teacher seemed oblivious to the disturbance he had just sensed. Anxiously, he turned to the shadows that lay beyond the Gothic arch behind him, towards the hidden form of Mr Kreb, who was lurking there. Kreb, who also possessed powerful psychic perception, appeared unmoved, his eyeless face expressionless. There was no acknowledgement of the disturbance from him either. *Nobody's noticed!* The disturbance had been very subtle and short-lived; he started to doubt if he had actually felt anything himself. *No! There was definitely something there. How could they have missed it? The fools!*

He cast his careful eye over the proceedings once more; his mind moved amongst the gathered cultists. *What was that disturbance?* The ceremony was continuing unhindered. Edward looked on solemnly as the Disciples chanted, rocked and gyrated. The wormhole spun as fast as ever, crackling with energy, throwing off bolts of electricity. Then, from the blackness at the portal's very centre, there emerged a pin-point of brilliant light; there was a collective gasp from the gathered. It was the first sign of the manifestation of Orbok, and the sheer joy of the moment fuelled the dance of the Disciples. Edward Devilliers' features softened again, and he even managed to smile. He raised his arms into the air. "*Ente gresgnit artum!*" he cried out, and blue-white lightning leapt from his body and into the wormhole to be absorbed by the sacred glow at its centre, increasing it in size fractionally. A renewed madness gripped the cathedral chamber; the chanting shifted to a higher pitch. He moved his attention momentarily to the three virgins, they were breathing more quickly and mystic winds from the wormhole tossed their hair. Their bodies were undergoing physiological processes never intended by nature; the resulting biochemical changes would allow them to receive the Demon King's essence. The brightness at the centre of the spinning wormhole grew steadily and was starting to take on form; no longer a single point of light, it was now an irregular glowing shape. This slow transformation was space–time being moulded into a region that could accommodate the physical presence of Orbok; only once the glow had taken on the dimensions of the Demon King's body would he be able to occupy it and complete his journey to Earth.

All eyes in the chamber were now fixed on the events taking place around the wormhole, all except those of Edward Devilliers, who continued to sense subtle anomalies that bothered him. Even the most capable of his minions remained oblivious to the worrying Presarium shifts he could detect; maybe he was expecting too much of them, sometimes it was easy to forget how far his ability exceeded theirs. He put these concerns aside briefly and turned his attention back to the ceremony. "More!" he ordered, his great voice projecting all the way to the furthest Disciple, and the chanting, gyrating figures became manic. "Orbok! Orbok!" their cries echoed around the cathedral. They were the giant, living generator that powered the wormhole, and their actions hastened the arrival of the Demon King.

**

Boyd, wrapped in chains at the centre of all this commotion, witnessed everything. With the wormhole fully activated and the arrival of Orbok imminent, it looked unlikely that the Disciples would need another sacrifice. He found some consolation in this, not for himself – for the three innocent girls. Remaining alive meant he was still in with a chance of stopping the dark proceedings and preventing any harm befalling them. His thoughts were interrupted when he felt the chain around him inexplicably loosen; he wondered if one of the mighty links had broken through his struggles. Then it started to slowly unwind by snaking away from his body, and he knew this was no chance occurrence; there could be only one explanation – Johnny! His friends must have made it here! Even in his injured state, his body battered and bruised from road accidents and battles with demons, Boyd managed to grin. Whether he would live or die he did not know; whatever happened, he would make sure there would be some payback first. The chain stopped moving. Although it still covered him, it was now loose enough to be thrown off. He felt the circulation and sensation return to his body; it made him feel stronger. *One more round*, he thought as he lay there, *one more round* …

Chapter 40

The feverish excitement gripping the crowd suited the three intruders; it made them even less likely to be noticed. Probing the mind of the Disciple on the stone stairway had most conveniently revealed the layout of this underground labyrinth to Johnny, and it allowed him to warp with his companions to the very rear of one of the enormous viewing balconies. To do this and remain unseen, he had distorted space–time to the point that they were able to move merely as a ripple through the air. Before infiltrating the ceremony, Johnny and Sascha had disguised themselves in the robes of the Disciples while Baccharus had concealed himself by hovering low amongst the folds of his keeper's new garb. Once they were amongst the enemy, the two humans had edged their way forwards through the seething mass of bodies, and the familiar had flitted to the shadows high up in the ceiling; in this way, each was able to look down onto the central region of the cathedral.

The companions had arrived just in time to witness the fearful scene of the naked, injured man, whom they did not recognise, being stretched across dimensions. Johnny regretted not being there soon enough to aid the poor wretch. The sense of horror he had felt at the unknown individual's fate was equalled by the awe inspired through his first sighting of the wormhole – the source of the psychic disturbance that had started their journey. Recalling Theodora's words from his vantage point, Johnny saw first-hand how the once placid pool of the original portal, so necessary for balancing Presarium levels on Earth, was entirely dominated by the malignant spinning dimensional corridor of the wormhole; a sight that filled anyone who viewed it with amazement and wonder. To those less psychically adept than him, it was mostly a visual spectacle, but he could also sense the link to the worlds of Disorder through it and feel the psychic hyper-stimulation that Edward Devilliers had experienced earlier. Once again, he understood how seductive the path of Disorder was to so many, although he could not bring himself to submit to it; he still found something obscene in it.

After managing to pry his eyes away from the wormhole, Johnny had taken the opportunity to examine the hall further and spotted Boyd, bound in the wooden cart. He had not been able to recognise the chained man straight away, only after carefully scrutinising his build and noting his blunt psychic signature had he concluded that it was indeed his friend lying there. Through a subtle exertion of his will he had set him free. Johnny had loosened the chain; it was up to Boyd now to decide how and when he would take advantage of his new-found freedom.

Johnny observed the proceedings closely. Outwardly, he looked a picture of calm; inwardly, his mind worked frantically as he planned his next move. The main source of consternation now was the glowing light at the centre of the wormhole taking on the shape of a giant humanoid, the form of Orbok. Although it did not yet contain the Demon King's substance, it was already terrifying in what it represented.

Johnny glanced up at his familiar, who was getting dangerously close to moving out of the Qrwshan amulet's protective range. Johnny hoped the high Presarium count here would cover Baccharus's tracks. He then looked towards Edward Devilliers to see if he had noticed their presence. The leader of the Disciples was becoming distracted from the ceremony; his dark, dangerous eyes glanced around the cathedral hall suspiciously, sure there was something going on. Johnny knew the psychic disruption caused by warping into the chamber and freeing Boyd had alerted Devilliers to their intrusion, however, at this range it was being seen which would be more likely to give him and his friends away rather than the detection of their auras. He had to act soon.

From Johnny's vantage point, Edward Devilliers presented a tempting target. He realised that opting to attack the Lord of Disorder directly would only give him one strike before he and his friends were overwhelmed by the legion of swaying and chanting Disciples around them. One strike to end an adversary as powerful as the High Lord was not enough; there would have to be an alternative plan.

Johnny appraised the situation further as he stood amongst the naked, heaving bodies of the enemy. He and his friends were still seriously outnumbered here, but something favourable had occurred. Earlier, the warp phantom Lord Arkkun had given the order for his guards to leave the cathedral and search the complex for intruders. The tunnels of this underground network were a maze, and so the guards would be gone for a while; slightly fewer enemies to face. Yet another factor to consider was how dangerously exposed the three girls were, still fixed in their chairs and positioned over the wormhole; in an all-out attack they were very likely to be injured, as was Boyd.

Unfortunately, Johnny could not see Mr Kreb, who remained hidden from view beyond the arch; his Fire-hound was there too, pacing restlessly as if it were pre-empting disquiet.

Hidden amongst the Disciples, Johnny knew he still had the advantage of surprise, and it would have to be exploited soon. He thought hard about a suitable plan of attack before finally deciding on an insidious strike. *Remain under cover and throw the enemy into disarray – fight Disorder with chaos.* He whispered his thoughts to Sascha who was standing beside him. In agreement with the proposed strategy, Sascha, with a pistol concealed amongst the folds of his hijacked robes, drifted away from Johnny into the sea of Disciples, even joining in with their insane chants at times to preserve his disguise. He was to remain under cover and look for an opening to covertly wreak havoc amongst the forces of Disorder. Next, Johnny communicated psychically with Baccharus, who was secreted amongst the gargoyles decorating the vaulted ceiling. His message was kept as brief as possible and timed to coincide with some particularly powerful energy feedback events from the wormhole so that it might avoid detection. His orders were simple, and moments after receiving them the familiar struck stealthily.

Johnny quietly watched Baccharus whip up the flames from a large brazier in a dark corner of the hall. Tongues of the psychically enhanced fire leapt unnoticed beyond the metal basket that held them. The robes of three Disciples who were standing nearby caught alight; they thrashed around trying to put out the flames with their flailing arms, unintentionally inflicting burns upon their nude companions in the process.

The wildly unpredictable fire threatened to set further robes alight, and in the resulting confusion the chanting started to falter. Since the recent enhancement of his psychic ability, Johnny had been in uncharted territory and was still learning how to fully harness his skill. With this in mind, he improvised his next attack, never having attempted anything like it before. If he pulled it off, it would be no end of help to them.

With eyes closed and a frown of deep concentration marking his face, he drew Presarium and any nearby matter into the shape of a dozen glowing orbs of thermal energy which he duly unleashed to race around the cathedral – a collection of miniature speeding suns. The chanting was replaced by the wails of the injured as each ball of hot plasma made contact with a body. Disciples scattered around the great hall, trying to avoid the lethal orbs; some lay on the floor, presumably dead, while many hid and nursed their injuries. Johnny even had the audacity to pursue the High Lord with his new weapons; it only took a casual wave of the hand for Edward Devilliers to deflect the orbs that were heading towards him. By doing so, he spared a whole section of the hall and many of his Disciples from the psychic attack. Earlier, Johnny had been observing the confusion on Devilliers' face; now he could see that his foe understood exactly what the energy anomalies he had previously sensed were.

"Show yourself, worm of the Equilibrium!" cried out Devilliers in anger, his powerful voice reverberated throughout the cathedral and was audible even above the screams and shouts of the burning men and demons. Disciples started looking at each other suspiciously, wondering who it was that their master addressed.

Johnny felt a nudge; Sascha had sidled up next to him and was pointing towards the wormhole. He had noticed an important phenomenon. As the chanting had faltered and eventually stopped following Johnny's psychic assault, the pulsing of the wormhole had slowed down a fraction and the glowing shape at its centre had ceased growing. Johnny acknowledged this observation with a gentle nod.

"Continue the chant!" cried out Edward Devilliers; Sascha drifted back into the confused throng. Johnny looked to the cathedral floor, some of the orbs were still dive-bombing the Disciples; most of their energy had dissipated to the point that they were becoming transparent and fading away. He observed the charismatic Edward Devilliers crying out to his people, rallying them. "True Disciples of Disorder, call out to Orbok – Demon King. Do not become distracted by what is happening in the cathedral. I, the one who loves you, will protect you as I always have done!"

Johnny would have to face this man soon; he had to find more room first or he would be trapped by his followers. As he looked around, he spotted Sascha, who was still under cover. Johnny watched his friend trying to disrupt the proceedings by bundling into a group of gathering chanters, acting as if he were one of the many in the cathedral injured by the orbs. With this tactic, Sascha managed to delay their attempt at restarting the chant. Regrettably, his determined actions had made little difference to the progress of the ceremony overall because the Disciples nearest Edward Devilliers, the ones who had escaped the worst of the orbs, already had the accursed mantras of Disorder on their lips again.

Johnny eventually found a way from his balcony to the large mezzanine. He carefully watched Edward Devilliers, whose hawk-like eyes continually scanned the cathedral for his enemies. He sensed the High Lord project a great psychic shield; it didn't alarm him, in fact he was mildly amused – he was already within its boundary. Devilliers must also have realised this because soon there was no shield present; instead, there was a probing field of energy individually caressing the aura of all those present, hunting out the unwelcome. Johnny became aware of what the High Lord of Disorder was doing. One could only hide from a potent psychic such as Edward Devilliers for so long.

Baccharus was the first to be discovered; he had drifted a little too far out from his hiding place. Johnny saw Devilliers raise an eyebrow and leer at the winged figure hovering amongst the shadows in the grand vaulted ceiling. Almost immediately a beam of purified psychic energy blazed a trail from the forehead of the High Lord to Johnny's little companion. The bright line of concentrated Presarium oozed with power, and Johnny had no doubt that it would disintegrate its target; he had anticipated something like this and replicated what he saw. Almost instantaneously, another similar line of energy shot out from under his cowl, and the two beams met, cancelling each other out in a shower of multi-coloured sparks. By sparing Baccharus from annihilation, Johnny had revealed himself.

Having forced the intruders from concealment, Edward Devilliers could not resist a satisfied grin. The beams remained locked into each other, his concentration deepened, just as Johnny's did, and the smile faded. Each combatant vied to exceed his opponent's psychic strength. The electrical disruption from the beam weapons sent most Disciples scurrying for cover while Baccharus managed to dart down from the ceiling to lose himself amongst the frenetic activity below. The strain showed on the faces of both psychics. The Disciples nearest to Johnny turned towards him; they watched as he projected the lethal energy, unsure what to do. To have an enemy amongst them, in this of all places, was unimaginable and some even thought he was a part of the ceremony.

"Kill him!" commanded Devilliers, obviously frustrated at the indecision from his followers. The momentary lack of concentration in giving this order weakened his beam, which was duly driven back by Johnny and threatened to blow his head off. The minions of Disorder around Johnny, faithful to their master's command, moved rapidly. They were a fanatical collection of naked, masked humans and sinuous blue-skinned demons who howled foul oaths and curses in the objectionable tongue of Disorder. A few of the robed guards, who were further away, advanced with drawn knives, and one, a pistol. Now it was Johnny's focus that was interrupted and Devilliers' turn to force his beam back. The enemy closed in and Johnny was trapped. His psychic power was focused on resisting the High Lord, he could hardly move; to do so would further disturb his concentration and then surely Devilliers' energy beam would make contact. The first of the cultists was almost upon him when there was a loud crack and he dropped to the ground. Further gunshots downed more Disciples and there was disarray in their ranks. From the corner of his eye, Johnny saw Sascha discreetly drifting amongst the robed and naked throng with pistol drawn, barely notice-able beneath his leather robes. On witnessing his followers cut down and further evidence of infiltration, Devilliers was enraged; it was all Johnny needed. With a supreme effort of willpower he drove Edward Devilliers' beam back, causing the High Lord to recoil suddenly before being thrown off his feet. Finally, Johnny was able to launch a psychic attack on the few Disciples who continued to threaten him despite Sascha's admirable defence. He pro-duced a giant wavefront of energy, similar to the one he had used earlier in the garden. It pushed out from around his body, repulsing the approaching Disciples, sending them tumbling away; many were thrown off the mezzanine and onto the hard stone floor beneath. As Johnny tried to recover from the effort of his psychic activity, more powerful adversaries made their way to meet him.

Mr Kreb had already reached the balconies of the gallery level; his long strides carrying him closer to Johnny, who was making his stand on the mezzanine. The Firehound rushed ahead of him, towards Sascha. For many of the Disciples, this was the first sighting of Mr Kreb and his familiar, and they parted fearfully to let the pair through. Johnny could see the Firehound charging at his friend with its muscles rippling and bulging. Fatigue prevented him from summoning an effective psychic strike so he shouted a warning instead. Sascha had just finished reloading the revolver, which was raised before him, and he started to fire. Each shot bit deep into the hound's flesh, prompting a howl. The creature advanced relentlessly; it seemed that all the bullets had achieved was to enrage it further. Sascha retreated whilst attempting to shoot, and the revolver was soon empty. Johnny tried to rush to his friend's aid, unsure if he would be able to produce anything psychically once he got there; the hound was well ahead of him. Sascha reached the edge of the mezzanine, and as he tried to reload again the creature pounced. Sascha raised his arms. Johnny shouted; it was all he could do. At that moment, Baccharus suddenly re-emerged from hiding; he was hovering over the balustrades behind Sascha. The familiar was on the offensive; his little arms were a blur of movement as he produced a hail of fiery psychic bolts. He managed to hurl a barrage at the creature's face as it leapt though the air, burning hair and flesh off bone. With parts of its skull exposed and dripping phosphorescent life fluids, the Firehound appeared more hideous than ever. It was a valiant effort on

Baccharus's part, but the familiar's projectiles did not kill the beast, and they could not stop its momentum. The hairy, muscular mass knocked Sascha, spinning, over the top of the mezzanine balustrades before following him over it, howling.

"Sascha!" screamed Baccharus over the noise, diving to catch up with his falling friend. As Sascha tumbled towards the ground, all the smooth stones, the psychic grenades, rolled out from the trousers and jacket he wore under his robes. They hit the cathedral floor with a massive explosion of psychic energy directly beneath him and the Firehound. The intense wave of released Presarium deflected the creature's body and caused its brain to implode. Sascha was also repelled by the explosion. The force of the blast beneath him actually helped to break his fall, and not being psychic meant he was spared any significant neurological damage, unlike some others in the cathedral. All Disciples with psychic ability on the lower level of the cathedral were sent sprawling to its edges, their higher cerebral function permanently impaired – most of Lord Arkkun's initiates were disabled in this way. On witnessing so many of the enemy overpowered at once, Baccharus celebrated.

Remaining higher up on the mezzanine level had protected Johnny from the full impact of the psychic explosion; this had also spared Mr Kreb, who was rapidly closing in on him. Johnny attempted to repel the demon-man's advance with a lance of energy that singed flesh and clothing. Kreb was powerful enough to absorb most of this attack, and before Johnny could launch another assault, psychic or otherwise, he was held in a crushing bear hug. He struggled for breath as he was shaken from side to side so hard that it looked like his head would disconnect from his body, and then Kreb released him, hurling him across the stone floor. As Johnny lay there winded, he tried to focus his mind on another psychic weapon; the demon quickly followed up his first attack with a stamp aimed at Johnny's sternum. Johnny rolled to one side and narrowly avoided the crushing injury; he looked back to see a crack in the stone floor where the demon's foot had landed. Kreb stamped again; Johnny stopped the foot with a psychic barrier and bought himself enough time to stand up, only to be on the receiving end of a fist. He managed to move his head quickly enough for the blow to merely brush his cheek. He retaliated by sending a psychic shockwave at the figure in black, an attack he was becoming quite adept at delivering. Kreb was thrown backwards, and Johnny pressed home his advantage by launching a psychic javelin that sent the demon burning and sliding across the floor. Johnny had recovered well from his earlier psychic exertions against Edward Devilliers. This was all new territory for him; prior to meeting Theodora, he could never have imagined operating at this level of psychic proficiency.

Mr Kreb, whose strength was not human, got to his feet and advanced once more, seemingly oblivious to his smoking clothes and flesh. Johnny began to muster an even more powerful attack; at the very last moment he sensed an incoming psychic force and urgently redirected his willpower into an impromptu shield which was just strong enough to absorb the energy beam Edward Devilliers had fired from the cathedral floor.

Upon recovering from his opening duel with Johnny, the leader of the Disciples had taken the opportunity to set the ceremony back in motion and left the warp phantom Lord Arkkun to preside over the summoning of Orbok. It was a double blow for Johnny. Not only had Devilliers returned to face him – the chanting had started up once more. Johnny didn't dwell on this unfortunate turn of events for too long, mostly because he couldn't – Mr Kreb had started projecting a chaos field, just like the one from their earlier battle. Johnny was suddenly overwhelmed by his own brain's neurological activity; the flood of sensations and emotions to which he was subjected threatened to cripple him – and then things got worse. Edward Devilliers levitated up to the mezzanine level to launch another attack as Johnny lay sprawled on the floor. Even in his weakened state, Johnny managed to fire random psychic bolts that struck light blows at both Edward Devilliers and Kreb, buying him just enough time to create another psychic shield against the inevitable onslaught coming his way.

Edward Devilliers pounded Johnny with psychic weapons: spears, beams, bolts – everything he had. He did this while Mr Kreb projected the chaos field. Each attack was absorbed by Johnny's shield; the effort of fending off so much energy was weakening him. Devilliers and the demon Kreb knew this, and they were happy to continue with what was now a battle of attrition. Johnny sat on one knee, locked in deep concentration; he was hardly visible due to the psychic activity flashing and exploding all around him. The enemy gloated, knowing it would only be a matter of time before Johnny's psychic shield caved in. The ceremony under Arkkun's direction was in full flow again. Soon Orbok would arrive, and to the Disciples of Disorder a favourable outcome looked inevitable. But they had made a mistake … they had forgotten about Boyd.

Chapter 41

It was not in Boyd's character to stand idly by while all hell broke loose around him. After his chains were slackened he had waited for the right moment to act, and now, with both Edward Devilliers and Mr Kreb attacking Johnny on the upper level, it was time for him to make his move.

Whilst bound, he had thought of a way to save Rachel and her sisters from the horror of the Disciples' ceremony; whether they knew it or not, his friends would be playing a pivotal role in the rescue. They had not let him down so far, and he hoped they would maintain that record.

Shaking off the last loops of chain, Boyd, still dressed in motorcycle leathers, slid his body unnoticed to the edge of the wooden cart. He looked around carefully; just as he had calculated, most of the Disciples were distracted by the brilliant pyrotechnics from the combating psychics, and many were making their way to the mezzanine to aid their leader in destroying Johnny.

Boyd leapt onto the floor and shifted stealthily to the edge of the wormhole. He moved around the low wall that surrounded it until he reached the suspended sedan chair on which Rachel sat in her trance. He crouched near the long handles that held it over the spinning purple tunnel, all the time keeping a close eye on the glowing form of Orbok manifesting in the air at its centre a few feet above him. He could not resist looking down, beyond the lightning, into the black depths of the wormhole. From this close it was both a truly spectacular sight and a feast of sensation. The multiple wavelengths of energy that radiated from it caused his skin to crawl and his hair to stand on end. Its emanating pulse could be felt through his entire body, and the wind that blew from its centre was strong enough to buffet him. He looked up towards the serene figure in the chair.

"Rachel," he called. She did not respond. Even with the background noise, she should have heard him; he suspected her trance was too deep. It was time to put his plan into action and remove her from the chair. He would have to work quickly because the wormhole was the central point of the chamber and the distraction from the psychic battle taking place overhead would not last forever. Boyd hoped that when the time came, his friends would notice him first, even though it was more likely to be the enemy who did so. He stood up from his crouched position, stepped onto the wall and stretched over the wormhole, reaching out towards Rachel with one hand while the other held the long handle of the sedan chair to support his body in this precarious position. Boyd glanced down quickly to steal another look at the spinning purple maelstrom that formed the impossibly long tunnel beneath him. He was closer than he would have liked to the forked lightning that crackled and discharged below and dreaded to think what one of those bolts would do if they made contact with him; he was pretty certain that the effect would be quite different from the one they had on Edward Devilliers. "Rachel!" he called one more time above the sound of rushing air, and still she did not respond.

With great effort, he extended an arm and grabbed the girl's wrist. He did all this with toes barely touching the low perimeter wall. His other arm tightly grabbed the sedan chair and supported most of his body weight. He gently eased Rachel's flaccid body to one side until she leaned out of the chair. From here, he gripped her around the waist and pulled her slight frame onto his shoulder. Boyd was now hazardously supporting his own body weight and also that of the girl.

"Stop him!" came the inevitable cry – he had been spotted. Disciples started to gather around him, most of them in long capes and leather robes. He had been observing the chamber long enough to work out that these were the ones who carried the knives and guns, unlike the naked ones, who were mainly involved in the chant. Close to him was a man with a cowl and leather mask through which puffy, sore eyelids were visible; he had his fingertips placed on each temple, a sure sign of psychic intent. Boyd surmised that so long as Devilliers and Kreb, the most powerful of the Disciples, continued to focus their attention on Johnny, he was in with a chance. Entirely exposed in the middle of the hall, hanging over the deadly wormhole with the unresponsive girl, and barely able to hold on to the sedan chair, it would have seemed to any onlooker that he had miscalculated, but it was this moment that he had willingly gambled everything upon. "Back off, motherfuckers! If I fall, then she falls," he sneered at the Disciples who slowly did as he asked whilst exchanging anxious words with each other. "No girl, no ceremony, right?" he said with a taunting smile which he managed to summon despite the burning pain in his arms. The nearby psychic initiate, with his swollen, scabbed eyelids, could only stand and watch – poised to strike; unable to take any action.

With Rachel positioned so dangerously over the lethal

spinning wormhole, the Disciples of Disorder could do nothing. If they lost even one of the girls then the events of this night that they had planned so meticulously would be worthless. None had the stomach to risk being blamed for the premature ending of the ceremony and facing Devil-liers' infamously labile temper; maybe he would forgive them, or maybe he would damn their souls for eternity – it wasn't a chance worth taking. They decided to wait, realising the intruder could not hold on forever. And if he became too tired, they did not know whether he would allow himself and the girl to fall and die or if he would claw his way back to the floor again and into their hands.

It was all as Boyd had planned. He was banking on a rescue by his friends. The worst outcome for him was either Devilliers or Kreb appearing on the scene: both were powerful enough to lift Rachel away from the trap and remove him permanently. He guessed that Arkkun could, until recently, also have dealt with him; as a warp phantom though, he was far too unpredictable and not an immediate threat. All Boyd could do was hang on. If help did not come, even he did not know if he could stop himself and the girl from falling into the depths below. But help did arrive, and few could have guessed the form in which it ultimately presented itself.

Of the cultists that had gathered around Boyd, most failed to notice the improvised weapon descending from above, and for the few who did there was little time to react. The main earthly source of light for the cathedral was from numerous, massive inverted metal cones filled with solid fuel and flame; they were mounted high up on the walls. One of these had detached and was floating through the air with intent to where Boyd was. It moved as if held in a pair of giant invisible hands. Once it was close enough, the massive torch was thrust into the heart of the throng surrounding Boyd; it whipped from left to right, scattering and felling many Disciples. Anyone foolish enough to approach Boyd and the wormhole drew the unwanted attention of this fiery death trap. The torch's movements were wild; it jerked at every conceivable angle, and its unpredictability made it even more terrifying. There were screams of pain; clothing and robes were set alight once again, and on witnessing their flaming brethren, the exposed Disciples were grateful for their nudity. It took only seconds to disperse the enemy from around Boyd as he hung over the wormhole with Rachel still on his shoulder. Another of Lord Arkkun's few remaining initiates tried to halt the thrashing torch with his will; he was brave – he was also far too inexperienced to overcome the momentum of the attack. The reward for his effort was to be struck on the head so that he was unconscious when his robes were set alight – most of his comrades had burned alive.

Boyd watched the confusion around him with some satisfaction; he knew his friends had a hand in all this. It was becoming increasingly painful for him to hang over the wormhole with Rachel's dead weight on his shoulder. His muscles were so fatigued now that to even consider clawing his way back to firm ground was a waste of time. His grip started to falter, and he found himself morbidly wondering what being swallowed by the wormhole would feel like. Soon enough, only his curved fingertips maintained any purchase on the chair, and he could feel himself sliding a millimetre at a time towards the spinning purple oblivion. It became painfully obvious to him that there was no point in hanging on any more; he would have to use any remaining strength in his overstretched muscles to try and throw Rachel clear as he fell in. But he wasn't quick enough. Boyd grunted as he lost his hold on the girl and her weight came off his shoulders.

"Hang in there, tough guy," implored a familiar voice unexpectedly. From the corner of his eye he could see a pair of hands with a firm grasp on Rachel; gently, they pulled her away from him and the terrible fate below, the relief he felt was indescribable. Boyd himself was not out of danger yet. The sensation in his arms and hands had disappeared from hanging on for so long, and he was not even aware of it when his tired fingers finally released their grip on the chair. His upper body swung down towards the wormhole and then slammed into the side of the wall where it hung suspended. The same hands that had lifted Rachel to safety were now grabbing one of his legs and the waist of his trousers. He was pulled slowly and with great effort back over the low wall until he finally came to rest on the hard stone floor of the cathedral where he collapsed, panting. He shook the sensation back into both of his tired arms before extending a hand to his rescuer, who helped him back onto his feet.

"I thought I told you to hang on!" said Sascha with a grin.

"You took your time didn't you, sunshine?!" Boyd replied as he winced in pain from one of his many injuries. "How's the girl?" he ventured.

"Appears generally unharmed. Although she's not particularly responsive I'm afraid."

Boyd nodded with concern at this.

"Let's find somewhere a little more discreet," suggested Sascha. They were in the middle of the cathedral and far too exposed at the moment; Boyd followed him without any argument. The floating torch, still lit, its flame dying, provided cover for the rescue. The friends moved away from the wormhole, and they found shelter behind one of the immense stone pillars that supported the upper levels and the vaulted ceiling. The torch burned itself out and crashed to the ground. Soon, Boyd and Sascha were joined by Baccharus.

"That was you, wasn't it?" said Boyd with a massive grin and a high five aimed at the familiar.

"Guilty as charged," Baccharus replied, returning the high five. The flaming torch had been a lethal manipulation. Disciples were sprawled everywhere; some were burning and others lay groaning.

"Where's Johnny?" asked Boyd.

It was a chance for Sascha and Baccharus to give him a quick update. The familiar described how they had become separated following Sascha's fall from the mezzanine. "Once I reached Sascha, we could both see that you and Johnny were in trouble," Baccharus explained. "After racking our brains, we decided to help you and Rachel first. We concocted the plan to use one of those great torches as a weapon."

Boyd nodded appreciatively.

Baccharus continued, "Regarding Johnny's whereabouts, as far as we know he's still on the mezzanine holding off Devilliers and Kreb."

"So he's still in trouble?" asked Boyd.

"I suppose so," said Sascha with a sad look.

Boyd was thoughtful. During the drama of Rachel's rescue he had paid little attention to the progress of the ceremony; now, sheltered behind the pillar, was an opportunity for him and his friends to catch their breath and reassess the situation. Opposite to them, on the other side of the wormhole, was a hard-core group of chanting Disciples focused on keeping the summoning of Orbok alive. They stood together, a naked choir conducted by none other than Lord Arkkun. A defensive line of guards stood in front of these chanters separating them from the wormhole and the intruders. Most were armed with the familiar long knives; a few carried pistols, and they took occasional pot-shots at Boyd's small group behind the pillar to keep them at bay. Sascha retaliated by returning fire sparingly with the revolver. Boyd watched him handle his weapon and was impressed; he was doing a good job considering the circumstances, and so Boyd did not ask for the handgun to be returned.

Boyd had to concede that overall things were not going well. The persistence of Arkkun's choir was showing frightening results. The pulsing vibration from the portal was rapid and the glowing light hovering above its centre was massive now; its height reached halfway to the ceiling, which was at least six storeys above them. The light formed the shape of a large muscular humanoid with a head that might have been from a wild animal. The Disciples took heart from the apparition materialising before them. A chilling cry made Boyd's heart skip a beat.

"Chant on!"

It was the warp phantom of zealous Lord Arkkun. Even though Rachel was no longer sitting in her chair above the wormhole, Boyd could see that so long as she was present in the cathedral the Disciples believed there was a chance their ceremony might reach completion.

Everyone's attention was suddenly drawn to a particularly large explosion from the psychics fighting on the mezzanine.

Sascha stopped firing and looked at Baccharus and then at Boyd. "Johnny is pretty stuck up there. We should really try and find a way to grab the other girls ... and someone should leave with them," he said.

"Well, then let's think of a way to do just that," said Boyd, knowing it was going to be no easy task. He directed a few quick questions at his companions and established that the way back was a mystery. None of them, Rachel included, had entered the cathedral through conventional means, each having been either transported by space–time warp or unwillingly brought in as an unconscious prisoner. With this in mind, Boyd looked around for a possible way out. His attention was drawn to five large, ornate archways nearby. They had been worrying him for a while, mostly because he could see that if any Disciples were to enter the cathedral through them then their little group would be surrounded; however, they also presented the tantalising possibility of an exit from this underground hell. As much as he wished to explore these arches, the gunfire from the Disciple guards was successfully pinning them all down and preventing any closer examination. For now, they would have to remain behind the pillar.

"Keep chanting!" urged the warp phantom of Lord Arkkun, his piercing voice audible over the psychic combat. Boyd turned from the five archways to look at him.

"There's all to play for yet," cackled Arkkun.

The hard-core chanters persevered with their dark mantra, and their defensive line of guards stood unwavering. The few remaining psychic Disciples had also fallen in with the mad choristers, and they were making a significant contribution to the summoning. This group included the last of Arkkun's initiates (recognisable by his swollen, bleeding eyelids). Arkkun gestured manically to different sections of the choir, creating an insane hymn. His psychic ability may have been crippled by Johnny's previous attack but his mind was as scheming as ever. He glared over his shoulder towards Boyd and his friends behind the pillar, daring them to cross the line of guards he had arranged. The glowing shape of the Demon King now filled most of the space above the wormhole. It would not be long before this mutation of space–time was filled with Orbok's actual physical form. It appeared to Boyd that the Disciples were no longer going to waste their energy on pursuit; they would rather complete their task and summon Orbok – the Demon King.

Rachel, lying on the ground at the feet of her rescuers, stirred. Boyd looked at her and then looked up again. "We've got to get the other girls soon," he said, resolved not to leave them to their fate. Sascha agreed.

"Then we get Johnny and get the heck out of here!" added Baccharus, nervously eyeing the vast demonic shape suspended between the three sedan chairs.

"I hope that lad is okay," said Boyd. "Why don't you go and check on him?" he suggested to the familiar. "And whatever you do, don't try intervening!" Boyd was worried Baccharus might injure himself, or worse, if he tried helping Johnny.

**

Baccharus flew up to a place where he could spy on Johnny and saw his keeper continuing to gallantly resist the psychic onslaught from Devilliers and Kreb. By now, most other Disciples had abandoned the upper levels because the Presarium fallout from the combat taking place there was causing all manner of neurological complaints amongst those in close proximity, complaints such as: convulsions, migraines and even unconsciousness. It was intolerable for all except the most hardened psychic practitioners – even Baccharus baulked as he got too close. Eventually, the familiar also backed away, impotent against Johnny's powerful adversaries.

Chapter 42

Under relentless bombardment, Johnny had subconsciously adopted the foetal position, the body's natural defensive posture. Forced to concentrate his mental focus on preserving the shield, he was not being given the opportunity to prime an attack of his own. As he considered his options, it occurred to him that his only hope lay in manipulating the strength of his powerful adversaries; what he had to do was try to redirect the megawatts of energy they were aiming at him. *Hallelujah for old kung fu movies*, he thought, as these were no doubt the inspiration for his next move. He saw his opportunity in a beam of Presarium projected by Edward Devilliers; with a single determined thought he managed to curve its trajectory and set it on a collision course with Mr Kreb. For good measure, he increased its potency by adding some of his own energy. The result was a brilliant flash of light and a fearsome explosion that blew away a large section of the mezzanine. Johnny watched the black shape of Mr Kreb as he was hurled from the upper levels all the way down to the cathedral floor surrounded by crackling blue-white electricity. An unearthly scream followed his hard landing beside the wormhole. Fierce bolts of lightning leapt from his writhing figure to discharge all around the ground level of the hall, forcing Johnny's friends and Disciples alike to duck away from the wayward, random strikes.

Johnny observed the outcome of his attack with horror, almost forgetting about the threat from Edward Devilliers. Kreb's limbs thrashed uncontrollably as the strange electric charge danced about his body. His screams became unholy wails that sent shivers down the spine until they gradually faded along with the electrical energy that so tormented him. Finally he was still. The dead body of Edward Devilliers' murderous helper was contorted in a terrifying way; the moment of death had evidently not been an easy one for him.

The Disciples wavered in their chant; they fell out of time with each other and slowly became silent. Johnny looked down from the balustrades at a few of them; some swallowed nervously and others glanced at their comrades, unsure of the implications of this loss. Arkkun was not going to be so easily confounded. "Our master, the High Lord Edward Devilliers, lives! Victory is ours!" he declared aloud, stirring passion within his choir. The cathedral filled with the sound of the damnable chorus once more.

Johnny turned to face Edward Devilliers; the High Lord had recovered from the unexpected violence of Kreb's death quicker than he had. All Johnny saw was a bright flash as he was helplessly thrust all the way to the far wall of the cathedral on the end of a beam of brilliant light that outshone even the lightning produced by the wormhole. The force with which Johnny struck the rock wall opposite produced a crater which radiated large cracks; the impact was enough to pulverise a man. Johnny had been psychically shielding himself and so only looked winded as he dropped back down to the cathedral floor. The chanting stopped.

"Johnny!" called Baccharus and Sascha while Boyd leapt from the safety of the pillar to run to his friend's aid.

"Stay away!" warned Johnny as Devilliers slowly glided down from the mezzanine to the ground level. Reluctantly Boyd turned back.

The two psychics faced each other across the wormhole. They both looked tired; neither was about to give up.

"Continue the ceremony!" Devilliers ordered the Disciples without taking his eyes off Johnny. "Every time you stop from now on, I will kill one of you myself!"

His associates needed no further persuasion, and the hall echoed afresh to their mantras. Johnny felt the wormhole's pulse accelerate until it was a constant beat that filled the cathedral. What really worried him was the light above it which had taken on the shape of a six-metre tall monster. His imagination went wild as it tried to picture the detail within this great outline and guess the appearance of Orbok, Demon King.

Devilliers proceeded to fire a barrage of energy beams at Johnny, who managed to deflect each one. Johnny had learned that Edward Devilliers was a master of the follow-up attack, and the High Lord did not disappoint on this occasion. Launching himself behind one of his beams, Devilliers flew straight at Johnny. Before the younger man could react, he had grappled him to the ground. He was strong, Johnny could certainly feel that, but there was something here beyond what mere muscles could achieve. Johnny sensed that Devilliers was enhancing the strength in each of his movements with psychic power; the High Lord's combat prowess was exemplary. Devilliers flung his victim, skidding across the floor, to the other side of the cathedral and into a wall, a move that would have killed Johnny had he not used his own powers to buffer the crushing impact. As Johnny struggled to try to sit up, he saw his opponent dematerialise. There was a barely discernible ripple that moved through the air in an instant, and suddenly Edward Devilliers was visible again, on top of him, pinning him to the ground. Johnny grabbed at Devilliers and rolled over; locked together, the two gladiators fought on, conducting their battle between the hellish choir on one side and the wormhole on the other.

**

"Right! This is our chance to grab the girls! They're fighting in front of that line of guards," said Boyd from behind the pillar. Sascha and Baccharus readied themselves: here was an opportunity to save the innocents and further interfere with this accursed ceremony.

Brushing aside the unpleasant waves of nausea triggered by the psychic duel, Boyd scurried over to the wormhole, trying hard to ignore the terrifying glow of Orbok's summoning. Baccharus flew alongside him. The titanic battle taking place between Johnny and Devilliers provided most of the cover Boyd needed; however, as a precaution, the cherub psychically shielded him as best as he could. Sascha remained behind the pillar with Rachel, who was now semi-conscious; he had his revolver at the ready.

Boyd, with Baccharus's help, pulled the youngest girl, Lisa, off her chair and onto solid ground before doing the same with Meredith. With an extra pair of hovering hands the job was much easier than it had been with Rachel, and this time there were no games to play. Disciple guards tried to prevent the rescue by firing a few shots past Johnny and Edward Devilliers; their bullets were inadvertently deflected by psychic shields and space–time disruptions generated as the psychics struggled. Boyd quickly returned to the pillar with Baccharus and the girls. He could not help stealing another look at the five archways, each presented the possibility of either exit or ambush; however, all were in direct line of sight of the enemy's guns, so, for now, he would have to leave them alone. Boyd glanced back at the empty sedan chairs with some satisfaction; unfortunately for him, the morale of the Disciples seemed unaffected. He could only assume that this was because Orbok, Demon King, was nearly here. The light at the centre of the portal was starting to fill with detail and colour, becoming ever more real and present; an encouraging sign for those aligned to Disorder, who chanted louder and faster in acknowledgement of the imminent arrival of their beloved.

"Fucking hell! They won't shut their mouths for five minutes, will they!" cursed Boyd.

"Why should they?" reasoned Sascha. "All they have to do is keep us here. They know that if Edward Devilliers beats Johnny then getting the girls back is no big deal. You've seen Devilliers' power; he could just pluck all three from us with a thought. We're safe behind this pillar; we are also stuck, so they might as well continue with the ceremony."

Boyd could see that the Disciples were doing whatever they could for their cause, just as he and his companions were for theirs. The final outcome would rest on the battle of psychic titans that was now taking place.

There was a groan from Johnny; Boyd watched his friend caught in what he could only imagine to be an invisible psychic lasso. Johnny was hurled from side to side by the wild movements of Edward Devilliers' arms. To Boyd it was plain to see that any non-psychic would have been crushed by the first impact if subjected to such an attack;

the only reason Johnny could survive was through buffer-ing the forces at work with his own psychic ability. There was movement beside Boyd's head; it was Baccharus, the familiar was about to fly to Johnny's aid. Without even thinking, Boyd reached out and grabbed the cherub by his calf in a firm grip. Baccharus turned to face him, incensed.

"Don't go out there, friend; you're lucky you weren't killed when Devilliers spotted you the first time around," said Boyd, holding on tightly.

"I've got to help Johnny!"

"Flying out there and getting hurt is not going to help anybody!" insisted the big man and Baccharus stopped struggling against his grasp. Their exchange was abruptly interrupted when Johnny landed on his back only metres away in yet another heavy impact; it was a bad hit and he looked dazed. Sascha automatically leapt out from behind the broad pillar to assist; Boyd and Baccharus screamed after him to come back. As he broke away from the safety of his cover, the Disciple guards opened fire. He kept his head low and, against the odds, reached Johnny. He had made it to his friend's side – just as Edward Devilliers was about to deliver the death blow. From each of his raised hands the High Lord of Disorder summoned two great beams of energy which crackled and glowed white-hot, dazzling all those who beheld them. The lines of raw psychic power traced their way through the air, to where Sascha leaned over Johnny. Screaming, Baccharus flew towards his keeper and friend using all the strength of his will in an attempt to project a shield; not only was he too late, his defence was also useless against the power com-manded by Edward Devilliers. Boyd witnessed all of this, convinced that it was the last he would ever see of Johnny and Sascha. He knew that only a potent psychic could resist an attack like that; had he been fully conscious, Johnny might have done it, but he was only just coming round. Boyd couldn't leave the girls; he bellowed a final, desperate warning as the beams hit home. All of the gathered Disciples yelped with joy at the impact, which was spectacular. It created a glowing sphere of brilliant white light that engulfed Johnny and Sascha completely, masking them from view. When the beams stopped and the sphere faded, Boyd could hardly bring himself to look; when he did he was entirely unprepared for what was before him: Sascha crouching over Johnny, holding aloft the silver cigar-shaped device he had been tinkering with in the motorhome. Its once shiny body was smoking and crumpled. His homemade creation, designed so elegantly to interfere with psychic energy waves, had saved them. A broad grin slowly crept onto Boyd's face as he figured out what just happened. Baccharus chose to express himself rather differently. "Fuck you!" screamed the familiar at Edward Devilliers. "Fuck you!"

In frustration, Devilliers fired a stream of erratic psychic bolts at all those who opposed him. Boyd grabbed the girls and they huddled together behind the pillar as chunks of masonry were torn away from it and sent raining down upon them. Baccharus narrowly avoided being hit as he flitted acrobatically through the air. Johnny was lucid once more, just in time to psychically deflect this fresh attack, giving Sascha a chance to follow Baccharus and shelter behind the pillar again with Boyd. Devilliers focused his onslaught on Johnny, and whenever the opportunity emerged, he would aim a few shots at his friends behind the pillar, being careful not to strike Rachel or her sisters.

Chapter 43

Wearily, Johnny managed to project a wide-ranging shield that extended as far as his companions. Struggling for survival meant he had lost track of the ceremony; it was swiftly brought back to his full attention again when the chanting reached a sudden crescendo, and the pulsing beat of the portal began to feel like it was penetrating to the very core of his person. A blood-curdling roar exceeded every noise before it and visibly shook the great underground cathedral. It signalled the climax of the summoning – Orbok, Demon King, had manifested. The awesome moment brought all activity in the great hall to an immediate halt – chanting, combat, movement and even breathing for some. The wormhole rotated slowly again, its pounding beat replaced by a gentle ebb which might have restored a sense of calm had it not been for the immense creature hovering over it where the light had once been. Four storeys tall and almost as broad shouldered, its torso was humanoid. The beast possessed an extra pair of arms beneath those it shared with the human form. Its muscles were grossly exaggerated; so enormous and inflated were they that each one's outline could be traced with anatomical accuracy. Massive thighs and calves, broader than oak trees, ended in cloven hooves around which thick tufts of black fur grew. The demon was covered from head to toe in an even layer of shiny, jet-black scales; it was impossible to say whether they were actually its skin or some form of alien suit. Orbok's appearance was terrifying; a thick sinuous neck supported a huge black head that vaguely resembled a terrestrial big cat, possibly a panther, with two great black bull's horns sprouting from either side all covered in more of the shiny scales. The Chaos deity observed its surroundings and the scattered multitude of lesser beings with sapphire-blue eyes that exuded a cold intelligence. The expressionless stare of an animal would have been a mercy compared with those eyes, so human in their appearance. The only other sound besides the slow ebbing of the portal was the deep snorting breath of the demonic deity echoing around the hall. Orbok took a step through the air above the portal to stand on the solid ground of the cathedral; the contact of hoof with stone floor shook the hall. Johnny watched in horror with his friends. The creature's physical power was undeniable; Orbok would have been a match for a hundred men. The most frightening aspect about the Demon King, however, was his superiority to humankind in both intelligence and psychic ability. Johnny knew this from the aura Orbok projected; it was like no other he had ever felt, a force of nature in itself.

Johnny bitterly resisted the sense of helplessness that threatened to overwhelm him. He saw the expressions on the faces of his companions, such good resilient people; it was the first time that he had seen them looking so cowed. He had defeated Mr Kreb and countless other Disciples, he had doggedly faced Edward Devilliers; now, with the Demon King present, all he could do was project the shield that guarded him and his friends.

Theodora, the Earth mother, had put so much faith in me,

thought Johnny, *she was wrong* … From the beginning, Johnny had questioned his suitability to carry out this most exacting of tasks. His previous doubts and vacillations now appeared justified because Edward Devilliers and the Disciples had successfully opened the gateway; the demon had been summoned … *the old woman's faith in me was misplaced.*

"Aid me, Orbok, Demon King!" implored Devilliers, breaking the ensuing silence. "Destroy those who would challenge Disorder."

With a maddened scream, the High Lord unleashed beam after beam of psychic energy from each of his hands, digging deep into his psyche for a final withering onslaught on Johnny and his friends. Johnny could feel each strike fractionally weaken his shield and he winced from the effort of resisting. Shouting incoherently like madmen, the rest of the Disciples advanced upon the small party crouched behind the pillar, testing the limits of Johnny's shield themselves, trying to physically force their way through it, hurting themselves in the process and not really caring.

The Disciples were no longer bound by the need to continue their chant so caution had been thrown to the wind. They were emboldened by their supernatural ally and a favourable outcome now seemed inevitable to them.

**

Orbok the mighty was still orientating himself to this new plane of existence he now occupied, this alien world to which he had been summoned. Journeying through the wormhole meant having his substance rearranged into energy waves and then transcribed across dimensions to take physical form again on Earth; it took time to adjust following such a process.

Ponderously, the Demon King turned his great head towards the commotion. Orbok had heard Edward Devilliers (whom he recognised as his affiliate and partial carrier of his genetic code) call to him for aid. The demon had no need to understand language; sensing Devilliers' brainwaves when he had spoken was more than adequate for perceiving his intentions. In fact, Orbok could sense the neural activity of every living creature present within a hundred-mile radius from gnat to human, which meant the ancient Demon King also recognised the power that lay in Johnny, his affiliation to the Equilibrium and, most importantly, the threat he posed.

**

Johnny watched Orbok lift a pair of his four bulging arms, each larger and heavier than a man. There was a glowing fireball of energy taking shape within the palm of each hand, almost ready to be thrown at him and his allies. Straining to maintain his shield, Johnny did not doubt that the Demon King's psychic weapons would obliterate this defence. He guessed that Orbok would first remove the shield, and once it was gone he would kill him and his friends with a single thought, sparing the girls to fulfil the Disciples' dark purpose.

Johnny prayed to whoever might be listening for help. He knew that other life-forms opposed to the Demon King existed in this universe and many were as powerful as the deity; he also knew that such beings generally paid little attention to a planet like Earth. Here and now, it was only he and his friends who could confront this terrible being of Disorder. Already, Johnny had implemented all the psychic potential that lay within him, and it was nowhere near strong enough to overcome the enemy he now faced. He longed to manifest one final devastating attack that would stop the Demon King, Edward Devilliers and the mad cultists. To find a way, his thoughts moved back to Theodora's mystic trance; it had taught him how his own limited perception, his inability to believe in what could be achieved, had stifled his psychic growth. He had put this lesson to good use in fighting Edward Devilliers and harnessed power he had never before known himself to possess; now, for the strength to defeat Disorder, he would have to look deeper, both into and beyond himself. He would need to fortify his psychic ability from elsewhere – *but where?* He knew the answer to this lay in the short time he had spent with Theodora – not the trance – in her words. In their brief meeting she had tried to impart as much of the weighty and profound knowledge that she possessed as she could. The depth of her understanding meant that it had been impossible for her to give him any specific advice so she had chosen to explain some essential principles central to her view of the universe; it was the best she could do in the limited time they had. It was up to Johnny now to meditate on what he had learned; he needed a moment of deeper insight to find the means to defeat Disorder.

Think, man; the answer is there. Think! What did she tell you? As he urged himself to recall the old woman's lessons his concentration shifted away from the shield he projected and it wavered; he ignored this because he was on the verge of an epiphany. The old woman had spoken of the spirit that lay within the planetary sphere, how it was the source of all power and knowledge. "Earth is a living entity," she had said. "There is strength that lies within it. When the time comes, harness it." In this most desperate of moments the meaning of those words became clearer.

So far he had been relying only on his own innate power; considerable though it was it could not compare to the might of the Demon King, who was a force of nature from another planet. Theodora, it seemed, was telling him of a more ancient force he could manipulate: the power within Earth. Johnny opened his mind to all the energy that resonated around him and entered the unknown; here he discovered what the old woman had called the 'Earth spirit'. It was so vast and omnipresent that it escaped the notice of all besides those who specifically set out to seek it. A constant vibration that permeated every ounce of matter around him, he sensed its origins from deep underground, within the very substance of the planet – its presence suddenly seemed so obvious. Audaciously, he used his mind to move this energy. It required a technique that was very different from normal psychic manipulation. You could not force it with willpower, the Earth energy had to be harnessed by gentle coaxing. It was like directing a giant beast, he imagined an elephant, a creature so large that it could not be lifted or forced to go where one wished it to be. The trick was to persuade it to move of its own volition. With this in mind, Johnny attempted to direct the planetary force to act against the Disciples of Disorder and initiate the destruction that would end the evil of Orbok and Edward Devilliers.

So distracted were they by the Demon King and the confrontation that no one noticed the fine cracks that were forming in the ceiling and walls of the underground cathedral; no one except Johnny, who had caused them. The cracks widened and spread rapidly through the rock, and within seconds huge, gaping chasms had started to open up. Just before Orbok could launch the great balls of psychic power from his hands, he was knocked over by a massive section of falling ceiling. Tonnes of rock and earth poured into the cathedral chamber burying the deity and all those around him. Johnny's companions looked on with relief and terror in equal measure. The debris moved as Orbok strained to lift the gargantuan piece of ceiling off his body; rubble tumbled away to reveal the demon underneath. His mighty muscles flexed against the weight, veins thicker than hosepipes bulged with the effort and he managed to free himself. Orbok stood once more; he was terribly injured, and black fluid oozed from multiple wounds all over his body.

Panic-stricken Disciples scattered everywhere as further cracks and fractures appeared in the chamber. More rock started to rain down; Devilliers watched in horror. It was no miracle that Johnny and his friends were spared from the cave-in; this was not a random collapse, this was a psychic phenomenon of higher purpose, a mighty living power acting under the guidance of Johnny M., Agent of the Equilibrium. So far, the orchestrated destruction was as Johnny intended, but already he sensed that this great force his mind wielded would slip out of his control at any time.

Johnny was barely able to move as he concentrated so deeply. He was only vaguely aware of what was happening around him. It was like viewing a distant movie projection: something far away with which he could not directly interact. He could just about see Sascha, Boyd and Baccharus watching in amazement at what was going on around them. He sensed their uncertainty regarding the origin of all the devastation they were witnessing. He saw Baccharus point at him eventually and heard his friends call to him; he did not dare respond. And when the realisation dawned on his companions that it was indeed he who had brought about the collapse and that he was not to be disturbed, he saw them turn away again. A few

Disciples persisted in advancing on his friends, and they were caught either by Sascha's gunfire or by falling rock. Johnny noticed a shadowy figure who seemed to be having a few lucky escapes from the collapse; he realised that it was actually Lord Arkkun warping randomly between energy states. In one instance, Arkkun just about avoided being crushed by a tumbling wall as his body flickered from solid to wave form. The wide scope of the destruction around him meant that it was only a matter of time before he was caught; in the end, a Gothic arch falling in on itself bisected him as he tried to escape the broken cathedral.

It was becoming increasingly difficult for Johnny to direct the destruction away from his friends. And even though he desperately wanted to urge them to escape he could not; to do so would break his concentration and cause him to relinquish whatever little control he maintained over the carnage, most likely killing them all in the process. It would be up to his friends to take the initiative and leave.

Chapter 44

With the enemy thrown into confusion, Boyd saw an opportunity to break cover and head towards the five archways; he still did not know which one would lead them to safety. He turned to Sascha to see if he had any ideas; his friend shook his head and told him that only Johnny knew the layout of the complex through the mind probe he had performed earlier. Boyd turned to Johnny and hesitated when he saw his glazed, unblinking eyes and the unnatural stillness with which he stood.

"Don't disturb him," whispered Baccharus. "I think it will be dangerous if we do." Boyd did not argue with this advice. Johnny appeared completely cut off from the events around him: he was dwelling in a world of purely psychic perception. Boyd averted his gaze only when the mighty pillar that had been faithfully sheltering him and his companions slowly started to crack. He agonised over which way to turn next, unwilling to let his friends and the girls down. Just as he was about to select an exit at random, a voice from one of the arches drew his attention. He spun around. A beautiful woman dressed in the robes of the Disciples with her hood drawn back stood in the third archway. She was beckoning and calling for him to follow her in a gentle voice that was barely audible over the din of destruction. *Who was she?* Her dress alone was good enough reason to be suspicious of her.

"Please, you must follow me; it's a way out of here." She was almost begging.

By now, Sascha too was aware of what was going on. "Who's that?" he asked. They both looked into the pleading eyes of the woman in the archway, unsure what to do. Boyd turned away from her and looked back across the cathedral to see what the options were. The Disciples were now more concerned about their own survival and were ignoring the little group behind the pillar. They remained mostly on the other side of the hall and seemed to be scrambling over each other to leave through a broken doorway in the opposite wall of the cathedral; so dangerous was the route to this door that most of them did not make it. This did not deter the rest from also taking great risks to try to pass through it. *That door must lead back to the surface*, Boyd thought to himself. He turned around again; the woman in the arch was gesturing for them to come to her. *Who is this Disciple? Why would she help us?*

"Please follow her," said a weak voice from near to him. Both Boyd and Sascha looked down abruptly; it was Rachel – she was awake.

"It's my stepmother; you can trust her," Rachel said feebly.

Boyd turned to Sascha and Baccharus; they nodded slowly. Rachel's recommendation was all they had to go on.

Boyd and Sascha shepherded the three girls, who were all slowly regaining consciousness, to the arch through which their would-be saviour awaited them. Baccharus psychically shielded the group from the worst of the falling rocks. The Disciples were in too much disarray now to provide any real resistance, and those that did met a swift end from the revolver which had been returned to the hands of its original owner. It was the third arch through which they proceeded, and it led them into a large, undecorated stone room with a brazier in the corner beside which stood Elizabeth Devilliers. There were more archways in here, each with a flight of ascending stairs. "This is the way out," she said, pointing to one of them.

"You stopped the Disciples from coming through the arches, didn't you?" Boyd asked, finally understanding why they had not been surrounded as they hid behind the pillar. The woman simply nodded and gave him a serene smile. Sascha and Baccharus were already leading the girls up the staircase. "Come on, let's go," Boyd said to Elizabeth, expecting her to escape with them. Gracefully and without a word she shook her head.

"What? You can't stay here!" Boyd argued, hoping that he might have misunderstood her intentions. Rachel, still looking groggy, returned to the foot of the staircase with Baccharus in swift pursuit, urging her to go back up.

"Mum, come with us," she pleaded.

"No, Rachel. Go now; go with your friends and sisters. I belong here; I can't live with the knowledge of what I have done. Go! All of you!" The room shook fiercely; its walls cracked and the ceiling started to crumble. It too was succumbing to the destruction and would not last very long.

"Thank you, Elizabeth," said Boyd, remembering the name of Martin's sister; he did not want to think of her as Edward Devilliers' wife. Elizabeth walked out through the archway. Baccharus and a distraught Rachel were already moving back up the stone stairs as they desperately tried to reach Sascha and the other girls. Boyd watched Elizabeth a little longer as she returned to the great cathedral hall. He saw her carefully pick her way through the broken masonry with purpose and wondered where she could possibly be heading. He frowned when he saw her objective; it was the High Lord of Disorder himself. As Edward Devilliers staggered about in disbelief at the ruins of his cathedral, Boyd raised his revolver. Devilliers was in his line of sight. He started to squeeze the trigger but released it when Elizabeth inadvertently blocked his view. Devilliers hadn't seen Elizabeth yet, his form started to flicker momentarily, and it looked like he was going to warp away; Boyd cursed. At that very moment a section of falling balcony landed on Edward Devilliers, crushing the lower half of his body and pinning him to the ground. Boyd lowered his revolver. He heard Elizabeth scream, "Edward!" as she rushed to her husband. Devilliers was grimacing and barely alive when she reached him. Boyd could have sworn that he saw Edward Devilliers manage a smile at the sight of his wife. Elizabeth frantically tried to pull Edward Devilliers out from the rubble; it only caused him more pain so she stopped and instead placed her head on his chest. Tears streamed down her face and created channels in the dust that covered her cheeks. Gasping for breath, Edward Devilliers reached out with his hand and touched her face; he wiped away some of the tears before his body became suddenly still. Elizabeth remained with her husband, oblivious to all that was taking place. Boyd turned away to join his companions as they made their way to the surface; he could not bear to witness Elizabeth's inevitable fate.

**

Since instigating the process of collapse, Johnny had barely moved, and his eyes stared unblinkingly into space. Controlling the Earth's energy with his mind was like guiding an ocean liner with the rudder from a dinghy. He hoped that with most of the pillars gone it would not be long before the entire mass of earth above the complex fell in, covering the portal once and for all. Johnny had set in motion a chain reaction that was now out of his control. Finally, he broke his concentration and once again perceived the world through the five senses; he shuddered at the sight of Orbok, injured and very much alive. He could see that the Demon King had managed to free himself from the great section of ceiling and rubble that had threatened to bury him earlier. The wicked deity continued to be bombarded by tonnes of falling rock and earth. Orbok was badly hurt, and his once proud body looked soiled and damaged. Johnny thought he could sense Orbok drawing upon his psychic power to deflect further punishment; it must have been difficult, even for a creature of his incredible ability, because of the injuries he had sustained. The Demon King limped to the edge of the slowly spinning wormhole, determined to return to his own realm. He stepped onto the edge of the low wall, ready to leap into the tunnel of purple ether; just before he did so, he turned around to look Johnny straight in the eye. For an instant, Johnny felt himself linked to the great, boundless consciousness of this being; it caused him to gasp and stagger backwards. Orbok had allowed their two minds to become momentarily bonded, and once more Johnny felt removed from the world around him. His thoughts moving in parallel with Orbok's, he could sense the Demon King was considering destroying him. As he readied himself for his final breath there was a last-minute reprieve, Orbok had experienced a brief vision of the future, a mere flash; it had given him a glimpse of Johnny's destiny and it was tied to the way of Disorder. With the approximation of a smile upon his alien features, Orbok said something in the coarse tongue of Disorder, his deep bellowing voice drowning out the noise of the cave-in. The language meant nothing to Johnny, but he was still patched into Orbok's great mind, and the alien being's message found its way directly into his brain.

"We shall be avenged tenfold," was Orbok's final communiqué, and with what was definitely a wide leering grin, Orbok, Demon King, dived back into the wormhole. Johnny felt a jolt shoot through his head and down his spine as Orbok broke the psychic link. Why the link had been initiated in the first place, Johnny did not know for certain. Maybe it was how Orbok would have killed him, joined to his victim's mind so he could feel his death first-hand, or maybe it was just how he communicated – it would have to remain a mystery. Johnny watched the dimensions of the Demon King's body warp and twist until he became a narrow thread of light, rather like Martin's dead body had, and then Orbok disappeared altogether. As soon as he was gone, the collapse of the massive cathedral hall accelerated, confirming to Johnny that Orbok had been resisting the power of the Earth energy with his own will and slowing the rate of destruction.

The only Disciples still in the cathedral were dead so Johnny tried to warp himself to safety; he failed, his mind was too exhausted from the efforts of battling Disorder. He still had the layout of the underground complex memorised from his mind probe and stumbled through the third arch, just like his friends had, and then started up the long staircase that would take him back to the surface.

Johnny discarded his Disciple disguise and made his way lethargically; the steps rumbled underfoot, and he was peppered by falling stones. The ebbing noise and vibration of the portal faded the further he climbed. He could just about see his friends in the distance, far ahead of him, so much closer to freedom than he was. They were moving slowly because the girls were still recovering from their sedative drugs. At the halfway point of his escape, Johnny heard a roar from behind him. It sent a tremor up the stairway and a rush of air; he turned around to see the passage caving in on itself. The destruction worked its way steadily up towards him and was preceded by a cloud of billowing dust. He still did not have enough energy or mental focus to attempt a warp and so moved his aching limbs quicker, legs pumping away as he tried to stay ahead of the approaching collapse. He looked up and was relieved to see that his friends were now out of sight, they had managed to clear the stairway; for him, it was still too early to celebrate.

Suddenly, he saw Baccharus emerge at the top of the passage; they looked at each other. "It's Johnny!" screamed the familiar before flying down to aid his keeper. "This way! Follow me!" urged Baccharus excitedly once he finally reached him. Too tired to respond, Johnny staggered on without a word. Baccharus grabbed the collar of his long coat and started to drag him up, psychically deflecting falling debris as he did so to make sure his exhausted companion didn't slow down. In this way, they made it to the entrance chamber with the two pillars, just before the passageway collapsed entirely. Having come this far, Johnny tried to sit down and catch his breath; Baccharus, fearfully eyeing the cracks appearing in the wall carvings, did not let him. Shouting encouragement and directions and even resorting to prods from mildly energised psychic bolts, the familiar led his keeper into the house proper, through the utility room and then into the kitchen. As they made their way to the broken window, the whole house started to quake, rattling all the lights and ornaments. Pictures fell from the kitchen walls, and crockery tumbled out of the cupboards, smashing to pieces on the floor. Sheer tiredness meant Johnny was making a mess of climbing out of the window and was left hanging halfway through it. Baccharus did not hesitate in pushing him the rest of the way in an undignified roll.

Outside again, Johnny felt a wave of cool night air wash over him, a relief from the stuffy underground atmosphere he had been in for the past few hours. It was still dark, and he had lost all track of time. He saw his friends resting on a section of patio that had managed to stay relatively intact during the Bar-Shiyq's death throes. He staggered to them; they looked just as worn out as he felt. When they finally met again, Boyd could only manage to give Johnny a feeble pat on the shoulder while Sascha exchanged a weak handshake; breathlessly, Johnny thanked Baccharus for his rescue, without him he simply would not have made it. Johnny noticed the girls anxiously watching him. The fresh air was helping them recover from their drug-induced trance; Sascha and Boyd were doing their best to reassure them.

There was a slight tremor underfoot. Johnny, who knew the full extent of the underground network, could see that they were still too close to the house. "Get up! We need to move right away from here," he warned. Without a solid foundation, he feared the building and indeed most of the land surrounding it would be unstable, and as if to emphasise his point there was a deep, distant rumble and the ground beneath them shook. The weary group needed no more prompting. At once, they all stood up and made their way as quickly as they could across the wrecked garden towards the perimeter wall. The girls were too traumatised by recent events to even question the metres of thick tentacle that protruded from the ground. They even ignored the miniature hill that was the dead body of the Bar-Shiyq. On this night, unimaginable terror had already been realised in the shape of the Demon King, whom they had witnessed for only a short time through a semi-conscious haze. In the future, these girls would come to appreciate the sedative effect of the drugs in their system, for it spared them the full horror of these memories.

Johnny found it easier to move outdoors – there was no climbing to do, although the ground here *was* pretty uneven. He and his companions were only metres away from the wall when a deafening sound caused them all to stop in their tracks and turn around in time to see the roof of the house falling in. As they watched, large cracks shot upwards through the walls of the grand old building, its windows shattered and glass flew out of distorted frames. Within a few seconds, one whole wing imploded before them while scattered pockets of garden were sucked into the ground, showing them exactly how extensive the subterranean network of chambers and tunnels was. Just as they were about to leave through the gate in the wall, there was a deep boom and the ground quaked – the Devilliers' country mansion was wholly swallowed by the earth. Ruptured gas pipes, diesel fuel and electrical wiring caught light, producing indistinct orange flames within dust cloud plumes. Strange and unearthly screams pierced the night air as the alien creatures from the world of Disorder trapped inside the house were also destroyed in the collapse. The friends had seen enough. They walked through the gate; Johnny led them to the motorhome and away from the destruction. Nobody looked back again.

Epilogue

Johnny had been driving for five hours; it was late, almost midnight. He preferred being on the road at this time; the traffic was so much lighter. It had been about two years since he first travelled here. A few more minutes passed before he saw the sign: HILVERN 22 MILES. He had seen it many times before; it still made him quietly reflect on the events that had taken place in the old Devilliers house. He had been on several assignments before that one and a few since; to this date, the Devilliers case had been his most formative. It was the one in which he had matured significantly as a psychic and come to a fuller realisation of his ability. It was the case that gave him a truer understanding of the universe and awakened him to the beautiful and terrible beings that dwelt within it.

He and his friends had been exposed to extreme danger in the old house. Without good friends there that night, by his side, he would not have overcome the forces of Disorder. The Council of Seven recognised all of their work, and there was material benefit in this; however, the real reward for them, Johnny included, would always be in maintaining the Equilibrium and playing their small role in preserving the universe.

Johnny remained in regular contact with Sascha.His

childhood friend had moved out of London to continue working as a much sought-after academic and researcher in his field of electronic engineering. He lived in the West Country now and had informed Johnny that the increased demand for his work had prompted him to move out of the city so that he would not be so 'available' all the time. Johnny knew it had been Sascha's long-standing desire to set up a quiet laboratory somewhere, and it amused him that the Devilliers affair had not deterred his friend from entering any rural environment altogether.

Johnny was also in touch with Boyd; he spoke to him rather less frequently than to Sascha. Boyd had always been a loner, that was his nature, but his joint experiences with Johnny had forged a tight bond between the pair. Boyd had returned to his Scottish home and continued working as a paranormal investigator, a cover for his true role as a priest of some worthy rank now within the mysterious Order of the Earthly Eye; he remained, as ever, a servant of the Grimoires. He still consulted with Johnny, sporadically, on matters psychic concerning his investigations. Even to this day, Boyd had not revealed his real name.

It had been a few months since Johnny had received any communication from the Council; in fact, it had been so long that a few days ago he had suggested that Baccharus treat himself to a holiday. His sidekick took up the offer without a moment's hesitation and was currently off-planet somewhere amongst fellow familiars. Things were quiet; Johnny liked it that way – it gave him time to relax, play the axe and catch up with friends.

The journey was nearly over. To Johnny, the long drive had been worth every second. He drove into Mrs McGuiness's farm just as he had two years ago and many more times since. Excitedly he adjusted his hair in the rear-view mirror of his car before grabbing his overnight bag from the passenger seat and walking briskly past the farm shop to the adjoining cottage. He did not have to knock; someone had been up waiting for him. Serena, Mrs McGuiness's granddaughter, opened the door. He smiled and she beamed back; they embraced and kissed each other.

"You should have gone to sleep," Johnny said.

"No way," she replied and gave him another kiss. "Aren't you glad I'm up?" she asked suggestively. He smiled again. Serena locked up, and they made their way to her bedroom. A slight figure with ruffled hair and puffy eyes emerged from another room and entered the hallway, her sleep disturbed.

"Hey, Johnny, how are you doing?" asked Rachel as she walked over to give him a hug. "I was asleep, but I heard you come in so I thought I would just say hi."

"I'm glad you did; good to see you, babe," said Johnny as Rachel drifted sleepily back to her room.

**

The collapse of the Devilliers' house was reported in the local press as having been a tragic accident with the blame falling on old mine shafts. The incident remained in the local news for some time as coroners' inquests and police investigations were carried out. The extent of the destruction had been so great and so deep that a full excavation had been deemed impractical. A list of the dead was made from vehicles at the scene and a tally of missing persons associated with the Devilliers; it included plenty of notables from the local community. The Hilvern region would be without some of its MPs, council officials and senior police officers for a while. A few masked, robed and naked bodies were recovered, presenting a conundrum for the authorities, but enough powerful friends of Edward Devilliers had survived that night to ensure these inconvenient details were promptly covered up.

The survival of the three girls was hailed as a miracle. Johnny and his friends were celebrated as heroes. TOURISTS OUT TO ENJOY THE HIGHLANDS; IN THE RIGHT PLACE AT THE RIGHT TIME was how the headlines of the local press had summarised their apparent involvement. Their carefully fabricated story described being awakened by the motorhome shaking and then going out to investigate, only to discover the fallen building and the girls trapped within. Neither the authorities nor the media pressed them further on the matter.

Following the deaths of the Devilliers, Rachel and her sisters had needed new fostering arrangements. By this time, Serena had almost completed her university degree and was going to be living and working with her grandmother, Mrs McGuiness. Together, they were the nearest thing Rachel had to a family (except for her wayward father, who was once again awaiting sentencing). It was decided by social services that Rachel would receive adequate care and supervision from Mrs McGuiness and Serena until she reached adulthood; their case was helped in no small way by Rachel's refusal to accept any other alternative. Once Rachel had moved in with Mrs McGuiness, Johnny would come to visit, just to make sure everything was okay. It was how he met Serena, and things just happened from there – very quickly.

**

When Rachel had gone back to bed, Johnny entered Serena's room. Locked in an embrace, they fell onto the bed together. Serena pulled her lips away from Johnny's for a moment. "Johnny, I forgot the light," she said.

"I'll handle that," Johnny replied. With a quick focus of his will, he switched it off without leaving the bed.